After the Rain

"Hard-edged and gripping. *After the Rain* . . . is miles ahead of the Clancy and Flynn novels . . ."

—*Washington Post Book World*

Homefront

"Seriously, the last sixty pages of *Homefront* are heart stopping, heartbreaking, and heartwarming, sometimes simultaneously. This is one that you absolutely should not miss . . ."

—Bookreporter.com

South of Shiloh

"An intensely gripping story of greed, manipulation, family dysfunction and murder. Highly recommended."

—*Library Journal* *Starred Review*

CHUCK LOGAN

AUTHOR OF *HOMEFRONT*

FALLEN ANGEL

Conquill Press

St. Paul, MN

FALLEN ANGEL
Copyright © 2014 by Chuck Logan

Cover and Interior Design: James Monroe Design LLC

Library of Congress Control Number: 2014947575

Logan, Chuck

Fallen Angel: a novel / by Chuck Logan

ISBN: 978-0-9800017-9-2

Conquill Press/ October 2014

Printed in the United States of America

10 9 8 7 6 5 4 3 2

*For the Jos and Andreas out there
flying the Kiowas and the Hawks.*

And for Ernie and Brian.

PROLOGUE

Every once in a while a truly talented sociopath comes along who puts up normal scores on all the tests. That's what the CIA psychologist quipped when he culled Morgon Jump out of Special Forces six years ago. And now even the old agency hands agree: Morgon's easy smile conceals personality dynamics that can make him a real bad boy.

So when it's a Morgon-type situation, you don't even want to know the details; you just watch the faint whisper creep down a basement corridor at Langley. You strap in, pass covert, and take a hard right on the far side of black. Nothing gets written down or passed via satellite, encrypted or electronic links, landline or telex, or anything except direct word of mouth. An hour after he receives the verbal order, Morgon is on his way to the nearest airport.

Now he's thirty thousand feet over the Atlantic flying economy on Swiss Air to keep it anonymous and sitting in an exit seat to stretch his legs. He's on his way to Baghdad to make someone disappear.

Morgon packs 180 pounds on a lean six-foot frame topped by slightly longish russet hair. His dry hazel eyes default to bemused detachment and reveal not a crumb of where he's been or what he did there. He turned 39 last September. The woman he's been seeing tells him that his face in profile reminds her of Alexander in the mosaic, charging Darius' chariot. He has a preference for turtlenecks to cover the small but distinctive star-shaped scar on the lower right side of his neck that he picked up on a bad night in Mogadishu in 1993 as a young Army Ranger.

Morgon works the politically sensitive nether regions of the targeted kill business. Some of his jobs can take months of careful planning, or—like this one—they can pop up on the fly, compartmentalized like a Chinese box. The contact waiting at Baghdad International will provide the face, the location, and the reason. The ambiguity does not bother him. *Last December a Mexican drug lord caught a 1200-yard shot from a Remington .308 at his villa outside Juarez. Earlier that year a vacationing Iranian nuclear physicist dropped on a crowded street in Karachi. That was arm's length with a silenced .22.*

The gold Rolex on Morgon's wrist is not a fashion statement. It's a blood chit — a universal barter item that will bring an instant cooperative smile to the face of the most illiterate peasant in the remotest back forty in the world. The Rolex tells him he'll land in Kuwait in six hours and then board Air Iraq for the hop into Baghdad. The Canadian passport in his pocket is issued to David Baker, a resident of Winnipeg. Occupation: security consultant. Baker has a ghost file in the DoD computer that identifies him as a subcontractor with DynCorp. He's entering Iraq on a business visa. His return reservations are scheduled for two days out after his arrival.

Briefly he considers the Iridium Global sat phone in his carry-on bag that is loaded with X.9 One Time Pad encryption. It's reputed to be NSA-proof, and his handler has a matching unit back in the States. The phones are to be used only in an extreme emergency.

Then he signals the flight attendant and asks her for a bottle of water along with a ginger ale chaser for the electrolytes, to offset dehydration.

Once his drinks arrive, he switches on the reading light and opens a thumbed paperback titled Stone Work *and relaxes into the author's paean to building dry bluestone walls in New England.*

CHAPTER ONE

Morgon is still hours away from Kuwait when captain Jessica Kraig wakes up in her sandbagged trailer at the Balad Air Base in Iraq. As she sits up and knuckles her sleep-mussed hair, there's not much to knuckle. She wears it in a yellow-bronze crop that prompts the older women in the unit to recall Audrey Hepburn. Her dad compares it to prairie Indian grass in the fall.

The crop fits her head like a swim cap and complements her no-nonsense persona. She swam competition for a while in high school but gave it up for dance. The way she sees it, in swimming all that counts is winning. It doesn't matter how you look. In dance, athleticism is a given. It's form that counts. Jesse likes to win, but she wants to look good enough to stop your heart doing it.

Short of winning, she believes in cutting her losses. She holds up her left hand, which is trim and tanned like the rest of her, and studies the pale circle on the third finger, where her engagement ring resided until she mailed it back. Extra Coppertone might banish the lingering white stripe. When she runs her tongue over her teeth she tastes the talcum-fine sand that sifts in through the air conditioner . So begins her 167th day in-country piloting a Black Hawk in the flight company of the North Dakota National Guard's 4/143rd Helicopter Assault Battalion.

Her roommate, warrant officer Laura Double Bear, also a pilot, is already up and out taking a run before breakfast. Mornings are cold in the desert, even in April, so Jesse slept in her old, baggy U of North Dakota Fighting Sioux sweatsuit. The first thing she does is look out the window.

3

The day dawns clear. A good thing. The rainy season is over, and now the dry, dusty Sharqi winds can gust to sixty miles an hour and throw up wall clouds 1,000 feet high. When the freakin' sand is up, Balad can look like a howling red airport mall on Mars.

The base, once home to more than 20,000 American soldiers and contractors, sprawls over six square miles on either side of what once was one of the busiest aircraft runways in the world. Now, with the drawdown, whole sections of Balad are reverting to the Iraqis or becoming desert ghost towns. The Subway remains, along with Pizza Hut, Burger King, a Starbucks, sidewalks, a giant PX stuffed with electronic goodies, endless concrete blast walls, and sporadic incoming mortars. It's still a war, but nobody has been killed at Balad by hostile fire for a long time. A few years back this smart-ass *New York Times* reporter suggested the most dangerous place on the base might be one of its four huge mess halls. Troops rotating out of Balad gain an average of ten pounds.

Jesse peels off the sweats, keeps the T-shirt, pulls on her running shorts, grabs a towel and a wash kit, exits her trailer, and heads down the duck walk to the shower for a quick scrub and shampoo. She carries her Randall survival knife, unsheathed, under her towel as a practical precaution. On her journey from being a grounded farm kid through college smart to army taut, she's learned to keep her eyes open and her head on a swivel. Men run the military, and the stats tell her she has a one-in-five chance of being sexually assaulted. And then there's the evil camel spider that lurks in the T-wall joint near the shower and likes to pop out and glare with its beady little eyes.

Back in her room, Jesse dries her hair and verifies, in her locker mirror, that she has kept the mess halls at bay. At 5'7", she holds to a tidy 125 pounds. She prides herself at maxing the army PT test. No guy carried *her* gear at survival school. She swings a 16K kettle bell, runs in the 120-degree heat, and rates in the top two on the enlisted men's informal hot-female-officer list.

She reaches in her locker, removes her flight pants, and shakes them out. Bingo. A middling-sized scorpion drops to the floor. With no more compunction than flicking a june bug, she whips a magazine off the locker shelf, drops it on the critter, and stomps twice with her bare foot.

After shaking out her tunic twice, she gets dressed, and the slim curves disappear in anonymous digital camouflage of her Nomex flight suit and desert boots.

Jesse's ticket out of the North Dakota wheat fields involved joining the Guard in college to do her bit, sure—but mainly she wanted the aviation schools. It turned out she liked the people, and she really liked the toys. She went to officer training and then to the helo flight school at Rucker. At 27, she's reinvented herself as an army aviator who likes to go fast. She'd prefer to fly the Kiowa Warrior, a scout aircraft that zips around like a bumblebee with a side-mounted 50-caliber stinger. But the mission calls for her to pilot the utility UH60 Black Hawk.

She can play it cool and demure—even bat her pale blue eyes on occasion—but when messed with, she has a short fuse. Her soon to be ex-fiancé, Terry, got a whiff of this blowback trait when he tried to talk her out of reenlisting. He wanted her to tag along with him to grad school. Now she's flying the Hawk in Iraq, and Terry is wandering off in search of himself as an assistant English professor at the University of Iowa.

Terry got off easy. Two weeks ago, on a night mission, some insurgents sent machine-gun fire her way. She doubled back into the tracers to verify the enemy position. Then she called a brace of Apache gunships down on their misguided *hajji* heads. Ground crew got to patch some holes in her Hawk, Tumbleweed Six, that night.

She slaps her Velcro captain's bars in place on her chest, tugs the brim of her soft cap low over her brow, leaves quarters, and strides through the battalion area, which is a tin-roofed maze of plywood, duck walks, corrugated tin huts, endless concrete blast T-walls, sandbagged trailers, and more plywood.

As she joins a parade of soldiers headed for the mess hall, a female sergeant falls in step beside her.

Sergeant First Class Marge Bailey is of a certain age that shows in the crow's feet ironed into the firm skin at the corners of her eyes. A spray of freckles dots her nose, and she wears her chestnut hair in a practical shag. Marge is a crew chief who sometimes flies in Jesse's Hawk.

"So?" Marge asks.

Jesse thrusts her left hand in the air, fingers rigid. No ring.

"So you did it. Now what?" Marge prompts.

"I e-mailed him, setting up a call time. I should be able to get a line out at the Internet café. Not as good as being there, but it'll have to do."

"So you're over him?"

Jesse squints at the gravel crunching under her boots.

"Pretty much."

They walk in silence for a few steps, then Marge says, "So, going forward, *Captain*, what are you going to do different?"

"Well, *Sergeant*," Jesse says, "the mistake I made with Terry was getting thrown by his laid-back act and figuring that his deep brown eyes could complement my, ah . . ."

"Sharp elbows?"

"Yeah. Turns out those soft brown eyes were, ah . . ."

"Full of passive-aggressive spite," the older woman suggests.

Then, after another interval of silence crossing the gravel, Marge says, "Maybe it's time to set some new ground rules for men in your life?"

"Like, what do you suggest, Sergeant Mom?" Jesse grins.

"Well, just my opinion, but I'd suggest a gal with your running pattern would do better with a guy raised with at least one older sister."

"I'll think about it," Jesse says.

Right on, Marge. Terry was an only child.

CHAPTER TWO

The asset, a smiling young man in slacks and a blazer, waits past customs. He is clean-shaven, his dark hair is neatly trimmed, and he introduces himself as Ahmed after he removes a photo of Morgon from his pocket and studies the likeness. Morgon takes out his photo of Ahmed and goes through the same ritual. They shake hands and greet formally.

"*Marhaba,* Ahmed. *Salam wa alaikum.*"

"*Wa aleikum ah salam,* Morgon," Ahmed says before switching to easy Stateside English. "This way, please."

The two security men who accompany young Ahmed have obsidian eyes and faces the texture of orange rinds. Unsmiling, they escort Morgon from the terminal through a wall of brown heat to the parking lot, where they stop at a freshly washed and waxed Mercedes limo. Morgon notes that the car's tires strain under the load of armor plating.

"Unfortunately this ride will only take us halfway to where we're going. It'll get more hot and dusty after that," Ahmed comments as he opens a rear door and extends his hand for Morgon to get in.

As they climb into air conditioning and plush upholstery, Ahmed leans forward and taps the driver on the shoulder, and the car eases forward into the sultry afternoon. The security guards drive a lead Suburban. More of them follow behind in a Jeep. Heavy on the horn and accelerator, they merge into the demolition derby that connects the airport to the city. Beneath the once modern skyline, they convoy through a maze of streets beset by gridlock, uncollected garbage, rubble, and checkpoints.

Morgon dials down the window to get a whiff of battered air that reeks of open sewage and the exhaust of thousands of generators that whir in lieu of reliable electricity. Baghdad is probably the future—the infrastructure crumbles and public order is a mere wish as the desert reclaims the outer suburbs. Then his attention retreats into the limo's air-conditioned cocoon and leaves Baghdad's five million souls to swelter beyond the tinted windows.

"So fill me in," Morgon says.

Ahmed hands him a photocopy of a dazed man caught blinking into the camera flash. He is in his mid-forties, with askew hair and a round face in need of a razor. Another photocopy of a Tennessee driver's license is appended to the first. The license photo ID matches.

"Richard Noland, from Memphis, Tennessee. He should have stayed there," Ahmed says.

"How'd he get famous?"

"He's a salvage contractor. A sheik up north subbed out a job to him, cleaning up an old oil-pumping station on land he's developing. Noland is a hands-on guy. He was driving the backhoe that snagged on a cache of buried artillery rounds." Ahmed smiles tightly. "Some of them were just rusty high-explosives, but most of them had these little death's-head icons stenciled in yellow . . ." He leans forward for emphasis. "Which means they are loaded with VX nerve agent. When Noland figured out what he had, he turned into a greedy bastard and started putting out feelers to see what it was worth on the black market."

"And you know this how?"

Ahmed's dark eyes glow briefly and he purses his lips in a modest smile. "Sheer luck. This involves my family. The sheik up north who hired Noland is an uncle. We offered to put him in the hole in the ground with his find. We only have the whole

Syrian Desert to work with." The young Iraqi shrugs. "We were told to wait for you."

After a quick assessment Morgon understands why he's here, why the suits are sitting on their hands and playing it low-profile. "And you will put him in that hole after I verify he's who you say he is and that what he found is real and that it's been destroyed."

"So it's about trust." Ahmed takes his lower lip between his teeth.

Morgon leans back, measuring this Ahmed kid with his snappy language skills and his iPhone. He says, "I read once where the Emperor Domitian had the palace walls covered with mirrors so he could see everything around him at all times."

Quickly catching the drift, Ahmed lowers his eyes in deference. "Nobody knows about this except Noland's work crew and inner-circle members of my uncle's tribe."

"And we'll keep it that way," Morgon says.

Chastened by the flick of menace implicit in Morgon's glance, Ahmed bobs his head. "For sure. But what's the big deal? They've been turning up odd lots of chemical munitions for years, mixed in with regular ordnance." Then, more slowly, he reflects, "But, okay, this is like 400 rounds on the original pallets. We thought that chemical junk was destroyed back in 1991. Some Republican Guard supply officer got lazy and just dumped it in the sand."

"Exactly," Morgon says. "You turn it in, and here come the cops and the army. There'd be an operation order to come collect the stuff. They'd vet the intelligence. Too many people would be in the loop. Word would get out. *Reporters*, Ahmed. In the current political climate back in the States, Noland and his rusty batch of old shells could stir up hype, possibly even revive the old WMD boogeyman in the midst of the troop drawdown." Morgon smiles and pats Ahmed on the knee. "Buck up, lad. It appears we're protecting the president's poll numbers."

Ahmed nods. "Among other things. But this is dangerous stuff Noland found, if it got into the wrong hands."

"Goes without saying. So where is he?"

"We have him secured in a tool shed on his work site." Ahmed's eyes alternate between Morgon's face and reading the text on his phone. "We'll be there in about five hours. I'm thinking we'll make it look like Noland was kidnapped."

"Have you ever been around this kind of play before, Ahmed? Like in the new Iraqi military or the insurgency?" Morgon asks.

"Actually, no," Ahmed says. "I missed the war. I was doing undergrad and getting an MBA at Boston College when they recruited me. This is my first real-world assignment. I'm here because of my family connection. Don't worry, the guys with us are some hard dudes . . ."

"Right, inner-circle members of the tribe." Morgon takes a weary breath. It's not the first time a nervous suit in DC has put him in the middle of amateur hour. "We'll do just fine," he says, running his hand along the leather upholstery. "Nice wheels."

"Yeah," Ahmed says, "but they'd draw the wrong kind of attention where we're going."

"And where are we going?"

"It's called Turmar, north of Samarra."

CHAPTER THREE

Forty-six miles north of Baghdad, Jesse Kraig sits in a phone cubicle waiting for her call to go through. The calling station is built along the Internet café's back wall. Behind her, soldiers, Guard primarily, lounge at row upon row of computer stations playing video games or chatting online. The regulars have mostly been pulled off the base. The café is more popular for calling home than the AT&T trailers where they gouge you on the phone cards.

Trying not to be impatient, which might show in her voice, she studies the cubicle's plywood walls, and it occurs to her that her main memories of Iraq—apart from a few edgy nights playing tag with *hajji* tracers so far—will involve a monotony of sand, T-walls, and plywood. It's versatile stuff, plywood. During WWII, the British used it to build the Mosquito Bomber. Probably where they started calling aircraft "crates."

She shifts the receiver from one ear to the other.

The Defense Switched Network phone system will connect to the army base nearest to Iowa City, which is the Iowa Army Ammunition Plant next to Burlington. That way she'll be billed with a local call. Terry finds it amusing that their phone conversations are mediated through a munitions factory.

Whatever. She drums her finger on the plywood desktop. Then the connection pops in her ear.

"Hello, this is Terry."

"Terry, hi; it's Jesse . . ."

"Hey, how's it going? You okay?"

"I'm fine." Pause. "Terry, we need to talk . . ."

"We *are* talking," he says with slow precision, getting the range.

She takes a breath, lets it out. So much for preamble.

"Jess?"

"I sent back the ring."

"Okaaayyy . . ." he responds, drawing it out. She can tell by his tone that he is not surprised. And in the suspended silence she imagines him calculating his options and deciding to wait. There's always a chance she could stumble on an emotional hurdle.

"Look," she says firmly, "I applied for Fixed Wing and got accepted. If it works out, I have an eye on a pilot slot in the King Air Group . . ."

"So you're thinking of extending?"

"I already have, for two years."

"Then what? Drive a bus for Delta?" And now his voice betrays the slightest undertone of resignation.

"That's not the point, Terry."

"Right, it's a question of where and who you spend your time with." As a correct afterthought, he adds, "It's your choice, of course."

She expects this. His style is to say the appropriate thing, play the aggrieved party, and let her be the bad guy. That way he can lay back and hope that remorse might set in. Then his control slips slightly and he asks, "You sure?"

"I'm sure. I report to Rucker for Aircraft Transition two weeks after I demob out of this place." She listens to silence on the line, then says, "C'mon, Terry. This was always in the mix."

"What you really mean is that I wouldn't make a good pilot's wife, huh?" He manages to insert a lilt of dark humor in his voice. This is what happens when two self-contained people are forced to face the obvious. "I assume you've thought this through," he says.

"C'mon, Terry; it's been there for years, hanging fire . . ."

"So, *bang*. You're pulling the trigger, huh?"

"Bang."

"Better than a whimper, I guess." His voice turns breezy. "Okay, then. I won't drag it out, because I suspect you're standing in line with some terribly nice boys from Armpit, Kentucky, and such. So you take care of yourself over there, hear?" He mocks a Southern accent.

"You too, asshole," Jesse says with a slip of grudging fondness.

"See you around, Jess. Watch your six."

"Will do. See you, Terry."

The connection goes dead. Jesse hangs up the receiver, gets up from the chair, turns, and studies the soldier standing behind her. "Where are you from, Specialist?" she asks.

"The fuckin' Georgia National Guard, ma'am," he answers without batting an eye.

When Jesse exits the building, staff sergeant Marge Bailey is waiting in a dubious rectangle of shade next to the door. Seeing Marge, Jesse shivers in the heat and says, "Not exactly ideal, a long-distance phone call."

"Some people would have just changed their personal status on Facebook to single. But you're sure, right?"

Jesse stares at her. "What, is there, an echo going around? Yes, I'm sure."

"Just asking. You were with him for like . . . three years?"

Jesse tugs her cap lower over her eyes. "Look, he's a lot of fun to hook up with. And he's got all the right moves. Like, he puts down the army—but he enlisted right after 9/11 and did a tour with the 173rd in Afghanistan." She narrows her eyes at the horizon where the dust is stacking up like beige blocks and adds, "Probably joined up to spite his parents. Like when he dropped out of law school."

She turns and points a finger at Sergeant Bailey. "See, the thing about Terry is, he's always going to get his way. And he's going to loosely interpret the forsaking-all-others clause. In the end, he'll model on his parents. His dad is an attorney for North Dakota Mill and Elevator." She shakes the finger for emphasis. "And his mom gave up a teaching career to be a corporate wife." Jesse clears her throat. "Pardon my venting, Marge, but I'm not going to be Mrs. Terrence Sherman."

They start walking toward the intelligence shack. Instinctively they both want to get a read on what's building up in the western sky.

"So now it's Fixed Wing," Marge says.

Jesse nods. "It's the smart move. Being Guard I won't have the obligation I'd have in the regulars. And I get the same schools."

"And when you break free of all this bullshit?" Marge swings her head to take in the sprawling ranks of containerized housing units landscaped with T-walls.

"Might be fun to fly a news chopper back home. Or maybe get on with Life Lift. The oil and power companies are always looking for pilots. Some of the bigger contractors are putting together helicopter fleets . . ."

"That sounds like signing on for more sand," Marge says.

Jesse cocks her head and momentarily yields to a daydream. "I've always wanted to fly the Dehavilland Beaver in Alaska. My bush-pilot fantasy, huh?" Then, in a more practical tone, "If nothing else works, there's the airlines."

For several beats their boots go *crunch* on the gravel. Then Marge says, "Fixed Wing makes sense. Aviation is a track where women are underrepresented. You'd have a leg up."

"I'm aware of that," Jesse says, "but I'm not counting on it. I intend to pull my own weight."

"A suggestion, Captain?"

"By all means, Sergeant."

"You've got the competent part nailed. But you might want to work on being just a tad more low-key . . ."

Jesse grins. "Say what you mean, Marge."

Marge shrugs. "If you present less ego, there's less chance of snagging on some flight instructor's macho tail feathers."

"I'll put it on my list," Jesse says as she evaluates the incoming weather and quickens her stride. "C'mon, I don't think anybody's going up in that . . . uh-uh."

CHAPTER FOUR

North of Baghdad they stop at a safe house to switch vehicles, and now Morgon rides in the passenger seat of a gray GMC Suburban headed north on National Highway One. Ibriham Construction is lettered on both of the truck's doors, in Arabic and English, just like the place names and the mileage on the passing road signs. Ahmed has doffed his blazer for a safari shirt and, wearing a Red Sox cap, sits behind the wheel. Morgon has changed his travel loafers for a worn pair of Timberland boots and has stripped down to a T-shirt. Now they both wear Kevlar body vests. Over the kid's objections, Morgon's cranked down the windows and switched off the AC to adjust to the heat.

The security men in the escort vehicles are thorough if not real talkative professionals. They have passed through half a dozen Iraqi National Police checkpoints with only a cursory inspection.

As they enter the slums on the outskirts of Samarra, Ahmed, slightly more edgy, explains the scenario thus far. "About the nerve gas, we brought in a crew of strictly innercircle clan members. It took us two nights to unearth and inventory the artillery rounds. We did it right: full hazmat suits, regulators, nerve-gas antidotes, everything. Tonight, after you verify, we'll finish entombing the stuff in cement, just like Chernobyl."

"Fine," Morgon says. "How much longer on the road?"

Ahmed nods toward the afternoon sun. "Two more hours."

Morgon settles back as they slow to pass through a cluster of houses partially fenced with concrete T-walls. More of the slabs spill off the blackened wreckage of a lowboy trailer. They pass a long line of cars queued up at a gas station. The sullen drivers lean on fenders, beyond bitching. A woman in a burka scrubs a large X from the wall of a house. As the convoy rolls by, she scurries for a doorway. A young man crosses the road talking on a cell phone, oblivious to the raw sewage beneath his high-top tennis shoes. Behind barricades of piled garbage sacks and the dark houses, Morgon hears the hum of a gasoline generator. A smoky stain curls in the air, redolent of burning refuse. Somewhere a plaintive voice chants Arabic in an amplified call to prayer.

"Virtual Iraq," Morgon quips.

"How's that?"

"New therapy the VA's experimenting with to desensitize vets to combat stress. They strap you into this head-mounted display and headphones. Like being inside a video game. Then they dial in terrain, weather, urban landscapes, sound, even smells. And threats, of course."

"Does it work?"

"Probably for the company who's marketing it."

Ahmed cocks an eyebrow, amused. "Here I think they give our guys two aspirin and a kick in the ass."

Ten minutes later Ahmed points to the sky ahead that has reared up into an adobe wall. As traffic empties off the road, he turns to Morgon with a pained expression. Morgon just shrugs and takes it in stride, saying, "You live in a desert. The wind blows."

So Ahmed pulls to the side of the road behind the lead vehicle. The driver jogs back, his face now protected by a headdress. They converse fast in Arabic, and then the security man, his silhouette already disappearing in the flying sand, leans into the wind and trudges back to his Suburban.

Ahmed frowns. "We're stuck here until this damn storm passes." He points at the brake lights in the gloom as the lead car slowly explores a way off the road. "He's going into the village to locate some food. We might be here a while."

Morgon takes his book from his bag along with a clip-on reading light as the world beyond the windows turns to grainy night.

Ahmed is apologetic. "We could try to muddle our way through, but my guys aren't real keen about driving through these Shia districts blind. Less so hauling an American."

"Relax, Ahmed. Mr. Noland isn't going anywhere. So sit back and enjoy the weather show."

"Don't worry, it'll clear. I'll have you back to Baghdad tomorrow afternoon."

CHAPTER FIVE

Nobody has just one job anymore. If Jesse isn't flying, she's tidying up administrative flight company details. She's walking through the fitful dust storm looking for the battalion quartermaster. One of his enlisted men had his ankle broken by a forklift when a work detail was unloading pallets of water and Dr. Pepper. If this is true, the battalion has now incurred its first casualty in the war zone. If you don't count PFC Joan Camp, a company clerk, who came down with a terminal case of missing her period and was shipped home.

About six steps from the supply hooch, a headquarters specialist jogs up to her and says, "Capt'n Kraig, Master Sergeant Dillon's looking for you."

"What's up?" Jesse says, reaching for the door.

"It's, ah, Toby. He just got in a dustup on the flight line with two wrench monkeys from that Alabama maintenance unit. Now an officer's come over and wants to talk to Toby's direct superior. That's you."

"Wonderful." Toby is Spec Four Toby Nguyen, her door gunner on Tumbleweed Six. He's also the company comedian. Jesse lets the door swing shut. "Where are they?"

"By the day room, and, ah, Capt'n . . ."

"What?"

"The officer who came over, he's a chaplain."

"Great." Jesse spins on her heel and heads across the gravel apron toward the company day room. Looking up, she sees sunset emerge from a momentary lull in the gloom. But she doubts if it's clearing; the reports predict a huge storm. Rounding a pod of sandbagged trailers, she spots master sergeant Sam Dillon rolling her way with purpose.

20

Sam, the flight company top sergeant, has his own way of doing things. Worse, he's older than her father. And the last thing she needs is a surrogate father figure mucking up the landscape. So here comes Sam with the bearing of a weathered ramrod because he carries three combat stars jammed in the wreath over the Combat Infantry Badge on his chest. A widower, he's the oldest trooper in the battalion and, at 60, he's pushed the max age limit the Guard allows a soldier to fly combat. The men in the unit, officers and enlisted, refer to him as "Grandpa Dillon," their Neanderthal, a relic of the drafted army. But they don't say this to his face, because he's logged more bullet time over the last four decades than the whole battalion combined.

Sam did twenty years active, then another twenty as an investigator with the sheriff's department in Grand Forks. He always kept his hand in the Guard. Most of the time he can be found flying in Jesse's Hawk as crew chief.

Sam should be off fishing, playing golf. Instead he's watching her approach behind his aviator sunglasses. As she stops in front of him, he rolls his tongue to shift the cud of Copenhagen tucked in his lower lip.

"I been meaning to ask," Jesse starts casual. "You dip that stuff back in the crew chief bay, right? I mean, you the kinda guy who spits or swallows?"

"Skipper's a sharp lady as usual this morning," Sam says.

Thing about Sam is, he hasn't quite made the transition to the modern all-volunteer army. Sam is culture-bound, hung up on gender. Like, he has a retro habit of opening doors for women. Jesse squares up, taps the insignia on her chest, and announces, "You see female written on these railroad tracks, Sergeant?"

"No, ma'am."

"We've had this conversation before."

"Yes, ma'am."

As she sets off walking again, taking the lead, she's not quite satisfied that Sam gets the point. She increases her tempo, putting a slight swing to her shoulders, and asks over her shoulder, "So what'd Toby do now?"

"Don't have the details. Sounds like he got into a punchout with a couple born-agains."

"Ah, for Christ's sake." Jesse stops walking and grimaces. "I thought we ducked that stuff here?"

Dillon shrugs. "We have—in the flight company, for the most part; we're strictly a bunch of hard-assed prairie Lutherans, from Chaplain Lundquist on down. 'Course we do come from farm stock and spend a lot of time watching the weather —so we're probably contaminated by Sioux sky gods."

Jesse is eyeing the next pod of trailers. Once she gets past them, it's a straight shot to the day room. This chaplain is a potential wild card who could be tight with a colonel or general in his prayer group up the chain of command.

Sam reads her mind and says, "Thing is, Skipper, if this takes a funny bounce, it could wind up on your proficiency report—and you being ambitious and all, gunning for Fixed Wing . . ."

Jesse clears her throat. "Say what you mean, Top."

"Yes, ma'am. Sounds like a garden-variety soldiers' fight. So maybe you could trust me to cool out this sky pilot— seeing's I got zero career to protect."

Ordinarily, Jesse would resent any man stepping in and playing at chivalry. But just thinking about Toby and a chaplain in the same grid square makes her eyes go wide—so she guts her pride and nods to Dillon. "I appreciate the gesture, Sam," she says.

Sam taps a finger to the brim of his soft cap, pivots, and heads for the day room. Jesse, relieved, turns the other direction and makes back for the Supply Hooch feeling just a wee bit sorry for what's coming the chaplain's way.

Rounding the trailers and approaching the day room, Dillon sees Spec Four Toby Nguyen standing outside. He's tall and gangly and immensely strong, sprung from the intersection of a shitkicker North Dakota dad and a Vietnamese mom his father met in college. He got his brawn from his daddy and the skin color and wraparound angle of his eyes from his mom. He is also, to the chagrin of all the officers in the company, possessed of a comedic streak for which the army provides endless material.

In his other life, Toby is a Grand Forks city cop who attends night law classes. This morning, Toby has a swollen bruise on his left cheek and his hands are stuffed in the pockets of his flight trousers. An amiable-looking, bespectacled captain stands next to Toby and appears to be trying to hand him something.

Seeing Sergeant Dillon approach, Toby stands a bit more erect but still keeps his hands in his pockets. Since Balad is technically a combat zone, Dillon holds the opinion that the saluting etiquette is relaxed. So he merely nods courteously to the captain, who wears a chaplain's insignia Velcroed on his chest.

Sam turns to Toby and asks, "How bad?"

Toby shrugs. "Not bad; routine ten fifty four chickenshit."

'Ten fifty four' is copper Ten Code for 'livestock on highway.' "Watch your mouth," Dillon warns.

"Working on it, Top," Toby says.

"Get your hands outta your pockets. It ain't military," Dillon says. Toby removes his hands, revealing skinned, slightly bleeding knuckles. Then Dillon turns to the captain and says, "Master Sergeant Dillon. How may I be of service, sir?"

The captain smiles and says, "This young man needs to appreciate we're all in this together, fighting a common enemy. Not each other. Perhaps you could convince him to benefit from some reading." He hands Sam the book in his hand.

Dillon skims the cover, which bears an army insignia and the title *The Soldier's Bible*. Respectfully, he returns the book, clears his throat, and says, "Sir, by virtue of those bars you're wearing, you can order Spec Four Nguyen here to do a number of things, like stand at attention. But you can't tell him what to believe."

"I'd never order a soldier to read the Bible, Sergeant. I'm merely offering it as a timely gift."

"And it appears Spec Four Nguyen is politely passing on your kind offer," Dillon says.

The chaplain turns the book over in his hand and says, "I take it, Sergeant, you and this soldier don't have a personal relationship with Jesus Christ?"

Dillon makes a slight coughing sound in his throat. "I'm good with the Sermon on the Mount. I suspect Toby here falls somewhere between a lapsed Buddhist and a Jon Stewart wannabe. Now just exactly what happened that brings you into our area, sir?"

"This soldier belittled the religious faith of two men in my unit and then physically attacked them. They'd be here, except they're both at the base hospital."

Dillon's eyes click on Toby.

Toby says, "Coupla pussy Fobbits. Just minor cuts and bruises, same as me."

"Let's hear your side of it," Dillon says.

"Well," Toby says, unable to curb the infectious grin spreading across his face. "I was walking down the flight line, coming back from the Hawk, and I see these two guys with a laptop. So I wander over, and they're playing this computer game. The new Left Behind Tribulation Forces."

"No law against that if they ain't on duty," Dillon says.

"Nope. So I was cheering them on, you know, getting into it. Way the game works, the good guys zap the heathens with the power of prayer—'cause if they just shoot them, then they lose some of their spiritual power and gotta restore it hitting their prayer buttons. So I used the line off *The Simpsons*, you know, when Rod Flanders is playing Bible Blasters and Todd tells him you gotta hit 'em dead-on 'cause if you just wing them, you'll make them a Unitarian . . ."

"Yeah, and?" Dillon says.

"They took offense, it got heated, and then they called me a name and a few punches got thrown."

"Like I said," the chaplain says, "belittling and sarcasm followed by physical assault."

Toby dramatically hangs his head. "The chaplain is one hundred percent right. I was definitely insensitive to those guys and way oversensitive about myself. Like, I didn't realize that the term 'Unitarian' was a swear word that could incite them to riot. And I definitely overreacted when this one dude called me a 'slant-eyed sand nigger'—which I shoulda realized is just normal talk where they come from. So I apologize for being culturally inappropriate."

Dillon, struggling to keep a straight face, removes his aviator sunglass and tucks them in his tunic pocket. "They called you that, huh?"

"Fuckin' A, Sarge."

Dillon turns to the chaplain. "That the way you heard it, sir?"

"I didn't hear anything about racial slurs. It's his word against the two men he assaulted," the chaplain begins, but now the earnestness fades in his tone.

"You making this up?" Dillon asks Toby.

"No, Sarge."

"Why should we believe you?"

"Because I been trained to accurately report on . . . stuff."

"How trained?"

"Back home I'm a cop."

Dillon clears his throat again and addresses the chaplain. "Still, sounds pretty serious. Let's round up the other two troops and question them and march all three over to my company commander. Then, if you're still so inclined, you can bring Toby up on charges."

"On second thought, Sergeant, I'll accept his apology if you follow up on your end and evaluate him for anger-management counseling," the chaplain says.

"I appreciate the guidance. I'll get our own chaplain right on it, sir," Dillon says.

The chaplain holds out *The Soldier's Bible*. Dillon just smiles patiently, waiting for the man to leave.

They watch the chaplain walk from the company area, and when he's out of sight, Dillon says, "You are one dumb shit. No telling when hair-trigger born-agains are going to pop up, and you pull a stunt like that. You got an alligator mouth, son; problem is you got an alligator ass to back it up." For emphasis, he cuffs Toby—hard—on the back of the head.

"Ow, shit," Toby protests. "You ain't allowed to do that."

Dillon whacks him again. "Oh, yeah? Tell it to the chaplain." Then he puts his sunglasses back on, splashes the gravel next to his boot with a spurt of Cope, and shakes his head. "Least, that's what we used to say."

CHAPTER SIX

Davis is late again, so FBI special agent Robert Appert strives to maintain his cool. A square, middle-aged man, he stands looking out the window of an eighth-floor room in the Al Rasheed Hotel in the Baghdad International Zone. His shoulders slope into thick, muscular arms, his short red hair is parted, and busted capillaries bloom on his freckled cheeks. A holstered .40 cal pistol juts from his right hip, and a leather cuff bearing a five-pointed gold star is fixed to the other side of his belt buckle. In keeping with the informal nature of this assignment, he wears jeans and a faded yellow T-shirt with a red USMC emblem. He's working a joint task force with Colonel Whalid Nasir from the Iraqi Intelligence Ministry; their brief is going after corruption, fraud, dope trafficking, and $9 billion in missing Iraqi development funds.

Nasir, knife-thin and mustachioed, sits on the couch watching the flat-screen TV. The latest remake of *King Kong* plays on DVD, with the audio turned off. Naomi Watts screams soundlessly as the big gorilla wrestles a tyrannosaurus.

"I truly love Americans and their movies," Nasir says in clipped Oxford-accented English. "The detail on the lizard is exact, but look, that's the tenth crotch shot of the big ape, and he has no balls. Just empty space down there."

"I wouldn't read in too much, Nasir," Appert says in a weary voice. "The guy who made it is a Kiwi."

"I'm just saying . . ." Nasir's voice trails off as he glances at his watch, then at his cell phone sitting on the couch. "He's late. He doesn't call . . ." He goes back to watching his movie.

Appert mutters "Fuckin' Davis" under his breath, turns back to the window, and stares at the brown, steaming city. Except it isn't steam, it's a slow-moving dust storm, and he can barely make out the shadows of the Great Ziggurat and the slender minarets. Like a new species of Iraqi birdlife, a Navy Sea Stallion chugs across the gritty sun.

They are preparing for a raid involving a large shipment of heroin and possibly a cache of missing IDF funds. Nasir's men are prepped and ready to go. But where? As usual, they're waiting on their mercurial "undercover asset."

On paper Davis is an independent security consultant who ostensibly works for Nasir, but Appert is inner circle and knows Davis is really one of Mouse Malone's Rainmakers. Malone is a silent partner in the task force. He presides over a Skunk Works operation secreted in the bowels of the National Security Agency. The essence of the clandestine shop Malone runs is demonstrated by how deftly he conceals its black budget between the lines. Since NSA is prohibited from running field agents, Malone employs Davis as a contract asset—an investigator— who follows up leads gleaned from international intercepts. If Davis turns up actionable material, he calls in old-style cops like Appert to play catch-up in the wake of his freewheeling cowboy boots.

"Ex–Force Recon Marine," the paperwork says. Wounded in Fallujah, in Afghanistan, and in other arid and/or jungle-rot places. The record is murky, the kind of dissembling Appert associates with the CIA's Special Activities Division. He glances across the room at the messy pile of gear on Davis' desk and shakes his head. *Damn scofflaw spook never puts anything away.*

But he admits that Davis has a flair for playing it alone in the black-market netherworld where the drug gangs, bad-apple contractors, and insurgents intersect. The grudging thought is preamble for Davis shoving through the door coated with sweat and red dirt that he shakes from his floppy bush hat and then dusts from his curly brown hair. Davis hides his scarred face behind broad sunglasses that he removes to reveal intense green eyes. In his early thirties with the build of a skinny six-foot python, he tosses his M4 carbine on a chair and holds up the iPhone in his hand.

"Hey, Bobby, you gotta see this. Talk about a new take on the car bomb. A chick in Riyadh just posted it on Facebook, and it's streaming live on Al Jazeera English. She filmed herself *driving a car*, man, in violation of that ordinance they got." Davis grins. His face is out-of-focus handsome, redesigned by high explosives. Cosmetic surgery has given him a reasonably repaired nose that is mostly centered in the braided ripple of scar tissue that meanders diagonally across his face and trails off into his right cheek. The right corner of his smile droops slightly. "Arab spring is bustin' out all over," he says.

"Al Jazeera?" Appert repeats in a perplexed voice. Then he holds up his hands in a questioning gesture and nods toward Nasir.

Davis shrugs and says, "It's going down up north, in Ramil, tomorrow at noon. Word is they got a ton of heroin coming in. My informant got inside the house where the meet is set and saw a closet full of shrink-wrapped hundred-dollar bills. So far there's just goons guarding the place."

"You sure about the buyer?" Appert asks.

"Just a hardworking guy from Dubuque picking up on a passing advantage, huh? He's in food services at the embassy," Davis says. "You know, the new 600-million-dollar, 121-acre embassy we're building as we pull out." Davis baits Appert with a droll wink. "Like I've been telling you, Bobby—this whole war is just one big financial instrument . . ."

Appert ignores the smart-ass remark and asks, "So where's Ramil?" He walks to a banquet table strewn with files, a computer, several cells, a satellite phone, and a military radio. He digs around and finds a map.

"It's up north of Samarra," Nasir calls from the couch, "on the big canal. It's about eight kilometers past the ruins at Turmar. Once the storm clears, we'll need a helicopter."

"You can't get a helicopter. They come in pairs," Davis says.

Appert picks up a phone. "What do you think? Call special ops at Balad?"

"Naw, some of those guys might know me from the old days. Let's get a good old down-home Guard unit. Use your flash clearance. Throw in a code name. Those Guard boys get all fired up about code names," Davis says. As Appert makes the call, Davis flops down on the couch next to Nasir and stares, exhausted, at the TV.

"*King Kong*," he says, "classic white-bread paranoid rape fantasy. Cool."

CHAPTER SEVEN

Downtime. Girl time. Miranda Lambert is singing "Gunpowder and Lead" on the iPod. Jesse hunches on her cot, knees drawn up, stripped down to a sports bra and panties. Right now she's inspecting her toenails and thinking the paint job's looking shabby.

She raises her head and listens to the storm grumble against the trailer walls. "You think the freakin' sand can blow right through my boots and chip my toenails?"

Laura, similarly dressed down, sits cross-legged on her bunk across the trailer, staring at a laptop. A full-blooded Lakota out of Standing Rock, she's a Grand Forks EMT in her other life. Without looking up, she answers, "Don't see why not. Blows into everything else: gauges and our watches and various nooks and crannies the guys joke about." In the morning, the two women will be flying side by side in Tumbleweed Six.

"Number four grit in the old nooks and crannies will separate the men from the boys, *every time*," Jesse observes.

"Who said that?"

"Think it was Sam." Then Jesse methodically works on her toenails with polish remover and cotton balls.

Laura goes back to her screen and says, "According to this, the first American female soldier was a Deborah. Except she went by 'Robert' . . ."

"Oh, yeah?"

"Yeah, this was like in the Revolutionary War. Says Deborah taped her breasts down . . ."

"Uh-huh."

31

"And she carved a musket ball out of her leg to escape being detected by the guys. Hmmm." Laura cups one of her ample breasts under her gray T-shirt and hefts it.

Jesse raises an eyebrow. "No way you'd make it in the Revolutionary War, girl."

"Why's that?"

"They didn't have Gorilla Tape back then."

Laura flings a pillow across the trailer. Jesse ducks and heaves the pillow back. "You got any of that Blue Iguana nail polish? I'm out," she says.

After digging in her toiletry bag, Laura flips a bottle. Jesse snaps it out of the air, opens it, and starts applying the paint. Laura turns back to her laptop and states, "Says here the army's designing a new uniform for chicks. For flat-chested captains mainly, so they don't look baggy across the front . . ."

★ ★ ★

The storm has passed, moving several cubic tons of Iraq downrange into the desert. A little before dawn, Jesse is walking out of the mess hall carrying a cup of coffee when she sees Major Greg Colbert, the flight company operations officer, talking to Lt. Col. Sampson, the battalion commander. Something about their posture and the cloistered nearness of their heads makes her look twice.

Then Colbert breaks away from the colonel and jogs over to her. Greg's usually impassive face is decidedly animated. He says, "Hey, Jess, glad I caught you before the intel briefing. They just scrambled the whole mission schedule," he says.

"What?"

"This FLASH order came down to us *bypassing* Corps and Brigade. High-profile spook stuff. Apache escort. We're flying a code name."

"We?"

"Actually, ah, me. I'm sitting in as commander on your mission set. You get to fly lead. I'll be on trail." He taps himself on the chest with mock seriousness. "And I thought the war was over. Major Greg Colbert, from Williston, North Dakota, is gonna haul a goddamn code name."

"I thought Task Force Brown handled that kind of mission." Task Force Brown is the off-limits special-operations compound on the base. Jesse lengthens her stride to keep pace with Colbert's long legs as they hurry back toward the battalion and the intel briefing in the mission shack.

"Don't know. Brown must be saturated," Colbert says.

"So what's the code name?"

"Busted Flush. Cool, huh?"

Inside the shack, Colbert, the plans officer, addresses the company pilots. Sure enough, he explains how they've been tasked with a short-notice, high-profile mission. So now the plans section has to reconfigure the pickup and delivery schedule around the standard ring route the company flies. Chaplain Lundquist offers a prayer for the day's missions. Colbert tells the pilots to check back in half an hour.

As the pilots file out grumbling, Colbert motions for Jesse to stay. When they are alone, he pulls up a tactical map. "I just talked to Busted Flush by sat. We're going in somewhere around here. By Samarra."

Jesse studies the map. "Who we hauling?"

Colbert waffles an open palm. "Sounds like a cop thing. You'll fly in empty. If it's a bust, you haul out the prisoners."

"Iraqi cops?" Jesse looks dubious. "Okay, just as long as they load their rifles after they get off the aircraft . . ."

"C'mon, these are special cops; they got an American with them. Guns are laid on as a precaution because of the mission status." He taps the map. "They won't give us an exact location until we're in the air."

"So where are they?" Jesse wonders.

"Catching a hop in from Washington." Meaning the Green Zone.

"They'll meet us on the flight line. That's it. Get your crew briefed."

Back out in the sun, Jesse admits to a slightly elevated pulse—spooks, code names, and all. Usually the missions are daylong milk runs—a minimum of two Hawks flying mutual support, ferrying troops and civilians from one forward base to another. Jesse lives in an American bubble, on the base or in the air. This could be different.

CHAPTER EIGHT

At 4 a.m. the veil of blowing sand dissolves into a crisp predawn stacked with twinkling stars. After sleeping in the Suburban's front seat, Morgon breakfasts on a thermos of strong Iraqi coffee and a Camel straight as Ahmed drives through the darkened outskirts of Samarra. The two escort cars with the security men stay behind. Now they rendezvous with a battered Toyota pickup packed with tribal militia armed with AK-47 rifles and RPG grenade launchers. Morgon glances at Ahmed hunched over the steering wheel and his cell phone. For the next two or three hours they are on their own.

Like Ahmed, Morgon now wears a loosely fitted tan *dishdasha* pulled over his Kevlar. His face hides in a checkered *kaffiyeh* headscarf secured by a plaited cord.

Under a pale sickle moon they race west through a hard-scrabble warren of villages, then slow and stop as a flush of blue-pink washes the eastern horizon. Morgon smells pungent, sluggish water. The roadbed creaks. They cross the spidery superstructure of a rickety, cantilevered bridge.

"Don't worry. It was built to handle heavy armor," Ahmed assures him when they halt on the far side. "We wait here 'til we can see."

Morgon takes advantage of the break to get out, stretch his legs, and look over the bridge that spans a 50-yard-wide canal with sides heaped in steep sand berms. Shadowy groves of date palms line the tops of the twin embankments.

Ahmed gets out, hugging his shoulders. "Cold, huh?" His words eject little white puffs in the chilly air.

A little past 5 a.m. the top of the sun pokes up in the east, and for a moment the blaze coexists with deep blue-lavender

35

shadow. Then Morgon feels the tingle of sunrise on his cheek and watches it slowly uncover a jumble of muddy red brick ramparts, narrow passages, and collapsed stairways. The ruins cover an area roughly the size of two football fields, and now that the sun has cleared the horizon, they merge into a switch-back maze of light and shadow that resembles the wreckage of an M.C. Escher Babylonian labyrinth.

Noland's work site is two hundred yards beyond the ruins, where piles of cinder block, corrugated steel, and scraps of twisted cyclone fence litter the desolation. Several men stand next to a truck, stamping their feet to keep warm. There's a shed, a dumpster on a lowboy, an old Land Rover, and a six-axle cement mixer with the drum turning.

"I'd send a couple guys to sweep through this brickyard, to make sure we don't have company," Morgon suggests. Ahmed barks an order in Arabic. Four of the tribals unsling their rifles and pad silently into the ruins.

Slowly the dawn creeps over the flat hardpan and uncovers a fragment of mud brick wall jutting up midway between the edge of the ruins and the work site. Like somebody could have built it last week. Or two thousand years ago, Morgon reflects. It's the dry climate. Out here you can't tell.

Half an hour later the scouts report back: all clear. Ahmed talks on his walkie-talkie to the men guarding the site. Then, after he posts six men to watch the bridge, he decides it's safe to proceed through the ruins.

Pulling up to the parked truck, Morgon shoots a glance at Ahmed. The truck is full of rusty artillery rounds.

"Don't worry," Ahmed says. "Like I said, we had to sort the cache. This is regular high explosive. We come across a lot of it in the construction business. We'll turn it in, say we found it on another work site."

Raising his eyebrows, Morgon indicates the welder's rig sitting next to the truck, twin tanks of oxygen and acetylene on a dolly. Ahmed shrugs and points past the truck, at two broad ground cloths stretched on crosspoles over what appears to be a long trench.

"We welded rebar in the excavation, to elevate the chemical rounds. So we could pour under them to make it tight all around."

As the workers pull back the tarps, Ahmed leans over and pops the glove compartment that contains a 9mm Beretta and a magazine. He looks at Morgon once, expressionless, then nods toward the tool shed. Then he exits the truck and walks over to the trench to watch the cement-truck workers unlimber the chute.

Morgon removes the pistol and tests the top round against the magazine spring with his thumb. Then he inserts the magazine, pulls the slide, releases it, and sets the safety. Out of the truck, he tucks the weapon in the belt that gathers his tunic as Ahmed motions him over to the pit.

"See," he points, "we didn't make this up."

Like a crop of dragon's teeth growing in concrete, the rows of artillery shells are buried up to their nose cones so only the death's-head stencils on the tips are visible. One of the shells lies horizontal and has been dismantled to reveal the nerve-agent components.

"So you can assure them back home nobody will ever use this stuff," Ahmed explains.

Morgon briefly gives the young Iraqi his full attention. Ahmed throws up his hands in protest. "Hey, we're Sunnis; some of my family has ties to the former regime. Nobody is gonna say shit about finding this."

Morgon nods, turns, and walks toward the shed. As his boots crunch on the hardpan, he's thinking how the last time he did this it had been a tactical exercise, reminiscent of the military. He'd had to creep up on the house outside Juarez. There were security guards to evade and terrain, distance, the sun, and wind direction to factor in. That target was a tier one scumbag and putting him down was doing the world a favor. Now the shed is only a few steps away and he's thinking how the guy in there is just a jerk who had too much sun, who had an idea and you could explain it to him all goddamn day and he wouldn't get it, why he has to go away.

A bearded man in a headdress stands guard in front of the shack. A screwdriver is jammed into the lock hasp that secures the corrugated metal door. Half-assed. Like parking a gas and air rig next to the high explosives. The guard removes the screwdriver and opens the door. Morgon steps in.

Richard Noland squats on a dirty bare mattress in a sudden rectangle of blinding light. Squinting, he can't make out Morgon, who makes a black silhouette backlit by the rising sun. Fat, shiny bluebottle flies buzz around a pail used as a toilet. The steel walls are heating up, and the pail reeks. Empty plastic water bottles and tinfoil food wrappers clutter the cement floor. Like Ahmed said, Noland should have stayed in Memphis. But here he is, wallowing in filth, chasing his get-rich-quick dream.

Noland blinks and raises his hand in a futile attempt to see better as Morgon removes the folded photocopy from his pocket. He's grown a little more beard, his greasy dishwater hair is a bit more tangled, and his face has added a layer of grime.

"Who the hell are you? What are they doing out there?" Noland blurts. "I hear them digging. I been in here for days, crapping in a bucket, for Christ's sake . . ."

"Richard Noland?" Morgon asks as he folds the ID sheet and tucks it in his pocket.

"Yeah, right. Quit screwing around. You're an American, right? So get me out of here," he almost shouts.

As Morgon eases out the Beretta, the thought occurs that Noland wouldn't be in this fix if he'd remembered he was an American too.

Of all the possible words a man could choose at a moment like this, the best Noland can summon up is "Hey—shit?" Blinded by the blazing sunlight, he probably can't even see the pistol leveling at his face.

The first shot strikes left of the nose, punches through his throat, exits the back of his neck, and plinks a hole in the corrugated wall. As he pitches to the side, a thin spoke of laser-bright light pops from the bullet hole and bisects the dark interior of the shed. Maybe it's the arch scent of cordite or the seep of blood. The flies rise in an agitated swarm. Noland has fallen on his side, quivering. Morgon steps forward, places his boot on the twitching shoulder, pushes him on his back, and fires twice more into his chest. Then he squats, quickly retrieves and pockets the three expended casings, gets up, turns, and walks from the shed.

The guard and another tribesman enter the shed, and each grab one of Noland's ankles and drag him out into the sun and then toward the excavation trench. Morgon follows behind them.

Ahmed joins him as the two draggers toss Noland's body over the edge, where it does a ragdoll tumble and winds up spread-eagled on the nose cones. Ahmed gives a signal, the cement mixer revs up, and slushy, greenish-gray cement pours into the pit. Two men in tall rubber boots take hoes and step gingerly among the dragon's teeth, spreading out the pour, covering the nose cones and Noland's body. In the dry desert air the cement coursing down the chute gives off a damp odor somewhere between dirty socks and yeast.

"You verify the rounds are being properly disposed of?" Ahmed asks.

"Looks good to me," Morgon says. "What about him?" he nods toward Noland's half-submerged corpse.

"On the way out the boys will shoot up his truck and put an RPG into the shed. A couple of these guys worked for him.

They'll go to the cops in Samarra and say they were attacked and Noland was taken."

"So how long do we have to stick around?"

"Well, the truck will be through in another twenty minutes, but we should stay after it leaves. Maybe two hours." Ahmed points to a Bobcat that is spreading and smoothing excess dirt from the trench. "That's the minimum amount of time for the pour to set up. Then the Bobcat can fill it in and clean it up. After a few days the wind will do the rest."

"Two hours," Morgon repeats. Then he walks to Ahmed's Suburban, reaches in for a liter bottle of water, and takes a long drink. He shakes the thermos, which is still half full, so he pours some coffee into the travel cup Ahmed provided. Then he walks away from the gravel swoosh of the cement truck and seeks relief from the sun in the shadows of the ruins. Pausing, he runs his hand along the pitted adobe-colored bricks. In his travels he has visited Stonehenge, Angkor Wat, Giza, and Machu Picchu. Stone is the only thing that lasts. Everything else turns to dust. *How old are these bricks?* he wonders as he takes a sip of coffee. *Have to look it up. Not real fancy. Lacks the power of, say, Inca stonework. But old.*

Again he touches the surface of the wall and tries to imagine the men who built it, their brown hands setting the bricks. And he wonders what they were thinking out here in all this silence, with all this sun and sky?

John the Baptist came out of this emptiness, and Jesus and Mohammad and Moses. Bound to happen; you stare into this big sky long enough, you're going to start building castles.

Morgon checks his watch and reaches for a cigarette. Two hours, Ahmed said.

CHAPTER NINE

An hour before liftoff, Jesse is walking to the crew briefing when Sergeant Bailey sidles over to her. "What's up, Marge?" Jesse asks. Marge isn't flying this morning.

"Might be a good idea to check out Sam," Marge says. Jesse turns and peruses Master Sergeant Dillon, who is bringing up the rear. Sam is looking particularly rough in the morning sun. His leathery face is pasty, and his eyes are hiding, as usual, behind his sunglasses.

"He got a hangover behind those shades?" Jesse asks.

Marge shakes her head. "Been up all night on Skype with his daughter in Grand Forks. About Ella."

Jesse raises an eyebrow. "So he's operating on zero sleep?"

Marge shrugs. "Well, you know how he dotes on his grandkid . . ."

"Yeah." Jesse nods, mindful that Sam keeps a picture of the little girl, five-year-old Ella, taped inside the chopper door next to his M240 machine gun.

"Ella's running a 105-degree temp. Which means he'll be going into the mission distracted and burnt to a crisp," Marge says, perfectly masking her concern in a matter-of-fact military tone. In her other life, Marge is a bank loan officer in Grand Forks. She is fond of Dillon, and Jesse suspects the two of them hook up in their off hours.

So Jesse weighs the peculiar vicissitudes of the National Guard deployed in the instant-messaging war. They are about to fly what could be a real combat mission over the Iraqi desert. And Marge is worried about old Sam, who is worried about his five-year-old grandchild in Grand Forks, North Dakota.

41

"I'm up on rotation. I could sit in for Sam. Let him get some rack time," says Marge.

Jesse mulls it and nods. "I'll talk to him, then run it by Major Colbert." Then she slows her pace, falls in step beside Dillon, takes a breath, and lets out, "Do me a favor and dial down the shades."

He removes the sunglasses.

"Those are some eyes, Sam," she says.

"Well, Skipper, I was up kind of late."

"Marge filled me in. So how's Ella doing?"

"Still running the fever. But, you know, kids can shake a high temp . . . bounce right back."

Jesse smiles tightly. The many things she knows do not include insight into a five-year-old's fever resilience.

"I'm thinking you should take a break today," she says.

"That you talking or Marge Bailey?"

"You see anyone else standing here?" Jesse says, the thin edge coming into her voice.

"No, ma'am." Sam shakes his head. "Just . . . ain't that life in the Guard: a forty-nine-year-old female sergeant and a twenty-seven-year-old female captain stand down the old guy. Hell of a note."

"Can't have you flying on no sleep." Jesse is adamant. "I'm switching Marge in to take your shift. Now grab a reset day and go get some rest. You're off the mission, if Major Colbert agrees, and I'm sure he will. We clear?"

"Clear, Skipper."

Before the briefing Jesse tells Major Colbert she's got a problem with Sam flying the mission. "Goddamn Sam," Colbert says. "He put in for the waiver to keep flying past sixty. Word just came through they turned it down. When we get back, you have to tell him."

"I'll put it on my to-do list," Jesse says. Then she tells him about Marge's concern, and Colbert concurs with her assessment. He okays swapping Dillon out and putting Marge in Jesse's ship as crew chief. Jesse sends word to Dillon: it's final; stand down and get some sleep. The way the new crew equation works out, Jesse's Black Hawk, Tumbleweed Six, will be flying with her roommate Laura in the other front seat—so two female pilots and a female crew chief. This crew mix is called pulling a 'Medium Minnesota,' a tribute to the historic mission the 2/147—a Minnesota Guard helicopter assault battalion—pulled off on Christmas Day 2007, when they sortied two Hawks out of Balad totally crewed by women.

After briefing on weather conditions—which are real good—and the threat level in the mission area—which is real low—the crews ride to the flight line and start gearing up with weapons, ceramic body armor, and survival vests.

The fourth crew member, door gunner Spec Four Toby Nguyen, strikes a pose and observes, "Now that you upset the hormone balance on the aircraft, I'll have to take my anti-estrogen poisoning pills."

"Put a zipper on it, Toby," Jesse shoots back. "You're still on probation."

"So you sent Sam home to take a nap," Laura says as she pulls her hair into a ponytail.

"Yep. He's tuckered out and needs a long rest," Jesse says.

"Oh, I don't know," Laura grins.

"You just like him 'cause he's old and toothless," Jesse counters.

Laura bats her wide, dark eyes over her wide cheekbones and treats Jesse to an enigmatic Great Plains smile. "I kinda like the way he *walks*."

"Yeah, how's that?" Jesse asks.

A few feet away, Marge Bailey glances up from her clipboard and says, "Like a John Wayne movie, Captain. Before your time."

"Yo, daddy," Jesse drawls. "I saw *Green Berets* when I was a kid. That's the one where they have the sun *setting* in the east over the South China Sea behind old John's fat ass."

"Figures. Vietnam was fucked up 'cause they didn't have GPS," Laura quips.

Then, more serious, Jesse tells Marge to get on with her checks. Toby sees to his and Marge's machine guns. Jesse wipes down the cockpit windows with Windex and a paper towel. Then she pulls on her flak vest and web harness and loads her pistol. She stows her flight bag and M4 rifle into the cockpit and is about to climb in when two Humvees roll up and eight armed men get out next to Colbert's chopper. Seven of them are pretty mean-looking Iraqis turtled up in body armor and web gear. The eighth man wears a vest jammed with magazines for the M4 Carbine slung over his shoulder. He's this wiry American in a black T-shirt, jeans, and a shapeless bush hat with a low brim. Dress code rule of thumb: the more clout you got, the sloppier clothes you can wear. So that must be Busted Flush. The low-hanging hat and his outsized sunglasses effectively conceal his face.

"Snake Eater," says a familiar voice to her right rear. She turns and sees Sam standing behind her, removing his sunglasses. Wrinkled and red-eyed, he points at the American climbing on Colbert's Hawk. "See the watch? Them Snake Eaters always wear them gold Rolexes."

"Sam, you're supposed to be in quarters. Take off."

"Hoo-ah," Sam says, raises a finger to the brim of his cap, and decorates the runway with a stream of Copenhagen. Then, after he has a brief word with Marge, he ambles away. Jesse watches him depart, studying the swing to his still broad shoulders and narrow cowboy hips.

Get serious, Jess.

All business, she climbs in the cramped cockpit and puts on her helmet. Pilots adhere to ritual, and the last item on Jesse's checklist is to inspect the duct tape that holds the male hula doll on the dashboard in place. Sam again. When the guys in the battalion started sticking hula girls on their dashboards, Sam located the hula boys on eBay and gave one to each of the women pilots. When the chopper vibrates, the boy toy wiggles his plastic butt.

Onward. Jesse pulls on her fire-resistant Nomex flight gloves and checks the comms again: VHF, UHF, an electronic digital pad fastened to her knee, Blue Force tracker, MERC, the texting chat room if needed. She confers with Laura, who marks the flight route to the rally point in yellow magic marker on her map. Flying the aircraft is a full-time job, so she hands off navigation and comms to Laura.

Before Laura puts on her helmet, she grins and holds up a tin of Skoal. Jesse makes a face and shakes her head. Their personal joke. She tried the stuff once on a night mission when she was at the ragged end of her endurance. Once was enough.

Ignition. The composite titanium and fiberglass four-bladed rotor slaps the desert air. In a bloom of sweet-scented fuel, they rush through the remaining preflight checks. "I got it," Jesse says, taking the controls. Wheels up at 0700 hrs.

With twenty-two hundred pounds of fuel on board, Jesse eases up on the collective with her left hand, jockeys the cyclic with her right, and lightly toes the pedals. Her slope-nosed, six-ton, six million dollar ride heaves up from the strip like a muscle-bound predatory bus. As the base runway falls away, the familiar, flat checkerboard of tan on green on brown stretches out in a grid of farm fields and canals from horizon to horizon.

As the two Hawks motor over the base perimeter, they run their "Wall Check" to make sure weapons, lights, and aircraft survivability equipment are in working order. Two Apache gunships are already aloft and will trail them at altitude.

"Red Side coming up. Keep your eyes open," Jesse tells the crew on the internal comms, just like she always does.

"Crossing wires," Toby calls out.

"Roger."

★ ★ ★

Fifty air miles north of Balad, they circle at the rally point, and the horizon stretches out in flat monotonous shades of tan hardpan, muddy canals, field green, and little turd-colored clumps of mud-brick houses. Out the right window, the Tigris River winds in the distance like an algae boa constrictor.

Colbert checks in, "It's confirmed. We're going to Ramil. We'll approach it from the south up the big canal. It's perfect for us."

Jesse keys her mic and points Tumbleweed Six north along the Tigris until Colbert signals the turn. A few minutes later, Marge calls out on the internal comms, "Tracers at seven o'clock, 300 yards."

"Diagonal or straight up?" Jesse asks, feeling a slight adrenaline surge.

"No sweat. Straight up."

"You copy, Tumbleweed Five?" Jesse calls Colbert.

"Roger. Some farmer pissed off we're over his field." The Apaches, nonchalant killers, merely key their mics in acknowledgement.

Jesse concentrates on flying. Tracers straight up are the farmer's equivalent of flipping the bird. Diagonal tracers could mean aimed fire. Aimed fire could be a lure to get the Hawks to swing down and investigate. Some *hajji* with half a brain could be waiting to launch an RPG or the much more accurate SA16, a shoulder-fired heat-seeking missile.

That could mean Red Screen of Death time.

Stateside, once a year she travels to Camp Ripley in Minnesota to check out on their flight simulator. You screw up on the SIM, and the windshield video pops bright red. You get the Red Screen of Death, it means you crashed.

Jess watches hula boy shake his tush on the dashboard. She hasn't crashed yet, SIM or real world. She's a natural pilot and, if pressed, will tell you that flying the huge Hawk is a delicate, sensory ballet played out with subtle pressure in her fingers and toes. Terry once likened her to a war witch flying a mean steel broom across the face of the full moon. The collective and the cyclic controls are her magic wands.

Maybe. But to Jesse, bottom line, it's a piece of machinery. Like Dad's old Ford 9N tractor she climbed on and mastered when she was twelve, standing up because she couldn't reach the pedals from the seat. It's all about balancing the competing consequences of centrifugal force with gentle pulses of pressure on the collective, cyclic, and pedals. Minding the instruments. Feeding in and decreasing the pitch and torque and throttle.

Back in the States, girls she went to school with are lining up at Starbucks ordering their lattes. Jesse's doing 120 knots fifty feet over the Mesopotamian hardpan by virtue of keeping two spinning discs in perfect sync—one over her head and another on the tail boom. Plus, unlike her suburban sisters, she's got a tender grasp on the cyclic jammed straight up between her thighs like a bad but potent Freudian joke.

You're a type A power-tripper; you love being strapped inside a war machine. Another Terryism.

Jesse glances over at Laura, who is coolly helmeted and visored and vested and armored and armed. If Laura bopped into that Starbucks in full battle rattle, those sisters would pee their Victoria's Secret panties.

Jesse swings her eyes and scans the desert floor, where the Hawks cast two black racing shadows and reflects that maybe Terry has a point. No denying the power thing.

Colbert calls, "Echo tango alpha to objective one zero mikes. Gunners test your guns."

Marge and Toby rip a few bursts down into the desert.

"Okay, Tumbleweed Six, check it on tracker," Colbert calls again. "We're coming up on the canal. It has high sides screened by palms. We'll shoot right up it. You fly lead, hugging the canal; I'll follow. Should cover the approach."

"Tumbleweed Six, roger."

A few minutes later, conforming to Colbert's flight path, flying right on the deck, Jesse spots the broad canal flanked by palms. Colbert drifts to the left, and Jesse takes the lead, drops into the slot, and contours north, date palms zipping past on either side.

CHAPTER TEN

Two raggedy children with dirty faces and eyes dark as the Black Stone of Mecca hunker at the edge of the ruins, minding five skinny camels. They stare at one of Ahmed's crew, a young kid, who is eagerly lining up his RPG rocket launcher at the tool shed. Ahmed breaks off, trots over, and sternly shoos the kids back to the north, beyond the ruins.

Morgon glances at his watch; it's thirty-five minutes past Ahmed's two hours. The cement truck has departed. The Bobcat has finished its job and is parked on a trailer along with the welder's equipment behind the truck. Except for the kid with the rocket and the truck driver, Ahmed's men have taken the Suburban and relocated to the bridge. Casually Ahmed raises his AK and fires a burst into Noland's Land Rover. The windshield shatters. The kid with the rocket laughs. Morgon turns and looks ruefully at the truck full of artillery rounds that is going to be their transportation up to the bridge. But the truck hood is open, and the driver is now arguing with Ahmed. Morgon gathers that the vehicle is flooded.

Slowly his eyes track the horizon. Outwardly he appears as undisturbed as the flat, empty desert. But he knows the desert's deceptive and relies on a frail skin of pebbles to hold it in place. Crack that "desert pavement," and it will gush dust.

The driver closes the truck hood, gets in, and this time the vehicle starts. Ahmed raises his hand, thumbs up to Morgon; then he signals to the kid with the RPG he can go ahead and shoot the shed with his rocket.

Morgon *feels* it at first, a vibration thrumming in his chest. Then he hears the unmistakable rotor beat of an approaching

49

helicopter. But muffled. Where? He swings his head. The sky is empty. Then he knows. *The canal.*

"Wait, don't shoot!" he shouts to Ahmed and the kid with the RPG. Too late. The rocket sizzles off, and the shed erupts in a deafening burst of flame, smoke, and dust.

Jesse is flying ten feet over the water when she sees the arch of the bridge. "Be advised, Tumbleweed Five. We got a high bridge coming up across the canal."

Then she hauls in the controls and brings the Hawk up to clear the bridge, and that's when the internal comms crackle with Toby's shout: "Explosion, ten o'clock, 400 yards!"

Next comes Laura's controlled yell: "Hard left, RPG twelve o'clock off the nose." On pure reflex, Jesse yanks in pitch and puts the Hawk on its side in an abrupt left turn, and the world speeds up in a blur of date palms and muddy water. Now she's flying over deserted ruins as the rocket flashes past the cockpit window in a rush of whitish, blue-gray smoke. *Wow, little pucker factor there. First time in daylight.*

Sonofabitch, that was almost close enough to touch.

Then it's Marge's turn: "*Hajji's* in the open."

Morgon is momentarily stunned when the Black Hawk jumps over the palm trees four hundred yards away—this black, roaring, sixty-five-foot-long steel flying insect attracted to the exploding shed. He recovers immediately and shouts, "Ahmed, tell your men at the bridge to do nothing, freeze—understand?"

Ahmed stares at him open-mouthed, his walkie-talkie hanging useless in his hand.

And then Morgon sees the rocket contrail race up from the cover of the palms along the waterway. Sees the chopper lurch toward them, taking evasive action. Shit. Some idiot back at the bridge has panicked and fired an RPG. And now the kid with

Ahmed has touched off a second one at the chopper that is still rocking on its side in their direction.

It's gonna be amateur hour.

"Holy shit! Another RPG, two o'clock," Toby yells into the comms.

Jesse calls her move to the gun bunnies overhead. "I'm breaking hard left. Contact my two o'clock," she croaks, suddenly dry-mouthed.

"Get out of there, Jesse," Colbert says urgently, stepping on her transmission to the Apaches.

Jesse finds her steady aviator voice that had momentarily got stuck in her throat. "You bet."

"Get your ass clear," Colbert shouts in the radio. "Guns are lining up."

"Hold on, it could get hot!" Jesse shouts on the crew intercom as icicles stitch a tight pattern between her shoulder blades and up her neck. Her heart bangs against the ceramic plate over her chest as she hauls in the collective and the two General Electric turbo-shaft engines surge. She's absolutely programmed to fly the Hawk but, back channel, her senses pound out an inarticulate battle prayer: *Our father red screen of death motherfucker!*

Do your job.

She puts the Hawk on its side, rolls away from the second RPG, and sees a truck down there. "Toby, Marge?"

"I count three *hajjis* by that truck," Marge comes back.

"One of them has another RPG," Laura calls out.

Jesse cranes her neck, catches a glimpse of three men running for cover, and marks the shape of the shoulder-fired missile one of them carries. "Keep them off me so we can get the hell outta here," she shouts to Marge and Toby.

"I'm on them," Marge answers in a tight, focused voice.

In a heartbeat Morgon adapts and calculates the distance and the angle. The left-side gunner is lining up on him. The only cover is the fragment of brick wall twenty yards distant. His hands move, seeing the solution before his mind catches up. He seizes the RPG-7 from the confused kid, snatches another long-stemmed rocket from the pouch on his back, loads the weapon, and motions to Ahmed and the kid to duck for cover behind the wall.

A string of machine-gun rounds kicks up sand as they sprint and hunker against the rocks. Morgon rolls, shifting position as the gunner hangs out on his harness and sprays more rounds. Sharp bits of silica pepper his face as he rises behind the wall and swings the launcher toward the truck full of artillery rounds with the tanks of oxygen and acetylene hooked behind. Not more than a hundred yards away. That's too close. But he has no choice.

"No, No," Ahmed yells. Terrified, he points toward the turning helicopter.

"There's going to be an explosion," Morgon yells back. "And one hell of a dust cloud. Should cover us to run for the ruins. Now get down."

Then Morgon takes a fatal second to orient because another Black Hawk has cleared the palms. The Hawks aren't a problem; they're just transports. He's tracking two more aircraft that are leveling out in the distance, their snouts heavy with armament. *Apaches.* A fraction too long, he watches the fleeing Blawk Hawk's sinister, rotating shadow flit on the hardpan near the truck. *Do it.* He raises the launcher, leans into the optical sight, steadies the reticle on the truck, and squeezes the trigger. Then he ducks. The ground rocks, his eardrums burst, and fists of sand hammer his mouth and eyes. A millisecond after the shock wave, the world explodes.

CHAPTER ELEVEN

The Screen of Death is not red.

The black crackling flash rips up through the steel cockpit deck, and the Hawk dies in a wrenching metal roar that drowns out Jesse's scream, "Tumbleweed Six going down!" Instinctively she jerks the cyclic to avoid the thrust of the blast. Big mistake. Now's she's in a bone-breaking struggle with the stick and jumping pedals to correct the violent yaw and right the ship from flipping. Lights flash on the console she's never seen before. Her helmet's gone in a violent shrapnel-studded rush, windshield's gone, *Laura's gone*. There's this sickening smell and then a more sickening vibration. The props are shredding, coming apart. Fighting the controls, she stares at her bare right knee—white of bone, red of blood. Looks up. Altitude? Level bubble?

No help. Somebody's guts on the instrument panel.

She's not flying the chopper. This little tin soldier strapped in her bursting heart informs her, *Captain, you better straighten this fucker out and get her down, or you're gonna kill your crew.*

She's blind in a pitching black maelstrom of dust, smoke, fire, leaking gas, sparks, and sizzling circuitry. Tumbleweed Six now has the aerodynamics of a plummeting safe. Riding it in, she reaches up and yanks the power-control levers. Fuel off. Battery off. Not aware she's screaming, she wills the Hawk to earth in a six-ton belly flop. A couple Gs of impact purees the marrow in her bones as blazing gravedigger dirt engulfs her mouth, her nose, her eyes. Nothing.

Everybody's yelling on the comms in Tumbleweed Five, how it looks like a freakin' ammo dump cooking off down there as Colbert fights to bring the aircraft in trim after being buffeted by the shock wave. The crew chief and gunner are re-straining Joe Davis, who's out of his seat gesturing furiously for Colbert to take it down. Colbert ignores the rumpus. Nausea rises in his throat as he watches the crippled, whirling shadow of Tumbleweed Six auger in at the edge of the mushrooming explosion, sees a second huge geyser of dust erupt on impact.

"Slow your roll. Can't do nothin' 'til all that shit clears," he tells everybody in a hoarse, controlled voice. Then he switches to the country-wide Safe Skies net and says, "Tumbleweed Five, grid line 38-Sierra—Lima Charlie—82824-80212. Fallen Angel. I say again, fallen angel."

Tumbleweed Six plows a trench into the dirt, and the front canopy disintegrates into plastic shrapnel and the rotors chew up the hardpan, beat themselves to splinters, and fling a huge cloud of dirt and sand that swells into the churning debris. Titanium/fiberglass razors the size of cookie sheets zing and slash through the cockpit and smash up the instruments. They ricochet off debris and miss Jesse. They carve Laura Double Bear's body to pieces.

The grinding wreckage convulses and shivers and slaps Jesse in and out of consciousness, and after everything else stops, it's still shaking inside her head and she has this awful taste in her mouth. Her first impulse from training is to try to get a grip. On what? Shock, pain, death? *Okay, you're still alive. You just can't move.* She's trapped between the armored back of her seat and the crumpled instrument panel. She's up to her nose in scorching sand and pebbles and shattered plastic. She can feel her feet and hands struggle to move, so she's not para-lyzed. Apparently the shock-absorber system in the seat actually worked.

Figuring this out only makes her more acutely aware of the dying electronics crackling all around. Fluids drip, and she real-izes in slow horror that she's smothered in body parts. Before the full effect of *that* takes hold, a loopy flash of flame sears the dirty sweat on her face, and she thinks, *Oh my God, I'm going to burn. Hyperventilation, tachycardia, the end.*

But the flicker of fire fades and she blinks away dirt so she can see a little now through the tangled rubbish of the instrument panel. And what her eyes focus on is this spectral figure that staggers in the dust.

It's Marge.

CHAPTER TWELVE

Morgon hugs the obstinate chunk of ancient Babylonian wall that saved his life. Then, slowly, he forces himself up on his elbows and knees. He lurches to his feet and, as the lore accumulated through all the bad close times kicks in, he feels himself for wet spots. He's momentarily disoriented, like in a sandstorm with his vision plugged. After pawing at his eyes, he can barely make out the broken Black Hawk stove in the dirt a dozen yards in front of him, with the stump of one rotor still vibrating and the roof sprung like a crushed steel coffin. Then he sees what he thinks is the kid running away, disappearing in and out of the billowing dust. Thinks to call out for Ahmed. But he isn't functioning yet, having trouble with his balance. Numb, he staggers toward the wreck.

Involuntarily he flinches and ducks as a sparkling pinwheel of flame illuminates the gloom. Jesus. Some of the artillery rounds are still going off.

Then he experiences a confused moment when he feels a pocket of air dislocate past his cheek. He doesn't hear the *snap-hiss* but something tells him *that was a bullet.*

He swivels his head and sees this tough-looking soldier clawing out of a gunner pocket. The dirt on his face is turned muddy by all the blood, and he rears up like an animated part of the wreckage—uniform torn, leaking what's inside him. But he's steadying a black pistol in both red hands, arms extended in the Weaver stance—like he knows what he's doing.

Survival reflexes trump conscious thought, and Morgon has the Beretta out as he crouches and sidesteps and rapid fires twice. The red figure drops. When he picks up movement in the corner of his eye, he rotates, swinging the pistol to his front like a divining rod. *Someone else is out there weaving in the dust.*

Suddenly Ahmed is next to him, feeling him for wounds. "Can you breathe okay?" he yells. Then he strips off Morgon's headdress and dumps a bottle of water on Morgon's head, wiping caked grime from his hair, face, and neck.

Morgon points to his ears. Can't hear. But his eyes work, because suddenly they are staring at an apparition that sways on unsteady feet in the smoke and dust.

"Shit, man," Ahmed blurts, "it's a chick."

Morgon blinks sand, shakes his head, and stares at the blast-burned, bleeding, barely recognizable woman. Her uniform hangs in black oily rags, and half her short, dirty-reddish hair is seared away.

A scoured ceramic chest plate dangles in shreds of webbing. Blood trickles on her bare soot-blackened torso, and her mangled left arm hangs limp.

But her right arm is working okay because she yanks a black automatic pistol from the smoking tatters of her survival vest and struggles to raise it. Morgon blinks, striving to get his bearings.

His control slips and he rages out loud, "Goddamn sonofabitch!" None of this was supposed to happen.

The woman gasps, maybe hearing him speak but definitely looking askance at his desert tunic and then staring at his face. "American?" she croaks. Trembling, unsteady, she drops her weapon and pitches forward onto her knees.

"Goddamn sonofabitch," Morgon shouts again to clear his blocked ears, and he claws dirt from his eyes as the moment turns weird and suspended and Ahmed and the woman drift in the smoke all covered in desert gunk like beige aborigines in a ceremony. Can hear a little now. Ahmed is yelling, "We have to go. In a minute this dust will clear. Everything in Iraq that can fly . . ."

Morgon nods and tries to think as the survivor stares up at him, dirty whites of her eyes like two blood-streaked marbles in her scalded face. Looking at him. Looking *into* him.

"Pilots." She makes the croaking sound again, struggling to rise. "Gotta help . . ."

Morgon blinks through an involuntary shudder. Dammit. It's all upside down; vertigo, nausea, vomit rising in his throat. Her damn accusing eyes. He stares at the pistol in his dirty hand.

"Leave it; she's dying." Ahmed pulls his shoulder.

Morgon shakes him off, shouting because of his blocked ears. "She isn't dying, and help's on the way. I've been seen. No loose ends, gotta make sure." To avoid her grave, bloodshot eyes, he steps behind her, raises the pistol at the back of her head, and fires twice.

★ ★ ★

Ten feet away, Jesse is entombed in the clutter of the smashed cockpit, going numb and out-of-body strange, and she's spitting dirt, and all she's got left is her eyes. If she hangs on—North Dakota tough—hard enough, her eyes, locked wide open, will work beneath the muddy veil of gore and sequins of shattered plastic and instruments. Moment of hope now, seeing Marge take labored steps. *C'mon, girl, I know you're hurting, but I'm just over here. You're my lifeline. Just keep coming.*

Then, aw shit, there's a *hajji* fucker in a filthy checkered headdress, and now Jesse finds herself alone in a place beyond any notion of fear she's ever known. The guy's got a pistol that he raises and shoots at something. *Not me. Past me.* Then he sees Marge, and then there's another one of them.

Jesse realizes by her frantic exhalations that she's raging to move her hands, but they're stuck immobile in dirt and debris. *Gotta get to my pistol because Marge's out there all alone with those bastards. But I'm stuck and can't move. Not even to look away. Never been here before. This godawful helpless.* The only thing she can do to fight back is will her eyes to stay open. Through the rush and ringing in her ears, she hears the one with the pistol yell muddy words through her fouled hearing. Sounds like he's swearing. The other one removes the first guy's headdress and pours water on his head from a plastic bottle, and that's no hajji because she sees strands of muddy hair shine like copper wire and in a moment of acoustic clarity hears him swear "Goddamn sonofabitch" in American English.

"Been seen," he rages.

And she suddenly realizes she doesn't have to stay here where it's real bad and getting worse, pinned in the present with the first sharkbite of real pain showing teeth through the shock. She can leave. There's endless room to hide inside, and the momentum builds to lose the outside and collapse toward endless possibilities opening inside. And why not, because *Oh Jesus God I got guts in my face and I wanna go home and I don't want to see what they're doing to Marge out there because the guy with the copper hair is raising the pistol again, and I want to help but I can't fucking move!*

Jesse can feel herself letting go, shutting down, blocking it out one piece of cloudy light after another. The scene in the dust tightens down to a tangle—raised, livid, red—pulsing like a pile of worms that writhe into the shape of a scarlet five-pointed star, and then she pulls her eyes in after her, and now she can stretch out free as she gently twirls into all this space that's there for her to get away, and it's soft and cool as she spirals gratefully into the darkness.

CHAPTER THIRTEEN

Morgon steps over the crew woman's body, pokes into the wreckage, and puts two more rounds into the gunner to make sure. Then he looks in the cockpit, which is pure *Texas Chainsaw Massacre.* Ahmed yanks him away, yelling, "Time to go, man."

Ahmed drags him in a loping sprint through the churning dust, and they trip and fall over a low wall. Okay, they're in the ruins. They scramble on all fours, then scuttle, bent over, deeper into the maze of collapsed brick. A shape rises up in front of them, and Morgon snaps up the Beretta, but it's the kid who had the RPG shaking like a palsied dog but grinning too. He waves to them and, panting, they pause and look back at the shadowy helicopters prowling the edges of the dust cloud. The tension releases in the form of spontaneous hysterical laughter, like juveniles who've pulled off a Halloween prank. Just as rapidly the sick mirth dissipates, and they stare at each other through the choking film of dust.

Panting, Morgon experiences a rare flicker of remorse. *She was wearing a US Army uniform.* Before he can explore the implications of *that,* he feels a cool slap on his cheek and he stares at a dervish of pure clean air that cuts a swirling hole in the dust, and suspended in the hole he sees this angry black dragonfly.

Shit. The Apaches!

Instinctively, he dives for deeper cover, grabbing Ahmed, dragging him down as a buzz saw rips the air. All around them, the thousand-year-old bricks explode and shatter into dancing gobs of sun-baked mud. Which is what happens when you wind up on the business end of a 30mm chain gun spitting out 625 rounds of high-explosive dual-purpose ammo per minute.

Panting and shaking, Morgon is crammed against another comforting thickness of Babylonian wall and sees that the dust cloud has enveloped him again, blinding the attack chopper.

"C'mon, we gotta move," he yells, tugging at Ahmed. But Ahmed doesn't budge. He's staring at a bundle of bloody rags that a moment before was the kid. Morgon rolls him over and checks the eyes, locked wide open. He looks just once at the shards of ribcage mixed with bits of mushroom pink. Sees a last air bubble go *pop*.

Quickly he yanks off the kid's blood-drenched Arab shirt and flings it aside along with the ammo bandoleer and the blood-streaked AK. And the RPG launcher the kid had retrieved from the crash site.

"What?" Ahmed is confused, gesturing.

"Leave some blood-trail evidence; give some credence to your kidnap story." He reaches out and grabs Ahmed's rifle and tosses it aside. Then he points to the walkie-talkie Ahmed still has clutched in his hand. "Call the guys at the bridge, tell them we're hauling a body they have to get out of here." As Ahmed makes the call, Morgon discards his own shirt and vest and hoists the smaller man's body over his shoulders in a fireman's carry. Not pausing to look back, they trot deeper into the ruins, toward the bridge and the truck.

CHAPTER FOURTEEN

A second after the explosion, Tumbleweed Five is slipping and sliding in the shock wave, and Colbert is fighting the controls. Joe Davis tears away the latches of his seat harness, loses his helmet and mic, and lunges forward over the equipment stowed between the gunner's pockets. As he thrusts his head into the cockpit, the crew chief rises on his flexible harness and tries to restrain him. Joe flings the man aside, pounds Colbert on the shoulder, and stabs his finger in a violent downward gesture.

"Take me down!" he screams. But voice communication is only possible over the engine noise of an operating Black Hawk in the movies. Now the crew chief and the gunner are on him, helmeted and visored and armored like *Star Wars* storm troopers, and they roughly manhandle him back to his seat. Colonel Nasir clamps a steely hand on his shoulder, and Davis relents, seeing the caution, warning, and weary pain in the Iraqi's dark eyes.

Davis lurches back down and replaces his helmet and mic. He understands, of course. The fuckin' military. There is a procedure that must be followed. So vital minutes are lost while they wait for the smoke and dust to clear. He has no use for procedure and rules. He resents the chain of command. Most of all, he hates the notion that orders come down from assholes removed from the event. He believes all events are unique and dictate unique action.

And so they circle and wait until the last errant artillery round shoots off and the dust settles like a shroud over the gaping crater, strewn debris, and the buckled wreckage of Tumbleweed Six. Through an opening in the dust, the Apaches spot the insurgents running away and swoop in low and hose down the ruins with their chain guns. Then the dust closes in again.

When the Apache commander decides it's safe, Colbert puts it down. Davis, Nasir, and the Iraqi intelligence cops leave the Hawk at gymnastic speed. They ignore the shouting crew chief. All veterans, they know you exit a Hawk at right angles to avoid the forward droop of the rotating blades. They fan out through the carnage. Davis heads for the wreck. Nasir leads his men toward the ruins.

The crew chief and the gunner detach their guns and set up a defensive perimeter to the front and rear of the chopper. The copilot stays on the controls, ready to leave fast if they have to. Davis follows after Colbert, who has sprinted ahead and now kneels over a ragged body in the dust ten feet in front of the wreckage. He checks for vital signs. He doesn't find any.

Davis catches up just as Colbert throws off his helmet and plunges into the broken aircraft. First he crawls across the buckled cargo hold and checks the gunner. He shakes his head. Then he comes around and confronts the crumpled cockpit, pauses to gather himself, climbs in, and gingerly tosses aside a portion of human torso. He plunges his hands into the loam of debris, reaches down, and probes with his fingers. Then he starts digging madly, jerks his head, and screams at Davis, "C'mon! A pilot's still alive!"

Davis joins Colbert and, inch by inch, they excavate the filthy ragamuffin head and shoulders of the slender pilot. Their hands are urgent and gentle by turns, clearing away dirt and debris, checking for wounds.

Now other aircraft arrive: First a brace of Kiowa scouts and two more Apache gunships. High up, F-18s circle. A medevac lands, and two medics rush out with a stretcher. Colbert and Davis step back to let them work.

Davis' shoulder mic crackles. Nasir's voice is as scratchy as the static as he says, "Joe, Nasir. We've cleared the ruins. Didn't find anybody."

"What the fuck happened?"

"Don't know, it was a freak. I don't know."

"One thing for sure, we aren't going to Ramil today," Davis mutters. Dizzy, drenched in sweat, he blinks to get his bearings. He identifies the problem and reaches for a water bottle in his cargo pocket. He thinks he has to call Appert back in Baghdad and tell him the Ramil raid went tits up. He'll do that later. Then he sees Colbert's hands, bleeding through his shredded Nomex flight gloves.

Without thinking, he removes the first-aid kit from Colbert's survival vest. He knows where it is. He knows how to strip off the gloves and bandage the torn hands. He knows a lot of things. In a pinch, he could even land Colbert's chopper.

Colbert is staring, loose-jawed, at the medics who strip away the prone pilot's filthy vest and body armor. Davis assesses him as he bandages his hands. Without something to do, the major has plateaued to the edge of shock. Davis helps him sit down, thinking he's an older guy, then glances at the carnage in the shattered cockpit. *Guard. Shouldn't be here looking at and smelling the remains of one of his pilots chopped up like sausage. Should be home flying people off roofs in floods and shit.* Davis takes a deep breath to center down, and it always amazes him how tourists to combat world love to rhapsodize about how all the sounds and colors and sensations punch up pins and needles bright and more intense than sex or drugs. *Fuckin' war poets are usually reporters or writers or officers who won't be sticking around for the fiftieth or sixtieth hookup when the glamour has long worn off.*

He catches himself. *You put these people in this. It was your idea to use a Guard unit selected at random, last-minute.*

64

Like an echo of his thoughts he hears Colbert say, "Never shoulda done it, put three of them in one Hawk." Colbert's fixed stare is stuck straight ahead.

"What?" Davis blinks, looks up.

Colbert jerks his head at the dirt-covered body in front of the wreck, at the cockpit, and then his hollow eyes return to the surviving pilot. "Put three women in one Hawk." More sober, Colbert shakes off the glide into shock.

Davis is ashamed of his sudden curiosity as he looks with new interest at the medics who work at great speed, scissoring away the pilot's flight suit, boots, and uniform. Carefully, they sponge away dirt and grime with sanitary wipes. Checking for wounds, they snip down to the bra and bikini panties, and she lays motionless as a drowned swimmer washed up on a filthy beach. Her smooth face is slick with blood from several deep gashes, bruising underlines her eyes and swells on her high cheeks. Dirt and worse fouls her golden hair. Davis breathes in sharp, pierced, when he sees the fresh blue paint on her toenails gleam in the morning sun below the messy bandaged knee. One of the medics picks at her hands and feet with a needle, then he says into his helmet mic, "Airway's clear, breathing okay. Deep wounds on her right knee and right shoulder, superficial wounds on extremities, and her face is real cut up. But she's unresponsive—looks like she's scrambled bad. She's urgent for TBI. Let's get her out of here fast."

Nasir has joined them and has heard the medic. "What do they mean?" he asks.

Davis taps his head and says, "Bad concussion. Probable brain damage."

"Too bad. Such a good-looking kid."

"What happened here, Nasir?" Davis asks, angry.

"I don't know." Nasir's voice is bitter as he shakes his head and looks away. A curl of smoke twists up from Tumbleweed

Six and flutters over the empty desert like a greasy black pennant.

★ ★ ★

Beyond the smoking ruins, across the bridge, in the shelter at the edge of a small shack town, Morgon hands the kid's body off to several of Ahmed's men, who quickly bundle it into the back of their Toyota, jump in, and drive off down a narrow alley. Morgon points to the pair of binoculars strung around Ahmed's neck. When he has them, he takes a moment for personal inventory. He's trembling from the exertion of carrying the body, burning up with adrenaline, figures he has fifteen or twenty minutes before he flames out. The Apaches' battle against the mud bricks sent the locals into hiding, so he climbs to the roof of a house and, keeping low, lenses the gathering helicopter convention through the binoculars.

And he sees them bringing a survivor out of the wreck on a stretcher.

"Shit."

★ ★ ★

Jesse does the dead man's float underwater, dreaming vague sensations of flight. Fangs of sunlight graze her cheek. She rocks to the vibration, engine noise, and the high-octane perfume of gas and sweat. Quick, determined fingers handle her, lift an eyelid; a needle of light probes her eye. A pressure cuff wraps her arm. Antibiotic astringent swabs her face, then fresh bandages press on her knee, her shoulder, her cheek, and her jaw. More pinpricks.

The medevac flares and lands on the hospital pad at Balad. The medics scramble to hand off the stretcher to nurses who run, heads bent, scrubs whipping, into the prop wash. They rush Jesse on a gurney to the trauma room.

This thing I gotta do. The American who . . . But the words that form in her head just mill around, and then the idea itself gets lost.

Voices come and go: "She been out, what, almost an hour?" "Score on Glasgow is not good." "We want X-ray, MRI and CAT scan. Check for swelling. Then snow her up and tag her for Landstuhl."

Swarming medics mob her and the bright lights glare down and astringent stings and needles prick. They suture the ugly wound in her knee, the flesh wound in her shoulder, and clean up and then stitch the deep gashes on her face. With a Valium IV drip running in her arm, Jesse is parked in a ward and scheduled to fly to Landstuhl Regional Medical Center in Germany. Diagnosis: moderate to severe TBI—Traumatic Brain Injury.

CHAPTER FIFTEEN

Go like hell, and don't look back.

Morgon drives the Suburban to give Ahmed time to recover from the shock of his first action. "You did good," he yells. "You lost a man, but you did good. You got the job done . . ."

"Two men," Ahmed yells back. "You forgot the truck driver."

"Okay. Two men."

He's shouting because his ears are still plugged and burning, and the adrenaline's flaming out, which screws up his timing. People yell their jabber talk and pound their horns and dive out of the way as the Suburban swerves, brakes, and burns rubber down the narrow side streets, racing through the warren of hovels west of Samarra. Red Arabic script flashes on an orange brick wall. Then, between buildings, he catches a sizzle of blue sky cut by wires. One minute his pulse bangs on fast-forward, then his heart downshifts into slow motion. Following Ahmed's shouted directions, he turns onto the national highway as the last of the adrenaline rush burns out and real time throbs in a hollow vacuum. Shock picks up Fatigue hitchhiking on the road to Balad.

Fatigue turns his eyelids to lead.

Hunched over the steering wheel, he's trying real hard to focus his sand-pitted eyes, and he can't hear and barely can tell where his sweat stops and the foul dusty air starts. Deaf, he searches the swirl of sunspots and the road ahead for the shadow of an Apache gunship. Any second he expects a missile up his tailpipe.

His mouth tastes like dirty melted copper, and blood fouls his trousers from lap to knee and reeks in the heat. More of it's all over his shirt and down his back, and the only good news is that it's not his. With difficulty, yelling to Ahmed to steady the wheel, he tears off the tunic and tosses it aside. Then he paws in the caddy Ahmed holds in his lap for his sunglasses. No luck. He finds a bottle of Visine and squirts the fluid into his burning eyes. Not much help there, either. The road is a gritty blur, going in and out. Traffic coming at him, bedsprings tied on top of decrepit cars, goats in the back of rusty trucks like an Okie migration doomed to wander through an endless Dust Bowl.

Blinking, he monitors himself for concussion. He checks his eyes in the rearview to see if the pupils are dilated. *Confused? You bet. Dizzy, light-sensitive, nauseous, ears ringing? Been here before. But you were younger then . . .*

The Visine helps some. His head swings on a swivel, checking the horizon to either side of the road, the rearview, the sky. If he hadn't blown the truck and created the diversion, they'd have never gotten out. In a lucid moment he thinks, *The choppers should be scouring the road to the highway. Insurgents resemble convenience-store jack boys—they like freeway access.*

Morgon turns to Ahmed. Some of the color is returning to the ashen pallor that had sucked the sweat from his brown face. "You okay?"

Ahmed nods. "I never saw up close what a gunship could do . . ."

"You'll be all right. Drink some water," Morgon says. "We're not done yet."

Ahmed dry-swallows and looks at him in disbelief. "What?"

"A pilot made it out alive. They'll take him to the hospital at Balad. That's where we're headed."

Methodically, Morgon swabs the dirt from his face, hair, and hands with a bottle of water and moist baby wipes. Up ahead an American convoy is throwing dust: three lowboys hauling Abrams tanks with Humvees front and back, headed south down Iraqi Route One. A green road sign printed in Arabic and English whizzes by: Balad 22 kilometers; Baghdad 90.

Cleaning up helps; his thinking, while painful, is more ordered. No detours into amnesia. The shock is wearing off.

"The helicopters," Ahmed says.

"If we're lucky, they were just coming up the canal on their way to somewhere else. One of your guys got carried away and took a shot, and it all went to hell."

"So an accident?" Ahmed asks hopefully.

"I think so, otherwise they'd be after us. Their first priority is the crash."

"So why are we going to Balad?"

"What if the pilot saw me?" Morgon explains, turning back to the road. He's never been to the hospital in Balad. And hospitals, even military hospitals, are relatively foreign ground. He'll need to use the forbidden satellite phone and talk to his handler . . . and to his handler's granddaughter, Amanda, the woman who makes pillow-talk comparisons to Alexander of Macedon. Amanda is part of their little team, is whip smart, and has three years of med school. He might need her expertise on this.

"We need to find a place to pull off. I have to get out of these dirty clothes and clean up."

Morgon slows for a checkpoint, and the grinning Iraqi National Police study his vehicle and just wave him through with the convoy. He's functioning better now, but the crud and sweat and filthy clothes are getting to him. He can't go into the hospital at Balad looking like a hairball mud pie. "C'mon, Ahmed, find me a turnoff."

After a few minutes, Ahmed calls out, "Next turn on the right, there's a side road along an irrigation canal."

Morgon turns off on a dirt road that skirts the canal. Iraqis on foot and kids on bikes avert dark eyes in their carefully neutral faces as he drives past.

He stops the big SUV where an irrigation culvert branches out from the canal. Ahmed gets out, takes an M4 carbine from the backseat, and leans across the hood, keeping watch.

Morgon digs in his carry-on bag for soap, strips off his filthy clothes, wades in the canal, and scrubs himself vigorously, swiveling his head to scan 360 degrees of approach. Then he dunks in the greenish water and surfaces and wipes suds from his pale, flat belly that is rippled with interlocking muscle and scars. Only his arms, face, and neck are marked with a faded professional tan. He picks up his towel and wraps it around his waist. In a few minutes he's shaved and changed into his extra shirt and trousers and clean socks. He bundles up the filthy shirt and pants and tosses them into the canal.

To compose himself, he forces himself to smoke a cigarette before he makes the call. Puff by puff, the Camel burns down. He'll cherry-pick the event, edit out his moment of hesitation that resulted in this clusterfuck. If he would have fired the RPG two seconds sooner the chopper might have survived. And he'll slur over shooting the crew, attribute it to his shaky Iraqi assets. Okay. He tosses out the butt and picks up the Iridium sat phone and punches the preset number. His ears still full of surf, he can't tell if anyone answers, but he starts anyway.

"We have a situation. The army happened by in some helicopters, and it got sporty." He knows he's speaking too loudly into the sat phone. The man on the other end is in Lakeside, Michigan, where it's early in the morning. He's an elderly man named John Rivard who is many things in Morgon's life: mentor, tactical handler, even a touch of surrogate father. He is also completely unflappable, because when he retired from the Central Intelligence Agency, John was the director of covert operations for the Far East.

Rivard says something. "Calm down," maybe.

Morgon shouts, "You have to talk louder. A chopper got knocked down. There was an explosion. Our local friends freaked and started shooting. What? I'm not hearing so hot. I thought the whole crew was dead," he shouts. Pause. "But there's a good chance *I was seen* by one of the pilots who survived the crash."

Morgon still can't hear properly; he's talking to himself. "They'd take him to the hospital at Balad." Another pause. "I know what I gotta do. Get Amanda and have her stand by; I might need some medical advice." Then he adds, "This all happened after the fact. The actual job went off without a hitch. No one will ever use that shit now. But maybe you should reach out, skew the reporting." He ends the call, trusting John to handle the hot-potato handoff and tie up the administrative loose ends. Then he tucks the phone back into his duffel and motions to Ahmed.

They get back on the road and pass a green freeway sign: Balad 12 kilometers. He watches an oily column of smoke curl over the flat. Something's always burning or blowing up, and the air smells like a smoldering gas station.

"I'm going to have to drop you on the road outside the base," Morgon says, trying to deliberately lower his voice, shake off the aftereffects of the explosion and talk normally.

Ahmed nods and says, "I'll get on the phone and locate the two cars that escorted us to Samarra."

"While you're at it, can you call the airport and change my reservations from tomorrow morning to later today? I'd like to get out of here as soon as possible. My ticket's in the zipper on the side of my bag."

Now he's caught up with the American convoy that has stopped by the side of the road. The soldiers are out of the vehicles setting up a perimeter. New kids, looks like, gamely learning to wear their sweat and riding the downside of a war.

Suddenly, passing the young GIs, Morgon is seeing the wounded woman from the helicopter on her knees in the dirt—

the look in her eyes, not fear even. Like she deserved an explanation.

Never killed a woman before. A woman with red hair. Thought a lot about it, though.

CHAPTER SIXTEEN

Morgon now struggles for focus, fighting the ringing in his ears, blotty vision and a nauseous swoon in his gut. He drops Ahmed at a roadside café and, as he pulls away, sees him in the rearview, hunched over his cell phone. At the Balad Camp gate, as Morgon waits in a line of vehicles for his turn with the security guard, he inspects his face in the rearview mirror. His cheeks and forehead are raw to the touch as if scrubbed with sandpaper, and his red eyes water. He finds his sunglasses. Some help. Outwardly he projects sun-dazed fatigue. Inwardly he calculates the odds. Will the gate guard pass him through with a cursory glance at his CAC—the Common Access Card issued to all contractors—that hangs in a plastic case from a lanyard around his neck? Or is the guard being fastidious today, in which case he might scan the electronically keyed ID and run him in the system? That would be a problem, because David Baker's subcontractor file with the DynCorp Corporation will not stand up to intense scrutiny.

His luck holds. The guard waves him forward. Morgon gives a weary smile and holds up the ID card. The air force policeman returns an equally sun-baked smile, nods his weary assent, and hands back Morgan's Canadian picture ID.

The base is bigger than he remembers it, so he drives around slowly to get his bearings, mindful that the ten mph speed limit is strictly enforced. After locating the hospital, he stakes out a remote stand of CHUs behind a nearby motor pool. After ten minutes, seeing no foot traffic among the pod-like units, he gets out and drifts down a wooden duck walk.

Without looking around, he opens a door and enters a unit. He's still lucky; it's empty. Immediately he goes to a wall locker and sorts through the uniforms. Too small. He goes to the next locker, where he finds an extra-large set of fatigues and a soft cap. But no desert boots. *Out of time. Have to fake it with the civilian boots.*

He pulls the uniform on over his clothes, returns to the Suburban, pulls the cap low over his eyes, then starts the truck and approaches the hospital. The rank on the sleeve is Specialist Four.

After he parks, he takes a moment to exercise his jaw and pop his ears. It's getting better now. The splashes of sound come closer, blending together. He tucks the sat phone in his pocket and takes a small notepad and a pen from his duffel. Then he freezes an anxious smile on his face, checks his uniform, and walks toward the hospital.

He leaves the heat and dust and blast walls and enters a clean, air-conditioned zone where the tile floors are shiny and the lights are bright and the nurses behind the admitting station are smiling. He skirts the front desk, checks a floor-plan guide on the wall, and locates the trauma room where med-evaced casualties are being rushed into surgery and ambulatory civilians line the walls. Then he falls in behind a wailing Iraqi extended family. A child with a horrific stomach wound is being wheeled on a gurney. Two bandaged men lean on medics. Triage staff slip and slide on a floor slick with blood and bandages.

At the entrance to a surgical theater, he grabs a harried orderly who rushes by with an armful of bloody clothing. "Hey," he pleads, "a chopper from my unit went down west of Samarra 'bout two hours ago. I heard only the pilot made it out. He come through here?"

The orderly blinks, stares, and hands the wad of clothing to Morgon. Then he nods at a computer on a table in a curtained alcove. "C'mere," he motions. A moment later the orderly has logged in and scans a screen. He bites his lip. "Sorry, only

American we got the last couple of hours is a female captain, Jesse Kraig. Went down by Samarra though . . ."

"Uh huh," Morgon ad libs. "Musta heard it wrong. The rest of the crew didn't make it?"

"That's her. Right now she's stable, in the holding ward awaiting transport to Germany."

"How's she doing?" Morgon asks with a genuine sinking tone in his voice. It's another woman. He's mostly hearing, sometimes lip-reading. But he's crossed the line of departure. He's working.

"They got her down for TBI. When they're that way, chances are they aren't receiving visitors," the orderly says.

"How long before she ships?" Morgon asks.

"'Bout an hour," the orderly says.

Morgon holds up the clothes. "What do I do with these?"

"Bin, down the hall, that way." The orderly points then rushes back to the triage room.

Morgon lingers briefly near the trauma room and spots a surgical cart that has been shunted aside in the controlled confusion. Moving fast, using the clothing for cover, he scoops up a bottle of fentanyl and a syringe.

Then he ducks into an unused curtained bed station, dumps the clothes, makes sure the sat phone is secure in his back pocket, draws a massive overdose of the drug, and uses a piece of cardboard backing from his notepad to sheath the needle and tucks the syringe carefully in his pocket. Blending in to the foot traffic, he walks rapidly, head downturned and constantly moving to confuse the security cameras fixed in the halls. He locates the holding ward and takes a moment to gather himself because his balance is still shaky. The bright overhead lights sting his watering eyes and blank pockets ascend in his ears, blocking sound like reverse depth charges.

Captain Jessica Kraig resembles a battered nun lying motionless on her back: eyes closed, her bruised, swollen face crisscrossed with yellow painted Frankenstein stitches and her head swathed in clean white gauze. An IV drip runs into her arm, and electrodes connect to a beeping monitor. But there's a problem. All these soldiers stand around her bed, talking in low hushed tones.

Morgon makes a show of looking in on one of the other patients and steps back and waits for the visitors, presumably from the pilot's unit, to leave. He overhears a tall major with bandaged hands quietly explain that surgery has been ruled out. They didn't find brain swelling. Then the major says that "Laura" never knew what hit her. The blast came right up through her side of the cockpit. Miracle it missed Jesse.

So the other pilot was also a woman. Like the saying goes, shit arrives in threes. Morgon retreats from the ward when a nurse shows up and shoos the crowd away from Kraig's bed. After checking the IV and the monitor, she curtains off the bed and leaves.

Okay. Dump an overdose of fentanyl into the IV and get out.

Morgon slips the syringe from his pocket, edges back into the now-empty ward, and walks to the bed, keeping the syringe just out of sight, tucked up his sleeve, balanced in his palm. Then he stops because Captain Kraig has a watchdog. This old, tired master sergeant stands behind the curtain, his boots hidden by the monitor cart. His red-rimmed eyes flick on Morgon, momentarily distracted.

Morgon avoids the glance and keeps moving. He checks the chart on the bed to confirm it's Kraig. Then he raises his eyes and notes the collection of camo badges on the sergeant's chest over the nametape: DILLON. The guy stands with a tight-wrapped posture that exudes veteran cadre. An expert at assessing men, Morgon decides it's probably not a good idea to trifle with this one.

Looking down the other beds, Morgon says, "I must have the wrong ward," as he palms the shot into his back pocket.

Then there's a bad moment when Captain Kraig opens her blue eyes and stares directly at him. Dillon shakes his head. "Random eye movement, maybe triggered by light or something. They say there's a chance she'll never wake up."

"Damn, man," Morgon says in sympathy.

Dillon doesn't hear him, speaking into the middle distance. "And if she does wake up, chances are she won't be who she was. Damn shame 'cause she was a good kid."

"Bummer."

This time the sergeant's steady gray eyes click on Morgon's sand-ravaged face, drop to his dusty nonregulation boots, then return to his face. Morgon responds by raising a hand to scratch his nose and then tugs his collar up higher around his neck, as if trying to retreat, turtle fashion, into the borrowed uniform. It's time to go. Clearly he isn't the only one present with a background of quick-studying people. And it looks like this Sergeant Dillon intends to stand vigil with his captain until they load her for Germany. So Morgon leaves the ward and tosses the syringe in a needle-disposal unit in the first empty room he passes. Then he retraces his steps to the hall outside the trauma room. Time to regroup.

After Morgon leaves the holding ward, Sam Dillon retreats to his default zone, where he long ago learned to function absent fatigue and emotion. He doesn't allow himself to entertain the thought that his captain swapped him out of Tumbleweed Six at the last minute and that's why he's standing here looking at her ravaged face—and not lying dead out in the desert.

Like Marge Bailey.

But even in this defensive zone he's still heir to a lifetime of hardwired habits, one of which is watchful suspicion. So who's this trooper who appeared in the ward at the foot of Captain Kraig's bed? Something about the guy bounced weird, like the disparity between the low enlisted rank on his uniform and his poised athletic persona. Like his sandblasted face being at odds with the clean uniform and the way the guy's bloodshot, hazel eyes moved over Sam's face like an X-ray machine. And there was something about the relative paleness of his face and hands, with just the barest blush of sun. The undershirt peeking above the first button of the digital camo tunic was a shade of dark-green olive more available in an upscale sports outfitter than a military supply depot. *And what's with the civilan boots?* He also noted a small star-shaped scar at the base of the right side of the guy's neck, peeking from his uniform just above the collarbone. Smudges of red dirt were swirled in the concha of his external ear but not a speck of it under the crystal that covered the gold Rolex on his wrist. And that was the second one of those watches he's seen today . . .

Out of place. That's what Sam's gut tells him. So, curious, he drifts into the hall and trails the guy, sees him step into an open office and just as quickly come back out. Sam enters the empty office and finds just a desk, an exam table, and a red sharps needle-disposal unit. When he steps back into the corridor, the soldier has disappeared.

Sam mulls it for a moment, then walks back to the holding ward. Before entering he notes the security camera that monitors the hall. *Maybe nothing, just another sloppy troop.* He shakes his head and takes up his post over Jesse's sedated features and watches the steady rise and fall of her chest.

Back in the trauma area, fortunately for Morgon, business is booming, and now more Iraqis are milling around wailing and gesticulating at a besieged-looking army translator. Gurneys with more civilian casualties scoot past. Everybody's working frantically, so if he keeps moving in this area, he probably has a minute or so to regroup before someone questions who he is.

Okay then, think; get it done.

He looks down the hall at an Iraqi janitor who is methodically swabbing blood off the floor with his mop. Then the janitor takes his bucket into a room and returns a moment later with a fresh bucket. Before he starts mopping again, he moves a wireless COW—a computer monitor on wheels—out of the way. The machine has been pushed aside in the rush to get the new casualties down the corridor. The screen is opaque gray.

Schluf-schluf goes the janitor's mop on the tile floor, moving crablike past him. The close triage air smells like crispy adrenaline-blasted nerves, disinfectant, blood, and vaguely of excrement. As orderlies hurry by on urgent business, Morgon eyes the computer ten feet away across the hall. It's worth a try. He walks over and taps the space bar, and the screen pops. *All right.* The desktop comes up. Somebody neglected to log out in all the bustle.

Moving fast, checking the hall, he wheels the computer into the laundry room the janitor used to empty his bucket and shuts the door. It's more of a supply closet—a sink and shelves stacked with cleaning solutions. With one hand he removes the sat phone from his back pocket and stops just short of thumbing the preset code. He's getting ahead of himself. These things only work if you can see the sky. He puts the phone back in his pocket and takes out the notepad and pen. Then he types *Captain Jessica Kraig/4/143rd* into the search window and hits *Enter.* When the chart comes on the screen, he copies the notes. Then he pushes the COW to the back of the room and tucks it behind a shelf.

Moving briskly, he leaves the room and walks down the hall like he owns the place. He exits the hospital, ducks in the shadow of a blast wall, and thumbs the preset on the sat. Eight time zones and 6,000 miles to the east, John Rivard answers the call in the kitchen of his big house in Rivard County, Michigan, on the shore of Lake Huron.

"Got you loud and clear," Rivard says. "How do you hear me?"

"Better. I've got maybe two minutes before I'm blown. I need to talk to Amanda *now*," Morgon says.

"She's right here . . ."

CHAPTER SEVENTEEN

"Amanda."

"Listen carefully," Morgon says. "I may have been seen when this thing went down. If that's the case, our business could be in the street. You fully understand?"

"I fully understand."

"The target is a female army chopper pilot who survived the crash. She's down the hall in a holding ward, waiting transport to Germany. I can't get to her, but I have access to her medical chart on an open terminal." He refers to his notes. "She's been diagnosed with moderate to severe traumatic brain injury. We need to deal her out of the game. If she wakes up, whatever she says has to sound like gibberish."

"How old is she?"

Morgon hears the hesitation in her voice and shakes his head. "What the hell does that . . ." he begins. Then he relents, checks the bio notes, and says, "She's twenty-seven."

"Okay." Amanda's voice is now cool and focused. "The computer you're looking at is on the DOD system. If you alter the chart now, the file will follow her to Germany for acute stabilization. Then it will transfer over to the VA system when they ship her home for primary care. Clear?"

"Clear."

"We can't tamper too much, or they'll catch it. So we'll just do a little foreshadowing and build on it later, in Germany and maybe Walter Reed. Are you looking at the chart now?"

"I made notes."

"Read me the doctor's comments and the medications."

"Under admission data there's a brief description of the crash incident, then it says she's unresponsive, six on Glasgow,

MRI, CAT scan negative for brain swelling. The meds are Valium 10 mm IV."

"Keep the crash stuff. Delete 'unresponsive.' Type in 'erratic cognitive function with violent overtures.' Delete 'six' on Glasgow. Type in 'six to ten.' Keep the MRI and CAT scan stuff."

Morgon quickly jots notes. He has the phone wedged in the crook of his neck to free his hands for writing.

"Now," Amanda says, "up the meds. Type in '15 mm Valium IV.' Make sure you save changes and close the file. Hopefully they'll bump the sedative before she ships."

"Got it."

John comes back on the connection. First he confirms the pilot's name, rank, and unit. "She's going to Landstuhl in Germany, right?"

"Right."

"We'll have somebody waiting for her. I'll make some calls, see if we can muddy the after-action report. Now get out of there." The signal goes dead.

Doing his confident military strut, Morgon goes back in the hospital, returns to the surgery hall, and enters the janitor's room. The computer is still parked where he left it and is still logged in. Quickly he alters the chart per Amanda's instructions, then he hits *save* and closes the file. He pushes the computer into the hall and walks casually down the corridor. Five minutes later he's in the Suburban, worming out of the borrowed uniform. In ten minutes he's pulling up to the roadside café where Ahmed is waiting.

★ ★ ★

In Michigan, Amanda Rivard looks her grandfather directly in the eye. "We're not killing her, right?"

John Rivard assesses Amanda, who is a touchy mixture of headstrong and fragile. The girl is rock solid here on home ground but tends to get frail when she leaves the estate. And the speed bump Morgon has hit is definitely off the family acres. She is involved to the extent that she arranges travel itineraries and the disbursement of funds. Her primary duties involve administering the day-to-day machinations of the Rivard Family Foundation. But they're in a pinch, and John needs her to step up.

"We have to tread lightly now that she's in the medical evacuation system. We need to *sideline* her for a while. We need to make her irrelevant," John says carefully. "What can we slip her to produce that result?"

"Do we have people who can get into Landstuhl and quietly give her a drug?" Amanda asks.

"You can always find people. It will involve some expense and using an old cutout in Germany," John says. "What are you thinking?" He's watching her carefully for signs of faltering.

Amanda, always good at taking tests, clears her throat. "Phencyclidine."

"Say again?"

"PCP. Angel dust. Hog trank," Amanda says with down-curved lips, not hiding her distaste. "In large doses, like 150 milligrams, it causes stupor, drowsiness, convulsions, and possible coma. A PCP-induced psychosis could last weeks. The stuff recycles in the body's fatty tissue. It would totally disrupt her thought processes. So hit her at Landstuhl and follow up when they ship her to Walter Reed."

"Disrupts the thought process? How?" John asks.

"Like severe memory and speech difficulties; that would be consistent with TBI," she says. "It might show up in a urine test, but I'm thinking, with the diagnosis, they'd be screening for brain damage."

"That's good, Amanda," John says, reaching for his sat phone. "I'll get someone cracking to Landstuhl who can be invisible."

Amanda turns and walks from the kitchen, down the corridor, and turns into her office. As she sits down at her Mac, she hears John's baritone echo down the hall, talking in German to someone named Agon. Dizzy and flushed with sweat, she self-consciously touches the skin on her upper arms and her throat that is strawberry splotched and tingling.

A tall, broad-shouldered young man sitting at his own computer station across the room turns from the Warcraft game on his screen. His ponytail and laid-back smile are misleading and conceal a high order of physical and mental agility. Kelly Ortiz completes the "team." He flies and maintains the helicopter John keeps on the premises, and as a qualified triage nurse, he backstops Amanda in monitoring John's health. Kelly is a veteran of two tours in Afghanistan with a JSOC Ranger group. Seeing her uncharacteristic disarray, he cocks an eyebrow.

"Morgon called," Amanda says. "He ran into a hitch."

"Not good," Kelly observes.

"Right. I just revisited Pharmacology 101 to help him set up a scenario to destroy a young woman's brain," Amanda says brightly. "She's a chopper pilot, twenty-seven years old." Then Amanda makes a face and lightly touches her cheek. "I had my first sexual experience when I was sixteen, but I really lost my virginity about three minutes ago, didn't I?"

Kelly winces and taps his teeth together. "Slow down. You want to take a walk? Smoke a joint? It goes with the territory, Amanda. In for a dime . . ." Kelly stops in midsentence, and they both look toward the hall when they hear the *tap-tap* of John's cane. Then he appears in the doorway.

"Now what?" Amanda asks.

"Relax, Amanda. Everything's going to be fine," John says. "We'll need Roger Torres at ASTECH; you recall he did the advance work on the Juarez job. He's just the lad to handle the Walter Reed end of this damn thing. Get ahold of him, would you, and ask him to give me a call on secure sat."

CHAPTER EIGHTEEN

Davis stands at the epicenter of the desert carnage, talking into his sat phone to Bobby Appert. "You know what happened here, Bobby? People are dead, and I put them in this."

"Slow down, Joe. They were soldiers. It's still a war. We got other fish to fry."

Davis blinks away sweat and a bout of double vision as he ends the call and tucks the sat into his vest and thinks he's gotta drink more water. He twirls an unlit cigarette in his fingers as his eyes track to where the remains of an unidentified body was dragged and bundled out of sight under a tarp. Flies gather. No idea where they come from out here.

A detachment from Army Graves Registration and several of Nasir's men slowly sweep the area between the crash and the crater. They are having more than language problems. Pieces of the unknown casualty have been found in the helicopter wreckage. A portion of a female pilot has been found at the blast site.

Never should have put three women in one Hawk. Colbert's words . . .

Davis walks to where Nasir stands watching his men rifle through the glove compartment of a blast-twisted Land Rover. Nasir shows him the singed registration and contractor license issued to a Richard Noland. "We've talked to some locals," Nasir says. "Noland was a salvage contractor. This was his work site. Apparently he was the object of the attack."

Davis points to the tarp where the flies buzz and cluster. "That him?"

"Don't know. That's just pieces; no head, no hands. How do you ID that? So for the time being, he's missing."

"Great." Davis spins on his heel and walks toward the relative quiet of the ruins. Halfway there he stops in the meager shadow of a wall fragment that juts from the hardpan and tries to reconstruct the timeline, from the first radio transmission to the explosion. *This is where they hid, the guys who brought down the chopper.* Pausing, he runs his hand along the adobe-colored bricks that are now freshly pitted by the strike of machine-gun fire. *A freak meeting engagement, that's what everybody is saying.*

His eyes click on a fresh cigarette butt that is squashed into a crevice between the bricks. He plucks it out and notes a portion of a Camel logo on the paper. *Does it mean something? You're reaching, man, reading tea leaves.* So he drops the butt, grinds it under his heel, and goes back to twirling his own unlit cigarette. *Too much imagination for this line of work, Davis. Always was your problem.*

Some of Nasir's men are picking through the rubble. They've laid out a poncho and pinned the corners with rocks. A bloody shirt, a headdress, a bandoleer, and two blood-smeared AK-47s are displayed on the rubber mat, along with an RPG launcher and a sack containing two rockets. The Apaches are thinking they got some.

Finally he lights the cigarette and grimaces at the hungry ache of tobacco smoke in his throat. *First one in over six months,* he thinks. *I am definitely going to hell in a pushcart over this botched op.* One of Nasir's guys jogs up to him—an earnest, skinny young guy in a baggy uniform.

"*Assalamu alaikum,*" the guy says courteously, bowing slightly.

"*Walaikum assalam,*" Davis responds with a nod.

"No English," the guy says with a game smile. Then he holds out a plastic baggie and places it in Davis' hand. The guy shrugs and points deeper into the rubble.

"*Shukran,*" Davis says. *Thank you.*

"No sweat," the guy says; then he raises a finger to his cap and returns to the search.

Davis studies the dirty baggie that contains several ounces of dust and what appears to be a twisted toothpaste tube with a sheathed needle projecting from the end. He's seen this before. It's an old version of a 2 mg atropine syrette. Atropine, he recalls from a bloc of training, is an extract of deadly nightshade. He furrows his brow and plucks a detail from memory about the officer conducting the class who'd mentioned that Spanish ladies used to put drops of atropine in their eyes to enhance the size of their pupils and give them a big-eyed allure—hence the term "belladonna." He also recalls that atropine is an antidote specifically used in cases of nerve-gas poisoning.

As he starts toward Nasir to show him this odd find, his sat phone rings. He answers, and it's Major Greg Colbert making good on his promise to call. Colbert informs him the pilot never regained consciousness and is now on air transport to Germany.

"What was . . ."—Davis corrects himself—"*is* her name?"

"Captain Jessica Kraig from Grand Forks, North Dakota." Then Colbert adds, "Are the people you work for taking over the investigation of the incident?"

"Like how?" Davis asks.

"I don't know. I just got debriefed by a colonel at Task Force Brown; that's way out of my chain of command."

"We were on an Iraqi special police raid. You were our only external assets. Don't know anything about special ops involvement." Davis thanks Colbert and tells him to take care of himself. Now he has a name to go with the image of the medic swabbing her feet. Again he feels the piercing sensation, the way her toenails twinkled bright blue against the smoky desert sun. Then he looks past the Graves Registration soldiers to where the truncated steel bones of Tumbleweed Six leak smoke and bake in the hot sun.

★ ★ ★

After a less frenzied ride south from Balad, and after switching the Suburban for the more comfortable Mercedes, Morgon shakes hands with the now subdued Ahmed and gets out of the limo holding his travel grip and an airline ticket. The black Mercedes eases from the airport parking lot, carrying Ahmed back into his family's close-mouthed intrigues. Without a backward look or thought, Morgon steps from the beige furnace of a Baghdad afternoon and enters the cool airport. An hour later, after rinsing his eyes with scrupulous care to remove pesky remnants of sand, he stands by the huge arrivals and departures board. His gaze wanders up to the stylized, tented grillwork on the terminal ceiling. Foot traffic eddies around him —Arab men in business suits and tribal robes, young Americans in digital camo. The smiling ones, he assumes, are going home. Like him. His eyes start to tear up and, blinking, he checks the concourse for the nearest place to pick up some more Visine.

Goddamn sand.

★ ★ ★

After they wheel Jesse away toward the waiting transport to Germany, Sam Dillon is leaving the ward when an orderly from the flight company hurries in and says, "Major Colbert needs to talk to you ASAP over at the company day room."

"What's up?"

"Don't know, just said it's urgent."

After driving across the base, the orderly drops Sam off in the flight company area. As the Humvee pulls away, Dillon sees Major Colbert standing with three other soldiers outside the day room—his crew from today's mission. They are stacking a pile of duffels and go bags.

Colbert motions to Sam, and they walk through the slanting late-afternoon shadows to a picnic table set under a plywood and tin sunroof. Sam jerks his head back toward the three crew members standing by the gear. "What's that about?"

Colbert gingerly removes a pack of Marlboros from his pocket with his bandaged hand and offers one to Sam. As he accepts the cigarette, Sam studies the major's angular face. The only other occasion on which he's seen Colbert smoke was right after the first time he took ground fire.

"It's like this, Sam," Colbert says in a certain tone of voice that acknowledges certain priorities, like—rank in the Guard notwithstanding—back home he's a dentist and Sam was a cop. He pops a lighter. "We just got immediate orders to catch a flight down to Kuwait; reassignment to Brigade Rear, to work on the drawdown."

Sam thumbs the cigarette filter. "Just like that?"

"Yeah, right after I debriefed the mission at Task Force Brown."

"Not our Battalion Intelligence shop?" Sam raises his eyebrows.

"Brown. They said it was because an American civilian was involved, the one who got kidnapped out there," Colbert says. Then he hands Sam a slip of paper. "Joe Davis is the code name I was carrying, contractor with the Iraqi cops. That's his sat number. He wanted an update on Jesse's status. Hold on to it." Colbert takes a drag, then exhales. "Got a little strange, all this out-of-channels shit," he says.

"How strange?"

Colbert shrugs. "This colonel over at Brown, he tells me there's no need to discuss the incident with anybody in my unit. And, oh yeah, they pulled rank; they'll file the after-action report, not us."

"Anything else?"

"Well, the colonel expressed his condolences that three of our people were killed in the crash. I explained to him that Marge and Toby survived the crash and were shot to death on the ground. Fucker pats me on the shoulder and tells me I been under a lot of strain."

Disgusted, Colbert flips the cigarette away.

"Tell me about it," Sam says.

CHAPTER NINETEEN

Jesse is trundled off an aircraft and into the army hospital in Germany wrapped like a mummy in a narcotic winding sheet. She takes a chance and opens her eyes. Just a peek. The light hitting her cornea ignites a hemorrhage of rapid breathing and accelerated heartbeat because the Bad Thing could be Right There waiting. All she sees is a glide of slow-motion people dressed in blue and burgundy scrubs. The walls are drab. The utensils are shiny. Exhausted by the effort, she pops back down into the comfort of her dark hole. Can't move out there. Hurts. Her right knee and left shoulder are stiff and heavily bandaged. Her whole body aches. The skin on her face is stretched mask-tight, sutured down over what feels like the enlarged bones of her jaw and cheeks and forehead.

She discovers that she has great difficulty forming the shape of simple words. Mouth hurts too much, full of abrasions. Not worth it. Stay down. It's protected where she is, down in the dark.

The Landstuhl hospital revolves slowly around her in a sedated blur of distorted faces and voices underwater. Words swirl like bubbles. Shiny, round, they float away to pop into sounds someplace else. Bedpans come and go. She's spoon-fed like an infant.

Then a shadow hovers near her bed in the dark, and something happens. First a stiffness, then this eruption inside her. The alarms on the bedside monitor shriek. Urine and feces gush into her hospital gown, and the funhouse-mirror faces and the bubbles gather, and then the bubbles burst:

"She's seizing. Put her on her side! Shit, man, she's choking!"

"Blood pressure 190 over 140!"

92

"Gimme five mil Valium IV push!"

"We need restraints here, people . . ."

"What happened?"

"She's convulsing, got violent as hell. Tonic-clonic seizure. Peed and crapped herself."

"Five more Valium."

"She's aspirating vomit. C'mon, let's intubate and get her to ICU."

★ ★ ★

Sam's on his fourth war: Nam, Desert Storm, Afghanistan, and this goddamn place. He doesn't count pissant deployments like Grenada or Panama. He knows how to suck it up and find refuge in routine and count the days until he rotates home. And now the verdict's finally in, and he will rotate early. They're showing him the door for good this time—sixty and out. But not so old that the dissembling up the chain of command after the crash doesn't gnaw at him; like now, as he props in bed, staring into the dark. He can't sleep or stop thinking about the stark circumstances of Tumbleweed Six going down. Before they deployed they'd rehearsed for casualties, even staged a mock funeral for one of the pilots. The reality has hit the unit hard; a bird splashes, and now there're four less people at breakfast.

And one of them should have been me.

From long practice, he does not allow himself to imagine Marge's face or the sound of her voice. Or Laura's or Toby's. The kids in the unit think he and Marge were hooking up, but it wasn't like that. Not yet. Marge was a circumspect divorcee who was mapping the dimensions of Sam's widower world. Maybe when they got home . . .

Change the subject, Sam. So Colbert is gone with his crew, and everybody is preoccupied with the daily work and soldiering through the trauma. There's no one left to talk to who was out there that day. He tried to call the number Colbert gave him—the code-name guy, Davis—but the number was out of service. Which all brings him back to the strange timing of the anomalous soldier who wandered into Jesse's holding ward with his Spec Four rank that didn't match his face and his gold watch.

So Sam rises, gets dressed, and goes to the company day room and signs out a Humvee. His destination is the base hospital. More specifically, he locates the office that manages the building's surveillance cameras. No one in the army pulls guard or KP anymore or mans the security apparatus on the base, so it's no surprise he finds a stout, white-haired retired cop from Charleston sipping Diet Coke at 1 a.m. at the desk full of monitors. Sam keeps his investigator ID from the Grand Forks County Sheriff's Department in his wallet for just such occasions. He bonds with Charleston around a few war stories, bullshits a little about the Entry PoE IP Camera System, and then floats a story about an asshole in his unit who might be pilfering medical supplies for sale on the black market. Soon Sam is seated at a monitor clicking through hallway and exit tapes for the afternoon of April 12.

His guy, when he finds him entering the holding ward, is tricky and knows how to face away to confuse cameras, but finally Sam isolates a full frontal frame and transfers it to a thumb drive. He thanks Charleston and drives back to the company. Because he's fixated on gold Rolexes and who wears them, he's thought out the next step. Instead of attaching the file to an email, he folds the thumb drive in a quick note:

Need a quiet favor. Run this guy through facial ID and see if you get any hits in military files going back ten years. Could you also locate a Joe Davis who recently worked in some capacity with the Iraqi police? This is a Casper-type request. Mail response to my home address.

Then Sam rummages in Chaplain Lundquist's desk and finds an envelope with a personalized military APO return address. He seals the letter and drops it in the company snail mail. The addressee is a colonel in the Pentagon's Criminal Investigative Division office. He and Sam go back a ways in the background-checks department, and the Casper reference will alert the colonel that the request is in the realm of "friendly ghosts" and identify Sam as the sender.

Now, as Sam returns to his quarters and climbs into bed, he's thinking it's probably nothing, but just maybe he'll have something to nose around in when he gets home.

★ ★ ★

A nurse charts that she *wakes up* at 10:36 the morning following the seizure, but Jesse has now lost even that tenuous connection. Nothing in her psychic wiring prepares her for the distorted sensory eruption of hallucination. It burns through the distinction between the inside and the outside, and she doesn't know she's swaddled in diapers and curled in a fetal position. She doesn't register that she's pinned to the bed by restraints or that she spent half the night tossing in a delirious rage, fighting the restraints, and has torn the stitches in her knee. At one point they started to intubate her again.

Worst of all, now the Bad Thing is not just lurking outside. Now it's everywhere. Her hiding place has been invaded, and huge slimy shapes rear and coil and wiggle out of her deepest childhood fears. She not only sees them, she hears them and feels them and even can touch them and taste them.

An exaggerated aversion of earthworms was a definite disadvantage for a farm kid whose family put in a large vegetable garden. And she was expected to weed that garden with her older brothers who delighted in finding fistfuls of the worms and chasing her, waving them.

The outside world is gone, and she's suffocating, buried up to her nose in the hot soil between rows of tomato plants that tower like triple-canopy jungle. The worms exude a ripe garbage scent as they sprawl and slither through the shadows all around her. They ooze right up to her face, soft and greasy and drippy red. Smaller spider worms dangle on silky threads in front of her eyes and squirm into different shapes—now a jelly-fish, then a snake. But they always knot together in the form of a five-pointed star.

So she must remain perfectly still, burrowed down in the dark. Even if she wanted to scream she can't, because her mouth is stuffed with dirt.

When anything touches her she lashes out with the exaggerated startle reflex reserved for snakes and spiders. In the grip of these seizures the questionable sanctuary of the garden is replaced by a sensation of tremendous pressure and heat and chaos; she's inside a fire hose in a rapids rampaging through an erupting volcano. She's plunging down on a burning collision course that never quite happens.

In between intravenous injections of sedatives, the pressure lessens and she calls for help. "The star killed me!" she screams, but it comes out gibberish as she thrashes in her bed. They tighten the restraints. They up her meds and give her high marks in hostility, suspicion, hallucination, and grandiosity on the BPRS—the Brief Psychiatric Rating Scale.

They rule out brain tumor.

They keep testing for brain damage.

A review of her medical history and proficiency reports shows no sign of mental illness.

The details of "the incident" entered in the chart notes are positive for severe psychological stress and exposure to a traumatic event—surviving the crash and possibly witnessing the violent death of her crew.

The kindest opinion ventured is that she's experiencing a short-lived psychosis triggered by these traumatic events, complicated by a yet-to-be-determined degree of concussion. So they "snow her and ship her" on a regimen of Seroquel—a powerful antipsychotic—to get her through the white water. The notes to the medics at Walter Reed recommend they continue to monitor for traumatic brain injury with psychotic overtures. If and when the psychosis subsides, she'll be a classic candidate for PTSD protocol.

★ ★ ★

The first few days at Reed are quieter. Then she has another night visitor followed by a violent seizure, and they start the round of testing again. One step forward, then a marathon of steps backward. They review her meds and continue to run the Seroquel drip into her veins. There is no ego in the combustible brew of sensations Jesse floats through; normal is mere fear. Above, below, and to the left and right of fear, the hallucinatory worms are waiting, as are the more aggressive spidery stars.

. But her muscles are starting to work, and so—zombie-fashion—she is hoisted behind a walker and, shepherded by an orderly with a lift belt, confronts physical therapy. Plodding behind the walker, dragging her feet and injured knee, she sleep-stumbles among a narcotic nightmare of faces and voices. Through the veil of sedation she sees but does not comprehend a universe of pain—burns, amputations, ghastly head injuries, and people suffering with what she has: a closed head injury caused by violent trauma that does not penetrate the skull. The staff appears not quite in focus. They ask her questions. The tongues in their mouths squirm like the worms.

After a week passes without a seizure or an outburst, they schedule a session with the speech therapist that involves a trek down the hall to the elevator, trudging behind the walker with a hovering orderly. After the elevator ride there's another hike to an office where, with the orderly's help, Jesse winds up in a chair. A woman sits across a desk that is bare except for a yellow legal pad and a large Sharpie pen. The woman rotates the pad, and the worm in her mouth curls and forms sounds.

"Hello, Captain Kraig. My name is Christine Morel, and I'm a speech therapist. We're going to take a first step toward an intake RIPA—that's a Ross Informational Processing Assessment."

Then she points to something on the pad, and briefly Jesse flashes on a memory of Miss Siple, her first-grade teacher at Langdon Elementary.

"Lurs," she mumbles. Letters. J-E-S-S-E K-R-A-I-G. But they could be Egyptian hieroglyphics, those letters . . .

"Very good," Morel says in a patient voice. Then she picks up the pen and hands it to Jesse. When Jesse doesn't respond, the orderly gently takes Jesse's hand and places the Sharpie in it, arranging her fingers in a writing grip.

As the swollen stitches bunch in perplexity on Jesse's forehead, Morel augments her helpful smile by licking her lips, and the worm jumps from her mouth and dances in the air. Then it twirls into the shape of the star. Jesse lurches back, then fumbles with the grip on the pen, clamps her fingers and thumb around it, and brandishes it over her head. Before the orderly can seize her hand, she stabs the Sharpie down on the pad with enough force to shatter it.

The orderly swiftly strips the broken pen from Jesse's hand but isn't prepared for her coiling and erupting from the chair and throwing a stiff forearm into his neck, and he goes crashing back against the wall.

Morel recoils from the snarl on Jesse's face and seizes the flimsy pad and holds it up for protection. In shock she watches Jesse raise her right hand and bite through the tip of her index finger. The orderly is on his feet and moving, but he's not fast enough to stop Jesse from tracing a sloppy but legible five-pointed star on the desktop in her own blood.

After more orderlies arrive and Jesse is ushered back to her ward, Ms. Morel types into the chart:

Captain Kraig demonstrates a complete breakdown in associa-tions. The semantic content of her minimal speech is disconnected, disorganized, and incomprehensible to the point of being mere "word salad." The session degenerated into a violent outburst, during which Kraig first threatened me with a pen and then bit her own finger and smeared blood on my desk.

I can't, at this point, attribute motive or ideation to the act. But she drew a definite shape, a star, like a kindergartener might make.

After a consult, they up her meds.

CHAPTER TWENTY

Joe Davis slouches against a pillar watching an empty baggage carousel go 'round and 'round in the Baltimore International Airport, waiting for his duffel to tumble down the chute. A lot has happened in the last two weeks, culminating in his being escorted to Baghdad International and put on a flight by the national police. Essentially they kicked him out of the country after his contractor license and visa were revoked.

Appert had been yanked several days previously and reassigned to a Counterterrorism desk at Quantico. They parted on a grumble. Appert didn't come out and say it but, clearly, he blamed Davis for his demotion.

His erstwhile comrade Colonel Nasir explained, perhaps sincerely, that Davis had become a liability. Suddenly there were too many rumors circulating that he had been skimming the very money and drugs he was supposed to be investigating. He didn't blame Nasir, who had to survive at crushing depths of political corruption.

To Davis it felt like the bureaucracy reacting, in Iraq and back in the States. Some tender place had been tweaked, and the pushback had been swift. It started snowballing his way after he began asking questions about the incident at Turmar. Nothing heavy, just simple queries about the disappeared American, Noland. Like, what was he doing there that day? And who was he working for, and who owned the land? Why did a truck full of artillery shells blow up? And what about the atropine syrette that had popped up and since vanished?

Davis is not surprised. He's been working the dark side for years in and out of the military. So long that when he was wounded the last time, he half expected to leak buckles and canvas straps and liquid vinyl. He understands how the system works: duty, honor, country, and Murphy's Law. Not necessarily in that order.

As a third-generation Marine he'd hewed to the old-time religion: you do not show emotion in uniform. That morning in Turmar it wasn't a few more dead bodies that got to him. It was the simple image of witnessing the medic swab Kraig's bare feet. When she took off that morning—on his mission—she probably thought the war was pretty much over.

His chain mail just flat froze up and flaked off. And, dumb shit that he was, he just couldn't get those blue toenails out of his mind, or the shapely foot they were attached to. He'd made some checks and discovered that the course he'd set for Captain Jesse Kraig—in addition to killing her crew—had ultimately resulted in her being under observation on a regimen of anti-psychotic drugs at a hospital in Germany. Wounded he could understand, along with the TBI diagnosis. But antipsychotics? Davis pretends not to be a sentimental guy, but Jesse Kraig's condition spoils his sleep.

So the usual perks of returning home in late April—mild weather, an abundance of green landscape, roads that don't blow up, and the girls getting out their summer dresses—are lost on him as he collects his bag and walks out to the curb and hails a cab and gives the driver a destination up the Parkway: Frank's Diner in Jessup, not far from Ft. Meade. He's not hungry; he's meeting somebody.

His elusive boss, Maury Malone, convenes an informal insurgency that has emerged among civil servants who've finally decided to fight back against the galloping fraud, corruption, and abuse spiraling out of control in the name of national security. After watching several of his NSA colleagues prosecuted for blowing the whistle, Malone, a survivor, has opted for a clandestine approach. He picks his fights and intervenes in the most excessive abuses that have piggybacked on the terror-war gold rush. Basically he closets with old-fashioned cops, like Bobby Appert, who believe assholes are assholes, regardless of rank, and should be held accountable.

Malone had recruited Davis into a unique niche where the shadows of NSA, FBI, and justice overlap under the increased candlepower of Homeland Security.

And now he's hit a snag, and it's time to regroup.

After he pays the cabbie and gets out, Davis spots Mouse in the shadows at the back of the restaurant's parking lot, leaning against his six-year-old gray Outback and unwrapping a Snickers bar. He's a pudgy man with a screen pallor whose chief form of exercise is clicking his index finger—hence his nickname. He's undercover in shapeless khakis and an ancient Trekkie T-shirt, and he doesn't look real happy when Davis walks up and tosses his duffel on the pavement.

"They took my gun," Davis says.

"I'll get you another one," Mouse says by way of greeting. He pauses to study the play of shadow caught in the ripple of scars on Davis' face. "You know you blew two months of preparation going after the Ramil thing too straight-ahead. That's what got you bounced out of the country. Somebody big had skin in the Ramil buy, and you pissed them off, and they sandbagged your skinny ass."

"Nice seeing you too, Mouse," Davis says. "And you have it wrong. Ramil was cool. It was what happened on the way to Ramil that fucked me up."

"I agree with the fucked-up part, but your grasp of motivation is skewed if you're gonna persist in that Turmar crap. I ran diagnostics on everybody—all the Iraqi ministries, their army, their cops . . . *our* army and Special Ops. Nobody was anywhere near that place. No drones. Not even worth a satellite flyover. It's like the after-action report says—a meeting engagement. You bumbled into a low-rent bandit raid on some scrap contractor who is now listed among the missing."

"You check him out?"

"Yeah. He had some speeding tickets in Memphis. When his construction firm failed, he filed bankruptcy and got divorced. When he left his wife and kids in Memphis, he was in arrears on his child support. Like a lot of people, he went to the sandbox to seek his fortune. Give it up, Joey. He was a glorified junk dealer, a sheeny man."

"What about the girl? The pilot? Anything new on her?"

"Absolutely. Now she's staring at the walls across town at Walter Reed instead of Landstuhl, Germany."

Davis turns toward the dome of light that glows over Washington, DC. "Just over there?"

"She really got to you, huh?"

"I put her in this. I made the call to use the Guard . . ."

"So put yourself on her visitors list. Take flowers. You're no good to me as long as you got her stuck in your craw." Mouse exhales, crumples the Snickers wrapper, and tosses it into the open window of his car. "I'm serious, take flowers."

"It sucks, you know. I thought the rough stuff was finished. I thought I was over there just cleaning up the garbage," Davis says.

Mouse steps forward and places his hands on Davis' shoulders. "Welcome home, Joey. You don't look so hot. You been out there way too long. It's time for you to come in and take some downtime."

"Maybe," Davis speculates, and all the while his eyes are still fixed on the lights of Washington in the distance.

★ ★ ★

He doesn't take flowers. The next afternoon Davis finds a few white crosses to medicate the insomnia and the jet lag and drives the government Crown Victoria that Mouse provided across DC to Walter Reed Medical Center on NW Georgia Avenue. He knows the way because he's been there himself in

2005 after a stairway blew up in his face in Fallujah. The Reed campus sprawls about the size of a Big Ten university and seems more orderly and low-key now, less the feel of a galloping meat-processing plant. Most of the guys he sees in the hall are older, from other wars.

Mouse has given him specific directions and made some calls to arrange the visit. Davis locates Kraig in the neurology compound on a fifth-floor ward, where she shares a room with another female soldier. He doesn't enter the room because, as he approaches the doorway, he sees her sitting upright in bed, propped by pillows, wearing a blue skullcap. Two nurses are affixing electrodes to the cap one at a time. As more and more of the electric leads are fastened to her head, she starts to take on the aspect of young Medusa whose golden hair has been replaced by menacing dreadlocks. He stands there as the nurses finish attaching the connections; then he watches them fiddle with a remote, adjusting a computer monitor.

Davis understands the object of the exercise: the electric leads connect to an EEG monitor. The electroencephalogram measures brain waves and is used to evaluate brain disorders. They're checking for brain damage.

That's when Kraig looks up at him standing in the doorway, and he has the distinct impression that if he doesn't remove himself immediately, her fixed, empty stare will indeed turn him to stone. So Joe Davis, who's never really run from anything in his life, pivots on his heel and hurries from the ward and goes down the elevator and exits the hospital and gets in his government car and drives until he picks a tavern at random.

Six hours later, when it becomes clear that all the Jack Daniel's in the joint will not ease the memory of looking directly into Jesse Kraig's dead eyes—and when the loud patrons start getting on his nerves—he calls Maury the Mouse at his home in Silver Springs and informs him, yeah, he probably does need some downtime and would Maury come collect him before his ace undercover boy goes off on a bunch of oblivious civilians and wrecks the place.

And Mouse says, "Stand by, Joey. I'm on the way."

CHAPTER TWENTY-ONE

Late on a Sunday night Jesse trudges behind her walker down the poly-trauma ward corridor. She has been granted some leeway to exercise because the violent freakouts have receded. She avoids sleep whenever possible because the wormhole terrors lie in wait in her dreams. Dragging herself from bed was not a conscious decision. Pure muscle memory forced her to plant her hands on the tubular strut of the four-pod. She doesn't really understand that her muscles are the only part of her that still reliably work.

Ka-thump. She scoots the walker forward then pulls up her good left leg. Then she drags the stiff injured right knee and gingerly tests her weight. The pain diffuses through the Seroquel. Beneath this antipsychotic straightjacket, an unknown invader still lurks in her fatty tissues, and occasionally, when her liver burns some lipids for energy, residues of the PCP release into her sluggish blood and it's freakout time again. But that hasn't happened for more than a week.

So she walkers the hall.

She doesn't want to go *clunk* up and down the ward.

But *she* isn't driving.

Her *body* feels an imperative to practice walking erect. And it's her *metabolism* that orders her liver and kidneys to keep scrubbing away in an effort to restore the chemical balance in her brain.

Ka-thump. She starts her crab-scuttle turn at the end of the hall. An orderly trails her, makes a quick assessment and decides to let her pursue her solo walkathon.

Ka-thump. Shuffle shuffle.

Attracted by a surge in sound and flashing light, she veers to the side and approaches a crowd of patients and staff who assemble by a wall-mounted TV.

One guy, like her, leans on a walker. He wears a patch over an empty eye socket, and a concave scoop is missing from the left side of his skull. A double and a quadruple amputee crane forward in their wheelchairs. Now more nurses and orderlies surge down the hall to join the increasingly animated group. Voices rise in a crescendo, and she feels a sensation, like sudden rain, pelt her face. She peers up at the television and can't separate out the sounds, not sure which parts originate with people next to her and which parts emanate from the flat-screen.

This tall guy in a dark suit and a red tie stands at a podium. There's more red behind him. A carpet. And on the left there's a cascade of red and white stripes. He's a black guy with close-cropped hair who looks vaguely familiar, and slowly she realizes it's the guy she works for. And now the people all around her are cheering. The ones who have hands pump them in the air. A patient standing beside her spontaneously turns and gives her a hug.

Yesterday she would have reacted violently to another's touch. But something has changed in the space of her walk down the hall. And now she enjoys the feel of his encircling arms. She wishes he'd do it again.

She blinks and concentrates on the screen, where letters crawl along the bottom. The B she gets right off, but the I and the N escape her. Okay. Next group. That's an L, and the next one is an A. Then there's a D. She misses that one, along with the E and another N. The next group hits her eyes like a handful of rocks: D-E-A-D.

The general excitement swirling around her resonates inside the passages of her skull. Her ears and eyes pop. The muscles of her neck and jaw throb and strum. Giddy, she teeters, pitching off her feet, and immediately hands are there on either side to lift her and steady her. She does not shrink from the contact.

Her central orienting principle—fear—is still present. But now it has company. She senses something confusing—some factor of ranging, of ordering—that, after the newness wears off, she perceives as depth perception. Slowly she rediscovers how it works. Her skin is a boundary, and the people and the TV are on the outside and the snare drum beating in her chest is on the inside. The suffocating, encompassing worm world has flamed out. No crawly stars. No choking on dirt. She staggers and steels her grip on the walker and experiences a manageable fear of falling that is followed by a buoyant distribution of her weight.

Balance.

"Ha!" she forces a hoarse, jubilant croak though dry vocal chords.

Then an image—not a sensation—causes her to start trembling and pouring sweat. It's an old wooden shed with uneven, weatherbeaten boards and jutting rusty nails. Gotta be early spring because the rutted ground is turning mushy and catches pools of snow melt. An eight-year-old girl braces herself to enter the low doorway. Spiders in there. Other critters. Coons, maybe even an early snake. Gruff male voice, not unkind. "Go on, girl. Go in there and bring out that old hose. Do it now. Git."

In there is full of cobwebs and rusty saws and crowbars and pitchforks hanging on the walls and piles of rakes and shovels that are shriven by lingering frost, and way in the back in the dark there's the old garden hose, which is hopelessly tangled up and still stiff and frozen. And she's got to go in there and grab it and drag it out into the light. This fat leopard spider scurries from behind a roll of barbed wire, and she stomps it flat with her muddy tennis shoe. And then she has to take the dirty, knotted, impossible hose in both of her bare hands and yank. She blinks and finds herself back in the present, not real sure where the picture in her head went or where it came from or, at first, who the little girl was. And then she realizes that the girl was her and she's just experienced a memory.

So I'm back. Slowly the notion forms. *In my body.*

The memory prompts a fresh idea: *Got to untangle the dead freakin' worms.*

A flicker of hallucination follows on the thought like errant lightning. When it rears up, she stamps her good foot. *Get back. Squish your ass! Ha!*

The effort drenches her gown with sweat, and the loose hospital pajama bottoms cling, damp, to her legs, and her knuckles that grip the walker blanch white. It takes a full minute to accept that the runaway drum in her chest is connected to her rapidly expanding and contracting lungs. Air. Breath. Heart.

"Walk," they command.

Laboriously, she sidesteps, braced on her forearms, and turns the walker. Doubling back now, she makes toward the nurses' station. One last *clunk*, and the walker bangs against the desk. She grits her teeth, and the pressure in her cheeks threatens to bust the stitches in her jaw.

"What's she up to?" the nurse behind the desk asks the orderly who shadows Jesse.

"I'm on it," he says, hovering. He'd noticed her accept the hug from another patient in front of the TV and has accompanied her step by step on the way back. "Looks to me like Capt'n Kraig is trying to smile."

When her breath backs off to a manageable pant, she steadies herself with her left hand and reaches out with her right and tries to grasp a ballpoint pen that lies on a stack of printouts on the desk.

"Easy there, Captain." The orderly gently guides her hand away from the pen. "That's a no-no in your case."

"Ha!" Making eye contact with the orderly, she more slowly, deliberately extends her fingers toward the pen.

The orderly raises an eyebrow and exchanges glances with the nurse. "What the hell . . ." He stays his hand and watches closely to see what she'll do next.

Slowly, awkwardly, she touches the pen and then curls her fingers around the slim cylinder. In a clumsy movement she experiments with mapping shapes on the paper. What happens looks like a game of Hangman the cat got.

Deep furrows crease her stitched forehead, and again she grits her teeth. Now several more of the staff have torn themselves away from the president's announcement and gather around the desk.

Jesse takes a deep breath and looks past her nonsense scribble to the block of type on the sheet. For several long minutes she studies the thicket of black Caslon characters. The concentration prompts another crooked flash from the new time machine in her head, and she sees a cloud of ravens rising over the stubble of a winter wheat field.

Her palm is damp with sweat and smudges the page, blurring the type, as she positions the pen and bears down, drawing the tip in an erratic loop around a letter *B*. Rest. Exhale. Blink sweat.

Then she forces her hand further across the type and makes another scraggly circle around the letter *T*. Shaking with exertion, she trundles her palsied hand to one last letter. Almost cross-eyed with exertion, she manages to capture an *R*.

"Bee Tee Are," the orderly pronounces.

Again Jesse grits her teeth and strains her cheeks as she hugs the pen protectively to her chest in her fist.

"Bee Tee Are," the orderly repeats.

Jesse attempts a vigorous nod that comes off in slow motion, but she manages to raise the hand with the pen and points her index finger at her head.

"BTR. Better, get it?" the nurse says in a hushed voice.

The orderly drops his jaw and exclaims, "Well, no shit, girl. No shit!"

The second celebration that erupts at the desk is tempered by Jesse's refusal to give up the pen. When the orderly patiently attempts to extract it from her hand, she clutches it possessively and a defensive snarl comes to her lips. He has to pry it away digit by digit.

That's when they all look around and see the doctor watching with a frown on his tired face. "What the hell's Kraig doing with a pen? She tried to stab Christine Morel with a pen, for Christ's sake."

They try to explain.

"Okay, great. But no pens. Get her back to speech therapy in the morning. Flash cards good. Pens not good."

CHAPTER TWENTY-TWO

Joe Davis knows about the Serenity Prayer because, once, back before 9/11, when he was a precocious baby cop doing undercover in Bangor, Maine, he became enamored of a stripper who was working a serious meth jones and tried to get her into rehab. She passed on the program and on him but not before he took her to a few meetings, so he remembered the Alcoholics Anonymous prayer, particularly the part about accepting the things you cannot change.

And now that's where Mouse, whose bullshit detector is wired into NSA's multibillion-dollar satellite grid, has filed away the fiasco at Turmar.

Davis disagrees after his face-to-face with Jesse Kraig at Walter Reed. So he's sitting in his broom closet–sized office at the back end of a subbasement in a National Security Agency outbuilding at Ft. Meade, Maryland, talking on a secure phone to Mouse. He's trying to get him to turn over his file on Richard Noland.

"You're taking a vacation, right?" Mouse says.

"For sure, going up to Maine to see my folks," Davis says, glancing at his packed travel bag that sits next to the door. In fact, before talking to Mouse, he'd just gotten off the phone with a travel agent who'd booked him onto a flight to Memphis later this morning and signed him into a hotel and arranged for a rental car. He'd Googled Richard Noland and scanned the articles on his kidnapping from the cable stations and the major dailies. All of them regurgitated the conventional wisdom. Then he found a brief CNN interview with his former wife—Sally Noland—that was recorded by the Memphis CNN affiliate. He pulled a photo-grab of her, a hard-edged blonde who went heavy on the mascara, wasn't beneath displaying some serious cleavage on national TV, and appeared determined to carry her pinched good looks well into her forties. But mainly what piqued his interest was her flat, dead-eyed delivery when she said, "Like, me and Dickie are divorced and all, but what happened to him shouldn't have happened to a dog, you know . . ." He replayed the clip several times. As a seasoned investigator, he knew how to connect the dots. He'd grown up tracking and hunting whitetails in the Maine outback, and he'd been to sniper school. He could hit a dot at a thousand yards. But in the end he usually went with his gut. It was part subjective, part a memory of his days on the streets of Bangor. Every copper remembers a Sally Noland whose thorny charms curve inward. Some guys can't resist going back after the impossible to forget roses and get sliced up on the way out.

Davis figured the ex-wife was a good place to start untangling "the things you cannot change." And he was willing to pop for a round-trip ticket to follow his hunch that Sally Noland was one of the last people her ex-husband had talked to in this world. What he needed from Mouse was her address and vitals.

"And you're sober, right?"

"Absolutely." In fact Davis has a hangover along with a bad case of the Toenail Polish Blues. Jesse Kraig has taken up permanent residence in the Rorschach water rings left by his tumbler of Jack Daniel's that he tries to interpret on numerous barroom counters.

"Okay, I'll send you an encryption package with the stuff I pulled on Noland. Just reading material, right?"

"You got it, boss."

Five minutes later Davis prints out the email and finds Sally Noland's address in east Memphis, under "next of kin" in the bio workup. Instinct tells him the lady with the attitude and the telegenic chest is his best informant. Always thorough,

Mouse has listed Sally's last known place of employment, also on the east side.

Twenty minutes later he gets off the base shuttle at the gate and is hailing a cab when he figures Mouse probably isn't fooled. Mouse is letting him off the leash to go out and kick the bushes for land mines. As usual.

Several hours later Davis steps off the Delta jet into soaking west Tennessee heat that seeps up the walkway. Then he's in the air-conditioned terminal and out again into the steamy turmoil of a thunderstorm. Driving the Hertz rental into downtown Memphis, he's reaching for the words to the song about coming into this town, but they evade him. When the rain lifts, he watches an emerald-gray haze sweat off the wide Mississippi.

When he gets the directions figured out off the map from the travel agency, he stops in front of the Peabody Hotel that fills a whole block like a square, stately galleon. After leaving the car in the hotel garage, he takes a moment to have a cigarette and acclimate to the street action. Union Avenue stretches out in the friendly, shabby twilight with easy Southern smiles and hot licks wafting from rib shacks in the alleys and guitar picks going on the corners.

A pair of women in heels strut by with a sassy swish to their skirts like you never see up North—like they just pulled some man's life down around his ears and are on their way to inspire another blues song before the sun goes down. *And you know, a guy could get used to this.* But he has work to do, so he enters the plush, columned lobby, registers, and gets his room. After a shower and shave, he pulls on a pair of jeans and a denim jacket and pats the empty space beneath his left armpit where a shoulder holster would usually go. He'd decided it wasn't worth the hassle of taking a gun through the TSA checkpoints. Sally Noland came across on the video clip as a definite piece of work, and she's listed in Mouse's dossier as a waitress at an east Memphis joint called the Trap Rock Inn. So Davis figures, at most, he may have to duck nothing more serious than a beer bottle or two. He calls the home number first and a boy, perhaps twelve, answers.

"May I speak to your mom?"

"She ain't home. She's at work. Who's this?"

"Mr. Davis with Publisher's Clearing House."

"Yeah, bullshit." The connection ends.

Smart kid.

Next he pages through the business listings in the phone book, gets the number and address for the Trap Rock Inn. After a man answers in a low din of juke music and bar chatter, Davis is breezy, slurring his words to disguise his dry, taciturn Down East accent. "Hey, man, is Sally working tonight?"

"Depends who's asking," the guy challenges in a thick mid-South gumbo of suspicion.

"I'm a friend."

"She ain't got no friends who talk like you." Click.

Which sounds to Davis like a probably yes. So after he pulls on an Atlanta Braves baseball cap and a pair of scuffed Nike Frees, he debates whether he should wear the sunglasses. He decides the scars might buy him some cred in the Trap Rock and leaves the glasses behind. Then he gets his car and drives east from town until he finds a diner to have a quick supper. Consulting a city map on his iPhone, he has the route plotted by the time he's finished his chicken salad.

He locates the tavern in an industrial district where chain-link fences cage aggressive tribes of weeds that push up through cracks in the empty parking lots. It starts to rain again, which adds a neon glitter from the Trap Rock sign to the empty streets. Judging by the name of the place and the pickups parked in the lot and the attire of the clientele he watches come and go, the Trap Rock is a hard-times hangout for the building trades.

So he ambles in out of the rain, sits at a table with his back to the wall, and checks out the ambiance that consists of one part oxygen to two parts nicotine fumes and beer farts. There's a ten-point whitetail mounted on the wall along with an iconic framed portrait of Nathan Bedford Forrest. Rounding out the décor is a pool table and one widescreen TV in the back, blaring Fox News in competition with Jason Aldean singing "Big Green Tractor" on the jukebox.

Davis fits in as far as it goes. He can sit a bar stool like 500 miles of bad road, and he's got the scars to discourage idle chatter. He figures he'll be fine as long as he doesn't open his mouth too much, because he hasn't practiced dropping his Gs and saying "ain't" lately, and the only thing he can blend into down South is a dark night.

After his eyes acclimate to the gloom, he takes out the photo-grab of Sally from the video and locates her at the service bar. She wears a short skirt under an apron that shows she's kept her trim ankles and calves but she's having less success with her fried smile and hair dyed the color of burnt scrambled eggs. She's still fond of putting it out there with the low-cut blouse.

When a stool opens up next to the service bar, Davis drifts over to it and orders a tap beer. Sally heaves off to deliver a tray full of drinks and then returns, gives the barkeep her order, and takes a pull on a Merit Light she has going in the ashtray next to the counter. She leaves lipstick on the filter.

"Sally Noland, right?" Davis says, raising his voice enough to carry over the bar clamor.

And she shifts her eyes, which are deep brown from damage or experience or both. Alert behind the mascara, she gives him a priceless look up and down, followed by a quick smile that is genuinely amused. "Honey, no way you can hide the fact you're a Yankee cop. You another government man?"

Her new order is up, and she sweeps up the tray and leaves him with her last question to chew on. When she returns, she turns to him with a droll smile. "Well?"

"Won't bullshit you, Sally. I was there the day your ex-husband disappeared in Iraq. Three people with me got killed . . . and I have a few questions." Davis pauses, then adds, "And I was a cop, but that was years ago."

"Uh-huh, so now you're a soldier boy? That where you got the interesting face?"

"Something like that."

She looks him up and down again, weighs it, then calls out to the bartender, "Jimmy, I'm taking my break. Pour me a coffee, will you?"

"Can you make that two?" Davis asks.

Jimmy, the bartender, appraises Davis with the genial scowl of a cage fighter calculating time and distance. "Everything all right here?" he asks Sally. "This more of that shit off the TV about Dickie?"

"Something like that." Sally treats Davis to a game smile. After the coffee arrives, she says, "C'mon, we'll go out back. There's patio tables under an awning."

Davis takes the coffee cup and follows her down a corridor past the restrooms and out the back door. They sit on opposite ends of a picnic table bench and watch the rain beat down on the trucks in the lot.

"Don't mean to be rude, but you have some ID?" she asks.

Davis takes the fake military ID out of his wallet and hands it to her. She inspects it, hands it back, and removes another Merit from a pack in her apron. Davis takes an old Zippo from his jacket pocket and thumbs the wheel. She takes a lungful of smoke and exhales. "Don't see many of those anymore." She nods at the lighter.

"Was my dad's." He places the silver lighter on the table between them. "So?"

"All I know is this woman from the State Department came by to express her sympathy and like that, said they were on it and they'd keep me up to date. She explained what they thought happened. He was working salvage in a remote area. Musta tempted somebody. Then there were these two helicopters..."

Davis nods. "We were on our way somewhere else, and it blew up in our face. You said government *man* earlier?"

"Uh-huh. FBI. Which was weird. I mean, asking about any *contacts*, like I'm going to come up with ransom money or something?" She cocks her head. "It wasn't like that, was it? More like they grabbed Dickie for the money in his wallet. Or just because he was a foreigner in the wrong place?" She raises her eyes.

Davis acknowledges her remark by raising his coffee cup.

Then Sally reaches out and fondly touches the old silver lighter sitting on the table. "My granddad has one of these. Makes you think. He landed on Utah Beach, and a year later he was in Germany." She picks up her cup, sips, and then raises it in a salute. "But we just got bin Laden, huh? Only took us ten years."

After an interval, Davis asks, "You hear anything else from the woman from the State Department or anyone from the FBI?"

She shakes her head and takes another drag on her cigarette. "He's missing. That pretty much sums him up." She allows a bittersweet smile. "He was always missing right there on the other side of the bed." Again she gives him that vintage barroom look. "So what's this to you?"

"I'm just trying to figure out what happened that day."

"Like, is it personal? You lose a friend?"

"Something like that. Anything you could tell me about what he was doing over there would help."

"Not much to tell." She sighs and stares into the rain. "Lot of guys inside, they use to work for us. We had a decent construction outfit up 'til the bubble burst. Fuckin' Wall Street, huh? Business went to hell, the marriage went to hell. We lost the house. It's an oft-told tale."

Davis studies her for a long moment, captured by the sudden lilt in her language, her posture, her crossed legs, her hitched-up skirt, and her one elbow resting on a carved knee. The smoke twists up from the cigarette in her fingers and disappears into the Tennessee rain, and with the hooded, blacked-out factory windows for a backdrop, he catches a flash of Blanche DuBois in *Streetcar*. He'd studied drama for a while at the U of Maine and was good enough at it that a summer-stock company picked him up his senior year. Probably one of the reasons Mouse selected him . . .

Sally reaches over and touches the sleeve of his jacket. "Hello?"

"Sorry. So he went to Iraq?"

"Yeah, Dickie figured he could hit the lottery over there. One big score and out. To hear him talk, he was going to get the business back, and the house. Buy stuff for the kids. Thought he could get me back, too."

Then she raises her cigarette, stares at the ash, and shakes her head. "Dickie was always right on the verge, you know? He called me just before he was taken. Said he fell into a real pot of gold this time. Said we were going to be rich . . ." Her lips jerk in a non-smile. "He wound up hauling other people's leftover junk out of the desert. The man was out of touch . . ."

This time Davis absorbs her words without missing a beat and points to her cigarette. "Could I have one of those? Left mine in the car."

As she shakes out a smoke and he lights it, he asks, "The FBI guy you talked to, you remember his name?"

"Sure. Special Agent Mueller, out of the Memphis office."

"You tell him about the last phone call, about the pot of gold?"

"You kidding? He was right out of the movies, wingtips and all. Besides, what happened was bad enough without buying more trouble."

"But you just told me?"

Sally leans her head to the side, and now it's her turn to study him. "I size up men all day on my job, and you might have been a cop once, and maybe you're a soldier, but you strike me like what we call a Pilgrim. Honey, I ain't sure where you're headed with this, but right now you look sorta on the lost side." Then she stands up and flips the remains of her cigarette into the rain. "Any help?"

"Maybe. Thanks for the time." Davis gets up, pockets his lighter, drops the Merit, and grinds it under his heel.

Sally shrugs. Then more sincerely she says, "I'm sorry about your friends."

"Me too," Davis says.

After he walks her back inside and says good-bye, he goes out the front door and turns up his collar and hunches his shoulders on the way to his car, and now he remembers the lyrics that escaped him on the ride into Memphis, maybe because of Sally's comment that his Yankee ass has touched down, sorta on the lost side, in Blues Country in the driving rain.

CHAPTER TWENTY-THREE

Aphasia.

Jesse is en route via military transport to the Ft. Snelling Veteran's Hospital in Minneapolis because it has the closest polytrauma ward to her home in North Dakota. She flew into Walter Reed, unconscious, strapped into a gurney. She boarded this flight under her own power with the help of a cane, and she rides sitting up.

But she knows she's moving at quarter speed in a slow-motion glide to the low-key strum of the Seroquel guitar in her blood.

Aphasia is a disorder that results from damage to portions of the brain that control language, which she pretty much understands from the perspective of being inside looking out. Her condition impairs the expression and understanding of English as well as the ability to read and write.

She knows her name but can't pronounce it. She knows her service number but can't write it. She'd like to try to write it, but they won't let her have a pen.

The doctors speculate that she suffers from nonfluent Broca's aphasia. Their diagnosis is based on the observation that she can utter fragments of words that make sense, but it requires tremendous effort to get them out. And she certainly gets it when they say that people with Broca's aphasia can understand the speech of others fairly well. So she is intensely aware of her own speech difficulties and becomes easily frustrated. The frustration makes her irritable and sometimes erupts as anger, so they've got her down as having an attitude. Which goes back to the freakouts in her chart that they attribute to post-traumatic psychosis. So they keep her juiced on the

Seroquel as a precaution against her harming herself or others. So, okay, that part she tracks fairly well . . .

What's giving her real trouble is what came after the hallucinations receded. Whole pages of her mental scrapbook have fallen into place, but there are scary gaps. Like the black hole she disappeared into at the controls of Tumbleweed Six. At Reed she overheard the doctors talking about post-traumatic amnesia. If she was playing psycho poker, she'd be holding a full house.

Usually people with Broca's have damage to the frontal lobe of their brains, but repeated MRIs come back without evidence of such damage. She struggles with the implication. Her situation is not caused directly by physical injury. It's in her head in a different way.

She knows what they think: that she lost her mind when she got shot down. But since the hallucinations stopped, she's cobbled together enough of her personality to form an alternate opinion.

Didn't lose it. They stole it with their freakin' drugs! Gotta figure how to get it back.

So now that the seizures have ended and the wounds on her face, shoulder, and knee have sufficiently healed, she's scheduled for rehabilitation in Minneapolis.

As she offloads and gets settled, she perceives that Reed was a warehouse for wounded and that Snelling is a friendlier place. It has lots of open space and more light, and the corridors wrap around spacious glass-roofed atriums that resemble a palatial hotel more than a hospital. A huge American flag hangs flour to ceiling in the four-story lobby.

The polytrauma ward on the fourth floor is Jesse's new home.

Poly—more than one. Trauma. Got it.

She has her own room with natural light flooding in through a bank of windows. She's encouraged to walk to meals in the ward dining area with the other patients. Escorted by nurse's aides, she attends the first clumsy speech-therapy and physical-rehab sessions. She finds the physical rehab challenging. Speech is much more difficult. The sounds and letters hide, tucked out of reach, like Scrabble tiles in a black bag. She can rattle them, but she can't get them out. She especially has trouble sequencing her thoughts when she tries to span the gaps. When she speaks, her pronunciation is slurred and inarticulate.

It is during this period, when she's at her lowest ebb, that a procession of visitors drifts past her drugged eyes. A chaplain and a Guard colonel appear. Two medals are pinned to her pillow. Her parents arrive from Langdon, North Dakota, and for a whole day they hover as she shuffles the halls with them, trying to form words. Her dad has never been good with problems he can't solve with his hands. Her mother is more patient and spends a last hour alone with her. With a mighty effort, Jesse manages to say, "Bett'r, lat'r."

Then her mother tells her that her former fiancé, Terry Sherman, has contacted them and is planning to visit.

Oh, boy. That's just freakin' great.

Alone in her room—almost alone, she isn't allowed to close her door—she hobbles to the bathroom and peers in the mirror and explores the healing wounds on her face with numb fingers, the nails in need of trimming, rimmed in gray. Her mom brought a cosmetic bag, but she doesn't know where to start.

Despite her listless attempt to use a brush, her freakin' hair looks like a shaggy sunflower that survived a date with a wind tunnel. The fading bruises under her eyes and suture tracks on chin, lips, and eyebrow give her a mottled raccoon quality. Still, compared to some of the skin grafts she sees in the hall, she's the ward beauty queen.

She shifts from foot to foot. Wiggles her fingers.

Her hands and feet function; it's her mind that's numb, like when your foot falls asleep and you put weight on it and it gives out. When she tries to put thoughts together, it's like her mind falls over, like it can't handle the gravity of thinking.

She *knows* what happened, damn it; they've patiently led her through it. She just can't *remember* it on her own. Or express it.

Going down Tumbleweed Six . . .

She got shot down, is what happened. But she doesn't have the energy to focus and penetrate into the gap where a Black Hawk and crew disappeared. She tries to visualize the problem and gets a picture of her mind clattering like rickety machinery held in check by barbed wire and bailing twine, like some quick fix her dad slapped on the windmill to keep it running.

Slo-mo. No energy. Quarter speed. So how do you fix the lows that moved in when the hallucinations stopped?

She was raised to believe that in North Dakota the term "depression" referred to a low place in the terrain or areas of low pressure in a weather front. As a mental condition it was reserved for people from Minnesota or Iowa or even *South* Dakota—folks who had disposable time and income and never worked hard for a living.

She turns from the mirror, shuffles across the room, and sits cross-legged on the bed to test the stiffness in her knee. Every movement is an effort because the drugs they're giving her have turned her blood to sluggish, lead-based syrup.

As best she can, she focuses her attention on the doorway and tries to make Marge and Toby and Laura appear and walk through it.

When waiting doesn't work, she tries hope. Failing that, she employs a kind of bargaining that in childhood passed for prayer. The hospital's a big place. They gotta be here somewhere. There are flickers of aching memory—these acoustic, visual shadows that swirl up, sharply etched in the fog. *All of them together, joking on the flight line, gearing up. Toby bitching about taking estrogen pills . . .*

Slowly she appreciates the dimensions of a new fear, almost as if the more lucid she becomes, the more she rubs up against something more terrifying than the hallucinations. Compared to this new fear, the seizures were like grotesque bubbles detaching and floating away. This is the opposite and obeys the laws of gravity, like a crippled helicopter crashing to earth. It's a permanent seizure.

It's reality. And reality comes with a raw, ferrous dirt aftertaste that coats her mouth and tells her they won't be coming through the door. But she can't remember exactly why. And then it hits her full-force. Did she screw up? Is it her fault Marge and Laura and Toby can't walk through the door? Is that what they're keeping from her?

A new sensation clamps her chest and stops her breath and punches right through the drugged grief and shoots past panic or mere fear or civilan clichés about right and wrong. For one pure, insane moment, Jesse dangles, all alone, in deep space on the meat hook of the ultimate military sin. *Did you let your buddies down?* When no one's watching, she turns into her pillow and sobs.

The notion has a black, bottomless quality that could swallow her forever, and the only thing that pulls her back from the brink is noticing her finger compulsively tracing on the bedsheet—over and over—the shape of a five-pointed star. And it occurs to her . . .

Gotta fight back, gotta work the problem. Gotta steal a pen and some paper.

CHAPTER TWENTY-FOUR

Thirteen miles southwest of Baltimore, Joe Davis guides his government-car-pool Crown Vic off the Baltimore-Washington Parkway onto the exit marked NSA Employees Only, then cruises down Route 32 toward the gleaming glass-walled headquarters building of the National Security Agency at Fort Meade.

His eyes look like he rinsed them in V8 juice behind his sunglasses because he was up too late meditating with a bottle and his mouth is parched because he's been smoking too much.

His conversation with Mr. Jack Daniel's concerned the phone call he'd made to special agent Bobby Appert's personal cell right after he returned from Memphis. To his voice mail, actually. Calling Appert was going off the reservation; Mouse would not approve. Besides, his parting with Appert had cast a cryptic shadow in the 100-degree sauna of a Baghdad afternoon more than a month ago.

The farewell handshake had been pro forma. Appert, being old-time and uptight, probably believed the stories going round that Davis was dirty. The message he'd left inquired whether it was normal procedure for an Agent Mueller out of the Memphis office to question Richard Noland's ex-wife about receiving communication from drive-by kidnappers in Iraq. Did the Bureau really think Noland was still alive? That was five days ago, and total radio silence reigns on his cell phone and in his email.

Mouse wouldn't approve because Davis had no official status to initiate contact with a federal agency. His carefully crafted deep-cover persona was *supposed* to look "dirty" and

Sphinx-like and indistinguishable from the sewage he sometimes swam in. And Mouse thought the blowout at Turmar
was a nonstarter anyway.

Davis didn't.

After talking to Sally Noland, he was encouraged in his
suspicion that something was going on.

Waiting on Appert to call, he'd made a check at Walter
Reed, where a receptionist informed him that Captain Kraig
was no longer on the neurology ward. She had been kicked
down the VA pipeline, and her whereabouts were a matter of
patient confidentiality to non–family members. The information
was not unexpected but still hit him like a leftover pail of cold
Tennessee rain.

Now it's time to slow for the gate guard, and so he pulls
out his temporary NSA ID card that describes him as a "special
consultant." The guard waves him through, and he drives to
the nondescript building at the back of the campus and parks.
With a large triple-espresso Black Eye for company, he rides the
elevator to the subbasement and angles between cubicles occupied by mathematicians staring at video screens. There's just a
conventional lock on the temporary office door, and Davis is
convinced it used to be a laundry room. He turns his key and
goes in, removes his sunglasses and his sports jacket, and slings
his shoulder holster on the corner of the chair.

He sits down and is taking his second sip of coffee when a
tentative tap sounds on his door jam. This roundish fellow
wearing rimless spectacles stands in the doorway peering at
him. "Ah, Mr. Davis, if you're going to leave your door open,
we'd appreciate it if you didn't leave the, ah, gun hanging
there. It, ah, distracts some of my colleagues."

"Sure," Davis says, grabbing the holstered .45 and shoving
it in a desk drawer. "And I'd appreciate it especially this morning if you boys didn't plunk the keyboards so hard. I had a
rough night."

The gnomish crypy withdraws, pulling the door shut behind him.

For a moment he puzzles over his e-mail queue, which is totally empty, then he leans back in his swivel chair trying to read his future in a water stain on the ceiling. He twirls the chair and studies a poster on the wall that he calls his tongue-in-cheek "mission statement." It portrays a skinny, spectacled man in uniform who resembles Congressman Ron Paul from Texas. The paragraph underneath the picture proclaims in bold type:

I spent 33 years and four months in military service, and during that period I spent most of my time as a high class thug for Big Business. For Wall Street and the bankers. In short, I was a racketeer, a gangster for capitalism. I helped make Mexico and especially Tampico safe for American oil interest in 1914. . . .

The last three sentences read:

Looking back on it, I might have given Al Capone a few hints. The best he could do was to operate his rackets in three districts. I operated on three continents.

War Is a Racket, 1935
Major General Smedley Butler, former Commandant, United States Marine Corps, recipient of two Congressional Medals of Honor.

He raises his Black Eye in a toast to Butler—two ex-jarheads who've reached similar conclusions—and then glances at the silent cell phone lying open on his desk. It goes without saying that Special Agent Appert would not approve.

And he wonders if, down deep, Mouse harbors the same sentiments. Then, hearing the door crack open, he looks up and sees Mouse standing in the doorway, looking truly scary in a dark-blue three-piece pinstripe suit and polished Allen Edmonds.

"Mouse? Damn, man; I was just thinking of you."

"Yeah, it's a burden, this psychic thing."

"What's up?"

"Not much, just somebody did a search of your records. All your records. So I shit-canned your e-mails as a precaution."

"I noticed. I thought my e-mails were encrypted?"

"Exactly. Meet me in the parking lot. And Joey, bring your stuff." Then Mouse saunters off down the row of cubicles.

Davis spins his chair. *Bring your stuff.* He retrieves his gun from the drawer and straps it on and bids farewell to his spiritual mentor, Smedley.

Across the grounds, the main building's window glass scintillates like a square blue bonfire in the morning heat. Maury the Mouse stands in the sun fifty feet from the front door like the No Smoking sign on Davis' outbuilding specifies. "Act natural," he says as he peels the wrapper from a Snickers.

"Why are we standing out here in the open?"

"I got some guys I trust watching to see who may be watching us."

"Great. Who's digging around in my file?"

"No clue. Relax."

So he relaxes and takes out his American Spirits.

"Those things will kill you," Mouse says as he pushes half the candy bar into his mouth.

"And that stuff won't?" Davis points at the gooey chocolate. "These are natural tobacco, no additives, like health food." His eyes are sectioning and tracking around the lot.

"I said relax," Mouse says. Another reason Maury got his nickname "Mouse" is because of his large ears—a foreshadowing of his future as an international and now domestic eavesdropper. Mouse has the junk-food pallor of a kid who was in the basement playing Dungeons and Dragons and taking apart computers when his peers where learning to swing a baseball bat. He runs one of the top floors in the big building.

"So how was your vacation?" After they exchange frank stares, Mouse says, "You know if I can track your flight reservations off your MasterCard, so can anybody. I'm going to need your badge after you leave the reservation. You're going away, Joey."

"How far away?" Davis asks.

"Whole-new-identity away. Presto-chango. Tap of a key. Governments fall. Task forces melt away. Those on the outs are now on the in," Mouse says with an enigmatic grin.

"Christ, are we being monitored right now?" Davis wonders.

Mouse stabs a pudgy finger at the sky and says, "Hundred-fifty miles thataway we got a satellite that can watch flies copulate under the morning dew."

"So you gonna tell me?" Davis asks.

Mouse shrugs. "No rush, but if I were you, I'd start repacking my parachute, like in about an hour, because somebody is fucking with our thing . . ." He winks, mouthing the words like a Mafia don, which, in a way, he is. "I suggest you relocate your ass, posthaste, to someplace that does not fit your daily travel pattern." Mouse swipes a dollop of chocolate from the corner of his mouth with a finger. "So just finish your smoke, then let's walk to your car, drive through the gate, and hand over your ID card. I get out, and you head for a black hole. Ditch the wheels, don't go back to the place." He hands Davis a cell phone with a car and wall charger.

"What's this?"

"Cold phone, so we can communicate." Then he hands over a key with a numbered fob and the address of a Baltimore storage company. "I'm throwing this together kind of fast, but it's time for you to *reinvent* yourself and lay low. But hang on to your wallet for the time being. Clear?"

Davis narrows his eyes, "Clear. What's going down?"

"What's going down is I can be wrong. I overlooked your take on getting booted out of the Sandbox, but you poking around in Memphis stirred up some kind of hornet's nest. So what exactly did you pull out of Noland's old lady?"

"Only that he was hungry to score, and before he vanished he told her he was on to something really big."

"Really big, huh? The day after you talked to her, this trip wire I built into your bio data lit up. Somebody *really big* is checking you out, Joey."

"Define 'really big.'"

"Like hiding behind counterterror encryption I've never seen before. Which means they could be checking *us* out, what we do." He pauses. "Oh, and they gave you the runaround at Reed about the pilot? She's been sent to Minneapolis."

"You *have* been monitoring my calls."

"I've been monitoring your *breathing*."

"So?"

"So, like I said, could be you stumbled into something at Turmar and they don't like you going around like a loose cannon with the questions. Now these fuckers think they can brush us off, so we're gonna find out who's better in the black, them or us." He winks again. "You're gonna start earning your pay. Like General Crook said, takes an Apache to catch an Apache, huh, Joey?"

"Sure, boss, but when you get right down to it, there's like . . ." Davis looks around, ". . . just you and me and maybe Appert."

"Yeah," Mouse smiles. "I already feel sorry for the poor dumb bastards who are after us."

CHAPTER TWENTY-FIVE

Sometimes, like now, Morgon Jump almost believes he has insomniac goblins on patrol in his sleep, who "heard" the lights go on in the Rivard mansion across the lawn from his carriage-house apartment. He sits up in bed carefully, so as not to disturb Amanda Rivard, who curls at his side. But she stirs at his movement and wonders in a foggy voice, "What is it?"

"Shhh. Nothing," he says. "Go back to sleep."

As she sinks to her pillow, he gets out of bed, pulls on a robe, and picks his way to the balcony door. Outside, he pulls the robe tighter around his chest. It was unseasonably cold last night in Rivard County on the Michigan shore of Lake Huron, so this May morning the grass and shrubs shimmer with a faint patina of frost.

The Rivard mansion grins in the dark like a broken-toothed jack-o'-lantern as lights pop on helter skelter—John's upstairs bedroom, Kelly's room, the stairway, the downstairs hall, the kitchen. Morgon's first concern is that the old man is having a medical emergency. Then he hears John's voice carry through the chilly air. The rhythm of the coded profanity suggests he's yelling into a phone. Morgon checks his watch. Calls at quarter after four in the morning are not supposed to happen in John Rivard's carefully scripted world.

And helicopters aren't supposed to appear out of nowhere and crash in the middle of Morgon's missions.

Not "nothing," like he had told Amanda. Something's wrong.

So Morgon sits on the balcony stairs and lights a Camel and watches the stages of alarm play out. Kelly Ortiz jogs down the front steps, fires up the golf cart, and putts off across the estate lawn toward the hangar where he keeps his Bell helicopter. In minutes Morgon hears the turbines whine and props start to turn. Kelly is rushing his preflight checks. Minutes later he's back with the cart as John stumps down the stairs punctuating every step with a frustrated stab of his cane. He gets in the cart, they bump off into the night, and a few minutes later the chopper's landing lights rise above the hangar and rotor off to the west, in the direction of the Traverse City Airport.

Morgon shifts on the cold balcony steps and takes a meditative drag on his smoke. John's sense of privacy predates the plummy nostalgia of gentlemen who didn't read each other's mail. No one reads John's mail because he doesn't allow anything to be written down. Or be spoken on insecure or even— ideally—secure voice communication. All business is conducted strictly face-to-face.

Morgon can visualize what will happen. A nondescript man waits at a flimsy table in a food court at the Traverse City Airport. He comes from an office hidden in a subbasement below CIA headquarters in Langley, Virginia. Morgon has never seen one of these couriers or the office he comes from. The joke in the Agency's Special Activities Division used to be that if the office had a designation it would be called the Bureau of Perfect Crimes. It's where they pick Morgon's targets.

Worrying about it won't speed John's return, so Morgon goes down the stairs, enters the garage below the carriage house, and selects his work clothes from a locker. Once dressed, he walks across the sweep of manicured lawn and mist-jeweled shrubs to the three-story Victorian with a wraparound veranda. Now there's a hush of ocher in the purple mist, enough light for the house to strike a Gothic silhouette spiked with gables and turrets and frets of gingerbread.

As John is fond of saying, "After my grandfather had his fill of killing Rebels, he came home from the war and proceeded to kill all the trees in northern Michigan. By 1880 he was timber-rich enough to build this Queen Anne monstrosity."

And Morgon, who started out barefoot wearing hand-me-downs in Greenwood, Mississippi, muses that some of those Rebels were undoubtedly his wretched-ass ancestors.

Irony is one of the concepts he didn't really learn to appreciate until the Agency attached him to old John Rivard as his personal bodyguard, which is cover employment for his real job of carrying out the lethal wishes of that nonexistent office in Langley, Virginia.

He goes in and finds half a pot of hurried coffee remaining in the kitchen, so he pours a thermos cup full and goes back outside to watch a gloomy sunrise smudge the wall of mist that rolls in off the lake. Sipping his coffee, he watches a Chevy Suburban ease up the driveway. Martha Mundt gets out. She's a cheerful, stout woman who has kept house for the Rivard family for the last ten years. Her white-haired husband, Carl, waves from behind the wheel. Carl maintains the grounds.

"The bird's gone," Carl says, nodding toward the hangar.

"John was called away," Morgon explains. Then to Martha, he says, "I'm sure he'll appreciate some strong coffee when he gets back."

Carl leans out the driver's-side window and nods to Amanda, who has appeared on the carriage-house balcony drawing a brush through the sable hair that falls past her shoulders. She wears a red silk kimono Morgon picked up years ago in Manila that, on her, looks like a prop in an ad for something expensive. Carl's smile is differential as he turns back to Morgon and muses, "The way you're settling in here, you might have found a home."

"Could be." Morgon won't argue the point.

Then Carl points at Morgon's steel-toed boots. "You thinking of getting back on your rock pile?"

"Yes, sir. Soon as there's enough light."

Working with stone is the only release he truly enjoys. Feeling the weight and heft in his hands is like touching centuries of permanence and deep silence. Stone is what's left standing after everything else dies.

There's enough nip in the air for Morgon to see his breath ghost out in a white blur and dissolve into the pewter mist. He's panting in rhythm with the rolling surf as he lifts a chunk of limestone. A cubic foot of limestone weighs around 160 pounds, and this stone rectangle is close to twice that size. The weight sings in the flat muscles of his arms and shoulders and gut and legs and tests the limits of his strength.

More than a month back from the desert, he's still working out the vibrations since the explosion played tetherball with his skull. Among the residual concussion effects he's experiencing are headaches, dizziness, and sensitivity to light.

Amanda prescribes rest and acetaminophen. It will pass.

In the meantime he finds solace in the stone wall he's building in front of a gazebo perched atop a slight hill on the north end of the lawn. Dry-rock construction, done with care, is particularly demanding bull work. A haphazard pyramid of the rock is piled ten yards behind him, where the dump truck dropped fifty tons of the stuff. It used to be a retaining wall in nearby Lakeside. An assortment of stonemason tools scatter around his work boots: a heavy-headed mash hammer, chisels, a rock pick, a tape measure, and a level. Shards of chipped stone sprinkle the lawn, debris from his three previous attempts to get this beast to fit.

Grunting, he wrestles the rock into the prepared slot and perfectly times releasing his grip as the rock locks into position with a dull *crunch*. The wall has been brooding in him all through winter and into the muddy spring. Last November, after deer season, he vacationed in Peru to walk the Inca Trail. On the way out he lingered for a whole day, appreciating the cunningly fitted stonework of the Cuzco Wall.

His careful meditation is jarred by a sudden phantom of desert heat. *It's the goddamn pilot. That's why John got the call. I never should have left her to Amanda's medical theories. They subcontracted her out to Roger Torres, who gives periodic progress reports — first from Germany, then Walter Reed. Now, according to Roger, she's vegging in a Minneapolis VA hospital.*

The aroma of fresh-brewed coffee precedes the scuff of Amanda's tennis shoes on the grass behind him. He turns and accepts the steaming cup. She's six years his junior, with a trim technical climber's body now tucked in faded 501 Jeans and a simple white blouse. She's fixed her hair in a practical ponytail, and the top of her head comes up to his chin, a pronounced window's peak striking a comma in the center of her forehead. The descending clip of hairline is a Rivard family trait, as is the subtle extra length of jaw that rescues her face from being impossibly beautiful.

"So where'd he go?" she asks after she inspects the courses of leveled stone set into the hillside.

"Traverse City."

"To meet whoever it is?" She asks with a bored drawl that John explained she acquired at the Cranbrook Academy.

"Yeah," Morgon can't help grinning. "Whoever it is." She has this blasé, priviledged art of knowing it all but not really.

Then they hear the approaching *wap-wap* of helicopter rotors. The Bell helicopter clears the trees, flares slightly, and then settles its skids into the lawn fifty yards from the house. Kelly waits until the props stop rotating, then gets out, his ponytail swinging, as he saunters around the aircraft and opens the right-seat door for John, who struggles out with one veined, marble hand clutching his cane, the other holding an empty pipe to his lips. Doctor's orders. Cut out the tobacco. At ninety, John is rangy and able to remain active with the help of his cane. Sometimes anger brings a shadow of his robust prime to his shaggy face. Like right now.

Seeing Morgon and Amanda approach, he stirs a hand in mock agitation. "Bunch of paranoid idiots. They think the sky is falling." Every month there's more gravel in the old man's baritone. The wrinkles around his watery eyes tighten in a crocodile scowl.

"Is this about the pilot who survived the crash?" Morgon asks.

"No, her brain's grazing out where the buffalo roam. It's someone else." John grumbles, "I hope there's coffee. I'm seeing double." He opens the screen door and clomps toward the kitchen. Amanda gives a big-eyed Betty Boop expression—*I'm outa here*—and tiptoes into her office. Morgon continues down the hall and joins John, who has poured a cup of coffee and holds the carafe out to warm Morgon's.

"So?" Morgon asks.

"So it seems a certain party is snooping around in our business," John says as he removes a photo from his cardigan pocket and places it on the island. Morgon leans forward. The lighting is not real good, a night shot in the rain. A man and a woman sit on a picnic-table bench, talking. The man's face is obscured by the shadow of a baseball-cap bill. Physically he holds himself like a trained man. Morgon notes the signature Rolex on his wrist like a Spec Ops charm bracelet.

"Who is he?" Morgon asks.

John smiles tightly. "You know how it goes. We know who he is, and we don't know who he is. His name is Joe Davis, born 1976, Caribou, Maine. Graduated the U of Maine with interesting twin majors—criminal justice and drama. Two years with Bangor PD. After 9/11 he went to New York and spent two weeks on the Pile, then enlisted in the Marines. He got into Force Recon and made the cut into the Agency's Special Activities Division for a while. Just like you." He takes a sip of coffee, peers briefly into the cup, and looks up. "So he's a hard target; mistakes with Mr. Davis could be unforgiving.

"Wounded in Iraq in '05, twice more in Afghanistan. Then he left the service and went on the market as some kind of lone-wolf contract cop. He turns up in places where large amounts of money, drugs, and arms deals mingle with terrorist connections. After he disappears the Feds move in with subpoenas or Predator drones, depending. His covert work is also linked to some big contractor fraud and corruption cases."

"So we're on the same side?" Morgon suggests.

"Not this time." John taps his teeth together. "The other helicopter at Turmar? He was in it running a raid for the Iraqi cops when they bumped into you. Totally unrelated. And now it seems that Mr. Davis has taken the resulting dustup personally. He started asking all these questions over in the Sandbox." He pauses for emphasis. "The picture was snapped last week in Memphis. The woman he's talking to is Richard Noland's ex-wife. He's a regular bloodhound, this guy."

"So what's he know?" Morgon asks.

"In the big city they worry they aren't the only ones who have a phone intercept off Noland to the wife, in which he alluded to a big score. They're worried that Davis has picked up the scent. What's worse, they're worried he may have powerful friends."

"First the pilot, now this," Morgon probes his cheek with his tongue. "How deep does the damage control go? Like, are we worried about the Iraqi end?"

"They don't foresee problems with cleanup there. Davis found an atropine syrette at the crash site, but they quashed it same time we sanitized the after-action report on the crash. We called in some chits with the Iraqis, who put out a story he was dabbling in drugs and missing development funds. They tossed him out of the country." John looks him straight in the eye and says, "Bottom line, we have to make him go away."

"Somebody upstairs made a bad call, John. And I'm stuck in the middle of it," Morgon exhales.

John temporizes. "Now, now. It can't all be Hollywood raids into Abottabad. Sometimes they give you the scutwork. And the way they see it, Noland wasn't just a jerk trying to make a buck. He didn't care who bought that stuff." He tosses his head, taking in the surroundings. "Out here, we fall asleep listening to the crickets. At Langley, the Bureau, and Homeland Security, they toss and turn with visions of the dirty bomb. Timothy McVeigh took down a federal building with a truck full of ammonium nitrate—fuckin' fertilizer. What if the bad guys did McVeigh one better and added a hundred of Noland's artillery rounds to the mix? Imagine *that* Ryder truck parked in Times Square." He points the stem of his pipe at Morgon. "It was a legit targeted kill. The threat assessment was exemplary. You took 400 rounds of nerve agent off the table. Accidently losing three helicopter crew was not excessive collateral damage when judged against the military advantage obtained."

"*Obtained*? C'mon, John," Morgon interrupts. "You're the one who taught me only one thing is more sensitive than national security . . ."

"Indeed. Political security."

"Turmar was about swatting a WMD mosquito with a sledgehammer. It was a reach."

The old man's stooped shoulders heave in a Gallic shrug. "Sure, on hindsight, you can argue they should have handed it off to the Bureau, arrested Noland, and put him through the system. Sets a bad precedent, we go whacking some good old boy from Tennessee every time a White House staffer comes down with an early case of election-year butterflies."

John reaches into his pocket, pulls out a pouch, and proceeds to stuff his pipe with tobacco. "Fuck it," he quips. "This is worth taking a few days off my life." Wheezing with laughter, he pops the end of a blue-tip match with a yellowed thumbnail and fires up the pipe that once belonged to Hermann Goering.

Through the cloud of smoke, he chuckles, "Bin Laden is three weeks at the bottom of the North Arabian Sea, and Peter Bergen is on CNN predicting the demise of al-Qaeda. You know what they're afraid of? If Noland's stash went public, some nitwit would get up on cable and start braying about finding WMDs after all and Cheney was right. Just when our president, the College Boy, is flaunting bin Laden's scalp and is pulling out the troops." Recovering quickly, John ambles to the sink and knocks the smoldering tobacco from his pipe. "Okay, I've had my tantrum. Now we have to get to work."

Morgon gets up, crosses the kitchen, and looks out the window to where the sun is breaking through the clouds and dancing on the jumble of stone at his work site. When a glare of sunlight stings his eyes, he turns and asks, "Do we have a location on Davis?"

"He flew out of Baltimore International last week to Memphis and returned. That puts him somewhere in the DC orbit at that point. But beyond that, they haven't got a clue. They did a global search. He doesn't show up on mortgage or rental roles. He lists his parents' place up in Maine on his tax returns. Same with his credit-card statements."

"They run a credit history?"

John nods. "Except for the round-trip ticket to Memphis, his accounts are inactive for the last year."

Morgon thinks about it. "So maybe going to Memphis was impulsive, a slip. Could be he's off his game. They have any idea who he works for?"

"That's the question. Like, is he this solitary wing nut? For a guy operating on his own, he has a habit of winding up in the middle of things. Or does he have an inside player feeding him information?"

"So is it a capture or a kill?" Morgon asks.

"They'd like it both ways. They want to know who they're dealing with if Davis has a handler."

"They don't want much, do they? And here I thought we didn't do domestic." Morgon weighs it, exhales, and his voice turns laconic. "It's splatter from Turmar. I'm still at bat."

Later, John and Morgon sit on the porch and stare out across the lake and listen to the rollers break on the cobble beach.

"I wouldn't let the Turmar fiasco bother you. Like Sherman said, 'War is cruelty,'" John says.

"War my ass. This is turning into fucking thug work."

"But it has a piquant flavor of hide-and-seek among the federal agencies I find appealing." John leans back and squints into the middle distance.

"It's politics. I say again, thug work."

John sucks meditatively on his now-empty pipe and ponders, "So you hand it off to a thug . . ."

Morgon sits up. "Me?"

"Yes, you. I recommended that you move up a notch and start handling the operational details here. I'm getting too damn old to take 4 a.m. phone calls. So?"

"So," Morgon says after a moment, "we give it to Roger Torres. He has an endless supply of thugs, and he can keep his mouth shut. Plus his company is joined at the hip with half the defense establishment. He has the contacts to track Davis."

"And," John breaks in, "it has the added advantage of using his Zeta operatives. Mexican Nationals connected to the drug trade. And we've already floated a story Davis is dirty around drugs. Can't have Americans killing Americans on American soil, now, can we?" John sketches a diagram in the air with his pipe stem. "He can front it off as a head-hunting expedition. It would make perfect sense for Roger to want to recruit a knuckle dragger like this Davis. But you have to manage it carefully. Some of Roger's lads can get out of hand."

"Okay, so Iraq was my last field trip?"

John nods and then says circumspectly, "It's the smart move, Morg. My end of things is—shall we say—winding down here . . ."

"So that's it. I'm being kicked upstairs."

John grins and tips his head back toward the sound of Amanda typing in the office. "And whatever will you do after you hang up your guns, boyo?"

Morgon's eyes drift across the lawn to his jumble of old limestone. "How about I build a wall that lasts a thousand years and settle down with Amanda and live obscurely in the country."

John chuckles. "In that case, I'm not sure who to feel sorry for, you or her." He pauses and strokes his chin. "But seriously, you and Amanda have turned out to be a good team . . ." His eyes travel over the grounds. "As stewards . . ." his voice trails off. After a moment, he continues, "Brett and I have talked about what a good fit you'd be for the sheriff's department. It'd be the perfect cover for your new duties. My friends on the county board agree. It'd mean working patrol for a couple years, then fast promotion. First deputy. I might even last long enough to see you become sheriff."

Morgon nods and says, "It's come up." Brett Hamry, the local sheriff, is eyeing retirement. Morgon conducts classes for the department in grappling, marksmanship, and SWAT tactics.

"Think about it, son. You've spent half your life breaking every law known to man on your government's service. Maybe you should make amends by enforcing them for a change . . ."

A moment later Amanda appears at the screen door and asks, "What's so funny? Why is everybody laughing?"

CHAPTER TWENTY-SIX

Reinvent yourself.

After turning over his temporary ID card and dropping Mouse outside the gate, Davis clears the guard station and turns north on 295, the Washington-Baltimore Parkway. His eyes crank from the rearview to the side-view mirrors, looking for a tail.

Mouse had made preparations against this day.

Inevitably they would step on some really big toes attached to a really big foot that would try to stomp them.

Later. Focus. Check the mirrors. Watch your speed.

He doesn't go to the apartment, which is merely a safe house, a duplex owned by Mouse and his discreet allies in other federal agencies, to put up agents like Davis when they pass through town. He's left nothing of value there, just a bag with clothes and toiletries.

So get your butt to Baltimore. Ditch the car and the old phone—not the new phone—and take a cab to the safe garage and retool.

A flock of descending and ascending jetliners on his right tells him he's passing Baltimore-Washington International, coming up on the city. He follows 295 right into the heart of the spaghetti junction of downtown freeways and veers right on Patterson. After fifteen minutes working a jigsaw, he's reasonably sure no one is following him. Then he shakes out the copy of this morning's *Sun* on the passenger seat and checks the "Crime Beat" section. He scans a headline about a triple homicide on the northeast side, on East Monument Street.

Sounds like fruitful ground, so he takes a turn and trolls into an urban DMZ of overgrown yards and shabby houses.

Still early, so the street trade isn't out yet in force. But there'll be some lurking around; it'll do. He pulls the Vic over to the curb, kills the motor, and tosses his phone on the seat in the crumpled newspaper. That should lure in some enterprising day-tripping lad. People with the resources Mouse alluded to can track his phone through cell phone towers even if it's turned off. So hopefully some joy-riding kids will direct them on a merry chase. He leaves the keys in the ignition and the doors unlocked as he gets out, jogs into an alley, and works another jigsaw through the back streets.

On the lookout for a cab, he turns north on Patterson Park Avenue and picks up a trio of fine young men dressed like menacing clowns in their baggy butt-crack jeans and warm-ups and maybe one 9mm for ballast. They pace him for half a block, trying to figure out if he's lost or a cripple or a stray or just plain crazy. Then he hears their steps speed up, and two of them pass on either side, brushing his shoulders. One stays behind. The two in front turn abruptly and block his path.

Okay, they've decided I'm not a cop. Not sure how to process that. Ego's taking a regular beating this morning.

"Wuz up?" one of them inquires through lidded eyes that scour him like a TSA scanner at the airport, assessing for threat, weakness, panic . . .

It's a problem. This grunt on his old recon team would say, "Hey, Davis, don't take this wrong, man, but sometimes when the light hits you right, you can come off as a cross between De Niro in *Taxi Driver* and Woody Allen." And clearly these early rising gangsters are not seeing Travis Bickle.

Instinctively, Davis sidesteps and grabs some wall for a backstop. "Old Chinese proverb," he says with his best lopsided smile, removing his sunglasses—with his left hand—to give them a good look at his scarred face. "Do not remove fly from dumbass gangbanger's forehead with cleaver."

"Say what?" Some eye whites are showing.

"Okay, look," he explains to the trio crowding in on him, "I know I don't sound the part. And I probably don't look the part . . ."

In a blur, the .45 is out, cocked, and pressed up under the biggest one's chin. "But I assure you—*I am the fucking part!* Now take off."

After the lads boogie, Davis hails a cab, checks the address on the storage key, and gives him a long fare up around Timonium in the northern suburbs.

Acme Storage Garage. He turns the key, removes the padlock, and hoists up the door and finds a slightly used Ford Escape with good rubber and just enough mud streaked on the light blue chassis to make it down-home ordinary. The car has custom Wounded Vet Wisconsin plates and a sticker for state parks on the windshield.

Wisconsin? Always an adventure riding with Mouse.

A set of keys is lying on the driver's seat. Around back, he lifts the hatch, peels back the security flap, and sees a wallet on top of a stack of stapled pages. Under the pages, a black briefcase sits on an Apple laptop. Three long gun cases and a go-bag lie behind the briefcase. He unzips the cases and quickly checks the actions on a Remington 11-87 entry type shotgun, a Colt shorty semiautomatic CAR-15, and a .308 scoped rifle. Boxes of ammunition and magazines for the Colt nestle on either side of the storage pocket, plus rounds for his .45-caliber pistol and custom silencers for the rifles and his pistol.

Hmmm. Looks like things have escalated.

Upon flipping open the wallet, he discovers he is now William Lemmer who lives on Miflen Street in Madison, Wisconsin. According to the driver's license that bears a modified likeness, Lemmer has black curly hair and wears outsized horn-rimmed glasses that are reminiscent of Barry Goldwater. His eyes are brown. In addition to a Visa and MasterCard in Lemmer's name, the wallet also contains a health-club membership, a library card for the Madison Public Library, and a Veteran's Service Connected ID card. A Post-It note attached to the card explains that Lemmer has received counseling for his 50 percent PTSD disability at the William S. Middleton Memorial Veteran's Hospital, 2005 Overlook Terrace, in Madison, Wisconsin.

First thing, Davis unpacks and inserts brown cosmetic contact lenses from the briefcase. Then he checks the rest of the contents. There's ten thousand dollars in twenties, fifties, and hundreds. Two sets of the clunky horn-rims snuggle in cases next to the currency. Then he shakes out the contents of the go-bag that include changes of underwear and socks, a toilet kit, a tactical web vest, and—bingo—a box of Just for Men shampoo in "Real Black" hair color.

A basin sits on a workbench along the wall of the garage, along with a mirror, towels, and three gallons of water in plastic bottles. Davis strips off his jacket, T-shirt, and holster and starts unpacking the hair dye.

CHAPTER TWENTY-SEVEN

Janet George, PhD candidate, looks up from her desk in her office in the psychology department on the second floor at Ft. Snelling Veteran's Hospital as a large presence fills her doorway.

"Hi, Tony. What brings you down to the second floor?"

Tony, a nurse's aide on 4J, is a psych major at Macalester College getting some hands-on experience heading into summer break. He's on partial scholarship along with GI Bill money. Tony did a tour with the 82nd in Afghanistan as a medic before he opted for psychology. He's a light-skinned black man with a powerfully developed upper body. With frog-freckled skin and wisps of a beard stuck on his flat, smiling face like inky cotton candy, he comes across as a genial troll. He wears light-blue scrubs and sneakers. It's been Janet's experience that Tony is a careful watcher who doesn't miss much.

"I think I found you a live one," Tony says.

"Oh, really?" Janet leans back and points to the chair next to her desk.

Tony flops into the chair. "Captain Jessica Kraig, fly girl with the North Dakota Guard. Her Hawk got splashed in the Sandbox. Came in from Reed a little while ago with a full boat —TBI, post-traumatic psychosis, amnesia, and Broca's aphasia. They got her on 600 mg of Seroquel. You haven't seen her because she's just graduating from bedpans and learning to walk."

"And?"

"And I've been watching her. I caught her stealing a pen . . ."

"Stealing a pen," Janet repeats.

"Uh-huh, see, in her chart from Reed, there's a notation. She grabbed a pen from a speech therapist and threatened the lady with it. She was having these seizures at the time. So day before yesterday I was escorting her to physical rehab and saw her lift the pen and some sheets of paper off a cart as we went by."

"Did you report her taking the pen to the charge nurse?"

"Ah, no; I was curious about what she'd do with it. In fact, I worked a couple double shifts to keep an eye on her."

"So what did Captain Kraig do with the aforementioned stolen pen?"

"She hid it under her mattress, with this." Tony pulls a folded piece of paper from his pocket and smoothes it open on the desk.

Janet leans forward and studies the scrawled images on the sheet. Crude five-pointed stars cover the top. Beneath the stars, the bottom of the page is filled with clumsy letters, some backward but in a sequence that sounds out *A, B, C, D, E, F,* and so on. She looks up at Tony.

"What do you think?" he asks.

"It looks to me like she's trying to puzzle out a phonetic alphabet," Janet says.

"Yeah. I mean, with all that dope on board, this gal can barely grunt, and she's struggling to do this?" He taps the piece of paper and then adds, "There's more."

Janet opens her palms in an inquiring gesture.

"At night when she's supposed to be sleeping, I caught her out of bed on the floor doing sets of push-ups and sit-ups."

"Hmmm. So what do you think?" Janet asks.

"I think there's more to Kraig than her chart adds up to."

Janet raises an eyebrow. "Like what?"

"Like maybe she's figuring out her own agenda to work out of aphasia. In spite of us. Like maybe *we're* the problem."

Janet knits her brows. "And you're telling me this why?"

Tony shrugs. "Most people in these offices won't give a non-degreed former grunt like me the time of day, huh?"

"Okay." Janet mulls it. "Tell you what." She leans over, digs in her purse, and withdraws a ten-dollar bill. "Do me a favor. Go down to the commissary and get a loose-leaf notebook, a felt-tip pen, and, ah, some Post-It notes. Then meet me up on 4J in thirty."

Janet walks down the stairs, crosses through the cafeteria, enters the mental-health suite, and taps the doorjamb on Dr. Durga Prasad's office. Durga is a *real* doctor, the consulting psychiatrist on Jesse Kraig's file. His family migrated from New Delhi when he was eighteen, and his face has the acne-pitted texture of dark fudge set in a bald, bullet head. An old-fashioned shrink, he thinks many of his contemporaries are quacks who throw drugs at disorders instead of people. For Janet's purposes, this could turn out to be a good thing.

"Janet." Durga waves her into his office. "What's up?" His diction and accent have survived assimilation and sound like starch breaking on the BBC.

"Tony and I need your permission to try out a little project on one of your patients."

Durga leans back in his chair and steeples his dark fingers. "Which patient, and what kind of project?"

"Captain Jesse Kraig. I'd like to get her on my list for counseling."

Durga turns to his monitor, types an entry, and taps a button. "You see her chart yet?"

"Not yet."

He turns the computer on its base and makes a "c'mon" gesture with this finger and points to the screen. "Check it out."

Janet quickly peruses the notes entered from the moment Kraig was shot down, tracking her through Balad, Landstuhl, Walter Reed, and now here. The consensus coming through the pipeline is TBI with speculation about short-term psychosis along with post-traumatic amnesia and aphasia. All the tests come back negative on brain damage. She reads of the bizarre behavior with the speech therapist at Reed that Tony had mentioned. And a real stiff regimen of antipsychotics. There's a recent note entered by the nursing staff on 4J: *Resists taking meds.*

She looks up. "I'd like to do an assess on her."

Durga swivels his computer monitor back around, leans forward, and pronounces with great patience, "Janet, she can't talk."

Janet nods. "Tony and I have some ideas along those lines."

"Tony? The nurse's aide on 4J?" Durga clears his throat, a little testy. "Tony is a student. He can get ahead of himself." His implication is clear; as far as he's concerned, she's also a student.

"Oh, I don't know." Janet leans her head to the side. "Before Tony got into the mind-fixing business, he was in the stop-the-bleeding-business. You know, Durga, the part of all this we get to skip. Real, real; *bang, bang.*"

"What's your point, Janet?"

Janet withdraws the folded sheet of paper from her jacket pocket and smoothes it flat on Durga's desk. "She's teaching herself to write, in her room, when no one's around."

"Really?" Durga taps his finger on the scribbled stars and alphabet letters. He looks up. "She did this?"

"Tony found it hidden in her room. I guess she swiped a pen."

"Did he get the pen back?"

"Sure, he's on it."

"Hmmmm." Durga scratches his chin. "Okay, this is interesting. In speech therapy she balks at the flash cards."

"Maybe you should try giving her something to write with?" Janet asks.

Durga's eyebrow goes up. "She tried to stab a therapist at Reed with a pen. It's in the chart."

"And that's why we're giving her enough dope to kill a horse?"

"Well, *yeah*. You want someone to lose an eye?"

"What if all the drama with the pen isn't hostile acting out?" Janet waffles a hand. "What if it's, you know, something real simple, like she's trying to communicate?"

Durga knits his brows. "Just what exactly do you have in mind?"

"Give her writing materials." Janet shrugs. "Tony and the staff can keep an eye out. Give it a week or so. See what she does."

"A week." Durga mulls it. "Okay, we'll give it a week."

Jesse is doing lunges called "the dragon walk" down the length of the hall, trying to strengthen her bad knee. She's thinking that the exercise is only about fifty times more difficult than it should be. It reminds her of an assignment in sophomore philosophy at college, *The Myth of Sisyphus*. Each lunge feels like pushing the freakin' boulder up the hill. Sisyphus was condemned to an eternity of frustration because he pissed off the gods. She hasn't figured out her crime. Yet.

Then she sees Tony, the gargoyle aide, at the nurses' desk. He's pointing her out to a stylish brunette who wears a laminated staff card around her neck. Now there's a clotheshorse who packs her big chest in a spendy blouse. Cute little hip-length jacket and a fashionable short skirt to show off her legs, which are good.

Her footwear, tasteful but practical cross-trainers, is at odds with the rest of her apparel. In fact, behind the designer labels, she looks like someone who is constantly poised, listening for the starter pistol.

She has large brown eyes, naturally wavy dark hair, and a creamy complexion. Jesse is reminded of pampered town women who had the effortless knack of looking good in clothes. *She probably spends a lot of time shopping, matching drapes and carpets and furniture. No wedding ring, though. Are they talking about me?*

Then Tony walks over, carrying a shopping bag. "How's it going, Jesse?"

"Ha toe eee," she responds with difficulty. He reaches in his pocket and produces the pen that went missing from under her mattress. *Uh-oh. Busted.*

"I'll trade you," he says. "This pen for what's in the bag."

Jesse cranes her neck and looks into the plastic bag Tony holds open, and an awkward smile crinkles her healing face. After a failed attempt to say "Thank you," she signals thumbs-up.

★ ★ ★

The next day Janet pulls Jesse's schedule up on her monitor and confirms that she's in physical therapy, so she goes up to polytrauma.

"I'll be doing the assessment on Captain Kraig, and I'd like to see her room," she tells the nurse on the station.

"Jesse's a rough one," the nurse says, leading the way to the room.

"Any weird behavior?"

"Last night she cocked her fist at the nurse who brought in her meds. Then there's all the notes. The stuff Tony gave her? She's been busy."

When Janet enters the room, she sees what the nurse means. The wall next to the bed is plastered with yellow Post-It notes scrawled with reminders: *Mak bed. Bruss teth. Flos. Showr. Push-ups. Crunges. 2 sirkits.*

The loose-leaf notebook Tony bought sits on the bed table. Janet thumbs through it and finds a page of vocabulary words broken into syllables. Then another page of five-pointed-star doodles. More of the stars, scrawled on the yellow notes, festoon the bathroom doorway like elementary school Christmas decorations. She plucks one of them and puts it in her pocket. One note stuck on the bathroom mirror particularly catches her attention: *Gota hlp Marg!!!*

Janet will admit she probably spends a little more than she can afford on clothes at Nordstrom, but that's where Jesse's stereotyping of her ends. Sitting in her cluttered apartment, she studies Jesse's childish star doodle and is more than mildly curious about her prospective new patient, her Captain Star girl.

As she prepares for bed, she pokes through the books and magazines on her night table, looking for a vial of moisturizing lotion. She opens the table drawer and moves aside a loaded, holstered .40-caliber service pistol. No lotion.

After she graduated summa cum laude from Carleton on a full academic scholarship—and before she elected to study psychology—Janet was a cop. After three years on the streets of St. Paul, she decided she wasn't making a difference; she was just recycling the same human refuse through the criminal-justice plumbing.

She chose to do her internship at the VA because she knows the lousy choices that face people in front-line jobs. She knows that no amount of glib counseling fixes can redirect a bullet fired too soon or too late.

But some of her old street habits have spilled over into her new career. Like running a trap line. She's set up contacts with people who work the wards. Not just nurses, but people who push the brooms and the food carts and bright aides, like Tony.

Now the suspicious cop brain lurking behind her academic training has a hunch that Tony made a good call—Captain Kraig is more than the sum of the notations entered on her chart. Jesse is fighting against something more than residual concussion, aphasia, and post-traumatic amnesia.

Janet falls asleep visualizing a padlock on Jesse's head with a star-shaped keyhole.

CHAPTER TWENTY-EIGHT

At nine in the morning, start of business in her office, Janet holds a little ethical discussion with herself. *Okay. I'm not switching hats here and playing copper. Any alert psychologist would have suspicions about this case.* This disclaimer notwithstanding, she then spends the morning sifting through Jesse's chart with renewed interest, like it's a crime scene. She's looking for evidence. One notation nags her through lunch. The wild episode with the speech therapist at Reed: *Bit her finger and smeared blood on my desk.*

It takes hours of phone tag, but by the end of the day Janet finally gets a call back from Christine Morel, the speech therapist at Walter Reed. "Sure," Morel says, "I remember Captain Kraig. Thought she was going to stab me in the throat with a Sharpie. Tough kid. She actually put a two-hundred-pound orderly back on his heels."

"I've been reviewing your notes. It doesn't look like you got very far with her . . ."

Morel answers quickly. "I've never had anybody *bleed* in my office before. I remember that session very clearly. With every new patient diagnosed with acute-injury speech impairment, you look for some signal—meaningful eye contact, discreet hand movements, other body language. Not that lady. I wrote her name on a tablet and handed her the pen to see what she'd do. She went from frustration to rage to violence in like two seconds."

"Could you give me more specifics about the incident with her finger and the blood?"

"Of course. It was weird. She bit right through the tip of her right index finger and started smearing blood all over my desk."

"This was after the orderly took the pen away, right?"

"And after she fought him off."

"Is there anything about the blood smear that stands out?"

"I took a good look at that scribble before I reached for the 409. Sounds crazy, but I got the impression she was trying to draw a five-pointed star. I admit, I was very rattled at the time."

"That's not in your notes. And it sounds like an attempt to communicate, to me."

"Not in the notes? I distinctly remember it reminded me of a star symbol a kindergartener would scrawl. Look, sometimes the nurses' station here cleans up the notes, checks for misspelling and stuff like that. They could have hit the wrong key and lost the last paragraph. It happens. So does this help? I mean, how's she doing?"

"She's doing better," Janet says, "and thank you much."

After a conference with Jesse Kraig's attending physician, and after a consult with a more sympathetic Dr. Durga Prasad, they agree to sign off on a complete battery of TBI diagnostics. Jesse shuffles off for her third set of X-rays, CAT scan, and MRI. The tests come back with no evidence of residual hemorrhage, hematoma, contusions, brain swelling, or tumor.

Janet makes her case to Dr. Dennis Halme, the head of her department. "We're in a gray area, right? All the literature warns about combat trauma evolving into a maze of comorbidity that can blur the diagnostic picture and care plan. She's a definite candidate for psychotherapy. But for my money, she's in a drug-induced stupor. I think she's overmedicated."

"The delusional diagnosis came from somewhere, Janet," Halme says.

"Well, she did get out of hand at Reed. And she writes tortured notes to herself that suggest she believes her crew chief, a sergeant named Marge Bailey, is still alive," Janet admits.

"That'd do it for me."

"Right. *But* what if she has trouble chronologically sequencing events? If she has no memory of the crash that killed her crew, maybe she only remembers they're in danger."

"Okay, let's talk to Durga. Maybe he'll ease up on the Seroquel, and we'll see what develops. They dispense that stuff like aspirin at Landstuhl and Reed just to keep patients quiet. And most people on a max dose of Seroquel couldn't muster the resolve to hold a pencil, much less scribble nonstop notes to themselves," Halme says.

CHAPTER TWENTY-NINE

Located twelve miles northeast of Washington, DC, on Interstate 270, the Best Western Hotel & Suites in Rockville, Maryland, is hosting a workshop titled "The Challenge of Regulating Private Military Security Companies." As the audience adjourns for the noon break, Roger Torres sorts through the crowd of think-tank wonks and observers from DOD and State as they leave the auditorium and spots his contact. As a procurement analyst at DOD, Cate Lenon has a secret clearance and every reason to be seen chatting with men like Roger, who run global private security companies. The part of her job where she siphons off mercenaries into covert operations is less well known.

Privately, Roger finds the term "handler" distasteful. Publicly, he puts on a disarming smile.

"So you think these guys will put us out of business, Roger?" she asks, tilting her gaze down to meet his brown eyes. Roger finds her attractive in a competent, ambitious, top-heavy way. Elegantly below medium height, he is drawn to tall North American women. This one styles her hair cropped short like a Roman general and wears perfume that smells like refrigerated currency. Tilda Swinton, he reflects, playing at Amazon ice maiden.

"Eggheads." Roger eyes the foot traffic in the hall and lets his fingers trickle in a languid gesture. Then he treats Cate to a feline smile. "Someone should make an omelet."

"Concur." She hefts the manila portfolio under her arm and disengages the tie clasp. "I got more on your guy. My investigator says he's hard to get a line on . . ."

Roger smiles. "Which is why I need him in my organization."

"You want it here?"

"A crowded hall is okay for flirtations. Maybe not so good for passing papers. Downstairs." Roger's eyes drift toward the nearest stairway. "My man will direct you."

Two minutes later, on the lower level, Cate is ushered into an empty meeting room by an impeccably dressed, prematurely balding man with a heavy four o'clock shadow on his dour cheeks and a thick-veined neck that matches the circumference of his head.

"Not one of your amigos," she says, wrinkling her nose as she admires the bodyguard's light-footed retreat. "That man looks like an erection wearing a tie . . ."

"Close. Cawker is Australian," Roger says.

After closing the door, Cate cocks her head as she hands over the slim portfolio. "I love doing business with you, Roger. Hand-deliveries instead of e-mail. Sneaking around like this feels like I'm hooking up with a trick."

"I'm flattered." Roger's smile reveals dazzling but slightly diminutive teeth. Inside he curdles at the relative roles implied in her crude comment. Then more soberly he says, "You were discreet?"

She straightens up, all business. "I put a friend at the Pentagon on it. There's a sidebar. Someone in CID was looking for him, sort of out of channels. You want me to run that down too?"

Roger weighs the portfolio in his hand. "I'll get back to you on that. And I owe you," he says.

"We're always interested in trading material on your old buddies down south. Like the Sinaloa cartel's infiltration of the Mexican government and military. More names, safe houses, and links to gangs in the States would be nice."

"I'll see what I can do. Possibly we could discuss it over dinner," Roger says, fluttering his somewhat dainty hand in a light movement as if he's just caught a passing butterfly.

"Call me." She smiles tightly. "Once you have the report."

He returns the smile, wondering if she knows the shade of coffee lipstick she chose this morning is the exact color of dried blood.

"Now there's an American cow of a thing," Cawker says, watching the analyst stalk down the hall on two-inch heels.

"*North* American cow," Roger corrects him as he opens the portfolio and removes a thin sheaf of printouts.

"So?" Cawker prompts.

"It's thin. Mostly the bio stuff we already forwarded to Rivard."

"No phone, e-mail, address?"

"The guy's an ex–Special Activities asset; he won't leave fingerprints."

Cawker points to paragraph. "What's this about CID?"

"Old stuff, small beer." Roger is dismissive. Then he brightens. "Okay, here's something new. His last known contact with anybody we can reach out and touch is a special agent Robert Appert. Davis left a message on Appert's cell eight days ago. No return number; he called from a pay phone. They worked together in Iraq on an antifraud task force. Currently Appert's assigned to the counterterror section at Quantico." Roger looks up. "We have friends in the Bureau . . ."

"Absolutely, and we can put our electronic boys on this Appert . . ."

Roger nods. "We track his movements, his phone, his e-mails. If we get lucky, he and Davis will cross paths." He slaps the printouts against his palm. "That's our play."

CHAPTER THIRTY

"Okay, Jesse, here's the thing," Tony explains. "The last five days we've reduced your meds. So now you're going to a preliminary psych examination. You ready?"

Jesse nods. After the reduction, the lead body suit has lightened from a hundred pounds of extra effort to around fifty.

Tony escorts her to the elevator and down two floors to an office suite. Shuffling in baggy blue hospital trousers and a matching gown and slippers, she makes out the ward sign: Psychology. *Right. Now I'm nuts.*

A panel of photographs hangs on the reception-area wall, listing the psychology staff. Right off she spots the clotheshorse brunette: Janet George. An intern. Then Tony leads her into an office with a window that looks out over the hospital parking lot. She sees leaves on trees. People walking in shorts. Tony tells her to sit down and exits the office as the brunette walks in and takes a seat behind the desk.

"Captain Kraig, my name's Janet George. I'm a psychologist, and I'll be doing your evaluation . . ."

Don't need one. Even with the less oppressive narcotic riptide in her head, Jesse's face contorts with the effort to construct words that come out in a slur: "Doekneeun."

Janet watches Jesse cross her knees and fold her arms tightly across her chest. Nothing delusional there; it's typical defiant behavior for a war fighter with diminished capacity, resentful of being probed by a mental-health professional who's never had desert sand in her shorts.

Plus, one look at the set of her jaw tells Janet that this one comes with all the type-A hang-ups—an officer and a pilot, to boot.

"First we need to gauge how much of what I'm saying you comprehend."

Jesse nods.

"So hold up a finger, one through five, to signal how well you understand . . ."

Instant five fingers.

"Now use the fingers to tell me how well you think you can express yourself."

Jesse holds up one finger.

"We've cut back on your medication. Have you noticed a difference?"

Another nod.

Janet leans back and smiles. "You don't particularly like being here with me, do you, Captain?" she asks. "You don't have to answer. It's a rhetorical question."

With difficulty, Jesse pronounces: "Donlikheer." *Don't like it here.* Frustrated, she taps the desk, then twirls her finger to take in the office walls.

"Sure, okay," Janet says. "It's a new place, new person. Is this the first time you've talked to a psychologist?"

Jesse studies her for a moment, then points at the pen on the desk next to a sheaf of forms. Janet nods assent. Jesse picks up the pen and slowly prints on the edge of the form in reasonably legible uppercase letters: NOT PSYCHOLOGIST. INTERN.

"Ouch. Touché," Janet grins. "So you've been practicing writing?"

Jesse nods.

Janet pushes a sheet of paper and a pen across the desk. "This is an informed-consent form. Can you sign it?"

Slowly, laboriously, Jesse writes her name in scrawled penmanship on the checked blank.

"Okay. Now do you feel up to taking this test?" Janet opens a folder that contains a pamphlet thick with numbered questions and a scoring sheet.

Jesse scans the title: *Minnesota Multiphasic Personality Inventory—2.*

"There's 572 true/false questions. Can you handle that?" Janet asks.

Again, Jesse nods.

A few minutes later she's seated at a cubicle in the testing room down the hall. She peruses the list of questions. *I would enjoy doing the work of a florist. True or False.*

Oh, boy. She picks up the pencil.

After Jesse leaves the office, Janet reviews her observations. Jesse's visual orientation is excellent—she checks the time on the wall clock; she looks out the window and notes the weather. Physical therapy gives her high marks; her motor skills are improving. But when she tries to speak, Janet gets the impression she's watching someone trying to untie a complex knot.

This behavior plunks the suspicious chord. TBIs can go on tangents—everything from Tourette's-like piss-offs to repetitive gibberish to delusional stories. Janet keeps thinking, *This kid is trying to communicate, and something's holding her back.*

★ ★ ★

Janet watches Jesse enter her office ten days into the taper program and take a seat. She notes that her gait has improved and is almost normal. Gross and fine motor functions appear to be improving. She is neatly attired in jeans and a blouse, but in the course of exchanging greetings, it's clear that verbal presentation is still moderately inhibited. So Janet starts slowly to assess Jesse's alertness and orientation in person, place, time, and location.

"Jesse, do you know where you are?" Janet asks.

"Minn-ee-a-plus, VA hospital. Was before Walter Reed. Germiny frum ther. Went down, May 12th Eyerak." Jesse breaks sweat from the effort. She looks around, then asks, "Want to see my crew?"

Softly but firmly Janet explains, "Your crew's dead; they didn't make it out of the crash."

"Know that!" Jesse's voice accelerates, agitated, barely in control. "Have to explain . . ."

"Who's Marge, Jesse?"

"Cruz-hief." Jesse gnaws her lower lip and struggles out a complete sentence. "Don' know much, do you?"

"Only what you tell me."

"Marge nee me . . ." Jesse grimaces and presses her fingers to her temples, then she drops her hands, pitches forward with her fists balled, combative.

Janet waits for Jesse to compose herself, then moves the conversation to what she thinks might be quieter ground. "So why do you draw stars on everything, like on the cover of your notebook?"

"Stars . . ." Jesse shakes her head violently and searches for a way to say it. ". . . make me get stuck. Can't butin blou."

"Possibly what you call getting 'stuck' is a momentary paralysis, related to what we call 'dissociative amnesia.' It can occur when you get too close to the original stressor. Hopefully it passes quickly."

Jesse's forehead clamps in concentration. Then she shakes her head. "Makit wurse."

Seeing the level of Jesse's agitation, Janet decides to end the session.

After Tony takes Jesse back up to four, Janet sits for several minutes with her fingers steepled to her lips. Then she picks up her desk phone and dials Dr. Durga Prasad. "Durga, Janet. Would you be willing to convene a meeting with all the attending docs to review Captain Kraig's recent progress?"

"She has brightened up considerably. What are you angling for here, Janet?"

"I want to float the idea we take her completely off the Seroquel."

"Hmmmm . . ."

"Think about it; I'll be down later to talk." A light on Janet's phone blinks. "I have to take a call. See you in a while."

The call is from the nurses' desk on 4J.

"You know she can't receive non-family visitors," Janet says. Then she pauses, listening. "Who?" Then, after she mulls it for a few seconds, she says, "You know what . . ."

★ ★ ★

After Tony brings her back to the ward, he allows her to walk, alone, to her room. A moment later Jesse steps into a hole in the day where she levitates in limbo as folks move past her at normal speed.

Close to the original stressor, Janet said.

Marge needs me.

Your crew is dead.

Because of me.

With great effort she forces her eyes down to the notebook she carries in her hand and stares at the stars scribbled on the cover.

Stars. Marge. *Stuck.*

When she gets stuck she can't move.

Stuck is the opposite of frozen. It's this hot, buried sensation—near suffocation. Her breathing becomes shallow and rapid. Her chest constricts. She can't move her hands or feet. There's this ugly taste—gritty, coppery liquid dripping in her throat. Like her mouth is stuffed with warm, slippery dirt.

Getting stuck can happen any time—lying in bed, raising a forkful of scrambled eggs. It's the thing she fears most that lurks in the clean, brightly lit rooms and corridors.

"Hey, Jess, how's it going?" A soft voice. Tony's flat, homely, smiling face appears close to hers.

Her lips work soundlessly; no words come, not even sounds.

"I'm going to take your arm now," he says gently, "and just walk you back to your room so you can sit down."

So she winds up sitting on her bed while Tony and the charge nurse converse quietly just outside the doorway. Then Tony walks in, sits down next to her, and says, "Something just came up. So we're going to bend the rules a bit. Usually we only admit immediate family, but Janet is going to make an exception for this guy. You feel strong enough to see a visitor?"

"Who?" she manages, uncertain. Then Tony inclines his head toward the door where the charge nurse has been replaced by—*sonofabitch*—*that's Sam Dillon standing next to Janet George.* Talk about clamping freakin' jumper cables on her heart.

"We good?" Tony asks.

"Good." Jesse almost gasps because, seeing Sam, she holds her breath and now expels it in a long burst. With more energy than she's felt in months, she pitches up off the bed. Ignoring the measured eye contact between Tony and Janet, Jesse takes two quick steps and wraps her arms around the old sergeant.

Goddamned Sam. Whalebone, tobacco, piano wire, and mud in your eye. His weathered face is creased in a smile. He wears jeans, a loud Hawaiian shirt, Western boots and a ridiculous yellow cap with a plastic fish on the peak and "Devil's Lake Bass Tourney" printed across the bill.

She steps back, pokes his chest, and struggles, "You, ah . . ."

"Yeah. Out of uniform. They didn't go for the waiver. I'm all the way civilian now."

Janet says, "We'll leave you two to catch up. The visitors lounge is probably empty." Quietly, Tony and Janet withdraw down the hall.

"How?" Jesse blurts.

"Got a standby hop into the Cities and thought I'd just give it a try over the transom. I know you been on lockdown when it comes to calls and e-mail except family. The liaison office here briefed the unit," Sam says easily, showing no reaction to the fresh scars and fading bruising on her face or to her speech difficulty.

Jesse lowers her eyes, fighting off a wave of humiliation at being seen like this. Recovering, she darts into the room and retrieves her notebook, takes out her pen, and scrawls *controlled access*. Then she points at her head and makes a circular motion. Game grin.

"Right, well, they cut me some slack, I guess. The nurse routed my call to your shrink, who told me to come on up, so here I am." He looks up and down the ward. "So where's this visitors' room? They got coffee?"

Very un-officer-like, Jesse hugs Sam's ropey arm with both of hers and walks him to the visitors' room, which, like Janet said, is unoccupied. After Sam pours two cups from the coffee maker on the side counter, they sit at a table.

"Let's skip the flowers and get-well cards. So, no bullshit, Skipper; tell me where you're at," Sam says.

Jesse takes a breath, exhales, then points to her mouth and holds up one finger and shakes her head. Then she raises the finger to her ear and opens her hand. Five fingers.

"Got trouble with the talking part but you comprehend just fine, huh?" Sam asks.

Jesse gives him a thumbs-up sign. Then she opens her notebook to a blank page and writes, *Aphasia. Amnesia. Could be residual concussion or a problem with the meds. Not psychotic!* Underlined.

Sam nods. "The shrink gave me the short course; she thinks you're misdiagnosed and overmedicated. She's working on that."

Jesse nods in agreement.

"Something you should know, main reason I'm here." Sam turns serious. Jesse raises her hands, palms up.

"The shrink says you might be worried you contributed to the crash that killed your crew . . ."

Jesse winces and bites her lip. *Like wow, that's in my face.*

"So here's the thing. Keith Colbert saw you ride the stick in. You brought that airframe down in a controlled crash. Got that? You did your job. Clear?"

Jesse nods slowly.

"Other thing you gotta know is that Marge and Toby weren't killed in the crash."

Jesse blinks several times as a pressure ridge expands behind her forehead that feels like mushrooming thunderheads charged with electricity. Clear. What a strange sound, what a strange word. *Clear.*

Then Sam puts her on alert. First his eyes scan the empty room, as if reassuring himself they are in fact alone; then he leans in and lowers his voice. "Something stinks about the shootdown, Skipper."

Jesse cocks her head and poises her pen over the empty page. Her hand shakes slightly. Her eyes widen.

"First thing is," Sam says, "they skewed the after-action report to say Marge and Toby were killed in the crash. Keith Colbert was there. He said Marge and Toby were out of their harnesses. Look."

He twirls the notebook around and takes the pen from her hand. Then he sketches the outline of a helicopter and marks two Xs, one inside the outline and one to the left front, outside the diagram. The last X he draws is on the right side of the cockpit area.

"The blast hit the right side of the aircraft. Laura was killed instantly." He pauses to evaluate her eyes. "You with me?"

Jesse nods and maintains eye contact as a thickness builds in her throat.

He taps the inner X. "Toby, he managed to get out of his harness and was found lying in the cargo bay with his pistol in his hand. He had severe injuries from impact, but Keith said it was three bullets in his chest that killed him." He pauses to let this sink in.

The pen taps the X outside the outline. "That's Marge."

Jesse supposes that Sam is showing her his cop/soldier game face. Old school. No hint of emotion in his voice or his eyes about the woman he was involved with, who volunteered to take his place that day . . .

She drops her eyes to the X on the lined notebook paper. Marge. X marks the spot. Then she raises them, like, *Okay, you got my full attention, Top.*

Sam nods and continues. "Now, Greg says he found Marge's body here, six feet to the left front of the cockpit. She couldn't have been thrown out at that angle, not in her gunner harness. What's the first thing you think about in a crash?"

Not trusting her voice, Jesse retrieves her pen from Sam's hand and prints, *Help your crew members.*

Sam nods again. "So she had to get out on her own. That's where she was killed. Two shots to the back of the head. And her pistol was found on the ground next to her body. Keith's no medical examiner. He's a dentist from Williston. And he didn't see all that many casualties over there. But he can recognize point-blank gunshot entry wounds. Marge was executed. He meant to file a report that Toby and Marge had been shot *after* the crash. Then he gets called over to Task Force Brown, where they go through it again and amend his report. In the new report, everybody dies in the crash."

After a moment, Jesse prints deliberately, *What did Keith say about changing the report?*

Sam shrugs. "They transferred him and his crew to Kuwait the same night you went down, advance work on the drawdown. I couldn't locate him again before they shipped me out."

Jesse narrows her eyes and prints, *What else?*

Sam sips his coffee, sets down the cup, and says, "I tried to track down the dude with the code name Keith was flying, the one working with the Iraqi cops. He helped Keith dig you out of the cockpit."

Jesse holds up her hand and clamps her eyes shut. Something. Then she reaches over, taps her finger on Sam's wristwatch, and takes her pen and draws a squiggle on the page with a forked tongue coming out of the head.

With a grin, Sam says, "You got it. Guy was wearing a gold Rolex. Them Snake Eaters always wear them gold Rolexes, huh?" Jesse bobs her head and raises her split eyebrows.

"Couldn't find him either, just a name: Joe Davis, former jarhead. They booted him out of the country for some reason. But he was part of a task force involving the FBI, and I have some contacts I asked to run some checks.

"The Iraqi Intelligence Ministry, which sponsored the raid that day, wouldn't return my calls. Gotta understand I was working at a considerable disadvantage over there. I even tried talking to the State Department about the contractor, Noland, who was the target of the attack you flew into. Complete radio silence there too. I did manage to find out that a routine satellite overfly of the area where you got shot down was retasked that particular day. No eye in the sky."

Sucks, Jesse prints.

"Big time. Problem is, from the moment the blast went off until Keith landed was maybe four, five minutes for all the dust to clear." Sam's face is now set, implacable. "So only two people know what happened in that dust cloud: the shooter and maybe you."

Hearing that, she takes a moment to put both hands on the edge of the table to steady herself.

Then Sam reaches over and pats her hand. "I got a feeling about this so, for now, let's stay off phones and e-mail. So how about I send you old-fashioned letters? There's some other stuff I'm poking around in, but it's just a hunch at this point. I'll keep you current if I turn anything up."

Then, as Sam pushes the notebook to her side of the table, he cocks his head and points at the stars all over the cover. "What's this?" he asks.

Jesse shrugs, picks up the pen and prints *doodles* on the cover.

"Hmmm." Sam's eyes conjure briefly with the scrawled symbols; then they both look up at the same instant, sensing Toby, who stands in the doorway.

"Right," Sam says, "easy does it for starters. They only gave me half an hour."

As he starts to stand up, Jesse stays him with pressure on his arm, opens her notebook, and prints, *Sam, how you doing with Marge?*

Sam pats her hand again, but his expression remains stoic. "That's my next stop soon's I get home. Pay my respects."

That night Jesse waits for sleep, pressing the notebook containing Sam's diagram with both hands against her chest. Beyond her open door the ward is a hush of nurses making rounds on their silent cat-pad shoes and the muted beep of monitors floating in the vast white noise of a sleeping hospital. She repeats the word *clear* over and over under her breath, stretching out the phonetics: C-L-E-A-R as she visualizes the cluttered, gunked-up screen of her mind. *Clear* is basically downloading a freaking antivirus program.

Brought it down in a controlled crash. Did your job.

CHAPTER THIRTY-ONE

Davis, lying low, is on his third Motel 6 and has just finished a spinach salad at a Subway when the cold cell rings. He thumbs *connect*.

"Joey, it's Mouse. We caught a break."

"What's up?"

"Bobby Appert and some people are willing to give us a big assist. He left a message on your old phone."

"I left the phone in the car I ditched in Baltimore."

"So? Doesn't mean I can't monitor incoming signals. He wants a meet. So give him a ring. And Joey, go in heavy and be careful. It could get dicey. Like there could be some large carnivores sitting in on this meeting. Oh, and bring your old ID."

"What? Why?"

"Just do it."

"Gotcha." He glances through the restaurant window at the blue Escape parked in the Subway lot. *Large carnivores, Mouse said. Why else would he include an armory in my latest survival kit?*

Down the road he pulls into a Holiday station to top off the gas tank and calls Appert's cell number from an outside pay phone.

"Appert." Old time cop voice.

"Surprise."

"Joey not Joey," Appert says cryptically. "We gotta talk."

"Do I need my lawyer?"

"You need to *stay flexible*. You need to find the Patuxent Wildlife Research Center. Take Route 198 off the parkway, then take the first right. That'll get you into the north tract. The road ends at some picnic tables next to the Little Patuxent River. Six p.m. You got that?"

"Got it. See you at six."

CHAPTER THIRTY-TWO

"It's on," Roger Torres says into the encrypted satellite phone. "Six p.m. my time, Appert is meeting Davis at a remote location off the Baltimore Parkway."

"And you know this how?" Morgon asks in Michigan.

"Voice intercept off Appert's cell phone. We have solid copy."

"Certain people would like it if you could interrogate him. Find out who his handler is."

"What's your feeling?"

"Off the record, I just want the whole thing to go away. You're the man on the ground."

"So capture is not absolutely necessary."

"Capture could be a costly proposition; this guy's a pro."

"I understand. I'll be in touch." Roger ends the call and then studies the three very fit young men who stand at a picnic table under a flowering dogwood at the north I-95 rest stop between Washington and Baltimore. They study a map spread out on the cement table. They wear shorts and polo shirts, and until they started looking over the target area, they were kicking around a soccer ball. Now they converse quietly in Spanish but slip into fluent English if passersby stray too close.

To Brian Cawker, watching through tinted windows behind the wheel of the Lincoln Town Car, they look more like Olympic athletes from a small Central American country than seasoned operators. A Jamaican-bobsled-team kind of impression. Perhaps not quite ready for the bigs. True, they are clean-cut and polite and appear to come from the Castellan rather than the Indio end of the Mexican gene pool. "You sure about these guys?" he asks, turning in the driver's seat and giving Roger a polite smile.

"Best I could get on short notice," Roger says.

"They won't blow away some family out there on a picnic?"

"C'mon. They've been thoroughly briefed." Roger purses his lips and fingers a thin 18-karat Van Cleef & Arpels gold chain around his brown throat. Cawker is a complete professional. His opinion has weight.

"We'll see," Cawker says as he watches the trio swagger over to his car. Overconfident, they strut like teenagers. Then he zips down the window and gets a good look into the cold, merry depths of the brown eyes in their Conquistador faces. The Aussie shrugs and says, "They might be up for the job."

"I want him alive, if possible. I'd like to question him," Roger says.

"He's a trained man—on the run, you say?" one of them asks, holding up a file photo lifted from Davis' last assignment in Iraq.

"Oh, yes; ex–Force Recon. He's definitely trained . . ."

"Then capturing him could be difficult."

"Very difficult."

"And we're concerned about the FBI man. What if he's not alone?"

"Well . . ." Roger shrugs.

"*Precisamente*," the man says.

CHAPTER THIRTY-THREE

Davis drives the Parkway toward Washington, goes past the 198 exit, passes over the Patuxent River, and wheels the Escape off on County 167. He slows at a sign that announces "Main Campus, Central Tract." A wooden dispenser holds road maps of the grounds. He gets out, takes one, and learns that the Patuxent Wildlife Research Center is the nation's first wildlife experimental station, established in 1937. Maybe Appert has a sense of humor; Ft. Meade abuts the wildlife park to the north.

He locates the area Appert mentioned on the map, then explores the gravel service roads until he estimates he's a mile from the access route Appert specified. He's checked the sunrise-sunset tables on Mouse's iPhone and knows sundown will be at 8:33 p.m.

It's now 5:40. Davis wants to get a look at the opposition before he hooks up with Appert. An hour before sundown will do nicely.

He parks the Escape in the brush, opens the hatch, and shakes a long camo backpack, a pair of khaki shorts, and two plastic liter bottles of spring water out of an HTO Outfitters bag. He made the purchases after he got directions from Appert. He kicks off his tennis shoes, removes his jeans, pulls on the shorts, and relaces his shoes.

Then he threads one of the silencer attachments on the CAR-15 and breaks it down, detaching the stock receiver group from the barrel. In two pieces, the weapon fits into the pack. Then he screws the other silencer on his. 45 pistol and sticks four magazines apiece for each weapon in his web vest. The rifle, the pistol, and the vest go into the pack. The pack goes on

175

his back, and his old floppy bush hat goes on his head. He jams the park map in his back pocket and takes a moment to drain one liter bottle of spring water. He tucks the other bottle in a pocket on the side of the pack. Then he hangs a cheap plastic compass around his neck on a flimsy cord. He now looks like a backpacker out for a day trip.

Using a GPS azimuth and orienting off the degrading sun, which he keeps on his left shoulder, he jogs into the trees and heads northeast. His target destination is where Route 168 dead-ends at the Little Patuxent River. Soon he falls into a relaxed rhythm of moving and listening and evaluating the ground ahead. It's pleasant enough going, except for the bugs, and, overhead, a canopy of silver maples, birch, hickory, and an occasional towering white oak blocks the sun. Skirting thickets, checking his compass and the sun, Davis pads along on a shadowed carpet of moss and ferns and decayed leaf mold.

Movement right.

He pauses, slight crouch, eyes tracking. Then he sees a doe push up on her haunches and nonchalantly move deeper into the brush. Not used to being hunted in here.

He checks his watch: 6:25. The Rolex blazes gold in a beam of sunlight. Vanity purchase; old bad habit. He removes the watch and zips it into a side pocket on the pack.

First he smells and then sees the meandering river. He checks the compass and the park map. The river tracks roughly diagonal, north to south east. When he sets a new course north and west, more directly into the setting sun, he moves with more deliberation. *Heel and toe, and mind the dry branches that snap.* After fifteen minutes of this silent ballet, he catches a gleam of slanting sunlight on metal through a break in the brush. A few cautious steps closer and he picks out the windshield and grill of a blue Crown Victoria. And a flash of red hair. Suit jacket off, the FBI man leans against the car with his arms folded over his white shirt. Appert jars the eye against all the green.

You been too long in the city, guy; you're hanging out there like a bedsheet.

Davis takes a small pair of Zeiss binoculars from the pack and lenses the area immediately around the FBI man, then focuses on the car. There's a shadow hunched down in the passenger seat. Okay, he didn't come alone.

Appert is parked in a sward of mowed grass at the end of a gravel road. Three picnic tables are scattered in an open oblong maybe 150 yards long, fifty yards wide, and bounded on one side by the river and by woods on the other three. *If they're here, there's at least two of them—if they know what they're doing: one to the left and one at the bottom of the open rectangle. A basic L-shape—to cover the target area.* He doesn't think they'd put the river between themselves and the road, their exit.

A freshening breeze stirs through the foliage, causing the leaves to shiver and sigh; an advantage that diffuses specific sounds. Now every step is calculated and every patch of the ground ahead is scrutinized as he skirts the south end of the clearing. It takes fifteen minutes to cover fifty yards. He freezes when he picks up a twitch of movement that breaks the pattern of the wind-ruffled leaves.

A brown twitch.

Finds it. A deer's ear, rotating, directional. Then he sees the large liquid eye. Carefully, he selects a dry stick and heaves it into the thicket. The deer erupts from cover and bounds with the headlong survival instinct of a buck. Then, as the crashing recedes, Davis hears a sound that is distinctly out of place: A muffled *scritch* of static. Then a low voice: *"Relajado—carajo venado."* Then a double *scritch*, the unmistakable signal of someone keying a mic twice: *Roger that.*

Okay. Davis can dig it. *El Gallitos.* He's been on a few live-fire exercises against narcos in Columbia and Mexico. Now he is moving in slow-motion inches, homing in on the voice.

The man lies prone, folded into the roots of an oak; he wears a camo smock and a nylon skullcap, and his hard cheekbones are the color of mahogany. He holds a radio handset in one hand. A stubby Uzi submachine gun with a silencer is poised in the other. The tree he's using for cover is just back from the edge of the wood line. Davis can look past the man and see Appert's shirt in the distance like a white postage stamp.

Slowly Davis backs away. He figures whoever the guy was talking to on the radio is close enough to be startled by the deer. So two of them at this end. The Uzi tells him the guy isn't here to take notes.

Now he makes his way, ever so slowly, to the east, toward the river. After a brief scout, he finds a suitable ford, part sandbar and some rocks, and crosses to the other side. Moving faster now, with thirty yards of cover between his route and the river, he parallels the clearing and goes right past Appert, who is now pacing and looking at this watch. When enough woods screen him from the clearing, he studies the river again and fords across through water that never rises above his waist. Picking his way through the trees north of Appert, he notes a clump of birch across the road from Appert's car: three trunks splayed off like a sturdy fleur-de-lis.

Two minutes of careful watching, and he is reasonably certain the shadow between the pale white trunks is a man's head and shoulders.

So three.

Quickly, quietly he slips to the edge of the woods just north of Appert, looks around briefly, and selects a depression behind an uprooted oak, the sturdy trunk four feet in diameter, the exposed roots scraggy as a mud-caked hydra. The tree lies athwart a direct line to the birches across the road. He removes his backpack, assembles the CAR, loads one magazine, transfers another to his hip pocket, then lays the .45 and four mags on the tree trunk. Then he duckwalks up to the edge of the brush, six feet from the FBI man.

"Appert," he whispers loudly, "Don't react. *We are not alone . . .*"

"Wha . . .?"

"Wander toward my voice and unzip like you're gonna take a pee."

Appert swings his eyes into the brush. "What the fuck you doing in there?" he growls—too loudly—and Davis knows he's made a mistake because Appert is not a patient kind of guy, at least not tonight.

"You're an hour late, asshole!" Appert shouts. Worse, he points his finger directly at him.

So much for snatching one of them alive! Davis pitches forward, shooting out his hand.

CHAPTER THIRTY FOUR

Davis swipes at Appert's ankle to knock him off his feet as a muted stutter commences across the road and gets a handful of air. Appert's ahead of him, stretched out in a sliding-into-first dive into the brush. Bullets *hiss-zip-snap* through the overhead. Branch bits and green confetti shower down.

Wide-eyed, Appert tumbles over the tree trunk and lands in a hollow of rotted leaves and moss. He rolls up on his butt, and his first reaction is to brush dirt off his white shirt. Then, reaching for the .40-cal Glock in the holster on his hip, he blurts, "Well, no shit!"

"There's three of them. Until you shot off your mouth, they didn't know I was here," Davis says calmly as he pulls the charging handle on the CAR, cedes a round in the chamber, and does not set the safety. In a crouch now, ready to move. "Your guy is in those birches across the road. Keep him occupied. I'd hold about a foot and a half high with that .40."

"You would, huh?" Appert scoffs, cautiously peering through the muddy roots, across the road.

"And there's two of them at the other end with automatics." He nods at the clearing, then frowns as he grabs a fast glance through the foliage at the silhouette still slumped in the front seat of Appert's Crown Vic. "Who's in the car, and why's he still there?"

"It's a surprise." Appert expands his adrenalized grin.

Davis cuffs his shoulder. "Hey—this ain't no drug bust taking down a door with fifty guys—we're fighting for our lives here . . ."

"Wrong." Appert continues to grin.

It is only then that Davis notices the shoulder mic fixed under the collar of Appert's shirt along with the bulk of a Kevlar vest. Appert leans into the mic. "The package also counts three. Let the one in the birches sky out of here when we take the other two."

"What the fuck?" Davis mutters as Appert pops up and fires three quick shots toward the birches. Then he ducks as a burst of return fire slices through the trees. Instead of firing toward the birch trees, Appert turns his pistol on *his car* and methodically blasts five holes in the gas tank.

"What's . . ." Davis is rotating from side to side, scanning the brush. The sweet stench of draining gasoline now seeps into the brush from the car twenty feet away.

"Trust me," Appert says as he reloads. Then he reaches under his vest, takes out a highway flare, uncaps it, and punches the bottom to ignite it. As it fizzes into giddy flame, he fires a few more rounds toward the birch trees. After the shooter in the birches fires back, Appert tosses the flare under his car, turns to Davis, and grins, saying, "Fire in the hole!"

"Holy shit!" They dive and huddle behind a log as the ground shakes with the explosion and a gasoline fireball swells into the twilight.

To the *whoosh* and crackle of the flames, a scratchy voice calls out in Appert's mic. "That got their attention. The two to the south are making their move."

"Take 'em," Appert replies.

"Roger that."

A second later a voice bellows, "FBI. Drop your weapons!" A volley of automatic fire answers the command. Two crisp shots bark in the foliage along the open area to the south. Then silence.

"They opted to fight. Two down," the laconic voice in the mic says.

"Copy two down, break; Jimmy, what's on your end?" Appert says into the mic.

"The guy in the birches is making a run for it."

"Let him go." Then Appert turns to Davis, grunts, and points his finger, casual-like. "You, ah, got this black streak running down your neck. And one of your eyes is green and the other's brown."

"Musta lost a contact," Davis grumbles as he dabs at his neck and his fingers come away damp with black hair dye. "Cheap shit don't stay fast when you sweat."

"Perils of undercover cosmetics," Appert quips, setting the safety on his pistol and returning it to his holster.

"Not to hit it with too big a hammer, but there's a guy burning up in your car," Davis says as he breaks down the CAR 15 and stows it in his pack.

"Uh-huh. You got your ID? Your old ID, not your new ID that goes with the hair-dye job?"

"Yeah." Davis fingers his old wallet from a side compartment on the pack, remembering what Mouse said about hanging on to his plastic and old Maine driver's license and thinking, *Why am I not surprised?*

"Where's that fancy watch you used to wear? With your initials engraved on the back."

"No way. Not my Rolex."

"Gimme," Appert insists. "And the Zippo."

"Uh-uh. It was my dad's."

"And the Zippo."

Reluctantly Davis digs the watch and lighter from his pack.

Appert takes the wallet, watch, and lighter, then steps from their hiding place and, crouching, gingerly approaches the burning car. Wincing against the heat, he tosses the stuff through a flaming window.

Then Davis sees two men approaching from the south and another coming up the access road. The two coming from the south carry a scoped rifle and spotting scope masked in burlap and look like Spec Op hobos trailing tatters of their guille suits. The third guy carries a wicked little bull-pup number that could be a French Famas G2. He also hauls an industrial-strength fire extinguisher that he unlimbers as he approaches the burning car. As Appert and Davis retreat from the flames, the third man commences to hose down the flaming wreck with fire-retardant foam.

"What?" Appert deadpans. "You think you were the only cowboy in town? They're snipers on loan from hostage rescue. Consider your ass rescued."

Davis points to the burning car.

"Unclaimed body from the Baltimore morgue we diverted from the crematorium. Gruesome, huh? We're still working on the statement, but basically it'll say that Joe Davis, an informant in a drug case, died here in a car fire in the midst of a dramatic shootout . . ."

"Can you pull that off? What about fingerprints, dental . . .?"

Appert, obviously pleased with himself, replies, "Due to the nature of the explosion, dental and fingerprints were compromised. We identified the deceased off fragments of a driver's license retrieved from a burned wallet. And other personal items."

Davis shakes his head.

"Somebody wanted you out of the way? Well, you're out of the way." Appert shrugs. "And, ah, we have an agent standing by to talk to your folks in Caribou, Maine. Let them in on this before they see a news report. They'll have to sign an NDA . . ."

"Thanks. Still, you set me up?" He scans the park area. Keeping a respectful distance, the two snipers quietly light celebratory cigars. The third guy casts aside the spent extinguisher and takes out his cell phone and makes a call. Then he holds up his hand and opens and closes his fingers once.

Appert nods and turns to Davis. "We got five minutes before it gets official around here."

Davis pokes a friendly finger into Appert's vest. "I didn't think uptight old guys like you did this kind of stuff."

"Uptight old guys," Appert repeats.

"Yeah, like, we used to argue in Iraq. You thought the problem was a few bad apples . . ."

"And you figured the whole apple cart had turned rotten." Then more serious, he says, "Listen, Joey, for my money you're still a smart-aleck risk-taker. But you ain't dirty, and that's the word someone is putting out on you. You always been solid. I just think your pal, Mouse, has you on too long a leash."

"Answer the question."

Appert shrugs. "Word's getting out. What happened at Turmar smells, so some people, like these guys," he nods at the snipers, "are willing to stick their necks out and choose a side."

"So you don't think Richard Noland disappeared in a drive-by insurgent ambush?"

Appert cocks his head. "That atropine injector you found and I sent to the Quantico lab? It went missing in transit. When I inquired, a guy I've known for years took me aside and warned me to steer clear of you—that you were a career-stopper."

Davis wrinkles his nose as a wind shift carries smoke his way. Before he can speak, Appert holds up his hand. "My take is somebody went too far, crossed the line. That crew chief on that chopper? Somebody faked the after-action report. Way I heard it, she would have survived her wounds from the crash. She was executed, Joey.

"Somebody big doesn't want it stirred up. So some of the boys decided to let you go stir it up. After you called me, our people picked up intruders hacking my phone and e-mails. Connect the dots."

"So you lured me in as bait." Davis doesn't pose it like a question.

184

"Don't get sentimental. We had them," he nods at the snipers, "to cover us. Which they did." Appert jerks his head and starts walking south. "Let's go see who we got."

Davis shoulders his pack and accompanies Appert down to the clearing. They pause when they see the two bodies; the nearest one sprawls on his back in the open, the other is curled under a cement picnic table. Davis pats his pockets and realizes he left his cigarettes back in the car. When they get to the bottom of the clearing, he walks to the first body and hunkers down. It's the guy who carried the Uzi. He ignores the stench of the corpse's bowels that released in a fatal convulsion.

The snipers tag along. One of them wrinkles his nose, puffs on his cigar, and observes, "Working conditions are still lousy in the shooting profession."

Davis watches a foraging ant scurry on the dilated pupil of the corpse's right eye that has started to film over and looks like a brown and white grape with a black hole in the middle. The busy ant explores down the claying face, enters the gaping mouth, pauses on a gold molar, and then runs in circles on the protruding tongue. *You unplug the electricity, and the food starts to get sticky and spoil.*

Then he notices the yellow nicotine stains on the fingers of the dead man's left hand. He stoops over and rifles through the trouser pockets. No ID. But he comes up with a blue pack of cigarettes. Gauloise. Then, in the other pocket, he finds a metal lighter, thumbs the wheel, lights a cigarette, and takes a drag as Appert joins him.

"Check it out," Davis says.

He rips the smock and shirt away from the corpse's torso. Next to the bullet hole in the sternum, an indigo tattoo, edged with blood, covers the left chest muscle: a grim reaper in a robe with a halo around the skull.

Then Davis holds the lighter up next to the tattoo. It's embossed with a circular emblem, a diagonal flourish across a parachute canopy. "Mexican Special Forces," he says, weighing the lighter in his palm. Then he flicks ashes on the tattoo. "And that, my friend, is Santa Muerte."

Appert gives an appreciative whistle and says, "The drug lord's patron saint of crime."

"Los Zetas—ex-Mex Special Forces working for the drug trade. They also hire out as hit men," the first sniper says.

"Real tough hombres. Only problem is, they tend to have more balls than brains," the second sniper adds.

To the west, toward the Parkway, a flurry of red and blue flashers slap the twilight. "We'll start forensics to print these guys and run them in the system. But, thing like this, I doubt we'll get any hits. So this any help?" Appert asks.

"Not sure, but I like the still-breathing part," Davis says, looking in the direction of the approaching emergency vehicles. Then they hear the sirens.

Appert's voice is now urgent. "Gotta ask. What yanked your chain at Turmar? The atropine? The ammo truck conveniently blowing up?"

Davis, gathering himself to leave in a hurry, gnaws his lip. *It was a girl. A girl with blue toenails.* But he can't say that, so he remains silent.

"Whatever. Now take off before we're all over in the Maryland State Patrol," Appert says. "Me and Mouse have your back. The way I see it, people who kill American soldiers are terrorists. And my job is catching terrorists . . ."

Davis asks, "What about the culture of headquarters?"

"Let me tell you something, kid. I worked the New York office under John O'Neill before 9/11. Headquarters ignored him on bin Laden. Fuck the culture of headquarters. This time the bullshit is gonna fall where it falls. Find me a bad guy, Joey; then call me on my cell any time day or night. I'll be there."

"Thanks, Bobby. I owe you."

"Yeah, yeah; screw you. Now get outta here before I start worrying about my pension."

As Davis sets off at a trot for the darkening forest, Appert calls out after him, "Whoever you are now, I hope you packed some mosquito repellent. And Joey, try not to break the friggin' law."

CHAPTER THIRTY-FIVE

The trouble with mental discipline is it's not reliable when you're asleep. Morgon lurches up on an elbow and paws his free hand to swipe away the image of the pilot stretched out on the bed in Balad like a statue reposing on a crypt. File it away under *occupational hazard*. Immediately he sorts the memory flashes into perspective. Army psychologists have rated him extremely high in the ability to disassociate and compartmentalize—to suspend empathy. He pretty much knew he was different by the time he was thirteen. By then he'd won enough fistfights to learn that while he didn't especially like to hurt people, it didn't bother him when he did.

But he's not a robot; he knows that all the deferred pain and fear and doubt have to go somewhere. So it accumulates in his sleep like compound interest, along with the faces of the people he's killed and the weight of their unlived lives.

Mogadishu was far worse. After that deployment he evolved a strategy for shaking the ghost willies out of his nervous system. He'd get on his motorcycle, tear out of Ft. Bragg, and head for an eleven-mile stretch of Tennessee 129 known as "the Dragon" because of the road's 318 curves. "Taming the Dragon," the good old boys called it. Lean into those turns fast enough and you could shake off all your hitchhiking demons . . .

He runs his hand across his chest, and his fingers come away tingling with the hallucinations that swim in his sweat. *What next? Giant spiders capering on the wallpaper?*

So he eases from the bed and goes into the bathroom, turns on the tap, and splashes water on his face. There's a bad moment looking into the mirror. He's read that a wild animal does not recognize its own reflection, only the threat of the other. Sometimes they attack the glass.

Disorientation is one effect of residual concussion. Along with sex drying up and inappropriate displays of emotion. He looks into the bedroom as Amanda shifts on the bed, slipping the sheet, and sprawls in a narrow stripe of light from the ajar bathroom door. The light skims the contour of a bare hip, touches thigh, bent knee, and calf, and falls across her cheek. Just watching her makes him ache, the way her hair tumbles loose and carefree as black ribbons against her smooth, unlined forehead.

More challenging for him, by far, than the visiting ghosts, is trusting this woman whose sleeping face is as cleanly formed as fine china. But nothing's perfect. He knows that she had a hard time in high school after her mother committed suicide. Migraines forced her out of med school. If he's a fugitive from the workaday world, so is she. Her porcelain complexion conceals invisible cracks of depression that have been glued back together with Prozac and Zoloft. The estate is her sanctuary, and John is her protector. Now her protector is aged and infirm, and Morgon has been trundled out as a replacement.

If they sanctify his guardian status through marriage, even having children, he can't shake the premonition he'll always be the hired hand on the Rivard plantation.

Whatever. Right now he needs some coffee. So he pulls on a light robe, slips quietly from the carriage house, descends the stairs, and walks barefoot across the damp grass to the mansion. Entering the house always reminds him that he came up hardscrabble in Mississippi until his dad had a vision of a Chrysler plant and led his brood to Warren, Michigan, on the ragged edge of the 313—which is to say, Detroit City. He's been all over the world, and he winds up here, upstate from where he grew up. The first time he entered this place the antiques, wallpaper, and swagged curtains had surrounded him like a three-dimensional Currier and Ives greeting card. *Like it's always Christmas in here.*

Morgon trails his fingers along the ledge of a hundred-fifty-year-old oak claw-foot pedestal, then inspects them for dust. When John passes, he'll be living here. He'll have to gradually change levels. Rise through the sheriff's department in easy stages. Trade in his 4Runner and upgrade . . .

Passing Amanda's office, he stops and studies the architect's drawing that takes up the whole end wall. The drawing is their shared vision to renovate the lakeside waterfront into an arts/vacation destination, as a tribute to John.

It's a big step, getting ready to contemplate a normal life with Amanda. The next time he leaves the continental US in search of prey, it will be to hunt the four-legged variety. A Kodiak, he's thinking, in Denali.

Martha, the housekeeper, is humming in the kitchen and points to a fresh pot of coffee on the counter, so he takes a cup out to the table on the back patio. Down the lawn, Kelly is a backlit shadow as he moves though the languid movements of a tai chi form. As the sun breaks the horizon of Lake Huron, he carries his coffee down toward the shore, where Kelly is finishing up his exercise. They are waiting on word from the latest twist in the operation from hell.

"Anything from Roger?" he asks.

Kelly points to the sat phone propped on the lawn with his towel. "He called an hour ago. He's flying in special to talk to you. Probably wants to show off the fancy new Bell 412 he bought for his company." Envy is palpable on the young man's face. "The 412 is quite a machine, carries thirteen passengers . . ."

Morgon reads between the lines. Kelly misses flying; more and more his duties here revolve around John's health. The estate helicopter's sole purpose now is to buy a few extra minutes in a medical emergency.

Morgon, Amanda, and Kelly do not talk about it directly. It's a waiting game.

Morgon leaves Kelly to finish his exercise and takes his coffee across the lawn to the pile of limestone next to his stalled wall. *Looks messy. Another loose end. Finishing this job is first on my list. It's time to start squaring this place away.* His eyes drift back to Kelly. *When the inevitable happens, we should start cutting back on expenses. Like, do we really need the helicopter and a mechanic coming in once a week from Traverse City making house calls?*

Morgon has changed into his work clothes and is two dusty hours into his stone project when Roger Torres appears in the eastern sky, coming in low over the lake. His new helicopter is, as Kelly predicted, quite a machine, painted red with yellow pin-striping flowing from the ASTECH pyramid logo like flames. Then the pilot flares and brings it down on the lawn a hundred yards from Morgon's wall.

Roger operates out of El Paso, where he was born into his extended family's drug business that spanned both sides of the border. By the time he was twenty-two he'd graduated from precocious DEA informant to being a trained counterintelligence operative infiltrating and playing the drug kingpins against each other.

The Feds were so pleased with the access he provided into the cartels that they tolerated his own low-key drug empire. In keeping with the practice of the region, he hatched plans in prosperous El Paso and worked them out on the dark and bloody streets of Juarez.

He invested his profits into ASTECH—American Security Technologies—and got in on the ground floor of the R&D that created the Predator drone. On the executive-security side, Roger courts an exclusive market, providing bodyguards to the new international mega-rich. If Bill Gates' father goes for a latte in Davos, the chances are one of Roger's impeccably dressed, well-mannered thugs is on escort duty.

More germane to this morning's business, Roger makes stone killers available to the bottom end of black ops deemed too dirty for God-fearing Navy SEALs and Delta commandoes. All smiles, Rogers gets out of his helicopter and removes his sunglasses. Morgon takes the smile as a positive sign. A husky bullet-headed dude built like a rugby player learning to wear a sports jacket walks at his side. Roger, by contrast, wears a two-hundred-dollar haircut and five-hundred-dollar shoes and a soft gray Kiton suit with his collar open to display the gold chain around his neck. As he approaches, his alert brown eyes assess Morgon and the wall in progress. Then he reaches up and grips him fraternally by both shoulders.

"Morgon, it's been too long."

"Almost a year, since Juarez."

Roger looks up toward the house, where John sits on the front porch with Kelly, who is unstrapping a blood-pressure cuff from his arm. "So how's His Eminence doing?" he asks.

"Advanced atherosclerosis. So far he's beating the odds with meds and all . . ."

Roger nods respectfully. "We are all standing in line, my friend. John is just a bit in front of us . . ." Then, switching up the mood, he peruses Morgon's work clothes and the courses of fitted stone. "Really, Morgon? Is this your idea of being a country gentleman?" He winks. "Dontcha know we have Mexicans to do this sort of thing?"

Encouraged by Roger's buoyant demeanor—the news is obviously good—Morgon plays along and arches an eyebrow.

Just as playfully, Roger holds up his hands in mock surrender. "I apologize. I understand; you're evolving. Miss Amanda Rivard has taught you how to use the proper fork and—when the old man passes—she will inherit." He casts around. "So where is the pretty lady?"

Diplomatically Morgon answers, "She's around some-where." In fact, Amanda has retreated into the house. She finds Roger distasteful and sees him as a dark reminder of Morgon's profession.

Former profession, he corrects himself. *Now I delegate.*

Only then does Roger turn to the man next to him, who has stood by polite and patient as a loyal wrecking machine. "Meet Brian Cawker, my current number one. He'll bring you up to speed while I go up and pay my respects to John." After the introduction, Roger turns and walks up toward the house.

"Pleased to meet you," Cawker says, extending a hard, square, callused hand that is also manicured.

Morgon smiles, now certain that if it was bad news, Roger would feel bound by etiquette to deliver it himself. So he can observe the amenities. "Where'd Roger round you up from?" he asks, but he can tell by the man's nasal drawl.

"Second commando out of Sydney. Six years. Being a spear-carrier got old after a couple turns in the two-way rifle range. Met Roger in Baghdad in '07. And, face it, the money in this game is too good to pass up."

"So where did we come out on this thing?"

"Done deal. Got a bit too messy for my liking, but it's done." He removes a DVD from his jacket pocket. "Recorded this off of NBC4 ten o'clock news, last night in DC. A spokes-man for the Maryland State Patrol went on air with a report that one of the three men killed at the shootout in the Patuxent wildlife area was an FBI informant identified as Joseph Davis. They ran a picture of Davis off a Maine driver's license. A rather singed driver's license, I might add. There's video of the Jacks extracting the body from a still-smoking car wreck. The other two fatalities, the alleged shooters, haven't been identified. The state patrol suspects drug involvement. That explanation is consistent with the disinformation that was spread about Davis, correct?"

Morgon nods. "That's right. How messy?"

"The FBI was there in force. As usual, Roger's boys were long on machismo and short on due diligence. The one who made it out saw the car go up. Musta hit the petrol tank."

Morgon now measures Cawker's bluff expression. "So you think it could have been handled better?"

Cawker shrugs. His blue eyes engage Morgon's steady gaze without blinking. "I keep telling Roger I know some SAS lads I worked with in the Sandbox who have a lighter touch. But Roger has a weakness for these Zeta dudes he came up with down south."

"It's Cawker, right?" Morgon reappraises this muscular, no-nonsense man with his head tonsured like a monk's.

Smoothly, sensing an opening, Cawker nods and then casually lowers his voice a decibel. "There's a minor detail that popped up during our research." Pause. Again their eyes meet. "Roger didn't think it was much, but I decided to run it out."

"Go on."

"Someone else was pulling files on Davis, so we tracked him, this senior colonel in Pentagon CID." Cawker shrugs. "Roger thought it was just some legal loose end from Davis' prior service. I thought it might be a good idea to get a guy inside and quietly toss the colonel's office. Check his desk and computer."

"You have this due-diligence hangup, eh, Cawker?" Morgon chides, revising his opinion of the man upward.

"Can't hurt. Smelly pot like this."

"You have a point," Morgon agrees softly, under his breath. "This thing with Davis is tied to a bullshit op in Iraq we never should have agreed to. Once John would have seen that . . ."

"Kenny Rogers' theory of executive longevity—gotta know when to fold 'em and walk away."

"And when to run. John got old. How's Roger doing in the executive department?"

"Off the record, he's acquiring a taste for the softer stuff. Executive security and the like," Cawker says quietly.

"So we'll keep this little fishing expedition with your CID colonel between you and me," Morgon says.

Cawker nods and the conspiratorial moment passes because, after taking leave of John, Roger gallantly accepts a tray of frosted bottles of Dos Equis from Martha and carries them down to Morgon and Cawker. Kelly has drifted off to talk to Roger's pilot. Amanda does not put in an appearance. John stays on the porch, attended by the housekeeper.

After the beer is distributed, Morgon tips his bottle and says, "Sorry about your loss, *compadre.*"

"They were big boys; they knew the risks. And there's a lot more where they came from."

"Any chance they'll trace them back to you?"

Roger smiles. "Not likely. They had no priors in the States, and their military and criminal records were expunged down south. It's a time-honored ritual all Mexican clerks understand —silver or lead, eh?"

"Price of doing business," Morgon says.

"Exactly. So this is the end of the project? As per your request, nothing written down, no insecure electronic communication, and now the report is strictly face-to-face."

Morgon nods. "And the pilot's condition is unchanged?"

"Ft. Snelling in Minneapolis has her diagnosed with traumatic amnesia and aphasia. We have a computer overwatch on her chart. My guy scrubs her blood and urine labs so nothing weird turns up. I wouldn't worry. She's in for the long haul, and even if she pulls out of it, how much credibility would she have?"

"So that's it." Morgon raises his beer.

"Congratulations. John tells me you'll be managing the jobs from now on. He's stepping down. *Salud y amor sin suegral.*" Roger clinks his bottle against Morgon's. Then for Cawker's benefit, he translates, "Health and love without a mother-in-law."

Pleased with his toast, Roger Torres misses the quick eye contact between the two other men.

CHAPTER THIRTY-SIX

Three days after they totally take her off the Seroquel, Jesse's eyes pop open at three in the morning and, trembling, she raises her hand to her face, and it comes away slick and wet. Awakening in slow rolling stages, her tongue tastes the moisture on her lips and determines that it's not sweat. It's tears.

In an unjarring way the thought settles in. *Sonofagun. I just had an almost-normal dream.*

Her face isn't the only thing that's damp as she discovers in embarrassed awe that she's touching herself in places she thought were dead. For a long moment she stretches out and savors the afterglow that hovers in the dark.

An erotic dream, yes, but so very modest.

Tentatively she explores the fading sensations in an attempt to recreate them in the blacked-out hospital room. Memory is a weak sister to the dream itself, and she can only salvage fleeting impressions. A time, a place, a boy, and a single kiss like a tiny, almost forgotten four-leaf clover pressed between the pages of remembrance.

His name was Johnny Merrill, and he was two years ahead of her in high school—a dangerously good-looking daredevil who straightened up on the rodeo circuit and then went to work as a roughneck in the oil patch to save up for school. Then 9/11 happened. That spring night in 2002 he was a Marine on leave headed for Afghanistan, and she was eighteen. They'd parked out on the prairie not far from Langdon, and Johnny had borrowed his dad's "James Dean car," a classic 1949 Mercury coupe that he left running with the lights off and the tape deck playing "Someday Soon" by Judy Collins . . .

As a pilot, she'd describe the moon that night at 100 percent illumination, but to an eighteen-year-old girl, it was a moon full of self-dramatic romance, and it illuminated the old Nacoma Radar Pyramid that rose out of the flat like a fantasy temple. So there was youthful magic loose under the big sky and circulating in the heady scent of early blooming alfalfa, and she remembered how the moonlight half-cupped his face and left the other half filled with the close shadow of death, and the fact was she was ready to give it up right there on a blanket spread out on the buffalo grass.

But Johnny, who was half-noble and half scared of her dad, said, "No, let's wait." So she didn't lose her virginity that night, and Johnny didn't come all the way back from Afghanistan, because he left one of his brown eyes there, along with an arm and both legs. She never had girlish thoughts about a young man ever again.

On the practical side, Jesse deduces that the dream is a positive sign that parts of her brain—and apparently all of her libido—are working just fine, but as to where it came from and what it means, she's initially confused. Which is not exactly a big deal, because she understands that dreams, along with other little things—like the origin of life and the creation of the universe—are mysteries.

But there are some theories, like she recalls from a psychology course that Freud thought that dreams were symbols of anxiety.

So she gets out of bed and paces her room and speculates how and why this erotic snapshot managed to squeeze up sideways through the roadblocks in her head.

And that's when she stops and looks at the vague shape of the bouquet of flowers that sits on her night table and was delivered yesterday with a low-key note from her former fiancé, Terry Sherman, announcing he'll be coming to see her tomorrow, with Janet's permission. So he sent wildflowers, prairie flowers, that fill the room with the scent of home: rosemary, sage, dusty miller, veronica, and blue delphinium.

That's Terry for you—a master of the double entendre, always working the angles. The bouquet is a thoughtful and appropriate gesture. But it's also the kind of posey a girl from North Dakota might hold at her wedding.

She worries her lower lip between her teeth and considers that he's the second non-family member to come to see her, and she has no difficulty remembering everything about him: how he's pleasant to look at and charming and an expert at projecting empathy for others.

And how, beneath his social skills, he's basically all about Terry.

CHAPTER THIRTY-SEVEN

Takes an Apache to catch an Apache.

It has a nice ring, except Mouse left out the part about *after* they caught Geronimo—how the Chiricahua Apache scouts were shipped to prison in Florida with the rest of the renegades . . .

After clearing the shooting scene, Davis decided to drive south into Virginia and booked a room in a Comfort Inn. He spent most of the night scanning TV and radio for reports of his death. And early in the morning, after checking out, he was driving aimlessly when he heard the confirming broadcast on a DC radio station linking the word *deceased* and his name. Which still left him tooling around in circles, working an edge, and trying to pick a direction.

Mouse must be hitting on all eight psychic cylinders, because in the midst of Davis' quandary, the cold cell rings—or rather, the whole car rings, because Mouse has paired the phone to Bluetooth. Davis taps the *off-hook* icon on the steering wheel, and Mouse's voice fills the interior of the Escape.

"You catch the news?"

"Yeah, WTOP outta DC on satellite," Davis answers.

"Joe Davis, FBI informant, deader than shit in the Patuxent Wildlife Research Center. And here you thought Appert was an old Elmer Fudd."

"I was suitably shocked and amazed. But you could have let me know they had it wired."

"Less is more where communication is concerned in this thing. But they did it up large. Gotta hand it to the Bureau; right or wrong, they're thorough fellows."

"Any word on the two Hispanic brethren who went down?"

"Nada. The trail's as cold as they are. Suffice it to say, they were pros."

"So what's your next bright idea? Where am I going?"

"Hayward, Wisconsin."

"Huh?" Davis' right foot involuntarily jerks on the accelerator. "What's in *Hayward, Wisconsin*?"

"They got a park in town with the biggest muskie in the world."

"Outstanding. I say again, what the fuck is the big deal about Hayward?"

"Because it's there—duh. Because I have *resources* in the area."

"That why you worked up the new ID?"

"Correct. You're gonna hide in plain sight while I beat the bushes for a lead on who targeted you. My department runs a retreat house outside Hayward. It's unbooked for the next month. It's remote, stocked with goodies, and it's three hours from the Minneapolis airport. Just clean up after yourself. So drive west, and when you stop tonight, check the laptop; there'll be a map to guide you in."

"Anything else?"

"Yeah, I'm getting one of my hunches . . ."

"Great. Does it involve me getting shot at?"

"Very funny. I'm putting together a capture program to find who's talking about what happened at Turmar, like everywhere in the whole friggin' world. Now, ground rules. This phone is secure long's we don't talk for more than sixty seconds a pop. You watch yourself, Joey. Gotta go."

Davis expels a long breath and shifts the road atlas in his right hand and studies the page showing the Eastern United States that looks like an odd, skinned animal, a llama maybe, with Florida for a foot, New Brunswick for a head, Michigan on its back, and blue interstate highways for veins.

Okay. You been to Kabul and Ramadi and Fallujah and all over Anbar and made stops in Yemen, the Philippines, Mexico, and Colombia, but Wisconsin is a first.

Interstate 80 looks like the straightest shot, so work up through Maryland and Pennsylvania, hop on it, and head west. Then he thumbs to the state maps and locates Hayward in the upper western section of Wisconsin. Does he really want to hit that rat's nest of toll roads around Chicago at rush hour tomorrow morning? So stay on 80, bypass Chi-town, and make his turn north on 39.

An hour after he heads northwest, he hits the leading edge of three statewide thunderstorm, so he settles into the road grind and searches the radio channels for suitable sounds to run with. He turns the knob and hits a classical station, Itzhak Perlman playing the theme from *Schindler's List*. With a triple-espresso Black Eye for company, he watches the windshield wipers beat against the dreary rain in solemn tempo to Perlman's strings, and the combination inevitably draws him into a meditation on a girl with golden hair who sits staring at a wall in a government hospital, and as he lights the last of the dead Mexican's Gauloises, he wonders what she was like . . . before.

CHAPTER THIRTY-EIGHT

The day after Roger Torres' visit, John's blood pressure spiked and he complained about severe chest pains. Amanda thought it serious enough to bundle him into the chopper and fly him to the Hurley Medical Center in Flint, the nearest level-one trauma center. Upon his return from intensive care, and over his objections, Amanda confiscated his pipe and tobacco and called in a local carpenter to add a wheelchair ramp next to the porch steps. Then an outfit came in from Traverse City to install a stairway lift to ride him back and forth to his bedroom.

Now on a regimen of enforced bed rest, John maintains a stoic distaste for all the fuss and grumbles, "You have to die of something."

Given John's medical issues, Morgon sees no need to burden him with Brian Cawker's side assignment to determine whether Davis had support in the bureaucracy. Best to remain positive and give no hint that the Turmar tar baby may drop yet another sticky shoe. So he's sitting on the veranda with his bare feet hoisted on a wicker ottoman, keeping it positive.

Through the screen door he can hear the muted *whoosh* of the kitchen-sink faucet, then the soft clatter of plates and glasses. The help has gone home, and Amanda is loading the dishwasher. Kelly is upstairs sitting vigil with John.

And Morgon's musing: *Just lookit this place, the way the freshly mowed acres stretch out in the humid evening like a golfer's vision of peace.* Amanda thinks he should take up the game. He has the hand and eye for it, along with a natural feel for ground and distance, and it would be useful for his future in the community.

Across the lake, the dark-veined clouds mushroom up on the horizon and, ever so slowly, blades of storm charge churn the air and spread an inky cool as Amanda pushes through the screen door. She's wearing a short, sleeveless paisley shift and no shoes. Her bare throat, arms, thighs, and calves gleam dull olive in the fading light, and a moist lemon steam of dishwashing liquid and hot water clings to her. "Look at you," Morgon says. "Talk about domestic."

His playful comment sails right past her as she rolls her eyes back into the house and up the stairway.

"It'll be fine; he's a tough old bird," Morgon says, coming forward in his chair.

"Don't minimize and don't baby me. He is a very ill old man," she says. "You, on the other hand, are young, healthy as a horse, and have options . . ."

"I'm not going anywhere, regardless of what . . . happens," Morgon protests, seeing where this is headed.

In the middle of composing her response, she cocks her head and watches him fold up the cuffs of his jeans. "What are you doing?" she asks.

"I've got an urge to walk barefoot on the grass. C'mon. With any luck we'll get caught in the rain."

Holding her hand, Morgon wanders across the lawn to the gazebo and his wall project. She surveys the plumb, interlocking pattern of stone, then turns her eyes toward the window of John's bedroom in the house and thinks out loud. "So now that, ah, Davis the loose end has been dealt with, it's over? The rough stuff, I mean. They can't call you back, can they?" For emphasis, she turns and scours his face with one of her gray-eyed practical looks. He takes a moment to compose his answer.

He understands that Amanda considers the "work" that her grandfather and he perform as being similar to her own philanthropic duties as foundation director. Cornball rhetoric aside, they were guardians who protect people's rights and property. And just as he knows there are two types of soldiers —the ones who fight and the other kind—there is a natural division of citizens bred into her Calvinist DNA. She assumes a destined few are born to wealth and privilege—like her—and then there are all the rest. And she expects him, as her consort, to continue in his role as protector.

So carefully he explains, "I'm separated service. They can ask favors . . ."

"Don't be coy. You mean the Agency," she says.

"Yes." Now he turns and looks at the second-story window, behind which John Rivard lays in his bed hooked to a beeping monitor. "It's all based on trust, on a handshake . . ."

Amanda nods and recites, "Nothing written down, strictly face-to-face. Before he went in the hospital, John told me you'll be giving the orders from now on, not carrying them out."

"Strictly case by case. They can ask, and I have the option to refuse."

She folds her arms across her chest and prods at a limestone slab with her bare toe. "So you've been promoted. What if you get tired of moving rocks around and become bored?"

Morgon shrugs and says in all honesty, "I had to change once before. I can do it again."

She drops her eyes, then slowly raises them to his. "You mean from working for me to working with me?" A faraway blush of heat lightning molds their features, and they are standing as close as two people can without actually touching.

"Is *work* really the word you want here?" he asks.

"So-o-o," she draws out, "come up with a better one."

He just smiles, and Amanda can't suppress a tiny thrill the way his tawny eyes travel over her face and down her body. It's more than an intimate glance. It's primal and triumphal, like encountering a lion's stare—a happy lion that's standing outside an open cage door.

She had dropped out of the migraine-plagued grind of med school to make her father comfortable as he sunk like a stone into the death spiral of Stage IV malignant glioma—the worst kind of brain cancer.

In the process she'd closeted with her grandfather, listened to his concerns, and then audited the foundation books and appreciated the shambles her father's reckless ventures into real estate had made of the estate. With John's blessing, after the funeral, she threw herself into the task of restructuring the family investment portfolio.

Morgon understood she was attracted to strength, to rectitude, to reliability and, because she was John's granddaughter, not a little bit to danger.

It didn't hurt they were good in the sack.

"I guess you're all better?" Amanda allows as she flops back on the rumpled bedding.

"Just your basic Motown Double Scream Back Crawler," Morgon says with a mussed smile. "Probably didn't catch many of those when you were hitting the books in Ann Arbor."

"You," she slaps his arm. "Answer the question. The headaches, the insomnia?"

"All better," he admits as he studies their grass-stained bare feet. "I think we ruined the sheets."

They slowly untangle, get up from the bed, and step, naked, onto the pitch-black carriage-house balcony. Morgon lights a cigarette and smiles because it's nice out. The smell of approaching rain in the breeze cools his sweat. Then he blows a stream of smoke and raises his hand. "You hear that?" This haunting string tune carries across the lawn . . .

"There, on the balcony off John's room. It's Kelly playing his violin," Amanda says absently as she plucks the cigarette from Morgon's fingers and tosses it over the rail. She insists that he quit. An occasional cigar would be okay, say during a round of golf with the county board.

Morgon slowly shakes his head. "No, darlin', that's fiddle music. That's 'Ashokan Farewell.' Remember, from the PBS Civil War . . ."

"Yes, I do," Amanda says, hugging herself. "It's a little spooky."

"Spooky's a bit strong, but it's sad and it's pretty. It's a Scottish lament," Morgon says.

"No," Amanda says, "it's spooky, because John's in there with his heart flopping in his chest and there's nothing we can do about it but wait. It sounds like Kelly is practicing for the wake."

Morgon reaches out and affectionately fluffs her hair. "You know what Roger said? We're all standing in line . . ."

Amanda wrinkles her voice. "Roger is an animal."

"That's more hyperbole. Roger just gives you a peek at a different world that's out there, beneath the everyday. John lived in it all his life. So did I, for a while. Roger still does." He raises two fingers of his right hand in a reflex, finds them empty. "You want to insure your car, you call Allstate. You want to safeguard your dirty op in the desert, you call Roger. It's just a more elemental level of reality." He laughs soundlessly and waggles his fingers in a booga-booga scare gesture. "Dark energy. Subatomic political particles. Invisible little shits like Roger make the world go 'round."

"I'm just worried it'll come back on us," Amanda says.

Morgon softly kneads her shoulder. "Don't worry. You'll be fine."

"You promise?"

"I promise. You'll always make a soft landing smack in the middle of that plush oriental carpet you picked out for John's living room."

Their eyes meet in the dark, and Morgon thinks, *Not that I planned it this way, but soon it'll be our living room.*

Now it's time to watch the storm explode over the lake and wait for the rain. Far off, silently, a lacy tendril of lightning shoos the dark, and towering cumulus clouds appear like giant chess pieces. Then it goes black again. A second later, smaller flashes trip and, in the flickering light, he turns and sees Amanda methodically draw a brush through her tangled hair.

A huge flash lights up the whole horizon, and he counts, "One-one-thousand, two-one-thousand . . ." until, after eight-one-thousand, the thunderclap shakes so loud they instinctively duck.

"First you see the flash," he says. "You get hit, you never hear the bang."

"Lightning," she says. It's dark again, and he can't make out her face.

"Yes," he says, but he's thinking of the soft light of an early Mexican evening refracted through a ten-power scope and the man sitting on a golf cart on his estate outside Juarez watching his children play croquet on a brilliant, green, chemically drenched lawn in the fraction of a second before the bullet hit him.

Then Morgon puts his arm around her shoulder and gets lost in the second round on the fiddle Kelly is serving up as a treat, rushing it a little to beat the rain. It's one of his favorite songs in the world. If there's a heaven for Americans, that song should be nonstop on the jukebox. And now that he thinks about it, Amanda is probably right: it is a little spooky, and sometimes—like now—it makes him think of walking through a graveyard.

And obviously it's having the same effect on Amanda, who chooses this exact moment to remark, "It was necessary what we did to the girl in the hospital, right? I mean, we're not bad people . . ."

Morgon thinks about it for a moment, then says, "Not anymore."

CHAPTER THIRTY-NINE

Okay, Captain Kraig, you have to do this. It's part of recovery and you're on stage and the show must go on. Jesse is kibitzing with her image in the bathroom mirror, fussing at her hair with a comb. What she sees is more like a head full of golden weeds that sprouts, tufted and untended, over her ears. She probably should have gotten it styled. But that would look like primping —and she isn't about to give *him* the satisfaction. So she'll have her hair done as a reward, if she survives this morning's little exercise.

She smiles. She's been smiling more lately, since Sam told her she rode Tumbleweed Six down, since she's been repeating the phrase *You didn't lose control* over and over like her private little mental-health rosary. Just saying it, and stopping the meds, the pressure in her head is clearing like a plugged sinus.

Onward.

Okay. Terry Sherman is, at this moment, waiting downstairs in the lobby. They'll have lunch in the cafeteria and then perhaps walk the grounds. It's like a date—a formal kind of date chaperoned by a light-footed ogre. Tony will trail them and undoubtedly take copious mental notes on her behavior and then report back to his keeper, Janet.

She places the comb on the sink and cocks her ear. Out the doorway, down the corridor, she hears a scrum of staff go into scramble mode. A patient is screaming, and his hoarse, slurred howls bounce like a basketball down the brightly lit, waxed hall. The outburst is followed by the clatter of something tipping over and crashing to the floor.

It's just a little hemorrhage of time-released terror hosing down the drugged ambiance of the polytrauma ward. Perhaps the guy is tormented by "intrusive memories" that have punched through the buffer of his meds.

As she applies a light coat of lipstick, she almost envies the screaming soldier; at least he has specific memories of the thing that turned his life upside down. And she's got this tip-of-the-tongue-type cloud where shadows stir like uneasy undersea shapes. Like Tantalus in the myth, the shapes move away when she reaches out.

Jesse sets her jaw. She'll get there, but first she must pass the Terry Sherman test.

She steps back, turns, and inspects herself in profile in the glass and plucks a piece of lint from her crisp white blouse that still has the creases down the front from when her mother ironed it, folded it, and tucked it in a package along with the short denim skirt that is a relic from her freshman year in college and still fits her.

The skirt's hem falls two inches above the knee and showcases the fact that grueling attention to exercise has restored the tone to her legs. Terry always rated legs, like sex, on a sliding scale from mediocre to good to great to "to die for." So she's curious how he'll judge the thick scar that curls out of her lower quad, zigzags across her right kneecap, and burrows into her upper shin like a slick purple eel.

She turns back to the mirror and mugs her lips to blot the lipstick. The cosmetic does not quite span the sturdy bright scar that splits her upper and lower lip and puts a deep dent in her chin. Another scar, like an accessory to the one that cuts through her lips, cracks her right eyebrow. Compared to what she sees every day on 4J, the scars are superficial scratches. She got off easy on the outside, but the fact is—and this she says out loud to the mirror—"You're not what the boys call pretty anymore, are you?"

No eye shadow, no mascara. It'll be a come-as-you-are party. Her feet are bare in flip-flops, and she's put off applying new polish to her toenails because she has a distinct memory of painting her toes the night before the flight into amnesia, shooting the breeze with Laura in their quarters. She catches herself going into a glide, staring at a chip of the old polish that still obstinately clings to the nail on her left big toe—this little curl of blue like a comma. Still there, like an abrupt punctuation to her life. Then, in a single ringing heartbeat, Jesse shivers as, first, she flashes on the hula boy doll that she kept taped to her cockpit dashboard, then the thrum of a thousand hours of Hawks' and Kiowas' motors in her blood. And it's like a shadow flies through her chest.

RPG two o'clock!

Laura's voice—her headset-cupped voice—echoes in the bathroom as if it's trapped inside the mirror. Sonofabitch. She peers at her face's startled reflection. Imagination? Playing tricks? No, that was a freakin' *memory.* No fanfare, no big deal. Just. There.

Both hands extended, she steadies on the counter. Talk about cold shivers. Then, shit! Another acoustic ambush: *Keep coming around, I'm on him.* Now it's Marge's voice that momentarily freezes her in place. Low and cool, a Chuck Yeager aviator voice in a radio.

Gingerly she touches her face and gets a numb prickling sensation like after the dentist when the Novocain wears off. Needles yanking out all at once.

And okay, no foolin', this is no hallucination. Her knuckles whiten, gripping the counter. And suddenly she's right there in the sensation of gut-churning free-fall, breathing pure adrenaline and smoke and the blades coming apart.

Very clearly the entombed moment is back. Buried again, yes. Helpless, yes. But now something more. A white-hot anger because she sees Marge Bailey suspended in the cloudy mirror, horribly burned, strips of flesh hanging on her raw arm and belly, her flight suit and vest in tatters. Blood dribbles with oil and mixes in the adobe dust.

And this guy is standing over her in a dirty tribal head-dress. Then he removes the scarf. There's another Iraqi, who pours water from a bottle on the first man's head, to clear dust from his face. Now she can see the back of his head, his reddish hair, the muscular column of his neck. She can hear him swear in English. He's taking out a pistol. She hears Marge's voice in a croak of pain: "American."

"Yo, Captain." She snaps alert. It's Tony's voice echoing from the doorway. "Time to roll."

Tony waits in the hall that now has returned to drugged status quo with only a few residual whimpers to punctuate the shuffle of walkers and wheelchairs.

"So the captain's got her war paint on." Tony's flat face is split by a game grin, just trying to ease the tension.

"Screw you, Tony," she quips back, striving for normalcy because it feels like she has to hide the sudden memories, like she just shoplifted them. "Let's get this over with."

As they sign out and exit the ward, he asks, "You good?"

"Good." They bump knuckles as they get on the elevator. "Doctor's orders. He may be totally pleasant, or he may try to mess with my mind . . ."

"And either way it breaks?" Tony raises an eyebrow.

"Smile where appropriate, don't pick my nose, practice my social skills. C'mon."

"Okay, here's the drill. I lay back a couple removes. You get to hang in the coffee shop and go out on the lawn. You get un-comfortable, shoot me a look, and we'll work it out from there."

Jesse nods. "Let's do it."

Jesse's trip to the first floor means Dr. Prasad had to sign off as well as Dr. Halme in psych, and, of course, Janet, who had gone out on a limb letting Sam in for an unscheduled visit and now feels vindicated. Jesse seeing her old sergeant worked a tonic effect, and Janet was feeling pretty good, having trumped the senior staff with her educated guess that Jesse had been misdiagnosed *and* overmedicated.

Now they'll see how she'll handle a social situation, off the ward, that presents some moderate stressors—like meeting with her former fiancé who might harbor feelings of being jilted. Jesse is determined to finesse this challenge and mind her footwork, her recent memory eruption notwithstanding.

So she squares her shoulders and steps off the elevator into the bustle of the lobby. She pauses to get oriented. This is the first time since admission that she's been plunged into a throng of people going about everyday routine—outpatients, visitors coming to see inpatients, employees leaving or coming to work, and military personnel doing whatever. And it strikes her that a VA hospital is a big house full of people who get broken in a particular way. A regular hospital caters to the aged, the diseased, the victims of accidents. She's here because her government invited her out to play in traffic and she accepted—to go looking for it.

Hyperalert since the memory dump, Jesse swivels her head, checking out the crowd, and fixes on a young female army officer in digital camo who strides by. She's a major who affects a short, practical haircut similar to the style that Jesse favored, and she's moving with purpose, never missing a beat, as she checks the iPhone in her hand. And Jesse thinks, *Three months ago, that was me.*

The major is focused dead ahead, the rest of the world peeling off on the periphery, too busy taking care of business to worry about keeping her memories straight.

C'mon. Move. Tony's watching. There's no safety net down here like on 4J.

As Tony falls back several paces, she walks past the commissary, turns right, and spots a young man with sandy-colored hair standing at the entrance to the cafeteria. He has a medium build and medium good looks and a titanium bear trap for a mind hiding behind his mild brown eyes and the easy smile that parts his regular features as he sees her and hurries forward. She notes that he was careful not to overdress; he's wearing faded jeans and a T-shirt that molds his V-chest and lets her know he still looks good with his shirt off.

"Jess, damn, it's great to see you," he says.

She had practiced this moment and raises her hand, meaning to shake his, but he steps in close and hugs her with an appropriate amount of familiarity. It's a careful, friendly hug, but the pressure of his encircling arms and the smell of his aftershave ignites all these little fuses.

"I've been better," she says tightly.

"Look all right to me," Terry says with a perfectly calibrated smile.

He, however, does look different. The small earring he used to wear is missing from his left ear. His hair is shorter. She points to the haircut, raises one scar-split eyebrow, then tugs on her ear.

He shrugs and says, "I decided to go back to law school, so bye-bye English Department eccentricities, huh? Figured it was time to cut down on the ornamentation. C'mon," he nods toward the cafeteria, "let's grab some coffee and catch up."

So they order their coffee and find a table. For a moment Jesse is distracted, flatfooted because Tumbleweed Six is back, cranking in her chest, and she has to find the ignition and *turn it the fuck off*. For now.

"Ah, Jess." Terry points to the chair he holds out for her. She takes her seat, and he spends a few minutes in polite warm-up chatter, bringing her up to date on who's still together and who isn't in Grand Forks. Then, deftly, he turns the conversation to her.

"You were in *Newsweek*, you know."

"What?"

"Indirectly. They didn't exactly mention you by name. This article about some congressmen who questioned how many women the army should put in one helicopter."

"Soldiers are soldiers, Terry," Jesse says deliberately, looking past him to Tony's reassuring hulk standing at the corner of the service bar sipping on a smoothie.

"Sure, that's the company line, but, as usual, the culture hasn't caught up," he says. "There'll always be a double standard for some people . . ."

Jesse forces a smile and changes the subject. "So now it's law school. You thinking of going back to Grand Forks?"

"Well, Dad went to UND. And I put a semester in there. But since I'm over here, I thought I'd drive by the University of Minnesota and check out their law school."

"Out-of-state tuition," she mentions, which is the practical thing to say.

"True. But it'd only be for a few months. Maybe I could just audit classes."

"Why only a few months?"

"Because when they let you out of here, you'll go into an assisted-living situation, essentially a halfway house. I thought it might be a good time to get reacquainted, as you ease your way back into things." It comes out smooth and reasonable and sincere.

"So you've been checking up on me?"

"C'mon, Jess. Just because I didn't go through the VA system doesn't mean I don't know how it works," he protests, still smiling.

"You've been checking up on me," she repeats.

He takes a sip of coffee, puts down the cup, and looks her directly in the eye. "I just thought you might like some company going through the transition," he says.

"Transition?"

"Sure, you know, back into the messy business of civilian life."

"Last time I looked, I was getting a paycheck from the army."

Terry leans forward, and the luster in his eyes appears genuine. Then the warmth turns to concern. "C'mon, they've talked about this, haven't they?"

Jesse starts to pick up her coffee cup and realizes her hand is shaking. When she sets the cup back down, it rattles on the table. "Say what you mean," she says carefully.

Terry sits back in his chair and raises his hands, palms out, in a "whoa" gesture. "Maybe I'm talking out of school here. I just figured . . ."

"Figured what?" Eyebrows knit, Jesse has leaned forward across the table.

"I've been talking to your folks about what you've been going through, the progress you've made and the future and . . . all that," he finishes with a halting tic in his voice.

Jesse stares deliberately into his eyes. "Since when did you start having trouble expressing yourself?"

Terry circles his finger, taking in the surrounding lobby. "So they haven't talked to you about what happens next?"

"Sure, more rehab, the halfway house, like you said," she answers. From the corner of her eye she registers that Tony is now paying attention to the tense body language at the table.

"I mean where you stand with the army."

"Where I stand? *I got shot at and hit*, in case you didn't notice." The slippage is clear in her voice. She's becoming annoyed. Not in her plan at all.

"Jess, Jess, take it easy." He exhales, sets his teeth on edge, and taps them together. "All I mean is, I know how much you had your heart set on flying . . ."

Past tense.

217

Jesse takes a deep breath and plants both elbows on the table and places her hands alongside her face to compose herself. Talk about knowing exactly where to stick in the needle. "Oh, boy," she says as she lowers her hands.

Now Terry purses his lips and lets annoyance trickle into his tone. "That's government doctors for you, bunch of hacks."

Calmly Jesse parses through his meaning. "You're talking about my flight status."

He nods. "Army aviation medical standards. You've been treated for seizures. You've been given antipsychotic medication. I don't think they grant medical waivers for pilots with that profile in their records. There's language in the regs about a review of medical history for physical symptoms that can develop during times of stress."

"You researched it, I suppose?"

He nods. "I read a few things, talked to a few people."

For a moment they lock eyes across the table. And suddenly Jesse can't suppress a laugh–a deep, rollicking, you-gotta-be-shitting-me soldier laugh. She knows it's rude, but she can't help it because there's a tough, resilient feel to the sound in her throat. *It sounds like me.*

"Okay, look," Terry says patiently after waiting out the laughter. "I think you're going through a rough patch and you could use more support than these government bureaucrats are giving you."

And she's thinking how utterly sincere he looks, leaning slightly forward, every hair and word in place. More than sincere, actually; sure of himself. And she gets it. Terry, the army, the VA—they are all sincere to a fault, and helpful, and they all have an agenda because now she's certain that old Sam was right: *Marge Bailey didn't die in a helicopter crash because I saw her shot. And here's Terry telling me I'm basically crazy, huh?*

"You'd do that for me?" she asks, unable to resist putting a hint of purr in her tone.

He's more earnest now, leaning forward. "Jess, just say the word and I'm in it for the long haul. I'll help you get back on your feet."

"How sweet." She reaches out and pats his hand on the table.

Encouraged, his voice lowers a register and approaches intimate. "And down the line we'll clean up the damage on your face and your knee. You'll be good as new."

Leave it to Terry the leg man to remember to airbrush the knee. "Good as new," she repeats and smiles fondly. "Aren't you Johnny-on-the-spot now that you think my wings are clipped." Then, abruptly, she glimpses this tall young soldier in camos and desert boots who appears at the back of the cafeteria. Then he disappears, sidestepping a gaggle of older, overweight vets in motorized wheelchairs.

Christ, for a second there, that looked like Toby. Be careful now. Her mind, turbocharged on the new memories, is playing tricks. She catches herself staring at a background of tall schefflera, yucca tips, fiddle leaf fig, ficus, and bamboo palms that edge the atrium. *Throttle down, girl.*

She finds herself standing up, biting down on the scar on her lip. "I gotta go," she says as she ratchets her head back and forth. From the corner of her eye she picks up Tony setting his drink aside and moving toward her.

Terry is on his feet now, hands up, conciliatory. "Calm down. Seriously. I can help," his voice pleads.

"Thank you, Terry," she says, backing away, her own hands waist-high, palms out. "I mean it, thanks. But I gotta go."

Then Tony's there, his hand on her elbow, guiding her away, and just that quick, Terry is forgotten. "That good, huh?" Tony speculates deadpan.

"Hey, I landed like a cat." Jesse forces a grin. "On all four broken feet." Then she tugs his arm and asks, "Hey, can we go somewhere, not the ward, away from here and . . . talk?"

"Sure."

After a trip through basement corridors, they wind up outside on a long patio that overlooks a loading dock. Men and women staff in scrubs lounge at tables, smoking. When Tony eases a tin of Copenhagen from his pocket, Jesse puts out her hand.

"You sure?" His brow furrows and he says, "This is long cut; it's the strong."

"Gimme. It's not a boy-girl thing; it's a pilot thing. I only used it once, at the end of a long night mission. Pretty disgusting stuff, but like the guys say, it gives a little edge and smoothes out the jangles. Less downside than go pills." Jesse opens the tin and inserts a chew under her lip.

"I guess," Tony says, doing up himself.

Grimacing, Jesse probes the noxious cud with her tongue and feels the nicotine claw into her bloodstream. "Thing is, it's the closest I can get to putting my head in a cockpit in this place."

That gets Tony's attention as Jesse takes a deep breath, exhales, and laughs. "We'd have these maps loaded on our computer screens. When you fly off the grids and run out of map, there's a line where the map ends and everything past that is black."

Jesse leans over and spits.

"We used to call it 'flying off the edge of the world,' and we'd kid each other, like, 'Hey, that's where the monsters are.'" She turns to Tony with a frank stare he's seen before, in Afghanistan. "There's all kinds of maps with edges you can fly off and get lost in the black. No joke."

"Yes, ma'am."

Jesse nods and looks directly into Tony's patient eyes. "My memory is coming back, Tony, and it isn't coming back easy."

CHAPTER FORTY

Hot goddamn night in the Wisconsin woods. The dew point hovers, dripping at 80 percent, and Davis feels like he's growing gills on the bottom of a black, sticky ocean. Across the lake, a loon calls, and the thrilling avian cry pierces through the soupy air, only a little friendlier on the shiver scale than a howling wolf.

Blinking sweat, he looks up for relief among the icy stars and scans the constellations until he picks out the Big Dipper and sights along the arc of the handle, like his dad taught him as a boy, and spots Arcturus by its reddish-orange hue. He leans back in a deck chair and sips from a glass of Jack Daniel's sour mash. He's turned off all the lights, and the surrounding woods block out any sign of neighbors. A muted trill of insects joins the cry of the loon, and then he hears a far-off yip-yip call that is probably a pack of coyotes.

Mouse's hideout looks out over a medium-sized lake and is no shack. The e-mailed instructions contained a map and directions to locate a key hung on a hook behind a porch piling. More lake home than cabin, the place comes with four bedrooms, a fireplace, satellite TV, and a pool table in the basement. The freezer is piled with frozen steaks and salmon, and a pantry contains boxes of fancy freeze-dried dinners. After the wicked turn of events in Maryland and the long drive, he was grateful to discover a well-stocked liquor cabinet.

Lay low, the Mouse said, while I try to get a line on the people who are after you. He takes a long sip of the Jack and snuggles deeper in the chair.

Then a branch snaps in the dark and he is instantly alert and oriented toward the sound that he judges to be fifty yards into the tree line along the right side of the lake. Simultaneously he calculates the time and distance it will take to slip into the house and ease up to the kitchen island where he disassembled, cleaned, and reassembled his cache of weapons first thing after arriving this afternoon.

He processes all the possible moves in two seconds flat because he's learned to build lethal reactions into a mere startle reflex. But he's also learned to court danger with common sense.

Ease off, man. It's a friggin' deer looking for something to eat.

After another big swig of Jack, he lights a cigarette with the dead Mexican's lighter and shifts his eyes along the dark shoreline. Yep. The wild things are out there. He can sense their eyes ranging in on the flaring coal of his cigarette.

He takes another drink and relives the sensation from the old days of squatting in the dark, a night watcher with a knife in his hand, tasting the air the way a mountain lion tastes it. And he can almost feel the bright bundles of his nerves bunch, getting ready to pounce. Back then, obedient and patient, he'd wait for the hearth to burn down to embers. He'd been good at it, like he was good at a lot of things.

But it wasn't really him. And, for all his precision, inevitably there were the civilians who got in the way.

The sweaty reverie ends. He raises the glass again but decides he's had enough for tonight. So he sets the drink aside . . .

Snap, crackle, pop.

One of the night critters is making a move out in the thicket, but this time Davis just heaves to his feet, flings his arms at the sound in the dark, and shouts "Boo!"

CHAPTER FORTY-ONE

The wooden crate that arrives from Balad is the size of a small footlocker and has the whole flight company's signatures for a return address. It's so heavy that the mail room sends it up to 4J on a dolly pulled by a maintenance man from building services, who explains that he used a Wonder Bar to pry it open.

"Security got concerned about the weight," he says as he sets the lid aside. "After I got it open, they got concerned about the shape." He points to the 16 K kettle bell that weighs thirty-five pounds and looks exactly like a cannonball with a hoop of steel handle. The bell nestles in Jesse's old Fighting Sioux sweatsuit and is wedged in with her running shoes. But the real surprise lies hidden in the folds of the warm-up jacket. Pulling back a sleeve, she finds the charred, somewhat mangled remains of the hula boy doll that used to occupy the dashboard above the instrument panel on her Hawk. Now her former good-luck charm hangs together by virtue of several strategic wraps of duct tape. With Sam gone, she wonders who reclaimed it from the wreckage of Tumbleweed Six.

It's the first time she's been directly confronted by a relic from that day. The springs that allowed the hips to sway are broken. Hula boy has lost his tinsel grass skirt and now wears a duct tape sheath. But that doesn't matter.

Because he was there.

And survived.

And now we can talk about what we saw, you and me. The question is—how much do I tell Janet?

★ ★ ★

Six days off the meds. Two days after the encounter with Terry Sherman. The change continues to be dramatic. The young woman taking a seat beside the desk in Janet's office speaks and moves normally and is attentive to small details. Today she shows up for the session with a touch of foundation makeup to tone the scars on her chin and forehead. After months of ignoring her hair, she's been to the shop for a style. And instead of hospital blues, she wears jeans, a Nodak T-shirt her folks sent, and a pair of sandals that show a fresh coat of blue polish on her toenails. But Janet notes a quietly wary edge to Jesse's eyes and so begins with, "Tony tells me things got a little tense during the visit two days ago. And you told him your memory has improved?"

"Oh, yeah," Jesse answers with a guarded eye roll, "came back all at once like a load of hay crashing on my head."

"So tell me about it, starting with the visit."

"It was great. Terry came all this way to tell me I'll never fly again. Because of the diagnosis, the seizures, and the drugs I've taken. He offered to take me away from all this and install me in a suburban kitchen." She leans forward. "I'm curious why the subject hasn't come up—the not-flying part—here, in this office, between you and me."

"Because this is primary care. You're recovering from an injury. Vocational rehab comes later . . ."

"Jesus. *Vocational rehab?* You mean like weaving baskets? Terry's right. You *do* sound like a bureaucrat."

For a beat they engage in a stare until Janet purses her lips and says, "And you sound like a smart-ass officer dressing down an enlisted man. You must be getting better . . ."

"C'mon, Janet. Given the cards in my hand right now, will I ever fly again?"

Janet shrugs and gives it to her straight. "Go out to Minneapolis–St. Paul International and book a flight. Then, just after you strap on your seatbelt, ask yourself how'd you'd feel if you learned that the pilot had struggled with active amnesia."

"It's a gray area, right?" Jesse conjures with her hands. "Traumatic brain injury, concussion interacting with drugs. Hard to figure out what the real problem is. But at the end of the day, my medical records will say I had seizures, that I was treated for acting nuts and given antipsychotics. One thing's for sure: nobody's going to hire *that* pilot." Jesse shifts her gaze, studies a point on the wall under Janet's diploma, and enunciates, "Let's say the thing I'm struggling with right now is not my memory; it's the implications of what I saw."

"That sounds a little grandiose. Can you be more specific?"

"I'm not sure you want to know."

Janet raises her eyebrows.

"Okay," Jesse says, "it's like this. Lots of patients on the ward have more drugs on board and have been through things as bad or worse than me. But they don't all have the memory problems I did."

"We're on the same page there," Janet cautiously agrees. "You were overmedicated in a major way. That's on us, not you. And you're right, it is a gray area we don't fully understand . . ."

"Pretty convenient, too, I'd say."

"Hold on. Define convenient . . ."

"Like, what if I was deliberately overmedicated? I get pumped full of antipsychotics—no more flying, no more army. I'm just another crazy vet who imagines things."

Janet leans forward with a worry line denting her brow. "You're not crazy. Just wait a second. I mean, you're complicating it. We're talking about your flight status, and you get defensive because you couldn't control your memory, then you get mad at yourself for getting defensive."

Now Jesse also leans forward, so their eyes meet on the same plane. "For once why don't you throw the books away and just talk."

Janet takes a moment to evaluate the intensity in Jesse's eyes. "Sure. Street psychology. Give a tough kid a kick in the ass. So losing control is the worst thing in the world, right? You're a hot-shit captain in the friggin' army. Your records put you in the top 1 percent of your peers. And I know that it has to be twice as hard for you because it's still a bunch of men. Plus you're a pilot. Most army officers get distracted and nothing happens. You get distracted for a few seconds, and you lose control of the aircraft. You lost control. They shot you out of the sky, and your crew died in the crash."

Janet twists her hand in a reasonable gesture. "It's like aikido, using your opponent's weight against him—like to regain your control, you have to admit that you lost it. Could that be the step you're hung up on? Doesn't mean you're crazy."

Jesse maintains strict eye contact and enunciates each syllable. "I didn't lose control. Sam told me. I rode Tumbleweed Six down in a controlled crash. But what if I landed in a *crazy situation*? So crazy it doesn't fit in one of the neat disorders in your DSM-IV?"

Involuntarily, Janet eases back in her chair. "Like how crazy?"

"Like, say, I clearly remember seeing Marge die. Okay? And she didn't die *in* the crash, like the after-action report said. I watched her die *afterwards*."

"Afterwards," Janet repeats slowly.

Jesse nods. "She managed to make it out of the aircraft and was on her knees and this guy stood over her aiming a pistol at the back of her head. Not ten feet away from where I was trapped. And not just any guy. He wasn't Iraqi." She points a finger for emphasis. "I accept going into shock, concussion, whatever. It's waking up in drug world I don't buy."

"You watched her die," Janet repeats.

Jesse nods. "She needed my help, and I just watched her die, and she still needs my help."

Taken aback by the cryptic intensity of Jesse's last words, Janet responds firmly, "Marge doesn't need help. She's dead, Jesse. Along with Laura and Toby. They buried her eight weeks ago in Grand Forks. She got the flag, the firing squad, the works. You're the one who needs help. That's why you're here. Survivor's guilt . . ."

Jesse glowers and interrupts, "You work here? I *live* here! Some nights, when the helmet heads down the ward are moaning and I can't sleep, I get up and walk the halls. Don't talk to me about . . . fuckin' *flags*."

Janet pauses for several long seconds, recalibrating her balance, and replies, "You're angry."

"Damn straight."

"Mad is good. Anything not passive is good. Jesse, listen. I've *worked* in this place for over a year, and you're damn lucky to have landed here. There's worse hospitals in the system. A lot worse. Even here outpatient is stretched thin, takes thirty days to get an appointment . . ."

"What are you doing? Justifying your job?"

"Nonsense. Dozens of soldiers have sat in that chair. And what a lot of them came to understand is that survivor's guilt is manageable. It won't ever go away. It's like a cable channel on TV. But you don't have to watch it all the time. You can look at something else."

Jesse is unimpressed. "I swear to God I feel like grabbing you and dragging you off your shrink soapbox. You don't get it, do you? School's out, Janet. Forget the fucking books!"

The two women glare at each other briefly. For the second time in less than a minute, Janet feels control slipping away. "I'm not the one with my head up my ass, *Captain*," she shoots back.

Janet's frustration elicits a belly laugh from Jesse. "You talk to the guys like this?"

"Once in a while, the real stupid ones."

"Were you military before you started working on your psych degree?" Jesse asks, narrowing her eyes.

"I was a St. Paul patrol cop, kiddo."

"No shit?"

"No shit."

Jesse smiles. "Well, that's great. Let me know when you remember how to think like a cop because all this" —she waves a hand at the shelves of books and the framed master's degree —"is bullshit as far as helping me from here on out." Then Jesse spins on her heel and strides, swinging her shoulders, from the office.

After her outburst Jesse pauses overlooking a mezzanine lined with historical flags. She fixes her gaze on one of them: *Don't Tread on Me.* Then she watches an elderly man in a wheelchair who pulls himself along, methodically, hand over hand, on the guardrail fastened to the wall. Each grip and tug sends a plastic squeak echoing down the empty hall.

She takes the stairs up to four, signs in on the ward, and starts toward the dining area to check the supper menu. Coming around a corner she encounters a young woman, slightly fleshy in shorts and a sleeveless blouse, with a dark ponytail and a butterfly tat on her left calf. Her right hand rests on the shoulder of a scrubbed little girl, perhaps five or six. The girl's hair juts out at angles in short pigtails. She wears a party dress. They are standing outside the TV room, where patients receive visitors.

Jesse slows her pace, then stops. She can see the tendons on the top of the mother's hand stand out as she steadies her daughter. She can hear the hush but not the content of whispered instructions. The little girl nods and stands completely still.

Now two figures round a corner in the hall. A male nurse's aide steers one of the shuffling helmet heads with gentle pressure on his elbow. By now Jesse accepts these men's faces as part of the 4J wallpaper; this one's few remaining recognizable features struggle through the raw welts of surgery to find common ground between determination and vacancy.

"See, honey," the mother says in a carefully normal voice, "Daddy's home."

Jesse turns and retraces her steps. It's not avoidance; she doesn't want to intrude. Galvanized and absolutely centered, she reminds herself as she walks to her room, *Never feel sorry for yourself. You took a soldier's chance . . .*

And you got off easy.

CHAPTER FORTY-TWO

On a grand summer afternoon, Morgon Jump surveys the grounds of the Rivard estate from the site of his almost completed stone wall, and he's thinking, *I can do this.* He'd meant it when he told Amanda he'd had to change before and he could do it again. Last time he'd had to reinvent himself out of a heap of white trash in Warren, Michigan—the same environs that produced Eminem. When he was a kid his mom and dad's worldview was summed up by the painting of Jesus standing next to Hank Williams on black velvet that hung in the basement.

Mom kept a little box on the mantel over the fireplace that contained cards printed with Bible verses. She liked it when Morgon and his brother and sister would select a card and take the scripture to heart before they left for school.

He seemed to get one card more than the others, and it stayed with him: *Second Timothy 2:15: Study to shew thyself approved unto God . . . a workman rightly dividing the word of truth.*

First you study a thing. Like with this wall. He pictures in his mind's eye the seamless, famous twelve-sided stone that is the centerpiece of the Inca Cuzco Wall. Fast moving-clouds have smothered the sun, and he notices that he no longer casts a shadow. So he stares at the grass where his shadow should be.

★ ★ ★

Morgon spelled with an O because his father was loaded the night he was born and entered the name wrong on the birth certificate.

By the time he was sixteen he had a reputation for handling himself, and kids would come to him with their problems, and he would figure out a way to fix them—usually by backing off some bully. His favorite movie was The Godfather, *and he identified with Michael because Michael wasn't crude like the other guys, had cool hair, and surprised people big-time once he got going, and Morgon was like that, sort of.*

Looking back, there was really only one similarity between his life and Michael's because Michael's family was powerful and lived in a big house and Morgon's family was what you'd call "low ordinary living in a crummy rambler," what you'd call "Michigan hillbillies."

Michael's dad ran one of the five families in New York, and he made people offers they couldn't refuse, and Morgon's dad was a sad, get-along-go-along drunk who worked on the production line at Dodge Truck on Mound Road and rooted for the Detroit Lions. His mom worked the cosmetics counter at Horner's Drugstore on Ten Mile and Van Dyke and lived for her duties as an orderly at the Bethany Missionary Tabernacle, where she lined her three children up with her on Wednesday nights and Friday nights and twice on Sunday.

The similarity was that part of the movie story about Michael having no choice but to kill his brother, Fredo. Morgon understood how that could happen. Fredo broke the rules and betrayed the family. And Morgon had a brother, Billy, two years older. Billy was the favorite and was being groomed to be a youth minister in the church.

By the time he was sixteen Morgon had figured out that his brother said one thing in church and did another at home. And what really bothered Morgon were the times Billy would make their sister, Darlene, do things that Morgon had only secretly thought about— because, well, Darlene was real developed at fifteen. Billy would crowd her in the bathroom and grab her hand and make her touch him. Then he'd grab a fistful of her red hair and force her mouth down there.

Bad touch, like they taught you in school when you were a little kid.

This was a thing that did bother Morgon a lot. It kept him up nights, listening. So he told Billy, warned him like—"Don't be doing that anymore."

And Billy, who thought he was tough because he played football at Warren High, wiggled his fingers scary-like and said, "Oow, whattcha gonna do? Besides, you dweeb, she's a cunt and she likes it."

"No she don't, 'cause I asked her, and she hates it," said Morgon. And Billy just laughed at him and told him to grow up.

Morgon at sixteen thought football players were all pussies anyway because they wouldn't hit anybody unless they were wearing half a sporting-goods store—Morgon said, "You do that again to Darlene, and I will fucking kill you."

"Oh yeah," said Billy.

"Yeah," said Morgon.

So Billy kept doing it, and so Morgon killed him.

He looks up when Amanda calls from the porch. "You want something cold to drink?"

"I'm good," he yells back. Then he returns to his hammer and chisel and starts chipping away at a big obstinate stone that he's decided will be his foundation rock, that will crown the whole job.

Not just like that, of course. Killing Billy involved planning. Because sure, one on one, Morgon could beat up Billy easy. But then Billy would come back on him with half the football team, and there'd be a big scene. And Darlene was real clear that was not going to happen.

And the fact was he was a kid and didn't really know how to kill somebody and, more important, how to do it and not get caught. He read a lot and knew about crimes of passion and low impulse control, and that's how dummies got caught.

Morgon didn't have impulses. He had plans. And he was no dummy. The teachers in high school kept saying, "You know, you scored real high on these tests and you could get some scholarship money." And Morgon said, "Thanks, but I got something else in mind a little more practical. Like getting some training."

So it took a while—years in fact. During that time Billy kept at Darlene, who finally ran away and went back down South to Missis-sippi, where the family originally came from. And Morgon graduated from high school and joined the army and went through basic and then infantry and then airborne school and qualified for the Rangers. After he made sergeant he came back to Warren, Michigan, on leave, confident he could whack the whole football team if it came to that.

Except all that was over, and now Billy was a flabby salesman on a Toyota lot, which probably made Dad puke, his kid selling Jap cars. And Billy had this blonde wife with vacant eyes who stayed home and watched TV all day. And they had a little daughter. He was still living off Twelve Mile and Van Dyke about two blocks from Ma and Pa. See-ing that kid really bothered Morgon, thinking what she had to look forward to. And worse, what really bothered him was that Darlene had married this hamface crew-cut moron of a preacher down home who, swear to God, looked like Billy.

It wasn't like Billy knew he was there, or anybody else. Morgon came in real quiet. For two days he watched Billy's routine—at work, at the house. Then he looked over the old neighborhood. Both nights, after dinner, Billy, who was about thirty pounds overweight, would go for a power walk wearing a weight vest and carrying an eight-pound barbell in each hand. His route took him along the wooded edge of a soccer field three blocks from his house.

When Billy came huffing by, Morgon, wearing light rubber fish-ing gloves, was waiting just inside the tree line. He stepped out, whipped one of the barbells from Billy's fat hand, and used it to cave in his skull. Bang. No words passed between them. Morgon didn't come to talk. He was keeping a promise.

Then he just walked away, slipping through the trees back to his car. A couple hours later he was into Ohio on his way back to Fort Bragg, running out a week-long pass. Swung through Memphis. Checked out Graceland.

He looks up and sees Amanda striding across the lawn toward him with her usually composed face set in an unabashed grin. She's wearing the black Morning Glory skirt and the oyster top with the twist in front that accentuates her breasts. He knows this because he's studied the clothes she wears in the Patagonia catalog that is full of pictures of scantily clad women clinging to rock overhangs like flies. He smiles as he remembers what the catalog said about the skirt, how it's soft and stretchy and has a natural playful drape.

Across the lawn, he sees Kelly trundle John out on the porch in the wheelchair that's outfitted with a defibrillator and a tank of oxygen. Making eye contact, the old man raises a hand in a happy wave as Kelly eases the chair down the ramp.

"What's up?" Morgon asks, now curious.

"It's a gift," Amanda says, eyes bright. "He just received a call from a Senate staffer. He's been invited to testify at a Senate Oversight Committee. Special summer session. It's the first time he's been excited about something since the heart attack."

When John arrives, he leans forward, and Morgon agrees with Amanda's assessment: there's more light in the old crocodile eyes than he's seen in weeks.

"So what's this about a Senate hearing, you showboat?" Morgon asks, grinning.

"They're assembling a gang of us old dogs from the Agency, part of the ongoing review of that disaster at Khost in Afghanistan, among other things." John beams.

"I figure we all can go," Amanda says. "It'll be like a vacation."

"When?" Morgon asks.

"A week from tomorrow," John replies. "It'll be a chance to reconnect with my old gang of pirates."

"Sounds great," Morgon responds to smiles all around.

As Kelly wheels John back to the house, Amanda takes Morgon aside for a walk. "I know it's short notice, but let's throw an open house after the hearing. We could audition the architect's model of the Lakefront Project. I could start phoning out invitations today, and Martha could do the follow-up with the food while we're in DC. We can hire a crew of high school kids to help with the grounds work."

Morgon deadpans, "Don't think I can handle all the smiley faces breaking out all over the place."

Amanda playfully punches him on the arm and says, "Hey, I throw *great* parties, and it'll give you a chance to remind the local bigwigs what a handsome, useful fella you are."

So he relents and smiles. "Can't argue with you there."

"So it's a deal." She goes up on her toes to kiss him on the cheek, then, after she fondly touches the scar on his neck, she turns and runs back toward the house.

Gifts. Deals. Parties. It's all part of his transition to learn the art of untroubled sleep in Amanda Rivard's clean pale arms. So he keeps the energy of it like a bright light to poke into some dark crannies of his life. Stuff he generally leaves off thinking about, that Amanda would index under repression.

When word reached him about his brother's senseless murder, he was granted compassionate leave. The family gathered in Warren, and Morgon was surprised when Darlene showed up without her shitbird husband. They had a private moment in the church, Billy tarted up in the casket. She never asked him the obvious questions, like why he never married. Must have been a hundred people at the service, and they were the best-looking couple in the place.

After the burial and the food and condolences at the old house, they took a drive to catch up. And it just started to happen right there in the front seat. Darlene busting out of her blouse and shaking out her strawberry red hair and coming on like a slow sexual tremor pent up and now unleashed, and she went for his crotch with a practiced precision that took his breath away.

Shit, man; looking into an open grave will do that to people, bring up the appetites real sharp!

With a mighty act of will, Morgon pushed her away, and she was hurt and blurted, "I thought you always wanted this!" Morgon just shook his head and had two thoughts: Billy died for nothing, and people, women especially, will let you down every damn time.

So the way it worked out, Billy had been right. Darlene was a promiscuous cunt who did like it, and Morgon had killed his asshole brother out of a misguided sense of upholding the rules. Talk about a weird sensation, like he was back in the beginning of the Bible with Cain and Abel or some fucking equally desolate place. After the funeral he made two resolutions: He'd never see Darlene again. And he'd do something to make up for Billy's death.

One thing was clear. He had a big problem when it came to deciding who gets to live and who needs to die. What he needed was some hard and fast rules that wouldn't come back on him. Rules he could rely on, with hard-eyed men to back them up. So when the test came around for Special Forces, he was the first to sign up.

His eyes travel to the porch of the big house, where John and Amanda are engaged in lively conversation. Calmly, he looks over the grounds and the house and winds up staring into the future. The estate has the solidity of a feudal castle; the county is the Rivard's benign fiefdom. And he is being groomed to be the big dog who stands guard in the night. *So go with it, learn to whack a little white ball around and smoke an occasional cigar. Deputy Jump. First Deputy Jump. Rivard County Sheriff Morgon Jump.* Do a little discreet Agency work on the side to keep his hand in and get the big paydays. His eyes drift back to the porch, to Amanda's slender patrician profile.

CHAPTER FORTY-THREE

After Jesse puts in a fast kettle-bell circuit, she showers, gets dressed, pats hula boy on his charred head for good luck, and heads for the nurses' station to sign out for a meeting with Janet. In a few minutes she's walking easy in snug running shorts, a sports halter, and flip-flops through a crowd on the first floor that no longer intimidates her. She has her notebook tucked under her arm, and she's talking on her cell to her mother.

"No, Mom, Terry is a sweet guy, and we'll stay friends, but that's as far as it goes. About the hospital stuff, I'm not out of the woods yet." Pause. "The rooms are nice, better than a college dorm. It's like a halfway house where you do your own laundry, cook." Pause. "Hey. *I can cook*." Then Jesse leans back and winds a finger in her hair that now curls over her ears for the first time in two years. "Well, at least I can go shopping on my own." Another pause. "I don't know for sure; maybe I'll be living there in a month . . ."

Depending . . .

After ending the call, she shrugs off a few surreptitious stares because she's showing lots of double-whammy leg—shapely and disfigured. Her face is animated with determination because she's done her homework and, today, by agreement, she's setting the agenda in her meeting with Janet.

Automatically, she catalogs wars in the foot parade in the hall. The Gulf, Iraq, and Afghanistan stride. Vietnam is a mixed bag—some walk, some shuffle. Korea uses a cane. The Big One rides in a wheelchair with an oxygen tank in tow. The amputations, brain injuries, and real bad combat-stress casualties are kept pretty much behind closed doors. Out the windows she sees a bright July sky. A light-rail line runs by the hospital, people come and go, rush hour hums on the freeway.

She meets Janet at the visitor's entrance next to the diminutive bronze statue of Bob Hope commemorating his work on behalf of the USO. She wears loose denims and a casual blouse and tennis shoes. When she sees Jesse, she asks, "You sure you wanna go outside?"

"You got anything against fresh air?"

"It's hot outside."

Jesse scans the halls briefly, the people. "It's more open outside."

They exit the building and walk around the side to a quiet wooded area with old picnic tables. They sit down, and Jesse slaps her notebook on the table. "Okay, first the ground rules. How confidential is this conversation?"

"The bright line in the business is I have to report the risk of harm, to self or others."

Jesse appraises Janet. "Which could put you in an interesting position job-wise—say—if the harm reported is to your employer, the government."

"How do you mean, exactly?" Janet asks, watching Jesse carefully.

"I mean the guy who executed my crew chief wasn't some drive-by insurgent. He was speaking English like an American."

Now Janet nibbles her lower lip between her teeth, watching Jesse more closely. She narrows her eyes, and the nibble has become a slightly nervous bite. "The after-action report in your records was quite specific; your crew was ambushed by insurgents and killed in the initial explosion and the crash."

"Total bullshit," Jesse says, leaning across the table. "When you let Sam in to see me, he told me what really happened that day. That must have shocked the wheels to turning in my head, huh?"

"And he knows what really happened how?" Janet has crossed her arms across her chest.

"He did some checking around. He used to be a county deputy in Grand Forks. He talked to the mission commander that day, Major Colbert, who was flying the other Hawk, the person who got to the crash first. Greg, that's Major Colbert, saw me bring my Hawk down. I rode it in. But then Greg had to stand off while he called in the medevac, for like five minutes —waiting for the dust from the explosion to clear. He couldn't see anything through that cloud."

Jesse pauses for emphasis. "Also, the after-action report doesn't say it wasn't your ordinary milk run. It was a classified mission, and Major Colbert was flying a special operator working with the Iraqi cops. A spook."

"Now it's spooks?"

"You bet." Jesse nods. "Now Sam . . ."

"The old sergeant who used to be a cop," Janet interjects.

"Correct." Jesse flips open her notebook to a page on which the outline of a helicopter is sketched, dotted with Xs. "Sam drew this diagram to show me how it really went down."

"Okaaay." Janet shifts on the bench and listens while Jesse leads her step by step through Sam's scenario.

In summation, Jesse says, "So Marge's body winds up here, six feet to the left front of the cockpit. She couldn't have been thrown out at that angle, not in her gunner harness. She had to get out on her own. That's where she was killed." Jesse takes a breath. "Where I saw her killed."

"You're in a little danger of spinning out here," Janet says soberly.

"C'mon, think like a cop, remember. The asshole would have given me the same, except I was buried in debris, dirt . . . and Laura. See, the props came apart on impact and sliced through the cockpit . . ."

Janet stares at Jesse for a moment.

"Back off that look," Jesse cautions. "Not like we were soccer moms getting mugged on the way to Starbucks. North Dakota Guard ain't exactly Combat City, but we all knew this could happen, and it did. Clear?"

"Clear. Keep going . . ."

"So why do you kill the survivors?"

"So there's no witnesses," Janet says slowly. "But witnesses to what?" Then she shakes her head. "The report said the mission was on the way to busting a smuggling operation in a town miles from where you were hit."

"I'm just telling you what it says here." Jesse taps the notebook.

"If there's an alternative to the official report, the logical solution has to be that the insurgents came in and did it." Janet bites her lip. "Don't you think?"

"If that's the case, why change the facts on the report? Unless we flew into something we weren't supposed to?"

In the ensuing silence Jesse takes a moment to study her counselor across the table, and what she sees is a woman who has reached an uncomfortable boundary. "This isn't what you had in mind when you told me to get my head out of my ass, huh?" she asks carefully.

"This is beginning to sound like a conspiracy theory. My colleagues on the second floor might say you're manufacturing false beliefs in the face of superior evidence, like, for instance, the after-action report," Janet says.

"Sounds like the company line," Jesse says.

"They'd say you're flirting with delusions, and delusions typically occur in the context of neurological disorders . . ."

Jesse smiles, undeterred, and says, "Like embroidering around the edges of post-traumatic amnesia, huh?"

"It would come to mind," Janet says. "You tell this to anyone else on two, and they might put you back on the Seroquel."

240

Jesse shakes her head. "There are legitimate questions here," she says, pointing to the notebook sketch. "Sam thinks something stinks about Marge's death. He says no phones, no e-mails."

"Now you *are* spiraling out," Janet says slowly. "It's good you're motivated and taxing your memory to analyze the crash. The problem is—like I said—your conclusions sound delusional."

"Yeah, well, Sam's a lot of things, but delusional isn't one of them." Jesse is adamant. "So what do you think?" she asks.

Janet answers carefully. "I think anything that orients you, alert, in that crash site is helpful. But now you've brought *they* into the picture."

Jesse smiles again. "You mean the conspiratorial *they* of tinfoil hats and little green men in the mailbox?"

"Exactly."

"And now you're a bit concerned if this gets around," Jesse points at the notebook on the table, "like, your department head will chew your butt because it was your idea to take me off the meds, huh?"

"Let's say you have my full attention," Janet says, tapping the notebook page. "Can I make copies of this?" she asks.

"Sure."

As she closes the notebook, Janet pauses to point to the star doodles all over the cover. "You ever figure out what these were about?"

"Dunno. Must have been the drugs, huh?"

CHAPTER FORTY-FOUR

Davis has scared up a rod and some tackle from a basement closet and is casting a line off the dock when the cold cell rings at three in the afternoon.

"How's it going, Mr. Lemmer?"

"Gone fishing. I just caught a fair-sized bass. Threw it back. How's 'bout you?"

"Appert drew a blank on the two dead Zetas, which is no surprise. And nobody has a single hair out of place about your former persona dying in a car fire."

"So nothing's turned up?"

"It's real quiet out there, nary a ripple."

"So maybe I died for nothing."

"Think positive. The North Atlantic was motionless as a millpond before the big ship hit the berg. And besides, I'm working my trap lines. So hang tight and enjoy your paid vacation. I'll be in touch."

And he was gone.

The days blended together, lazy hot. In the morning cool he'd tuck a magazine into the AR and run the trails around the lake, then finish up with a swim and shower. In the afternoons he put himself through intense interval sets on the free weights in a corner of the basement. He skipped rope. He shadowboxed. He set up targets at 200, 300, and 400 yards down the lakeshore and burned a few rounds to check the zero on the scoped Remington.

Once he woke up at three in the morning with vivid images throbbing behind his eyes and literal sensations burning in his hands, of digging Jesse Kraig from the charnel pit of her helicopter cockpit. Unable to sleep, he'd made a pot of coffee and sat out in the dark firing up cigarette after cigarette with the dead Mexican's lighter.

Restless, he explored the house. Puttering in an upstairs bedroom closet, he'd discovered a battered, peeling steamer trunk. Inside he found a bundle wrapped in oilcloth that contained three ancient books and two mildewed picture frames. The books were a King James Bible, an edition of Shakespeare's plays, and a ragged copy of *Moby Dick*. One of the frames showcased a darkish, wet plate photo circa 1875, according to the date scrawled in ink in the corner. It portrayed a bearded man with hooded eyes standing stiffly next to a cramped homestead cabin. The small lake in the background was clearly the body of water the current house was sited on.

Preserved under glass in the second frame he found an abbreviated, typed history of the original squatter who homesteaded this location. Jeremiah Moffet had served with the Wisconsin Regiment of the Iron Brigade until a Minié ball took his vocal cords the first day at Gettysburg. Hence the local name: Dummy Lake. Moffet lived out his days a recluse, with only the three books for companionship. A sentence was devoted to the Melville, noting that it had been published in 1851 and that Moffet had carried it in his pack the first two years of the war. Intrigued, Davis opened the musty cover and traced his fingers over translucent pages that were smudged with dirt and soot and gnawed by sparks.

Peering into the opaque depths of Moffet's Gettysburg stare, Davis tried to imagine the man as a youth reading this very book, his lips moving by campfire light, as he drifted ever closer, not unlike the doomed crew of the *Pequod* on their ocean, to the big fight in Pennsylvania.

Which brought him to the current drift of his own life. He'd looked up into the bright summer sky and followed a hawk that floated on the thermals high above the lake. The hawk was not sightseeing. The hawk had one relentless forward gear and two ten-power scopes for eyes. As he tracked the gliding hawk, Davis mused, *Quo vadis, Buddy? What do you see waiting for me over the next hill? Where am I headed?*

And a cool premonition had insinuated in the warm afternoon air, and then, icy as a finger bone, it scratched the certain knowledge on his heart: *There are no old, tame hawks.*

CHAPTER FORTY-FIVE

Morgon wheels his 4Runner off the small Ford dealership at the north end of Lakeside, where he's just put money down and signed a purchase agreement on a new Expedition EL with all the trimmings. Buy local. There's no sense driving an import in this Michigan economy when he's about to matriculate into the Rivard County Sheriff's Department.

His next stop is a block off Main Street at the office of Danny Larsen, the architect who produced the riverfront sketch that hangs on Amanda's office wall. Danny gets up from his drafting table when he sees Morgon come through the door.

"Rattle the pots and pans. Amanda's decided to throw John a party," Morgon calls out, shaking Danny's hand. "Last hurrah kind of thing. He's been called to testify at a Senate committee, and when he returns, we want to give him a send-up. Be nice if we could reveal the riverfront project as a surprise. Can you pull out the stops and speed up work on the model?"

Danny takes Morgon into the office's back room, where a cardboard three-dimensional scale model is in progress. Over coffee, they spend half an hour discussing the proposed renovation of the empty Rivard Lumber Mill that overlooks the lakeside harbor. Amanda had been impressed when Morgon proposed rehabilitating the old post-and-beam structure into an airy galleria. Her interest increased when he suggested filling the building with boutiques, a dance studio, and an art gallery featuring summer artists. Morgon envisioned the mill connecting via a boardwalk to another Rivard Foundation property at the other end of the harbor—the former steamship line office. Morgon thought that the brick office would convert nicely into a restaurant.

After leaving the architect's office, Morgon drives down to the actual waterfront and parks next to the steamship office. He gets out, walks over, and sits on the office steps to have a cigarette. Only two sailboats are moored inside the breakwater, and the entire waterfront has the shabby feel of a deserted warehouse district. Most people shop and play at a strip of box stores a mile down the highway. Morgon envisions a carousel along the boardwalk, maybe some popcorn kiosks. Why not make it a friendly space for people to bring their kids? As long as he's on the general subject, he tries to picture Amanda as wife and mother. Just as he's considering the interesting prospect of being author of, and witness to, a happy childhood, his phone buzzes in his pocket. He brings it out, selects the message, and sees Brian Cawker's number at the top of the queue. The encrypted message cuts his fantasy to ribbons: "You know a master sergeant Samuel Dillon from the North Dakota National Guard?" *DILLON. Etched black camo letters on a tunic over master jump wings and a combat infantry badge with three stars. Balad. The hospital room. The old sergeant.*

Morgon taps the slideshow function, and up pops a photo of a weather-worn face off a military ID, and Morgon almost drops the cigarette from his fingers in a shiver of confirming recognition. He hits the call icon and keeps his voice steady despite his accelerated heartbeat. "Don't know him. Saw him once."

"Well, he's interested in getting to know you."

"Tell me," Morgon says tightly, between puffs on his cigarette.

"I got into that office we talked about, the one in the big city. Didn't find anything on Davis. But there was an envelope in the desk that contained a brief note and a thumb drive. The letter was postmarked from LZ Anaconda, military APO return address from a chaplain Kurt Lundquist . . ."

"Who's he?"

"Doesn't matter; it's disinformation. The anonymous note asks the nosey Pentagon colonel for a favor, to run a facial ID check off a photo grab on the thumb drive, to match it against military files going back ten years. I suspect these guys are in the game because there's a hint of inside baseball; the anonymous sender requests that a response be sent to a home address otherwise not mentioned."

"And?"

"We had our techies run diagnostics on the thumb drive the same night we found it. It's a frame from a security camera in the hospital on the Balad base recorded at 3:27 p.m. local time on the afternoon of April 12th. It's a shot of you looking a bit worse for wear, mate."

Morgon exhales audibly.

"Bad news?"

"Probably. Good catch."

"Like I said, I run out the slippery grounders; habit my old dad taught me. The rest was easy. We copied the drive and put it all back in the desk. Then I had some mates make some inquires at Balad. They found the contractor who was on duty that night minding the cameras. Friendly fellow, used to be a cop in South Carolina. He recalled this older master sergeant coming in who wanted to view some tapes from April 12th. Said it concerned some nickel-and-dime black-market bullshit in his unit. He didn't remember the sergeant's name, but he did remember he was with a North Dakota Guard helo unit and had been an investigator with the Grand Forks County Sheriff's Department." Cawker clears his throat. "And, ah, my guys made the tape go away, and they only found one senior NCO in Guard choppers at Balad who was a Grand Forks cop."

"You get a location on him?"

"They packed him back home to Grand Forks; apparently Dillon exceeded his shelf life—over sixty, too old for active duty."

"You get an address?"

"I did."

"You up to moonlight on the side?"

"I can do that."

"You ever snoop a hard target in Grand Forks, North Dakota?"

"Can't be worse than Alice Springs in July."

"I want to know what's under Dillon's fingernails and what's on his computer, like if he dug up anything on me. If so, this could get ugly."

Without hesitation, Cawker answers, "Understood."

Amanda finds Morgon in the carriage house inspecting the suit he purchased for the Washington trip. Always a thrifty man, he insisted on finding a bargain, which involved driving almost to Detroit, to the Neiman Marcus Last Call Clearance Center in Auburn Hills to get the Brioni. Amanda thinks the olive color in the weave complements his eyes. Twenty-eight hundred bucks and change, off the rack.

"How'd it go in town?" she asks.

"Made stops at the car place, Danny's office."

"You might think of joining the VFW."

"Okay. What else?"

"Sit in with me and the accountant. We may have to switch foundation status from private endowment to pass-through next year, to justify appropriating the initial start-up and construction costs for the lakefront."

Morgon raises his hands in surrender. "Mercy."

Amanda smiles. "We'll wait on that."

★ ★ ★

While Brian Cawker travels west to Grand Forks, Morgon flies east on an Agency Lear Jet outfitted with a lift ramp to accommodate John's wheelchair. A waiting limo ushers them to their hotel.

Getting dressed before dinner, Amanda chides him, "C'mon, Morg. Quit lollygagging." She's putting finishing touches on her hair.

"Lollygagging," he repeats, savoring the word.

"We're late," she says as she draws a light shawl around her bare shoulders. Her dress is understated but clingy, with just two slender spaghetti straps over her collarbones. Behind her, out the sliding door leading to the balcony, the lights of Washington, DC are just twinkling on.

"Look at us," Morgon says.

"What?"

"Come on over here. Give me a kiss," he beckons.

Amanda adds a coquettish sway to her hips as she crosses the room, goes up on her toes, and busses his lips.

"A real kiss," he says.

Her cool fingers ease up around the back of his neck. "You mean like this?" she says.

Dinner happens in a DC restaurant on Marker Square North with a string quartet playing in the corner and linen napkins folded like origami. Now the dishes have been cleared away and, across the table, John leans forward in his wheelchair and gabs with two old associates who are moderately in their cups. Kelly, silent and watchful in a charcoal suit, with his dark hair combed back in a sleek ponytail, sits at John's elbow and restricts him to one lightly watered whiskey. It's a pirates' reunion. They sound like they're playing Yalta, like they're dividing up the world.

Morgon and Amanda excuse themselves, leave John in Kelly's care, and take a cab back to the hotel and wind up in the bed.

"At some point this teenaged sex thing has to taper off," Amanda muses as she leans back, draped in a sheet, against the balcony railing on the sixth floor of the Westin Hotel. Morgon, stretched out on the bed, fancies that her exposed skin shimmers milky pale as the monuments he can see swelling up from a carpet of city lights in the distance. She could probably pose in one of those sculptures. Not Liberty or Freedom or Charity. More like a nymph in the background. He picks his memory for an appropriate minor goddess and decides on Tyche Fortuna, the patron of gamblers and mercenaries.

"Are you listening to me?" she calls out with feigned pique.

"Every word," he answers with an easy smile. In fact, he is thinking about Cawker, whom he has set in motion purely on his own authority.

The next morning is free, so they split up. Amanda checks some shops in Georgetown, and Morgon decides to look over the capital. No gun, no eyes in the back of his head; just another tourist.

It's warm, summery, a break in the heat. People promenade in shorts and sunglasses. He queues up and follows a group of sightseers into the Capitol Building. Inside, it's nonstop marble, and he puts a crook in his neck looking up to study the frescos on the rotunda dome. An informational handout informs him he's viewing *The Apotheosis of Washington*: Father George rising to heaven surrounded by a harem of liberty ladies.

Afternoon is showtime, so Morgon gets back in the new suit but opts for open collar and skips the confining tie. They rendezvous in the hotel lobby. Kelly smoothly maneuvers John and his wheelchair in and out of the limousine. At the Senate Office Building, Kelly ably negotiates the ramps and elevators and pushes John down a hall to the hearing room.

Kelly parks John's wheelchair at a table dressed with a green baize cloth, where he makes small talk with a gaggle of similarly aged, stooped mandarins of a departed era. The senators and their staffs file in and sit behind a raised, curved dais. A gavel bangs. The spectators quiet down and take their seats.

"The committee will come to order." The chairman peers over his glasses. He's a gruff Michigan senator who looks like the tough uncle everyone wishes they had in a pinch. "Will the panel members rise and raise their right hands to be sworn. Mr. Rivard, you may remain seated."

But John, with Kelly's assistance, presses both his gnarled hands down on his cane, and as he slowly rises to his feet and lifts his right hand, a hush settles over the chamber.

Amanda smiles and nudges Morgon's pant leg with her knee, and when their eyes meet, they agree they are easily the best-looking couple in this stuffy room. At that moment, when their foreheads are close together, Morgon can't help but notice that Amanda's gaze is rinsed clean of nervous glitter and, in the absence of medication, shines with what could only be happiness.

Just before John makes his statement, Morgon glances at his wristwatch. *Cawker should be in Grand Forks by now.* Then he composes himself and listens to John attribute the controversy that persists about the losses at Khost to an overreliance on drones and NSA intercepts complicated by armchair analysts who never stepped off the base or spoke the local language. At one point, he gestures with his reading glasses for emphasis and drops them. Morgon, sitting in the first row, quickly scoots forward, scoops up the spectacles, and hands them back.

CHAPTER FORTY-SIX

Sam Dillon has been keeping his electronic surfing low-profile, so he's using an Internet connection on a computer in the Grand Forks Public Library. He logs off and leans back, feeling vindicated. When he started down this path, in Iraq, it felt like he was tracking a herd of black cats in the dark. Now, with his Pentagon buddy's assistance, he's narrowed his search to one big cat, and his name is Morgon Jump.

A discreet visit to a friend at the North Dakota Bureau of Criminal Apprehension in Fargo put Jump in tighter focus. The state cop used his IRS connections to provide Jump's last 1040 form. Currently he's employed as a security consultant with the Rivard Family Foundation in Lakeside, Michigan. From his Pentagon contact, he's learned that Jump was previously CIA Special Activities Division by way of Fifth Special Forces. By the time Sam started Googling Rivard, he was not exactly surprised to learn that Rivard's bio included being a former director of covert operations Far East for the Agency. So Jump is a big cat working for an even bigger cat.

After chasing around on Rivard posts, he's just confirmed that Rivard testified yesterday at a special Senate hearing, and the hearing is archived on the C-SPAN website. What makes the hearing interesting is that Jump and Rivard appear briefly together, in the same camera shot.

He removes a photocopy of Jump's military ID card from a manila folder. It's the gift forwarded by his Pentagon friend. A frown creases his face. He'd made an extra copy on his home fax machine, and it's not in the folder. Quickly he runs a mental checklist. *Damn, Sam. You're getting old. You must have mislaid the other one in the study.* At the finish of this slug of research he'd promised himself a couple days downtime at Devil's Lake, eighty miles to the west on Highway 2. He's packed all the gear and has his boat out in the lot hitched behind his truck. But he can't leave that piece of paper lying around, so he'll have to go back and police it up before he leaves town. Then he smoothes out the blank space below the photocopy, thumbs the plunger on a ballpoint, and begins to write:

> *Jesse,*
>
> *Sorry to have taken so long to get back to you.*
>
> *I didn't want to mention what else I was looking into when I visited at the hospital because I was going on pure speculation. Now I have some hard information to back up my suspicions. The day you were shot down, this guy—see above—showed up in the holding ward at Balad, right at your bed. He was dressed like a troop, but he was all wrong. Can't say for sure, but I think me being there might have scared him off. After I talked to Colbert, I went back to the hospital and managed to pull the guy's picture off a security camera and ran some checks.*
>
> *Like the ID says, he was SF, then he worked for the CIA. For the last couple years he's been employed by a retired Agency honcho named John Rivard. Rivard runs this charity foundation in Lakeside, Michigan, that could be a convenient cover for all manner of rat fuckery. I can't connect Jump directly to what happened at Turmar, but maybe you can. I want you to watch this special Senate Foreign Relations Oversight Committee Hearing on CIA Field Operations. It was recorded on C-SPAN, July 23rd, and is available online. Pay attention to Rivard's testimony, because Jump will briefly be on-screen. Be thinking of those star doodles you drew all over your notebook. Maybe you knew all along?*
>
> *After you view the hearing, write me what you think, at my home address. Let's play dumb a while longer with phones and e-mail.*

*If you can ID this prick as being at the crash site, I have a
friend in CID at the Pentagon you can talk to for starters.*
   Good Luck,
   Be in touch soon,
   Sam

Sam grimaces and flexes his cramped hand; his damn ar-
thritis is acting up from the mere act of handling a pen. Then he
folds the sheet and puts it in a stamped envelope, which he addresses to Jesse C/O the 4J Polytrauma Ward at the Minneapolis
VA Hospital. He leaves the library and, on the way to the parking lot, drops the letter in a mailbox.

Totally relaxed, Brian Cawker pedals a bike down Seward
Avenue in a quiet residential neighborhood just south of River-
side Park, a green zone that meanders along the banks of the
Red River that divides Grand Forks, North Dakota, from East
Grand Forks on the Minnesota side. A blazing prairie late afternoon dims toward twilight, and people flock to the illusion of
coolness, jogging or riding bikes. In running shoes, shorts, a
tank top, and a Twins cap, Cawker blends in. He "borrowed"
the untended and unlocked bicycle earlier from the campus of
the University of North Dakota a few miles to the west.

He's traveling "cold"; he's unarmed and left his ID back at
the motel. If this truly gets ugly and he winds up having his
rights read by some hick cop, his only hope is Morgon pulling
out a Homeland Security get-out-of-jail-free card.

But he puts these thoughts from his mind as he circles the
block a second time and glides past well-maintained houses
and lawns dappled at this hour in fuzzy shade from mature
elms, oaks, and an occasional towering cottonwood. His target
is a neat stucco bungalow with a garage back that's in the
middle of the block nestled between tall lilac hedges. He turns

and coasts into the alley. The thick hedges are a stroke of luck. They fence in the rear yard and screen access from the alley.

Last night, after he drove up from Minneapolis International Airport in a rental Saturn, he made his first drive-by of Sam Dillon's home. Then he grabbed a Motel 6 room near the university. Later in the evening he made a second reconnaissance on foot. After the lights and TV went off in the house, he trolled down the alley. After checking the garage that contained a Ford F-150 and a trailer holding a fiberglass johnboat, he entered Dillon's small backyard and crept under the wall of lilacs. Gingerly he approached the kitchen windows and, by a light above the stove, observed no sign of a food or water container. So no dog. And no sign of a security system. Cautiously he hunkered to a basement window.

The travel brochures advertise Grand Forks as a great place to raise kids, with virtually no crime. So the first window he approached had no storm window, and the screen panel unlatched with an easy shove. And that would be his way in.

Now, slowing the bike, he acknowledges that usually this kind of job would involve a surveillance van, a street crew, and a backup tech network to monitor Dillon's phones and electronics—a commitment easily within the reach of Roger Torres' ASTECH resources. But he doesn't have time to track Dillon's local travel pattern or his connections. Morgon needs this to happen fast and dirty and invisible. So Roger is out of the loop. And he's very mindful that tonight's work amounts to an audition. Rivard has stepped down, and Morgon is moving up. That leaves the action arm for the mythic Office of Perfect Crimes an open position. And, on this warm early evening, Cawker is making his bid.

He dismounts the bike just past the garage and peeks in the window. There's enough light to see that the truck and trailer are absent. And the house windows are dark. He walks the bike into the shrubbery, out of sight, and pauses to listen to the muted sounds from the surrounding backyards—the hissing of a sprinkler, children's voices. It's just another peaceful early evening in Grand Forks.

Go.

He pulls on a pair of nylon gloves, then slips an extra-large pair of light nylon socks over his shoes. Hugging the lilacs, he cautiously approaches the basement window, pushes back the screen, and rolls in.

Crouching, he takes a moment to listen and acclimate his eyes. The only sound in the cool basement is the furnace fan circulating air. A night-light in a wall socket reveals cheap pine paneling, linoleum, furniture covered by sheets, and a small pool table. After clicking on a pencil flashlight, he goes up the stairs for a fast walk-through. Dillon's living space is part ship-shape barracks, part faintly musty museum. The living room and dining room appear unused, even preserved; china and knickknacks peer down from shelves like spotless statues. The same atmosphere prevails in the master bedroom, where the king-sized bed and sterile dressers could be a furniture display room. A single framed photograph sitting on the bare bureau top at the foot of the bed suggests an explanation. In a beach scene set against a moody vacation sky, a striking, dark-haired woman wearing cutoff shorts and a halter is captured in a moment of middle-aged vitality, smiling at the camera. Inserted in the picture frame a memorial card shows the same smiling face: Anna Grace Dillon, 1954–2010.

A spare bedroom across the hall has a double bed that looks lived in; a thumbed copy of *Guns and Ammo* rests beside the reading lamp, and underwear and socks wait to be washed in a plastic basket in the corner. Cawker sifts through the clothes in the closet and pauses to peruse an army dress uniform with combat badges and eight rows of ribbons. Then he moves to the dresser drawers without finding anything unusual. But when he slips his hand under the mattress, his fingers touch cold metal, and he withdraws a Colt .45. A quick check reveals that the handgun is locked but not loaded. Some ex-cops are control freaks, up to their asses in trigger locks and gun safes. And some are laid-back. The aging Dillon must be of the laid-back variety. He slides the gun back into its hiding place. A moment later, inspecting the hall closet, he finds the inevitable gun safe tucked behind the hangers.

The tidy kitchen cupboards offer nothing, but off the kitchen, a four-seasons porch is converted into a home office with a computer desk, printer, phone, and fax. When he taps the space bar, the screen saver pops up, so he selects the e-mail icon and reviews all the traffic coming and going for the last two weeks. Nothing but routine immediate-family stuff; e-mails from a daughter contain pictures of a granddaughter. The rest is the kind of raucous right-wing jokes you'd expect ex–law enforcement/ex-military to exchange for laughs. Then he trolls through the computer history. Again nothing. Dillon favors fishing sites, and that's about all. Only after he searches every drawer, every cranny, every book on every shelf does he spot the sheet of paper laying in the fax tray. In plain sight. He flips it over and puts his flash on a copy of Sergeant First Class Morgon Jump's Special Forces ID.

Immediately he takes his cell from his pocket, taps in a predial setting, and hopes the encrypted software is as good as advertised. Morgon answers on the second ring.

"It's ugly. He has your face off an old army ID. The rest of the place is clean. So what's the play?"

Morgon answers calmly, "I'm thinking this guy is not going to cooperate or be turned by money, and no way he goes gentle into a capture situation. A whole operation is riding on this, so you have to make him go away. If we have to, we'll backfill with his Pentagon contact in DC. So be creative . . ."

Cawker pauses to read between the lines. "Got it."

Morgon, standing behind his Expedition in the driveway beneath the carriage house lights, slips his phone back in his pocket and savors his first executive decision. As he reaches into the cargo compartment to remove his suitcase, Amanda comes around from the passenger side and cocks her head.

"Roger," Morgon shrugs. "Just some leftover housekeeping."

Cawker puts his phone away and takes a moment to center down. It's not his call and way above his pay grade; the people behind Morgon, for politically sensitive reasons emanating from the mission in Iraq, have relegated Sam Dillon to the wrong side of the Old Fickle Fuckin' Inshallah Factor. *Don't overthink it, mate. Go to work.*

Immediately Cawker folds the photocopy of Morgon's ID and slips it in his pocket. Then he goes to the spare bedroom and retrieves the Colt and sticks it in his waistband. Practical, he goes to the kitchen and checks the refrigerator to see what's on hand to eat. No telling how long he'll be here waiting for Dillon to return. He's eyeing a plastic deli container of meatballs when he learns that he won't be waiting that long.

First he hears the truck pull up to the front curb. He flips off the flashlight, and by the time the truck door slams, he's at the front door watching through the peephole as Sam Dillon walks up the sidewalk. The Colt is out. A slow metal clash sounds as a round jacks into the chamber. His eye never moves from the peephole. In the porch light the lean, hangdog-faced Dillon, at sixty, looks like he can still trade body blows and barely break a sweat. The house key comes out. Right-handed. Cawker exhales; he's got maybe four seconds. Then he squints in the spill light off the porch coming through the living room curtains. There's this heart-shaped pillow on the couch, the embroidered letters barely discernible, but he makes it out: *Anna Grace.* All speed and stealth, and past mere thinking, he crosses the room, seizes the pillow, and darts back to behind the door as the key turns in the lock.

Cawker has never been through the US Army's Survival School to be tested for resilience. So he's never paid much attention to the research about Special Forces types, like Morgon, who produce highly elevated levels of neuropeptide Y. NPY is an amino acid that, among other things, your brain employs to quash fear and keep you thinking clearly when people around you are paralyzed by stress.

Freud joked that the Irish were immune to psychoanalysis. Cawker accepts as his birthright that Australians have the same unfussy response to fear.

Sam Dillon steps through the door into his darkened house and Cawker kicks the door shut and then, feet perfectly planted, slams the pillow into Sam's face, smothering his startled cry. Almost simultaneously he hammers the butt of the Colt into the center of the pillow with tremendous force. Sam staggers back, knees buckling, flailing his hands up defensively. Cawker follows him down, left hand maintaining heavy pressure on the pillow. Keeping control of the trigger, he jams the butt of the Colt into Sam's groping right palm. The semiconscious man's fingers seize, explore, struggle as Cawker's sturdy, iron-bending fingers close over Sam's weaker grip. Now Cawker has pinned Sam's right arm between his knees—firmly but not overly so—and, using his knees as fulcrum, he leverages the pistol up and mashes the muzzle into the pillow that gags Sam's face. For a second Sam attempts a feeble rally, to steer the weapon away, but Cawker, grunting with the effort, plunges the barrel deep into the pillow, overcomes the resistance of Sam's frantic right hand, and presses the trigger.

Sam's body jerks rigid with the impact and then slumps back against the wall. Cordite sequins sparkle briefly in the close air, splattered bits of skull and brains dot the door along with skeins of burned thread and pillow stuffing. The shot was muffled—no louder than a car backfiring down the block—but Cawker stays crouched over his kill for several seconds, listening, as his heartbeat returns to normal. Then, slowly, he releases his grip on Dillon's limp hand and lets it fall, fingers uncurling around the pistol. The hand flops into the dead man's lap, and his shattered face effects a slightly tarred-and-feathered aspect, bearded in bloody tufts of the ruptured cushion.

Cawker presses the still-twitching index finger into the trigger guard and stands up to study the scene. The corpse is attired in faded jeans, an ancient gray T-shirt with an Air Cav patch, and tennis shoes. Cawker inspects the right arm and hand for signs of bruising or swelling and sees none. He spends a moment evaluating the angle of the entry wound just below the nose. The extensive soft-tissue and bone damage effectively disguises any evidence of a stunning blow to the face, and the shot angle is consistent with a self-inflicted wound administered by a right-handed man. The expended cartridge casing lies on the carpet. A forensic team will find gunshot residue on Sam Dillon's fingers. And something else. Cawker gets up, pads down the hall to the master bedroom, and returns carrying the framed photo of Anna Grace Dillon with the memorial card insert. He leans over and places the framed photo at Dillon's feet.

Five minutes later, pedaling his stolen bike through the dark, headed back to his motel, he recalls reading that an American veteran commits suicide every eighty minutes.

CHAPTER FORTY-SEVEN

Late afternoon, after taking some sign-off tests in speech therapy, Jesse's back in her room during a free period before lunch. The Post-It notes have long vanished from the walls and doorway to the bathroom. She plugs in her iPod headset and flicks on "Not Ready to Make Nice" by the Dixie Chicks. Then she takes a seat cross-legged on the floor and starts paging through her childish notebook. Exploring the scribbles and the clumsy words is like backtracking a staggering zombie. No brain damage. Slight concussion. Trauma, sure. It had to be the damn drugs.

At first, her ventures into memory retrieval were like sinking into murky water to locate debris, not unlike the video last summer as British Petroleum fumbled to repair its busted pipe in the Gulf—sending robotic submersibles down into the dark, where the pressure is a thousand pounds per square inch.

Then . . .

Huh? She looks up and sees Tony leaning over, shaking her arm. She removes the headset as he nods toward the hall. "Call at the desk from your mom; you didn't answer your cell."

A moment later she takes the phone the nurse hands over the desk. "Mom, it's me. What's up?"

Tony watches the blood drain from Jesse's face as she drops the receiver. He steps in, deftly catches the phone, raises it, and says, "Captain Kraig will call you back directly. She needs a minute." Then he turns to Jesse.

"Sam—the old sergeant who was my crew chief, who came to visit—he's dead," she whispers.

After composing herself, she calls her mother back to get the sketchy details. Then she goes to the computer station and brings up the front page of this morning's *Grand Forks Herald*. It reads: *Retired Grand Forks deputy Samuel Dillon was found in his Seward Avenue home last night by his daughter. Unconfirmed sources close to the sheriff's office speculated the death appeared to be self-inflicted. A picture of Dillon's wife, who succumbed to cancer last year, was found at his feet.*

Jesse walks aimlessly. Tony shadows her as she wanders down the stairs, and when the stairs end, she comes out in the basement corridor. Most of the people she passes are older patients, a lot of big bellies stretching the flags and eagles on their T-shirts. She blinks and stares and then focuses her gaze at a phone on the wall. A panel on the phone offers the helpful tip: LOST? CALL 2025.

Never really thought about it. Didn't even take all the army lectures seriously. Now she contemplates the black vacuum that is really all the way off the map. *Momentary depression? All-consuming world-weary melancholy? Sam could be cranky but dark?*

No memory problems now. This one night over the desert, flying with a Kiowa escort, the crews got into an '80s sing-along to break the tedium: Culture Club, daring the Iraqi night with joking lyrics about people who want to hurt you and make you cry. And Sam bitching on the comms: *Anybody know any Hank Williams?*

Just before the tears start, Tony is there. "You want to go upstairs? Janet cleared her schedule."

Janet sits and listens quietly. Her drawn facial expression suggests she is in the presence of her profession's most hated enemy as Jesse emits a sardonic laugh. "You pick up the phone to call the VA, and the first thing the recording says is, 'If you're thinking of harming yourself, call 911.'" She shrugs. "My mom told me that. I didn't know ..."

Janet passes a card with her cell phone number. "Anything. Later tonight? If you want to talk?"

Jesse accepts the card and scrutinizes the type: *Psychological Assessment. Psychotherapy. Consultation. Forensic Evaluation.* An enervating wave beats down her thoughts, like a black wind in the wheat. "Something I never told you. Maybe should have. That day we went down? Sam was scheduled to fly crew chief. Marge subbed in for him . . ."

Jesse shakes it off, stands up, and squares her shoulders. "I'll be okay." She turns and leaves the room. The sadness is palpable on Janet's face when she sees that Jesse left her card behind on the desk.

★ ★ ★

Workout. Work it out.

The next day Jesse stays in her room and skips her appointments. Dripping sweat, she picks up the kettle bell for the third muscle-burning circuit and takes a stance, feet spread, with the weight hanging in her hands between her knees. She starts by hiking the bell back, two-handed, between her legs. Deep squat, piston the legs straight and thrust with the hips on the upswing and fix on the point where the kettle bell reaches its apex at about her bra line. The bell comes up, hangs briefly on the momentum, and, as it starts to swing down, Tony walks in. He holds up his hand. It's an envelope, a letter.

Boom!

The kettle bell crashes to the linoleum floor like a thirty-five-pound cannonball—which it basically is. The flash of recognition is instant when she sees the return address in angular printing she remembers from army paperwork. *Sam Dillon, Seward Ave. Grand Forks.*

"You want me to stay?" Tony asks.

"No, I have to do this alone." She wipes sweat from her palms on a towel, casts the towel aside, and opens the letter.

If you can ID this prick . . .

Half an hour later, with Sam's words echoing behind the cold fury in her eyes, Jesse stalks to the computer station, opens Sam's letter, and puts it beside the keyboard. Then she brings up the net, selects the C-SPAN website, and finds the hearing Sam mentioned right on the front page. She starts the video, and the usual C-SPAN–type picture fills the screen like paint drying. Old guys sit at a green table in front of an audience. Steampunk wallpaper and draperies. Boring. Droning testimony.

Then . . .

An elderly man sits in a wheelchair at the witness table. Another man comes off his chair in the first row of chairs behind the wheelchair. He stoops, picks something up, and hands a pair of glasses to the old man. This man is lean, ruggedly handsome, with short-cropped reddish hair. Jesse's eyes drop to the ID card reproduced at the top of Sam's letter. Same guy in a nice suit but no tie. Casual. As he bends forward, the camera happens to zoom in, and Jesse sees the small star-shaped scar peek from his open collar, on the right side of his neck . . .

Our father Red Screen of Death motherfucker!

Two months of scrawled stars burst out of storage and fall in a shower that ignites a meteor storm. *That's what Sam meant. I saw you washing off the dirt, didn't see all your face because it was turned away. But I saw the fucking scar!*

Crazy.

No, I'm not.

That's the sonofabitch who killed Marge and probably Toby! Christ, and what about Sam?

That's where it gets crazy . . .

Janet's voice comes back, dismissive, saying, "So now it's spooks?" *Can't take this to her; she already thinks I'm nuts.*

Gotta do this on my own.

She hunches back to the computer and Googles John Rivard and reads that he's a former intelligence bigwig who, along with Brent Snowcroft, had been an early critic of the Iraq invasion. Yeah, yeah...

What I need is to confirm his location. Sam's letter mentioned Michigan.

Then she finds a YouTube promo for a TV interview and views the taped segment with Rivard by WPBN, an NBC affiliate in Traverse City, Michigan, that was recorded July 18th. *That's last week.*

The reporter stands beside Rivard, who sits in a wheelchair with a flat gray horizon line in the background. The reporter mentions he is talking to Rivard at his home in Lakeside, Michigan, about his upcoming Senate testimony.

Bingo.

But just as quickly, the tsunami of doubt is back, slamming her, and it's like the whole weight of the hospital, this government labyrinth stacked with credentialed health providers, not to mention cops with guns, is pressing down on her. Watching her even. She glances around nervously. No phones, no e-mails, Sam said. *Shit.* Immediately she deletes her search history from the computer.

You're reaching, Jesse. What Janet would call "spiraling out."

Am not.

Crazy.

Am not. Gonna look this fucker in the eye!

And she knows she's going to go for it.

CHAPTER FORTY-EIGHT

In the morning Jesse eats a hearty breakfast to fuel up. Then she sits in the flag atrium and takes an inventory of her resources. When she deployed, she set up a direct-deposit schedule with her bank in Grand Forks. Figuring she wouldn't need a lot of spare change in the Sandbox, she put 90 percent of her pay in a CD that's locked for a year. So cash on hand until her next payday is eighty-seven dollars. Worse, her Visa card is maxed and has an available balance of 196 dollars. Enough to eat on and buy gas maybe, but not enough for a rental car.

How serious are you?

Serious.

How serious?

Steal-a-car serious.

Just before lunch she drops by Janet's office when she probably doesn't have a client. She knocks.

"Yeah, who is it?"

"Me," Jesse says, entering the room. She hooks her thumbs in her sweatpants waistband and sort of cants her hips in a hem-haw gesture. "I just wanted to say I mean to talk to you about . . . stuff. But I'm not there yet."

"Sure. Take your time," Janet says, leaning back in her chair.

"Well . . ." Jesse drops her eye to the carpet briefly, then she looks up and points to the tall bookcase in back of the desk. "You have *Blackhawk Down*; I never got around to reading that. I saw the movie—all except the crash parts."

"Take it."

Jesse comes around the desk and fingers the book from the shelf. As she opens it and browses the opening pages, she watches Janet open the left bottom desk drawer and dig in her purse. She removes her wallet, then shoves the drawer closed.

But does not lock it.

"Thanks," Jesse says, holding up the book. On the way out, she asks the receptionist what Janet's schedule is tomorrow morning.

"There's a staff meeting at nine, then she's booked until, lessee, 2:30," the receptionist says, looking up from a schedule.

"Nah, thanks; I got rehab for my knee at two."

Back at the computer, Jesse prints highway maps of Minnesota, Wisconsin, and Michigan. She locates Lakeside, up on the western shore of Lake Huron, and considers a route. Interstate 94 cuts across Wisconsin, then angles down around Chicago into a tangle of interstate and toll roads. Then you have to drive up the whole length of Michigan. *Gotta be a better way.* So she works out a quieter route: Highway 8 across Wisconsin into Michigan's Upper Peninsula, then over the Mackinac Bridge and straight down into the Mitten State.

At five p.m. she shadows Janet as she leaves the second floor, exits the building, and walks to the staff parking lot. From the cover of a hedge, she sees Janet get into a blue Subaru Forester and can't help but grin. Minnesota's a blue state, right. Her dad always said that Foresters were the SUV of choice for the "Olympic lesbian ski team."

The FedEx van pulls away down the driveway to the Rivard estate as Morgon opens the just-delivered mailer. It has the return address of a men's clothing store located on the concourse of the Minneapolis International Airport. Inside he finds a red handkerchief monogrammed with the letters MJ. Tucked inside the hanky is the front page of the Grand Forks newspaper, which displays the story of Sam Dillon's death above the fold: . . . *probably suicide, according to an unconfirmed source in the sheriff's department.*

Morgon crumples the newsprint and allows a smile. Cawker's light, even elegant, touch isn't lost on him. He's good and he's applying for a job and he comes with his own crew of ex-SAS boys—a package deal. Morgon sticks the hanky in his pocket and then takes out his lighter and ignites the crushed ball of paper. As he watches it burn to ash on the driveway, he surmises there will be rumors in the wake of Dillon's death. But rumors don't generate retaliation in the form of, say, oversight subpoenas. For that you need a witness.

And like every *Sopranos/Godfather* groupie knows, without no witness, you ain't got no crime.

CHAPTER FORTY-NINE

In the morning Jesse bolts a fast breakfast, puts on her sweatsuit and her running shoes, and signs out for the exercise room. She has her wallet, cell phone, and a pair of shorts and her flip-flops in her fanny pack. The copy of *Blackhawk Down* is tucked under her arm as she enters the psychology suite at five minutes to nine. She lingers in the hall until she sees Janet come out of her office. She's carrying a laptop. No purse.

"Hey, thanks," Jesse says, holding out the book.

Janet, chatting with a colleague, one hand on the doorknob to the office door, just nods. "Drop it on my desk . . ."

Jesse goes into the office and tosses the book down on the desk with a loud *smack* to cover opening—yes—the bottom left drawer. Then she leans toward the bookcase, fingering the car keys from the purse, and quickly strips off the Subaru key as she calls to Janet, who stands half-hidden by the ajar door. "Hey. You've got *Chickenhawk* by Robert Mason. It's the first real helicopter book. Can I barrow it?"

"Sure. C'mon, Jesse. I'm late for a meeting," Janet says, getting impatient.

Jesse hurries back into the hall and holds up the new book. "Thanks," she says to Janet, who pulls the door shut and makes sure it clicks.

One last thing to do. Can't take a chance of being caught with Sam's letter. Back on the ward, she enters the patients' lounge, goes to the bookcase, and selects an ancient copy of James Joyce's *Ulysses. No one is ever gonna read that, not in here.* She inserts Sam's letter deep between the pages for safekeeping and slides the book back onto the shelf. Anything goes wrong, last resort, she can always call Janet.

Twenty minutes later she's in Janet's car expanding her horizons to include grand theft auto. Thankfully it's an automatic. Less things to think about while driving. Onward. With hula boy taped to the dash and her maps spread on the passenger seat, she sweats through the tangle of unfamiliar ramps and exits east of the Minneapolis–St. Paul International Airport. She finds a St. Paul exit, then takes Sheppard Road along the Mississippi and finds her way past the city to Interstate 94 and heads east into Wisconsin. Checks the map. At Hammond, she'll turn north on Highway 63 and take it to Highway 8, then turn right and ride it straight to upper Michigan.

After the turn on Highway 8, it's a straight shot east across Wisconsin, so Jesse puts aside her maps and tries to ease the tension in her hunched shoulders. *Relax*, she tells herself. *Breathe deep through your nose. For now, don't think, drive.*

The two-lane runs through rolling farmland that is reminiscent of home except the fields are cramped by tree lines, the sky somehow lower. She misses the horizon-to-horizon sweep of wheat, the summer oven perfume of yellow black-eyed Susans and lavender spiderwort and white yarrow and patches of bluestem scattered in the buffalo grass and a sky so freakin' big, how could a kid not want to fly away into it?

Just when she gets her shoulders to halfway relax, the dark wind is back, flattening her thoughts: *What if Rivard's not home? What if Janet goes to check her car before end of business? What if Sam did lose it and eat his gun?*

The drowsy fields humming with cicadas close in, and suddenly she's lonely out here on her own hook. No tactical-op center, no mission commander; just a flash on a computer screen and Sam's letter to navigate by.

It's a hot day, and even with the air conditioner it's stuffy in the bulky sweatsuit. So she pulls off at a rest stop, goes into the women's room, and changes into her shorts, halter, and flip-flops. Back in the car, she takes a moment to ask herself, *What am I missing? What am I not thinking about?*

She stops at a Holiday station, fills the tank, and grabs a road atlas, some energy bars, and bottled water. Back on the road, getting toward twilight, and she's crossing the state line into the Upper Peninsula. Long past the time Janet gets off work now. She imagines the moment in the parking lot. The 911 call. When will the staff on 4J start looking for her? She's put Wisconsin between herself and Minnesota. How much time will that buy her?

She doesn't have a lot of wiggle room when it comes to escape and evasion, but she can do something. She's in scrub pine country, and the roadway is darkened with recent rain. So she pulls off on a gravel road and floors it, aiming for every mud puddle. After five minutes she stops and gets out to inspect the Forester's chassis that is now splattered with mud and splash, dulling the blue paint, obscuring the license plates. Then she pulls back on the highway.

Pitch black now, driving desolate Highway 2 across the empty UP. Disorientation sets in. She's blinking, having trouble seeing. Stuff going jittery at the edge of her vision. It takes a while, but she figures it out. It's *night*-night. She's used to *green* night. *Night-vision goggles* night. Adjusting is like wearing someone's prescription lenses, and she feels the strain tug at her eye muscles.

C'mon, you've never been afraid of the dark, even in Iraq. But then, you never were out in it alone, either. She dials down the window, reaches out, and lets her hand windsurf on the cool rush of night air. Bad idea. The darkness is a tangible touch of black Braille that spells out all the futility in the fucking world. *Is this what Sam felt? Marge dying in his place, sent home to an empty house to stare at pictures of his wife? Too old to do his job?*

And what about you? Talk about driving off the emotional map, an AWOL polytrauma patient trying to make an argument that the

271

CIA killed your crew? Now there's a 911 call for the books. With aching clarity she recalls the exact moment she yanked the controls to evade the second RPG. Left. If she would have turned toward the threat, maybe her crew would still be alive. Maybe. *Damn, it's lonely out here in the dark.*

Jesse shivers and withdraws her hand, closes the window, and concentrates on the center line. *Focus.* How many hours has she been driving? Twelve, maybe? Road sign: St. Ignace, 11 Miles. The Mackinaw Bridge coming up. *Want to cross that in the dark, then grab a motel on the other side and get an early start.*

After an uneasy night in a Mackinaw City Best Western and a buffet breakfast, Jesse is driving Highway 23 along the Huron shore. Cheboygan, Rogers City, and Alpena are behind her. She's getting close and getting jumpy from drinking too much road coffee, sitting up foolishly straight every time she passes a cop car. At one in the afternoon she drives into Lakeside, Michigan.

It's a run-down summer town, the kind of place where people with boats live. Some nice brick houses, but along the shore there's a deserted feel, like whatever was happening here moved on long ago.

She pulls into a convenience store and searches for John Rivard's listing in a local directory at the outside pay phone. There's a Rivard Family Foundation but no residence number. Must be unlisted. She takes a deep breath and enters the foundation number. No answer. She passes on the voice mail.

So she goes in the store and asks for directions. The clerk is an older, obliging, talkative woman. "Sure. The Rivard place. It's on the National Register, a big house north of town on the water. Sits on two hundred acres. But it's hard to find; trees block it off." Jesse gets directions on how to find the private drive, thanks the clerk, and leaves the store. The clerk cranes her neck to see the car Jesse is driving, then picks up the phone.

"Probably nothing," she says to the switchboard at the Rivard County Sheriff's Office, "but I just thought you might want to know. A young, kinda nervous blonde woman was just in here asking directions to the Rivard estate. Ah, she's wearing gray shorts and, ah, a white halter top, and flip-flops. Oh, yeah. And she's driving a muddy blue Forester with Minnesota plates. What with the big open house out there today—thing is —she had one of those hospital bracelets around her wrist, like patients wear . . ."

CHAPTER FIFTY

Morgon needs a break. All morning he's been supervising high school kids setting up banquet tables, shucking corn, and bringing in deliveries of ribs, chicken, and ingredients for tubs of coleslaw. Now the double-wide gas grill is fired up, the rental patio tables and their umbrellas have all been placed to Amanda's satisfaction, and the coolers are filled with ice for soda and beer. Danny Larsen is waiting down the access road with the architect's model hidden under a tarp on the snowmobile trailer behind his Ford F-250, awaiting Morgon's signal to bring it in and set it up. John sits on the porch, and his vital signs are holding steady since the Senate hearing. He sips a mild gin and tonic and appears to have no clue about Danny's surprise. Then Amanda briefly emerges from presiding over the packed kitchen to ask him to drive into town, go to the party store, and pick up the balloons. Halfway back, the helium balloons come untethered and fill his new SUV, and he drives the rest of the way home batting at bobbling colored bubbles. That's it. He needs a break.

Kelly, just as frazzled, readily accepts Morgon's offer to take a run and grab some relief before the people start arriving. Quickly they change into Nikes and shorts and hit the old logging road that winds through the woods along the shore.

"Get used to it," Kelly advises. "She likes to throw parties."

"Yeah, well, next time you go get the balloons."

They circle back, sprint the last two hundred yards to the house, and then walk it off to cool down. Morgon realizes they are circling each other, which is Kelly's way of inviting a go at sparring some mixed martial arts.

"What?" Morgon feigns disbelief. "You feeling lucky?"

Kelly crouches into a fighting stance. "Feeling guilty. Taking advantage of an old guy."

Morgon curls his fingers into his open palms in a "gimme gesture." "Bring it on, Facetube."

Kelly, who has two inches and twenty pounds on Morgon, is ten years younger, and has a longer reach, darts in, and they slap arms looking for a grappling opening. Morgon lets himself be thrown, hits the grass hard in an accelerated roll, pops up on top, and then slams his running shoe down on Kelly's long ponytail, effectively pinning him to the lawn.

"Check it out," he says. "Alexander the Great had the Macedonian army trim their long hair and cut off their beards so nobody could grab them in close combat, huh?"

As he extends his hand to help Kelly to his feet, they see Amanda putt up on the golf cart. She is less than amused. "I've been looking all over for you guys. Danny Larsen's been trying to find you. He wants to know where to put the display. And the first people are showing up." She points back toward the house. A low stand of junipers obscures the view, but several red and blue balloons are clearly visible, launching into the sky.

CHAPTER FIFTY-ONE

The country road is hemmed in by trees, and the turnoffs come up fast. On her second try, Jesse slows and finds the address on a bronze plaque fastened to a boulder next to a sign that spells out Private Drive. A batch of helium party balloons bobs in the breeze, anchored to the mailbox.

Okaay . . . She keeps going and spots another sign—Public Access Boat Ramp—and turns right on a gravel road about a quarter mile from the driveway. Dense woods on her right, a cemetery on the left. She pulls into tall grass between some trees, kills the motor, and gets out.

Her knees tremble and she blinks to get her bearings in a sudden lassitude of heat and summer sunlight. *Okay, Jess, now what?* The last twenty-four hours have been about getting here. Having reached her destination, she realizes that she hasn't exactly thought through what comes next. *Confront them. But how?*

So keep it simple. First, creep in and scope the layout. See if Rivard's there and if he has security.

Okay. Here goes.

She takes a second to orient herself and then slips into the shadows of tall oaks and finds a game trail that runs parallel to the shore. *Deer in here,* she thinks. Almost immediately she hears music that gets louder as she comes to the edge of the trees. Squatting in the grass just inside the tree line, she maps out the property. To her left the trees thin out along the beach and end in acres of tended lawn that could be a golf course. She looks past the imposing Victorian house, when her eyes snap on a familiar marker, a windsock eddying next to a silver blue-pin-striped helicopter in front of a hangar and a fuel blivet. Automatically she identifies the chopper as a 206L Long Ranger, the stretch version of the military Kiowa.

I trained on that airframe, she thinks.

Then, *Get serious, Jess.* She waves a hand to shoo bugs flitting in the humid, itchy grass and blinks away sweat and a frazzle of fatigue. *Come all this way to stall in the summer heat. Dizzy. Shoulda drank more water. Feels like dehydration.* She looks at her bare feet in the flip-flops. *Shoulda wore my tennies . . .*

A bigger problem is, there's a lawn party in progress in back of the house. *Get closer.* So she threads through the narrow strip of trees and foliage along the shore. The cover peters out, and now about a hundred yards of open lawn separate her from the house.

Wiping sweat from her face with her forearm, she studies people gathered around a dark-haired woman in a red apron who wields long-handled grilling tongs at a grill. More of them stand around some sort of display set up in front of the tables on sawhorses. Then she squints to make out the old man seated in a wheelchair at a table next to the grill. He wears a wide-brimmed straw hat. *That's him; that's Rivard.* No sign of the other guy, Jump. *No way you want to tangle with him just yet, but if you can catch the old guy alone . . .*

She scans the crowd. Security? Hard to tell with all the people. Some kids are setting up a volleyball net. A guy is throwing a stick for his dog to retrieve. Others toss a Frisbee. One of the Frisbee players, a tall, broad-shouldered guy in shorts and a ponytail, is hamming it up between throws, dancing to a sixties tune—"Proud Mary." She's figuring how to use the wood line to get closer to the house when she hears a crackle of brush behind her. Turning, she sees a police officer dressed in a tan-and-gray uniform stepping out of the deeper woods. He raises his hand, not exactly a greeting, and calls out, "Ma'am, could you hold it right there."

CHAPTER FIFTY-TWO

Morgon's in the kitchen brushing barbecue sauce on a plate of ribs as he goes down a mental checklist. *The county commissioners are here, along with people from the sheriff's office, the school board, and the chamber of commerce. Danny Larsen is presiding over his three-dimensional cardboard display, complete with a blue mirror representing the lake.* He's having an animated conversation with the Reverend James Tindsdale, the pastor of the Episcopal church. Morgon's role is to look useful and play it low-key and let Amanda feed him slowly into the buzz about the waterfront project.

Through the window over the sink he can see Amanda in a loose light-green cotton dress under her red apron. Barefoot in the grass, she's flipping racks of ribs and chicken on the grill. Smiling, she's making small talk with a fastidious slender gent who's out of uniform in a loud Hawaiian shirt and a rakish straw Panama hat. David Handsvale is a second-generation accountant who, like his father before him, oversees the Rivard Foundation finances. Amanda has the tender job of preparing him for the huge outlay the waterfront will require.

Like the accountant, John also wears a wide straw hat, but, seated in his wheelchair at a banquet table, he takes it off and uses it to fan his face.

People drift in, and the women bring hot dishes and salads. The men haul coolers. Some guests are starting to gather at the grill. Others crowd around Danny's display. Cars park haphazardly on the lawn. Bursts of laughter erupt from kids who tug on lines and pound stakes, erecting a volleyball net. Kelly is showing off, making gonzo Frisbee catches.

Then, from the corner of his eye, he catches movement—a flash of pale skin. Bronze hair. Finds it. A long-legged young woman in shorts and a halter pops out of the woods and dashes across the lawn. No sign that it's a game of tag or a mother worried about a child. Then he sees a Rivard County deputy jog out on the lawn pursuing her. Kelly abandons his game of Frisbee and is already in motion, on an intercept course.

Jesse, running, favoring her bad knee, knows it's dumb and ultimately hopeless. The dog barks. Faces turn. The cop is behind her.

"Whoa, hold on there!"

Her head jerks right, and she sees the guy with the shoulders, the dancer, running directly at her. His right hand hovers at the ready over a fanny pack that's spacious enough to hold a couple sandwiches or a pistol. And he's gaining on her like a freakin' gazelle.

"Hey, take it easy," he says as he easily runs her down and grabs her arm.

Jesse skids, loses her flip-flops, and pitches facedown on the slick grass. She finds her palms and knees and starts to get up.

"Just stay put." A wheeze of breath, and that's the cop who flushed her from the tree line coming up. Now a third man—tanned, husky, older—jogs over from the crowd by the grill. A small radio mic is clipped to his shoulder epaulet. Jesse sits up and wipes a tickle of damp clover from her face.

"We got her," the older man says into the radio. He wears a blue yachting cap, and now she sees the leather cuff on his belt with the gold shield. "Could we see some ID, ma'am?" he says in a polite but even tone.

"Sure." Jesse digs in her own fanny pack, brings out her wallet, and hands over her military ID and North Dakota driver's license.

"Okay, get up and explain yourself," the dancer says, calmer now, extending a hand to help her up.

Figuring her only chance is to bluff through it, Jesse says, "I need to talk to Mr. Rivard."

"Concerning what, Captain Kraig?" asks the cop in the boating cap, perusing her ID. Then he points to the band on her left wrist and the other cop fingers it and looks up.

"Ft. Snelling Veteran's Hospital," he says.

Shit, Jesse thinks. *That's what I forgot.*

"Snelling," says the dancer conversationally, but his face hardens. "Nice place. I was there in '05. You, ah, okay, ma'am?"

Jesse starts to tremble, exhales, gets it under control, and looks past her interrogators at John Rivard, who is being wheeled toward them by the slim, dark-haired woman in the red apron. "What have we here, Brett?" Rivard asks.

"We have a Captain Jessica Kraig from the North Dakota National Guard coming over the transom," the cop says, holding up Jesse's military ID. "And she's wearing a medical bracelet from the Ft. Snelling Veteran's Hospital. Apparently she drove a missing car here from Minnesota. Left it over there." He nods toward the woods. "Says she wants to talk to you."

Hearing that, the woman next to Rivard teeters and her face blanches white and she puts out her hands, like she might lose her balance. Trembling visibly, she steadies herself on the chair handles.

Rivard, mildly curious, stares up at Jesse and asks, "Really? What's on your mind, Captain?"

Jesse takes a moment to review her limited options as Rivard's watery but piercing gray eyes peer out from under the broad hat brim. She knows her classic movies, and with his gravel voice and commanding air, she could be talking to John Huston in freakin' *Chinatown.* At least the cops are here to hear what she has to say. No sense coming all this way and clamming up. "Just curious, sir," she answers. "I saw you testify on

C-SPAN. When you were fielding questions from that Senate committee last week, how come they didn't ask you about CIA involvement in a helicopter shoot down on April 12th in Turmar, Iraq, that killed three crewmen?"

"I'm afraid I don't follow you." Rivard shows no reaction other than a sidelong glance to the man in the boating cap.

"Maybe you should ask the guy who works for you, who was at the hearing—the one with the scar on his neck . . ." With her shoulders squared, Jesse stares directly into Rivard's eyes and finishes, *"Since he was there."*

Rivard's eyes click to the young man with the ponytail, the dancer, who steps back, turns, takes out his cell, punches a button, then raises the phone to his lips.

Morgon, curious about the commotion, is starting out the kitchen door with his platter of ribs when his cell phone rings. He places the platter on the island and brings up the phone.

"Stay in the house, Morg," Kelly says. "We got a situation out here, and it'd be best you stay inside 'til we sort it out."

"What's going on?" Morgon asks.

"Remember the helicopter pilot? Well, looks like she just showed up out of nowhere asking about a guy with a scar on his neck."

"Jesus."

"Yeah."

Conversation has dried up, and Jesse feels diminished. Clearly she's overplayed her hand, and now she's sinking into the lawn and, all the while, she's involved in an odd staring trance with the dark-haired woman who has her arms clamped tight across her chest except when she raises one hand and nervously tugs at the widow's peak that marks her forehead. *Like she's looking at me but seeing something else?* When it goes on too long, Jesse lowers her eyes and watches ants crawl on her bare feet.

It gets worse. A police car rolls over the lawn toward them. Blue type on the side of the tan cruiser: Rivard County Sheriff's Department. A deputy gets out.

"Jenny at the QuikShop called dispatch about a young woman asking directions to the place," the deputy explains to the older guy in the boating cap, who Jesse gathers is the local sheriff. He nods toward the trees. "After we found the car I told you about, parked over off the public access, we were pushing the woods, and Carl"—he indicates the other uniform, the one who spotted Jesse—"saw her and she ran." When he's closer to the sheriff, he lowers his voice and says, "Mental patient."

Then he walks up to Jesse and asks gently, "Ma'am, are you Captain Jessica Kraig?"

Jesse nods and then goes silent as the cop explains she's a patient at the VA hospital in Minneapolis who apparently *borrowed* her psychologist's car. Jesse winces as she hears the cop say, "I talked to the shrink, who says she's not a threat, just maybe confused. They're making arrangements with the military to get her and the car back to the Twin Cities."

Rivard turns to the sheriff. "Let her down easy, Brett. I wouldn't file any paperwork on this. She's evidently got enough trouble."

"Sure. If that's the way you want it, John," the sheriff says.

It's all low-key now, in deference to the sick person, like charity or pity. Rivard's eyes drift back toward the curious crowd of people standing around the grill and banquet table. "Are you hungry?" he asks Jesse. "Amanda could pack you a plate for the road." At this, the dark-haired woman's face twitches deeper into startle.

"Thank you, no, sir," Jesse says, eyes lowered.

The young guy who caught her walks up and hands her the cast-off flip-flops. "You take care, Captain," he says. Maybe Jesse detects concern in his eyes and in his voice. Not real sure at this point; she's not tracking too well . . .

"Good luck to you, soldier," Rivard says politely as the deputy ushers her to the car. As she bows her head to get in the back of the police cruiser, she appreciates how strange it is where she finds herself when the bottom falls out and she's left with a sensation of mere folly.

Like they were waiting for me? She can feel the flush creep over her face, this awkward, preadolescent embarrassment, a sense of shame she thought she'd avoided all her life. Head downcast, she hugs her goosebump-speckled arms across the grass stains on her halter.

As the police car goes down the drive and exits the property, Rivard turns to the assembled guests and says, "Nothing to be concerned about. Just a little misunderstanding." Then he realizes Amanda has seized his shoulder with both hands to steady herself.

"It's *her,*" she mutters, her eyes wide and unblinking in her bloodless face.

"Yes, it is, and it appears she's off her meds." Rivard's breathing rasps shallow, labored, as he sees Morgon walking toward them, wiping meat juice off his hands on a kitchen towel.

CHAPTER FIFTY-THREE

When the secure cell jangles at quarter to three in the morning, Davis lurches up in the strange bed and grabs the phone from the bedside table.

"What?"

"Am I a fucking genius, that's what," announces Mouse.

Davis blinks, then squints at the red numbers stamped on the bedside clock. "Hey, asshole, you know what time . . ."

"Just listen. I been up all night on Ripped Fuel and just a wee bit of pharmaceutically pure cocaine, and I'm on my third bag of Cheetos. You listening?"

"How stoned are you?"

"Relax. Listen up. You remember Captain Jessica Kraig? Black Hawk pilot you got a thing for last April in Iraq? You with me?"

Davis' eyes click all the way open. "Go on," he says.

"Where's she from, Joey?"

Davis plants his feet on the floor. By the time he stands up straight, he's less groggy and getting oriented. "Grand Forks," he says slowly.

"Negative, good buddy. That's where she *lives*. She was *born* in this little town, Long Shot, North Dakota, and in this case, geography is definitely fate . . ."

"You're losing me, Mouse."

"Then allow me to find you. At 2:36 p.m. Eastern Standard Time yesterday, a call was placed from the Rivard County Sheriff's Department. That's in Michigan. The call went to a Janet George in Minneapolis, Minnesota. A Deputy Thomas Caniff informed George that her missing 2008 Blue Subaru Forester had been recovered in Lakeside, Michigan. The cop asked Miss

George, who is a psychology intern at the Ft. Snelling Veteran's Hospital, if her patient—a Captain Jessica Kraig, who swiped the car—had ever expressed any animosity toward Lakeside's leading resident, a John Rivard . . ."

Mouse's words thud like soft sledgehammers. "Who's Rivard?" Davis shakes his head, trying to catch up.

"When you were in elementary school, he was a heap-big spook. He left the Agency but not the work. Now he's a sort of elder-statesman, country-gentleman spook. He comes from old Michigan money—lumber, shipping, banking. And he lives like a baron on an estate and has a foundation named after him. Which is all totally legit as far as it goes. But the rumor from the shadows is he has a sideline, namely that he runs very black, very precise operations when absolute deniability is called for. Remember you telling me, when you were an asset for the Agency's Special Activities Division, how the boys would josh about this secret office?"

"The Office of Perfect Crimes," Davis says slowly.

"The same. It started as an idea under Clinton, who wanted to knock off Slobodan Milosevic in Belgrade. They actually had a working plan to whack Saddam, but the White House pulled the plug at the last minute. After 9/11 the Neo Cons turned them loose. At this point, Joey, you should be getting a bad feeling . . ."

Now dry-mouthed, Davis asks, "How'd you get on to this?"

Mouse's tone turns breezy. "The mechanics are way too elegant for a passé knuckle walker like you to comprehend. Face it, Joey, basically you've been replaced by nerds sitting in trailers in Nevada twirling remote joysticks on Predator drones . . ."

"Try me."

"Okay. Remember I told you I designed this little capture program that flagged every time Turmar or Captain Jesse Kraig showed up in electronic communication anywhere in the fucking world? That's how I reeled in the call from the Michigan cop about Kraig."

"So I guess she isn't brain-dead?"

"No, but crazy is a real possibility."

"Is it a coincidence I'm standing two hundred miles from Ft. Snelling, where she's doing rehab?"

"Let's say she's the one wild card we had to rule out. She's the only one who was there in the desert who lived. So maybe she knows something, but she was all banged up, and now she's getting better and maybe she's trying to put the pieces back together."

"So how'd she get to Michigan?"

"There was a follow-up call from Officer Caniff. Off the record, like just a concerned cop trying to help a veteran. He told the shrink that Captain Kraig had this obsession. Apparently she saw Rivard on C-SPAN. Some hearing. Get this: She questioned Rivard about a guy who works for him *who was involved in a helicopter shoot down in Iraq* . . . real crazy shit, like she saw him . . ."

"How the hell did she connect all those dots?"

"Exactly what we have to find out, huh? Welcome to the bigs."

"You're suggesting that making Noland disappear could have been a Rivard operation we interrupted."

"Given the way somebody came after you, we can't discard it out of hand, can we?"

Davis is now completely awake, and his voice speeds up. "The dust cloud. We couldn't land. Kraig was buried in the cockpit, which was, believe me, a mess. She couldn't move, but maybe she could still see. So they missed her."

"Yeah," Mouse says, "and figured she was a head case, permanently out of play, like no problem. Except now, apparently she came back and got hooked in to Rivard somehow—

enough to go AWOL from the hospital, steal a car, drive to Michigan, and confront the old man."

Davis assesses a contradictory rush of sensations; his spine has turned to a column of ice and his heart is expanding, filling his chest. "Christ. Where is she now?"

"She's en route back to the Minneapolis VA with an MP escort. But I got a feeling she could use some company . . ."

"If you're right, they'll get to her," Davis says.

"No they won't, because you won't let them. You have to get in there and find out what she knows, or thinks she knows. Get her clear and debrief her. If it's material, we call Appert. Maybe you ran the Ramil mission, but he signed off on it. That chopper went down on his watch. It's our only shot, Joey. Maybe she can unravel this whole mess."

"So I just walk in and buy her a cup of coffee? I don't think so."

"Jesus, I'm over the time," Mouse says. "I'll call you back in five." The signal goes dead.

Davis starts a pot of coffee in the kitchen. Then he takes the phone out on the deck and looks into the night sky, where he imagines Mouse's pudgy corpus forming a constellation made out of NSA satellites. His eyes drift toward the southwest. *Just over there, three hours away. Not a vegetable. She's warm and alive and wiggling her toes. And stealing friggin' cars. Sonofabitch.* Three drags into his cigarette, the cell rings again.

"Okay," Mouse starts back in, "William Lemmer's records have been transferred to the Ft. Snelling polytrauma ward, where's he's expected for an inpatient evaluation for traumatic brain injury."

"You can do that?"

"I already did. Now Joey, you have a shitload of home-work to do in the next couple days. It's what, Wednesday? The army will putz around, and they gotta get the car back—so a day on the road—figure she gets back, say Thursday. You gotta be ready to go in no later than Friday. Fire up the laptop. I sent you a floor plan of the hospital. There's background on Jesse Kraig, and you need to study Lemmer's bio. He's you—wounds and duty stations match. After he left the Marines, he went back to the Sandbox as a private contractor and started experiencing headaches and blackouts. He couldn't do his job, so he came home and checked into the Madison VA, who recommended the folks at Snelling take a look at him for possible TBI complications. They run the flagship polytrauma ward in the system."

"Hey, Mouse, kicking doors and shining dope dealers and dumbass contractors down the road is one thing, but that's a hospital full of *doctors*."

"You can do it. Go in quick, make contact with her, and get her out. They tried to kill you, Joey. You really think they'll give her a pass after the stunt she pulled? You gotta check her out. We can't go to Appert with moonbeam speculation; he's old-fashioned FBI. We need something solid."

"Friday," Davis says.

"There you go. And don't sweat times and dates too much; foggy memory fits in with the diagnosis. Main thing is, you have to internalize moderate TBI and balls-out PTSD. Shouldn't be a problem; you'll chart borderline antisocial on the MMPI walking away . . ."

"Very funny."

"Just saying. Okay, here's your big chance, you ham. One last thing—there's no metal detectors in the Minneapolis VA. That's all for now. Gotta go." Presto-chango. Mouse vanishes into the electronic ether.

With a tall cup of black coffee and a fresh pack of smokes, Davis sits down, turns on the laptop, and starts going through the files to construct the Lemmer role. So it's back to Drama 101—theory of mind, empathy, and emotional regulation. *Learn your lines and don't bump into the furniture.*

Okay, this kind of job you have to play it method to the max. Think real fucked up.

Davis always liked the original pre-Technicolor method actors. *So channel Montgomery Clift. Punctuate moody and twitchy with an eerie smile.* He turns from the screen, and his reflection stares back silvery-black as a negative from a night-filled window. *What was it Hitchcock said about Clift? He looks like he has the angel of death walking beside him.*

Timing is the problem. He has to spirit her out of the place without getting tripped up by staff, who are professional watchers and readers of records.

Captain Kraig.

Jessica Kraig.

Jesse.

Click goes the dead Mexican's lighter in his hand as he evolves a simple plan to kidnap her, after hours, when there's less staff around. Gotta be. *So read, chain-smoke, and chug coffee nonstop up until, and after, you get into the car and start driving around sunup on Friday. By the time you walk in that hospital and they strap on the blood-pressure cuff, you'll blow the mercury right out the top of the gauge and through the friggin' roof.*

CHAPTER FIFTY-FOUR

Four hundred miles east of Dummy Lake, it's five in the morning on the patio in back of the Rivard house. Trash cans overflow; paper plates, gnawed cobs of corn, beer bottles and plastic cups litter the grass. John Rivard slouches forward in his wheelchair with a shawl around his shoulders. An oxygen feed runs into his nostrils, and his jowls sag, parchment-veined, in the yellow glare of a yard light. Morgon and Amanda sit across the table. Both are smoking cigarettes. Kelly Ortiz stands to the side, his arms clamped across his broad chest.

John clears his throat. His voice wobbles, then steadies down. "According to Roger, the Ft. Snelling hospital is not what you'd call a secure facility. There are no metal detectors, and the on-site security is contract. In case of trouble, they call in local jurisdiction; that's the Hennepin County sheriff. Some of the wards are controlled-access. The polytrauma ward, 4J—where Captain Kraig is quartered—is one of those."

A clutch of colored helium balloons bobble from a ribbon tethered to a lawn chair at the edge of the patio. Kelly removes a jackknife from his pocket, opens it, and methodically pops the balloons one after another. Then he closes the knife, puts it back in his pocket, turns, and folds his arms across his chest. "So you're going to kill her?" he says.

"Not me." Amanda nervously tugs on her widow's peak.

"Yes, you are," John states matter-of-factly. "This is off the reservation. On American soil. Read the RICO language sometime about conspiracy." He smiles a tight, wrinkled smile. "We're going to kill her the way a politician does: by sending a message and some money."

"Fuck it," Kelly says. "I thought our mandate was strictly overseas."

No one speaks as the words fade into the damp, predawn darkness. Even the waves flopping on the beach sound exhausted.

"Fuck it," Kelly repeats. "I *will not* be a party to going into a VA hospital to silence a serving army officer."

"No need; we'll use Roger's cutouts," John says. "I've already talked to him. He's assembling the team. It should be easier than the Maryland fiasco. It's an unarmed woman in a hospital bed. She's already tried to run once. It'll look like she escaped again. They just go in, slip her a toddy, and roll her out in a wheelchair. Except this time she won't be found." After a pause, he adds, "One thing you can count on in a VA hospital is a lot of wheelchairs sitting around."

"Well, count me out. I'm packing a bag and vacating the premises. I'll get the rest of my stuff and settle up later." Kelly walks off into the darkness toward the house. Morgon takes his time lighting another cigarette, then turns to John and Amanda.

"Well, at least he didn't commandeer the mansion and set us adrift in a rowboat."

With an effort, John jerks his head toward Kelly's second-floor window where the light has come on and asks, like a surgeon evaluating a tumor, "Think he'll talk?"

Morgon shakes his head. "No way. He signed an ironclad nondisclosure agreement. This is just dragging out a bit too long."

"Absolutely. Jesus, talk about mission creep," John mutters in a thready voice, his chin slumped on his chest. Shaggy hair askew, with the oxygen tubes glistening from his nose, he looks like an old, shrunken, tethered bull.

"So this is all because she saw Morgon on C-SPAN? Where's that leave us?" Amanda takes a nervous puff on the unaccustomed cigarette.

John's knotty hands fumble, pulling the shawl tighter around his shoulders. "Calm down. She's not exactly the most credible witness, is she? Still, we can't have some farm kid from North Dakota with a pair of pilot's wings drawing attention to us." He turns and watches Kelly stride from the mansion with a duffel bag over his shoulder. A moment later a vehicle starts behind the house.

Morgon's lips form a silent laugh. *Amor fati.* The grunts said it better than Nietzsche ever did. *It's all good, bro* . . . His eyes wander out over the lake, where bleak sunlight now pokes holes in the dark and reveals a wreck of broken pumice clouds heaped in the cracked mother-of-pearl sky. "This whole op was upside down from the minute I landed in Baghdad," he says.

John nods. "It's been a real stinker. But you have to eat the bad ones because, the way the game works, the next time it could be the real thing." Then the old man's eyes wander back toward the taillights of Kelly's Jeep disappearing down the driveway. "Too bad," he says.

"What's that?" Morgon asks.

"Roger insists on talking to you face-to-face as a precondition. He'll be making a connection in Detroit, with his crew. I thought Kelly could fly you to the air link in Traverse City, but now you'll have to drive."

After Amanda gets John settled in the house, she returns and puffs experimentally on another cigarette as she paces back and forth.

"You promised me this stuff would never come back on us —me—here," she says. "If you want to go off and club terrorists and baby seals to death, fine, but they're not supposed to dribble in across *the fucking lawn*," she says. "You promised."

Morgon turns his head and stares out over the glittering horizon that's starting to look like the goddamn desert.

CHAPTER FIFTY-FIVE

Jesse makes the return trip from John Rivard's estate in Janet's Forester with two Michigan National Guard military police sergeants. One of them is a sturdy Chicana female, presumably on hand so Jesse doesn't try to escape through the window in the ladies' room at a rest stop. They trade off behind the wheel and drive straight through. She sits in the backseat with hula boy for company, staring at her hands.

Funny, she thinks, you stare at your hands long enough, and they disassociate—Janet's word—and transform into these odd, five-legged white spiders like something creeping back from the hallucinations.

So going back has to be the worst ride of her life, except for getting shot down. What she does know for sure is that stealing Janet's car is a deal breaker. Conduct unbecoming. So there goes her army career. And for what? To crash some friendly old man's lawn party? Make that a very smooth old man.

"Let her down easy," Rivard had said. "She has trouble enough."

More difficult to bear are the sudden mood swings that drag down the corners of her mouth and well up in her chest as, one after another, her thoughts sicken and step off a sheer drop. They tumble into the dark, where she imagines them piled up like flimsy suicides. And that brings her back to Sam, and she really doesn't want to go there, because if Rivard's man could execute Marge, why not Sam?

The MPs are easygoing and solicitous of her welfare and regularly monitor her in the rearview mirror. When she goes into particularly long stares, the one in the passenger seat turns and engages her in polite banter to bring her out of the glide. Is she hungry, does she need a rest stop?

Mainly they engage in what sounds like a graduate seminar on the near-perfect game Tigers pitcher Armando Galarraga had going against Cleveland last month. With two outs in the top of the ninth, a first-base umpire ruled a batter safe when the video replay clearly showed he'd been thrown out.

In a quiet way the endlessly debated point of baseball etiquette tosses her a lifeline. *The rules say you're off base, but you know you saw something, dammit. Okay, so you went about it dumb is all.*

Doesn't mean you were wrong.

The only direct comment the MPs make about her tri-state adventure is to casually suggest that the next time she pulls a stunt like this, she should swipe a better car. A Lexus, maybe. The message is clear: she is being delivered like a package, and life goes on.

Finally they wheel up to the parking aisle in front of the outpatient entrance to the Minneapolis hospital. She gets out and looks over the sprawling building with the green façade that's been her home for almost two months, and for the first time in her life Jesse Kraig sees herself as a small cog caught in the hopper of a huge impersonal machine. Make that a squeaky wheel that's been singled out for special scrutiny.

More to the point, the hospital isn't just where she rooms for rehab. She's an active-duty captain in the army, and Ft. Snelling is her "post." And now she's gone AWOL in a stolen car. And it was like they were waiting for her, like it's all connected —the hospital, the cops, the killer with the star on his neck, Iraq.

Congratulations, you just discovered the government.

So who do you trust now? The big familiar building looms impersonal and vaguely threatening. Everybody in it works for Uncle Sam. At the VA police office in the lobby, she is signed for like a piece of equipment.

"You understand," the VA cop behind the desk says, "even if Ms. George did not sign a stolen-car complaint, we had to report the missing vehicle with the Active Duty Liaison Office. And the VA police have the option to charge you even if the local sheriff's department is not involved." He's brusque and matter-of-fact in his blue uniform. Just doing his job.

After taking possession of her from the MPs, a VA cop escorts her to the second-floor psychology suite and knocks on Dr. Dennis Halme's door.

Halme dismisses the officer and invites Jesse inside. Janet —strict white blouse, hair in a bun—stands at the office windows that overlook one of the atriums. Her arms are folded across her chest. She is trying, unsuccessfully, to look non-judgmental.

"I'm just heating some water for tea. Would you like some?" Halme asks. He's a stooped, bearded man in his early sixties. Jesse isn't sure if his soft brown eyes are kind or just really weary from staring into the aftermath of the nation's wars for thirty years. His voice is only a few decibels above a hush.

Jesse shakes her head, and it feels like Halme and Janet are watching her like a magnified bug under glass. Scientific curiosity, maybe. Then she realizes it's just her appearance—two days unwashed, hair a mess, with grass skid marks still on her knees and a dashboard bobble doll covered with dirty tape clutched in her right hand.

"So," Halme asks, "what happened? Janet could press charges, you know."

Jesse lowers her eyes. She realizes she's been standing at the position of attention. She relaxes slightly and adjusts her posture and clamps her hands behind her back. *How much is paranoia? How much is humiliation?* Either way, she's seriously locked up.

"For Christ's sake, Jesse, sit down," Janet says.

"I'm fine," Jesse says. "Now what?"

"Well, I'm going to sit down," Dr. Halme says, which he does at his desk, dunking a tea bag in a steaming mug of hot water. "Now, we have some wiggle room. Perhaps we can finesse it over with the legal people. But you have to meet us halfway. After this . . . event . . . we have to take some precautions, you understand?"

"Yes, sir."

"This," he says, picking up a thick plastic wristband from his desk, "is a Wander Band; it sends an electronic signal if you approach any of the building's exits. Pick a hand."

Jesse extends her left hand, and Halme snaps the monitor in place next to her treasonous ID bracelet.

"Now, there will be a team meeting on your status." He consults a desk calendar and says, "Early next week, because Dr. Prasad is away, as is the team physiologist. In the meantime, you wouldn't want to discuss what was behind your road trip, would you?"

Jesse picks a spot on the spine of a book in Halme's bookcase.

"Jesse," Halme says quietly. "There are worse VA hospitals. This is not a loony bin, and Janet and I aren't Nurse Ratched."

"Yes, sir."

"Okay, then. We've decided not to put you back on the meds for now, although the full team could decide differently. If you can drive across three states without incident, you can handle yourself here. But for the next few days, you will be strictly monitored. For instance, you can go to the gym, but you'll have two aides for company. Pretty much you're on probation, stuck in 4J. Depending how you settle in, you'll resume seeing Janet. Clear?"

"Yes, sir."

Janet walks her to the door, then lowers her voice. "Look. I could get in trouble for saying this, but I think you should talk to somebody . . ."

Something in her tone impels Jesse to turn and relax her defensive posture. "Sorry, Janet, I've had it with the therapy jive."

"Where you at with cop jive?" Janet says pointedly.

Jesse drops her eyes to the floor because Janet's slang sends a signal, intimating she knows something. When she looks up, Janet holds up a folded slip of paper. "Tomorrow, at four, in the cafeteria when I get off. I need the time to follow up on some calls." She thrusts the slip of paper into Jesse's hand. "That's my cell. Now take off."

In the hall the biggest nurse's aide on 4J is waiting with old reliable Tony. When the door closes, the larger one, Neville, smiles. "Welcome home, Captain Jailbreak. You have fun? You get laid?"

Jesse unbends from her stiff routine and can't resist elbowing Tony in his barrel gut.

"Watch it," Neville says, "hostile patient on deck. Get out the cattle prods."

"They explain how there's gonna be some changes?" Tony says more seriously. "Like, we had to confiscate your kettle bell."

"Says in the Geneva Convention, cannonballs are banned from VA hospitals," Neville adds in a stern voice.

Jesse squares her shoulders and manages a scruffy grin. "You guys missed me, huh?"

CHAPTER FIFTY-SIX

The morning after the party, the cleanup crew gets rained out, and rubbish litters the lawn. Amanda stands at the kitchen window watching the soggy garbage churn in the wind-driven downpour. Morgon is next door in the carriage house getting ready to drive to the airport. John slouches in his wheelchair. Fluorescent kitchen lights ricochet off the stainless-steel appliances. It's been a depressing day, inside and out. And now it's getting dark.

Amanda goes over to her grandfather and turns up the flow on the portable oxygen concentrator that feeds into his nasal cannula. The supplemental oxygen reduces the workload on his heart. He glances up at her concerned expression and waves a dismissive hand.

So she turns and looks back out over the lawn. Now the windows go dark in the carriage house, and she sees Morgon, a purposeful shadow, descend the stairs and walk to his new SUV.

"He never complains," Amanda says.

John chuckles. "Oh, he has an opinion. Certainly he was against this thing from the start. But in the end, he does his job. Where else could a guy like him pull down this kind of money short of robbing the Federal Reserve? Or meet a girl like you?" John clears his throat. "And everything that goes with it."

"We're pretty intimate, and I've never seen him get mad. Have you?"

Distracted, John shakes his head.

Amanda persists. "I mean, I don't really know him, really. Like, is he a possessive guy? Jealous?"

John's smile is blank, the light in his eyes sinking inward.

"C'mon, John. You can tell me. Just because I'm the sane one doesn't mean I'll be the first to break down in the shadow of this nightmare." She cocks her head and forces a bright smile. "This isn't a coal mine, and I'm not a canary."

John studies her for a moment, then answers, "Let's say Morgon has acclimated to a line of work that puts him way past trivial control games like possessiveness, don't you think?"

"So what you mean is, there's no middle ground? I fold his socks wrong, and he puts a gun behind my ear? The point is— does it matter what I think? Or am I a perk that goes with a promotion?"

John grumbles, then wheels his chair to the windows and watches the red taillights disappear into the gloom.

"He's very good, Amanda. We need men like him, especially now . . ."

"Spare me the perils of everything that lurks beneath the everyday. Morg already gave me that speech."

"Well, he does clean up nicely, don't you think? A regular Gatsby."

Amanda sniffs and folds her arms across her chest. "Cold comfort, John. The way I remember it, Jay Gatsby lived *alone* in his big house and was found facedown in the pool."

Much later, after Amanda has tucked him in and taken his blood pressure and made sure he's taken his meds, the dreams come visiting like old buddies and shake him awake. His parents, two wives, siblings, presidents. Fading snapshots flicker; a German Tiger burning in a snowy Ardennes forest. Sunrise in the magical Laotian hills west of Khe Sanh . . .

So he plants his still-powerful hands on the bed rails and pushes himself to his feet and yanks the irritating oxygen tubes away from his nose. The walls of his heart tremble paper-thin with the effort, and he knows he's operating on the last ferrous vapors of his once-iron reserves.

When he's hobbled to the stairs, he refuses to use the damn motorized chair. The sound might wake Amanda. So the stairway almost defeats him. But finally, hand over hand, he makes it to the first floor, where he discovers Amanda in the living room curled into an armchair with her legs tucked under her.

Always a pretty girl, he thinks. *Almost a beauty. Just a little too strong in the chin.* He briefly studies the prescription bottles—Zoloft and Ambien—sitting next to her on the coffee table. Always a little too high-strung. John shuffles to the couch, retrieves an afghan, and drapes it over her shoulders. He stands for a minute listening to the wheeze in his chest, then reaches out and touches the widow's peak on her forehead. He raises his hand to fumble at his own descending clip of thinning hair. His son, her father, didn't have one. Skipped a generation, as they say.

But it's too late for sentimental bullshit, so with difficulty, he moves one leaden foot in front of the other and makes it to the front of the hallway, where he finds one of his walking canes and leans on it.

The storm has passed, and it's so silent in the house that he can hear the soft rise and fall of Amanda's breath, and he prefers not to entertain the image of one of Roger's *tiranos* smothering the young pilot with a pillow.

Once Kelly would have ferried Morgon to the airport in the chopper. But Kelly has departed on a point of personal principle, and the helicopter sits useless on the concrete apron next to the hangar. Kelly would not approve of his sleepless night, would be strapping on a blood-pressure cuff, would be doling out pills.

Fuck it.

Now where do you suppose she hid my pipe?

It takes all of ten minutes for the old spymaster to outwit Amanda's good intentions, and he finds the pipe in the bottom drawer of her office desk, along with a pouch of tobacco. Ignoring the numbness in his fingers, he lovingly packs the bowl. He savors the stringy aroma of the leaf and finds one of the ubiquitous blue-tip matches in his jacket pocket and flicks it with his thumbnail. His lungs clutch and strain as his lips pull on the stem to ignite the smoldering tobacco.

He opens the front door and pauses, gathering himself on the porch. The sky is overcast. The moon is obscure. No breeze nudges the fuzz of mist against his face. It's all opaque, and the murmur of the lake is the only reference point. *Well, here's to dark nights. And good men.*

He ignores the first twinge of stiffness that shears the left side of his chest as he stumps down the steps and out along the cobble walk. He focuses past the squirm in his chest and concentrates on the stronger heartbeat of the lake. It's the first lullaby sound he remembers hearing, even before his mother's voice. He takes a puff on the pipe and watches the smoke ooze from his mouth and nose, twisting in the dark. The Huron, who walked this shore before his family cleared the land, believed that ceremonial smoke lifted their prayers to heaven. The smoke from his pipe is indifferent, agnostic, seeping out horizontally.

And he recalls how the Vietnamese were funny folks who scribbled prayers on slips of paper and ritually burned them before going into battle. An incense-drenched culture, they thought the dead could only read smoke.

In the wreathes of smoke crowding his face, he strains to summon a last nuance of victory from the New Deal Valhalla of his youth that was lit by the stink of Dresden and Hiroshima burning down.

Then, *Oh Jesus God that smarts.* An iron oak has sprung full-grown between his shoulders. Rigid branches shoot down his arms and snarl up his neck.

He discovers that he's fallen and now sits unceremoniously on the damp cobbles. The pipe falls from his clay fingers. The surf laps, soaking his slippers, and metal stacks up in his chest, clamping off air, and he has just enough time to peer into the darkness and compose one last game thought: *Now what?*

CHAPTER FIFTY-SEVEN

Morgon is working off a day without sleep, and it feels like pure black coffee is pumping through his heart. He spent most of the night pacing up and down in the Traverse City airport because the damn weather followed him across the state and wind shear delayed his departure. Finally, he arrives in Detroit, wearing his new suit and the same shirt he wore in DC. Just grabbed it, wrinkled, off the hanger. As he walks off the concourse and is about to enter the Fox Sky Box Sports Bar, his cell phone rings. The way Amanda says his name, he knows it's going to be bad. Holding his breath, he strains to monitor her voice.

"John had a heart attack early this morning. He's gone." She sounds like a little girl being brave.

"Where are you?" he asks.

"I'm standing on the porch looking at an ambulance and three cop cars."

"The porch?"

"He must have got up during the night and made it down to the beach."

"Where were you?"

"Asleep, in a chair in the living room."

Morgon triages the information and sets his feelings for John aside. He thinks but does not say that there's a good chance if Kelly hadn't left the group, the old man might still be alive. He says, "Who's there with you besides the cops and medics?"

"Carl's here; he came in early. He found the body."

Carl Mundt, the groundskeeper, is no Kelly, but he's a retired Rivard County deputy and army before that. So he's a trusted Rivard family retainer. "Let me talk to Carl."

When Carl comes on the connection, Morgon says, "What's your assessment of Amanda? How's she holding up?"

"She's pretty rocky."

"Call Doc Merriman at Lakeview Emergency. She may need more prescriptions to get through this."

"Whole county might. Okay, Morg; I'm on it."

When Amanda comes back on, he says. "Carl will keep you company until I get back. There's no template for this, honey. It's something you have to go through."

"Don't patronize me, Morg. I buried my father and mother, and I'm perfectly capable of handling affairs here." The tart repost is unexpected and almost snappish. But Morgon can't worry about her now because Roger Torres, sitting at a table with three men, spots him and raises his hand. So he tells Amanda, "I'm real sorry, but I can't talk now." He ends the call as Roger gets up and pads smoothly through the clientele who hunch over their drinks sucking in their guts and watching high-definition gladiators rage in violent color on multiple flat-screen TVs.

In keeping with the ad-hoc nature of this rendezvous, Roger's smile is drawn in a thin line surrounded by stubble on his cheeks and chin. But his quick brown eyes flick on Morgon like a cougar measuring the distance to a moving target. Seeing Morgon's expression, Roger steps back. "What is it, my friend?"

Morgon gestures with his phone. "It's John. His heart quit."

"Dead?"

Morgon nods. "A few hours ago."

"*Mala suerte,*" Roger says under his breath and then places one hand on Morgon's arm. "But, you know, he was a man who lived a real life. We are pygmies by comparison. Look what he did when he was not much more than a boy—he captured Hermann Goering." Roger observes a moment of subdued silence, then declares, "I'll be honored to come to his funeral." After pausing for another interval, Roger motions and says, "Lousy timing, actually. I was going to give you shit about Grand Forks, cherry-picking my man, Cawker. My people monitored his phone. Don't worry, we left no fingerprints."

Morgon glances around.

"Not here, took some vacation," Roger explains. "Like a big snake, he crawls away to digest after he feeds."

"And?"

Roger shrugs, expansive. "But now, with John gone, I presume you'll be writing the checks. You can have him. I'll find a replacement. C'mon, I'll introduce you to the crew."

They enter the sports bar, and Roger points to three men who sit at a table apart from the other patrons sipping coffee. They are athletic, relaxed, and casually but expensively dressed for travel.

"They are the best I've got, not the bunch who were smoked taking out Davis in Maryland," Roger assures him. "The blond one, Hector, he's Chilean; his day job was nurse anesthetist. He's seen the target before. He was the one we put into Walter Reed to hotbox her IV with PCP. He knows his way around hospitals." Roger's cell phone rings. He answers the call and then waves to Morgon. "I have to take this. Go on. Fill them in. Show some canines to remind them where they are." Roger winks. "So far from God and so close to Morgon Jump, huh?"

"Who's in charge here?" Morgon asks the trio.

"You can talk to me. I'm Victor Jaurez," the tallest of the three speaks up.

"I see in the paper where your *compadres* are cutting hearts out of people down in Cancun. What's going on, a religious revival, some Aztec thing?"

Jaurez and his companions chuckle among themselves and salute Morgon with their coffee cups. Jaurez says, "So you have a problem you can't solve with all your furious *Nortre America-nos* and their expensive toys. A big problem," he says, tapping the dossier Roger has prepared, "that weighs about 130 pounds, has a pussy, and lives in a hospital lock ward. You are slipping, *amigo.*"

"I assume Roger explained she's already a runner. Shouldn't be a problem, getting her out of the hospital," Morgon says, tight-lipped.

Jaurez grins. "For what you're paying, I will overcome my dislike for skinny, flat-chested American women and personally fuck her to death."

"Be my guest. Just do it fast. She's never to be found," Morgon says coldly, staring down Jaurez's glib bravado.

"*Claro.*" Jaurez motions to his men to get up. "We have to make a connection to the Twin Cities."

"So," Roger says, walking up, "are we good here?" He places two cups of coffee down on the table.

Jaurez shrugs. "We should be in position tomorrow."

As they leave, Roger takes a seat across from Morgon and slides over one of the cups. Morgon catches himself staring into the black coffee, where his reflection flickers back at him, oily dark. Absent John, this is the first time, since Billy, he's been off the leash. He looks up. "Roger, I need some advice going forward here." He nods toward the exit, where the trio of killers have vanished in the pedestrian foot traffic. "I don't mean this kind of thing."

"If you're looking to branch out now that John's gone, I'm all ears. The world has changed in the last few years. The whole anti-terror apparatus is getting to be a top-heavy bore. But there's a new international elite zipping around in private jets chasing the next killer app. Hong Kong, Mumbai, Dubai." Roger shrugs. "They require high-end security, and the market is glutted with amateurs and wannabes."

Morgon shakes his head. "I like it fine where I'm at."

"Ah, you're still determined to settle down and play house with Amanda." Roger's smile is both resigned and sympathetic. "So how's she holding up?"

"Not so hot. She was already kind of a mess behind the pilot popping out of the woodwork, and now with John . . ." Morgon exhales. "I'm going to have to ride herd on the place for a while. Maybe you could sit with me and go over the books; you know the foundation, the portfolio?"

"No problem. We should wait a few days after the service."

"Of course. Tell you what." Morgon is feeling better now, and the shadow of a smile creeps across his lips. "I'll give you a deal on a Bell helicopter. Kelly gave his notice, and with John gone, we have no use for it now."

"Sure. I'll take it off your hands, find a buyer. My pilot's a qualified mechanic. He'll check it out."

Morgon's gaze wanders back to the entrance where Roger's three men disappeared.

"Don't think about it," Roger says. "Pretty soon it'll all be over." Then he fingers the cuff of Morgon's suit jacket. "This is nice."

CHAPTER FIFTY-EIGHT

Jesse pulls the hood of her old college sweatsuit up around her head so she doesn't have to look at people and heads for the computer station. She has retrieved Sam's letter, which is now tucked in her fanny pack that is tightly strapped around her waist. Along with Janet's cell number. She's decided to take a chance, so she called and confirmed the meeting at four this afternoon. She'll just listen to what Janet has to say. She exhales and looks at the wall clock. In an hour it'll be lunch.

She sits down and stares at her reflection in the blacked-out computer screen and snaps on the image of the dark-haired woman in Michigan, barefoot, in the apron, staring at her in stunned disbelief, looking at her like she wasn't even supposed to exist.

She logs on and Googles *paranoia* and opens the first file: *Paranoia is a thought process characterized by excessive anxiety and fear, often to the point of irrationality and*—the next word jumps out at her—*DELUSION. Paranoid thinking typically includes persecutory beliefs concerning a perceived threat towards oneself . . .*

Jesse stiffens bolt-upright in the chair when she senses someone behind her. She turns and sees this guy reading over her shoulder.

"Hey, what's up?" He's all edges and hollow eyes and wiry muscularity and looks like hunger. Six feet tall, he's dressed in an old pair of sweatpants, a faded gray T-shirt, and tennis shoes with his bare ankles showing. His lean face is twisted slightly by a crooked smile that droops at the corner. A braid of scar tissue runs diagonal from cheek to cheek, and his nose looks newer than the rest of his face. Completing this tapestry of hurt is a pair of black horn-rimmed Buddy Holly glasses. The overall effect is what happens when handsome gets seriously run over by the Wheel of Life and makes a bad decision on glasses frames. In what she assumes he thinks is a friendly conversational tone, he says, "What's the old saying? Just because you're paranoid, it doesn't mean they aren't out to get you."

Officer reflex: he's got an attitude, because there's a pack of cigarettes rolled in his right shirtsleeve, which gives her a better look at another scar that zig-zags down into his bicep.

Female reflex: his hair—short, dark, and curly—is too vivid for his eyebrows.

He leans too close and gives off a taut muscle-scented odor that reminds her of sleep deprivation and intense concentration. The way Tumbleweed Six's cockpit smelled after a long night mission. And then there's the smile: a Joker's smile full of death metal–emo-punk energy right off a deck of cards. Like something extra's going on. Like he's stoned on meds, crazy, or both—all of which are perfectly acceptable on 4J.

But.

The disturbed grin doesn't fit with his penetrating brown eyes. She checks the two small, faded words printed over his left breast on the shirt: *Force Recon.*

"Back off. What do you think you're doing?" she demands, getting up. Strangely, in rising to her feet, she doesn't move away but moves closer, and they shiver in a suspended moment with their scarred faces inches apart. She can feel his breath on her cheek. He's chewing gum. Dentyne.

"Meeting new people. I just got here," he protests.

"Go meet people someplace else." Jesse is taking a second look now. Behind the downbeat Iggy Pop act, he's older and harder than the trippy smile suggests. And the smile can't disguise the physical poise and kinetic focus of an elite athlete. He doesn't quite add up. In fact, he's a little on the scary side, but she in no way feels frightened. *Maybe it's something about the way he moves? A premonition that they've met before.* She needs some time to process this, so she spins on her heel and walks toward her room.

"Okay, I apologize," the guy insists as he follows her down the corridor. "Lame start. Let's try again."

At the door to her room, Tony catches up with them and eases the guy aside. "Whoa, there, Lemmer," he says. "Maybe they didn't explain the fraternizing policy, or maybe you just forgot. The women's rooms are off limits."

Jesse watches the new patient adjust to Tony's presence. He backs off and lets Tony walk him down the hall.

★ ★ ★

Joe Davis blinks his heavy eyes at the nurse's aide who wears an ID card on a lanyard around his neck bearing the name Anthony Grayson.

"Hey, how you doin'?" Davis says, letting an ambiguous edge glide into his voice. He has to stay in character with the chart Mouse inserted in the system. The chart says he has boundary issues, poor impulse control, and a tendency to get aggressive. "Don't worry, man. I get it," he tells the aide. "No bugging the female patents and no going in their private rooms."

"Okay, good. Now, did you get settled in?" Tony asks as his watchful eyes take their time, appraising Davis. He stands a little closer than is polite, as if to remind Davis of the considerable leverage spring-loaded in his roustabout's physique.

"Yeah," Davis says, "I brought my stuff into my room on the other side of the ward."

"You did intake with primary care this morning, right?" Tony says.

"Uh-huh. Checked vitals, took a medical history, peed in the cup, like that. Then they sent me down to the lab to draw blood." His eyes flit up and down the hall—then, with an almost palpable afterthought, he brings his gaze back and stares, unblinking, into Tony's eyes.

"You know your appointment schedule?" Tony asks, indifferent to Davis' stare.

Davis nods. "Got a printout in my room. Skate the weekend, then on Monday morning I see a psychologist in mental health."

"Mental health's down on one, past the cafeteria," Tony says. "I'm headed that way, so if you want to tag along, I'll show you where it is."

"So I can leave the ward, right?"

"Sure, just sign in and out. You don't have restrictions. Your chart says you're here for tests, so just make it to your appointments."

"So where can a guy take a smoke break around here?" Davis asks.

"There's a patients' smoking area, but I'll show you where the staff goes. Give me a minute. I'll meet you at the nurses' station."

As he watches the hefty aide trundle away, Davis figures this guy has a proprietary interest in protecting Jesse Kraig and wants to talk to him, man to man, off the ward, straighten him out to the program.

Waiting for the aide at the nurses' station, Davis takes a quick inventory. The ward floats, all easy colors, the sounds muted. A pulse oximeter chirps softly from an open doorway. A nurse pads by on silent moccasin feet. Less quiet is a young man who stamps—crow-like—up the hall on knees that end in steel struts. He nods to Davis, who nods back, and Davis catches a glimpse of red grit in his eyes that lingers from where he left his legs.

Focus, Davis tells himself.

Now that this Anthony guy is giving him the evil eye, he's worried they might run room checks in his absence and dig in his go-bag and find his tactical vest that contains a .45 automatic, numerous magazines, a small pack of plastic explosives, and a tidy drugstore of narcotics, tourniquets, and Kerlix combat bandages.

He looks around. The hospital is just too damn big, with too many people. His only play is to get her out. Tonight. With force if necessary.

Davis sags against the desk and enters a sign-out time and a destination: smoke break. *Think positive. You're inside and operating in your element, which, at the moment, is midair.* On the plus side, he's finally reconnected with Jesse Kraig in the flesh, and the encounter has left him a little stunned. His hands throb with the sensation of digging her out of that shattered cockpit months ago in a nameless patch of desert. She's no longer a phantom flirting in his imagination, not a memory of the manqué-like staring patient at Walter Reed. Even cowled like a monk in her hoodie, he could see that her embattled blue eyes were clear and focused. As for the scars stamped on her face, they only make her more crash-and-burn, heartbreak beautiful. And he can't help thinking that if he put his lips against hers, the drooping corner of his smile would hook into the scar that splits up her chin over her mouth and they would fit together like two lost halves of a treasure map.

Then Tony is back and leads Davis to the elevators, and they stop on one. Tony shows him the way to mental health, a suite of offices in an atrium flooded with green planters. They return to the elevator, and Tony hits the button for the basement. They get out and wander through a warren of industrial halls until they pass some vending machines, then exit a set of warehouse doors that open on a cement platform at a right angle to a loading dock. Tony leads him past a covered structure like a bus shelter that is filled with a scatter of newspapers, magazines, and a tired-looking man in blue scrubs who sits smoking by himself. They stop at the far end of the platform at a corrugated metal table. Davis holds out his pack of Spirits. Tony takes one. When Davis pops the dead Mexican's lighter, Tony studies the insignia briefly. While this inspection is under way, Davis takes in the loading-dock parking lot that is enclosed by twenty-foot concrete walls topped by a chain link fence. A sliding cyclone wire gate controls entry.

"So what's on your mind?" Davis says when they are both lit up.

"Don't crowd Captain Kraig," Tony says, speaking over turbines that whine along the wall venting exhaust from the hospital air-conditioning. "She's under a lot of pressure right now."

"I guess. A guy told me she's the ward celebrity. She jacked a car and went off on her own for a couple days and was brought back under military escort."

Tony takes a drag, makes a face, then tosses the cigarette aside. "That's right. She's in a lot of trouble, and we're all trying to figure out how to cut her some slack. So she doesn't need any extra bullshit coming her way. Word to the wise, Lemmer: we try to keep the boy-girl at a minimum on the ward. Do we understand each other?"

"Sure. Absolutely; I don't intend to take up permanent residence. I'm just here to get a clean bill of health so I can get back to work."

"So we're cool?"

"Chill out." Davis plucks up the aide's ID card, studies the name, then lets it drop, "Anthony. We're all in the violence-management business together, right? This hospital is just a big spare-parts depot. I don't need an arm or a leg; I need—what's the buzzword these days?—my resilience tweaked."

"Great. Any other questions?" Tony is smiling, but his eyes are unconvinced.

"Nope, it's all good." Davis flips his smoke over the platform, and they head back into the basement maze. About thirty paces from the dock Davis laughs out loud.

"What?" Tony asks.

Davis points to a sign—Inpatient Pharmacy—and the door under it that is controlled by a simple touchtone lock. "Now that's real smart," he says. "Put the class-A narcotics in the basement a hundred yards from the loading dock."

Tony can't help grinning. "Why am I not surprised at the way your mind works?"

Davis shrugs. "Just saying . . ."

Tony keeps the easy smile, but his eyes harden. "Save it, hotshot. I seen guys like you before."

"Oh, yeah?"

Tony lowers his eyelids a fraction. "Yeah. Guys with Mex Special Forces lighters. Guys who live outside the wire."

Back on the ward, first thing, Davis checks his room. He'd left a pattern of lint arranged on his go-bag zipper. It's undisturbed. Then a nurse finds him, asks him to follow her to her computer station, and gives him a form to fill out for mental health. He shows his veteran's ID card and recites the last four digits of Lemmer's Social Security number so she can access his file. The form is a medical history along with a combat-trauma checklist. At the bottom, the form requires a list of his decorations. He skips his other medals and scrawls, "Purple Heart, four clusters," which is, after all, the only one you can't fake.

CHAPTER FIFTY-NINE

Lunch in the 4J dining area. Seating is segregated according to who can eat under their own power and everyone else. Coming off the cafeteria bar, Davis spots Jesse sitting by herself at a table to the side. She has a book propped open as she picks at her chicken salad and cottage cheese.

He slides into a chair at the far end of her table and eats quickly. It's fuel. When he raises his eyes, she's staring down the table at him.

"Do me a favor," she says.

He grins. "What, move?"

"No, take off the glasses."

So he slips off the dark frames and tucks them in his pocket.

"That's more you," she says. "The glasses don't work."

Encouraged, he slides his tray down the table and takes the chair cross from her. Casually he gestures in her general direction with his fork. "I thought you lived in a sweatsuit?"

She's changed into a crisp light-blue blouse, jeans, a layer of makeup base to soften her scars, and just a touch of lipstick. "I'm meeting someone this afternoon," she says.

"Oh?" Alert, he studies her more carefully. "Family?"

"My shrink, after hours, down in the cafeteria with Tony and Neville as chaperones." She holds up her left hand with the plastic Wander Band.

"Tony? The big guy I talked to?"

"Yeah, and Neville, the bigger guy."

For a moment they both drop their eyes and toy with their food.

Then he reaches over and tilts up the book next to her tray to read the title: *Chickenhawk*, by Robert Mason. "Hey, I read that book. My dad had a copy." He squints slightly. "So you were in choppers, right?"

Her eyes go guarded.

Davis glances at the other patients in the room and says, "People talk."

She nods. "Kiowas and the Hawk. Mainly the Hawk."

"Uh-huh." He pushes his tray aside and, in a tight dazzling display of dexterity, fingers a cigarette from the pack folded into the sleeve of his shirt and proceeds to twirl it like a miniature baton.

"You nervous?" she asks, indicating the twirling cigarette.

"For sure." Then he looks directly into her eyes. "So what do you think?"

"About what?"

"The book," he says. "You think it's any good?"

She pushes her tray aside and lifts the book's cover with a finger and lets it drop. "Different world: Hueys, Vietnam. Compared to the Black Hawk, those guys were flying hot rods. Some of the stuff he describes . . ." she shakes her head. "Heading straight ahead into hot LZs with no body armor. It's like teenage kids drag racing or playing chicken. Makes me feel like a bus driver."

"Really?" he says to keep the conversation going. "Give me an example."

"Like chopping a hole down through trees with the blades to make an emergency landing. We'd never endanger an aircraft like that."

"Then again," he says, "there weren't exactly a lot of trees where you did your flying, were there?"

Their eyes meet. "No, there weren't," she says.

Davis continues twirling the cigarette. "Chickenhawk rules. Whatever it takes. They were in a serious war. Check it out. We haven't fought a real army since 1971 . . ." He ends the thought in mid-sentence because he's starting to draw stares from the next table. So he shrugs, stops twirling the cigarette, breaks it in half, and tosses it into his tray.

"So where are you from?"

"North Dakota."

He nods. "Oil patch. Only state that's added jobs in this economy. Known for its work ethic. Maybe because you guys stick it out through the winters and all that prairie wind."

"You seem to know a little bit about a lot of things," she says.

"I read all the time, *Doonesbury* mostly."

"So tell me something I don't know," she says.

It's a subtle thing, what he does with his face and his eyes and his posture. How he leans closer and changes from ward bum into this durable person with real serious heft to his face. And she realizes his brown eyes are always casually in motion, unobtrusively tracking everything around them as they talk.

Not telling her anything, but showing her something.

His voice loses the casual lilt and comes straight at her: "I do this mind-reading trick. And you're thinking how you'd like to get out of this place. And I can help you."

"Really?"

"Yep. Jesse, right now I'm the only friend you have in the world."

One second, two seconds, three seconds of silence.

She purses her lips and pierces him with a single blue, steel glance. "I'll have to think about that," she says.

"Do that," he says.

All right. It's time.

Davis paces outside his room, working an edge. His eyes monitor up and down the hall, tracking the patients, the staff. Then he checks the wall clock for the tenth time in two minutes. *Okay. When she signs out to meet her visitor, she'll have two staff as* escorts. *Tony, who comes on like Big Brother Shrek. And the other, bigger one, Neville. So Big Shrek and Bigger Shrek.*

He'll tag along, distract her keepers, get a good hold on her wrist, and make a run for it. Shouldn't be too hard. She said afternoon. Thank God it's Friday. The place clears out at four. The cafeteria is on one, near the exits. Snip off the Wander Band and disappear into the crowd.

So just do it.

The decision made, he enters his room, grabs the go-bag, steps into the bathroom, and shuts the door. He opens the duffel, removes the folded vest that weighs about fifteen pounds, and straps into the harness. Then he pulls on an extra-large hooded blue sweatshirt. The garment is roomy enough to disguise the compact vest and all its goodies. What else? Mouse's cold phone. A roll of fifties and hundreds. His car keys. He reaches under the shirt, slides out the Colt, inserts a magazine, jacks the slide to load a round, and sets the safety. Making a break with her could trigger an attack. They gotta be here, probably watching every move she makes.

He studies the nearly empty bag. *Can't bring it along.* So he takes out a roll of duct tape, mashes the bag into a ball, binds it in the tape, and tucks it under his arm. Then he spends a few minutes wiping down the room, erasing his fingerprints.

He closes the door behind him and conducts another hall check, then takes a brisk walk past her room, where he sees her sitting on her bed staring at a ragged doll she holds in both hands. He ducks in the TV room, which, yes, is empty, so he stuffs the bag in the bottom of the trash container. The minute he gets her off the grounds, he'll call Mouse, who'll make William Lemmer's VA file vanish. Just like that.

Okay. Here come the two Shreks marching down the hall like a couple of old-time big-house screws. They stop at Jesse's room.

Tony is placid with menace at the sight of Davis as he takes his turn at the sign-out sheet and says amiably, "Mind if I follow along? I could use a cup of that designer coffee. It's funny, from the East Coast all the way to Wisconsin, you put espresso in coffee, it's called a Black Eye. Past Wisconsin, they call it a Depth Charge."

"I got your black eye," Tony squints, knitting his brow. "Just keep your bullshit to a minimum."

"You got it," Davis smiles.

CHAPTER SIXTY

Coming less than four hours after her reckless conversation with Lemmer in the cafeteria, Jesse is blindsided when he joins them. Then, as they step off the elevator, he eases in close and whispers in her ear, "You thinking of relocating, now'd be the time." The little gesture is not lost on Tony, who shoulders between them.

The cryptic remark puts Jesse on guard, and now she is wary when she sees Janet George standing at the entrance to the Patriot Café. Without speaking, they shuffle past the counter and order coffee. Janet pays with a credit card, and they carry their cups to an open table. Lemmer, Tony, and Neville are still in line, ordering drinks.

As Jesse slides into a chair, she nods toward the Starbucks counter. "The guy in the baggy blue sweatshirt next to Tony? You ever see him before?" Jesse asks casually.

Janet shakes her head as she takes a sheet of paper out of her briefcase. "Who is he?"

"New patient, I guess."

Janet places the paper on the table between them. A name is written in legible longhand: *Sgt. Spencer Holstadt; Investigations; Grand Forks County Sheriff's Department*. And two phone numbers with the Grand Forks area code prefix: 701. After she's satisfied that Jesse has read the name, title, and numbers, Janet turns the page facedown. Then she takes a moment to raise her cup and blow on the hot liquid. She takes a sip, sets the cup down, and looks Jesse straight in the eyes. "Before we discuss what's written on this piece of paper, I have to ask you a question."

"Me first," Jesse says, leaning forward, ignoring her coffee. "In your previous job, you ever work undercover, like wear a wire, record conversations?"

"What? You wanna frisk me?"

Jesse gives a scar-broken smile. "You," she nods toward Lemmer, "him. Everybody."

Janet just gives her a cold-eyed stare and taps her finger on the blank sheet of paper.

"So ask," Jesse says.

"Do you think Sam Dillon committed suicide?"

Jesse drops one hand to her lap and presses the fanny pack. "No."

Janet nods at the paper. "Neither does he. Dillon's file landed on his desk. They knew each other. Dillon's truck was parked in front of the house with his fishing boat in back. He'd packed for a getaway. He had sandwiches and beer on ice in a cooler..."

"You talked to this guy, huh? What happened to the rules, confidentiality and all that?" Jesse asks.

"Let's say I loosely interpreted subpart 2 of the rules governing confidentiality—where it says I can disclose private information, without informed written consent, if it's necessary to protect against a clear and substantial risk of imminent serious harm being inflicted on the client by the client or another individual," Janet recites.

"Again, in English," Jesse says.

"I may have been party to information that could shed light on Dillon's wrongful death. So I passed it on to the relevant public authority."

Jesse points to the paper. "Could that get you in trouble?"

"There's talk-talk and there's real-real. Sam Dillon visits, and afterwards you start making real progress. You tell me what he's been digging up: the diagrams, an altered after-action report. His remark about no phones, no e-mails. Then he's dead. The circumstantial evidence at the scene is definitive for suicide. Then, Tony tells me, you get a letter from him, maybe the last communication he made in the world. The next day you steal a car, drive to Michigan, and confront a guy who used to work for the CIA. Sergeant Holstadt in Grand Forks would really like to read that letter."

Jesse bites her lip. "I don't know."

Janet leans forward and lowers her voice. "I'm willing to stick my neck out to explore the hypothetical. Like, say, what happened in Iraq—there's no way to get a handle on that through the army. If it was some special-ops fuckup . . ." Janet shakes her head.

Jesse nods slowly as she moves her hand back in her lap and fingers the shape of the letter in her waist pack. "Like Pat Tillman's death," she says softly. "The brass lies, gets caught in their lies, and then they all get promoted. Everybody moves on, and Tillman's grave is still covered in lies."

Janet shrugs. "Army politics is out of my league. But Sam didn't die in the desert; he died in Grand Forks." She taps the paper. "If you have anything that suggests someone had a motive to kill him, that could be where it starts to unwind."

Jesse clamps her arms across her chest and hugs herself. "Or this conversation could sound like you lost your shit to Stockholm Syndrome and I'm crazy as a loon." Her eyes flit over the cafeteria. "Are we being recorded?"

"Christ, no." Janet's jaw actually drops.

"But can you be sure?" Jesse shoots a look across the cafeteria at Lemmer. But as she stands up, she takes the sheet of paper from the table, folds it in quarters, and sticks it in her pocket.

"What are you going to do?" Janet asks.

"I don't know." Abruptly she turns and walks toward Tony, Neville, and the latest wild card, Lemmer.

The lobby throngs with people heading for the doors. Tony and Neville squire Jesse through the press of bodies; Davis, dodging people, moves closer to her side. When they get to the central elevator alcove, Jesse turns and faces Davis, who is tensed on the balls of his feet, eyes darting, monitoring the foot traffic.

"You still here?" she fairly spits.

"What?" Davis grinds his teeth, unprepared for the anger on her face that's pure Congreve—all hell and scorn and fury. Five of the six elevator doors open at practically the same time, and they are engulfed in off-loading people.

"What's with you? Stop dancing around. So you're the last friend I got in the world, huh?" Jesses skewers him with a look. "So tell me—Buddy—you're so good at watching everything, who's watching us right now?"

"I wish I knew," Davis mutters as they jostle through the press of bodies toward an open elevator going up. Tony and Neville are just stepping in when Davis shoots out a hand to seize her wrist.

Jesse, hyperalert, shrinks from his touch and skips ahead, squeezing in between the two Shreks, and Davis can only bring up the rear, swearing under his breath.

"Shit."

CHAPTER SIXTY-ONE

Just outside the door to her room, Jesse is down on one knee tying the laces of her gym shoe when Davis ambles up. She's changed into sweatpants and a gray ARMY T-shirt with cut-out sleeves. The fanny pack containing Sam's letter, and now Sgt. Holstadt's numbers, is still strapped tight around her waist.

"What're you doing?" he asks.

"What's it look like I'm doing, you moron?"

A few feet away Tony, standing with Neville, chuckles. "She's going down to the exercise room on three."

"I could do with a workout," Davis says.

"Fuck you, Lemmer," Jesse says, pulling the knot tight.

The exercise room is smaller than a handball court, but it crams in two side-by-side elliptical cross-trainers, a rack of weights, and a seated leg press. Jesse climbs on one of the machines. Davis gamely gets on the other. Tony and Neville lounge in the hall on either side of the door, which they have propped open, and Davis figures that's Tony's way of keeping an eye on him.

Jesse plods and stares at the columns of numerals on the control panel; ages keyed to your heartbeat. Pick a number and a pace. Burn fat. Or train cardio. No combination of numbers to tell her who to trust.

She steals a look at the exhausted man pumping away beside her. He stares straight ahead with eyes that resemble two proverbial piss holes in the snow. And she remembers the first words he said to her:

Just because you're paranoid, it doesn't mean they aren't out to get you. Which, she figures, is his warped sense of humor.

She exhales and considers the prospect of calling the Grand Forks cop, which evokes an image of Sam's weathered face and creates the homesick effect of making the institutional walls close in tighter.

After five minutes of pumping beside her, Davis is starting to pant.

"You smoke too much," Jesse points out with a tight smile.

"Yeah," he says. *And I've slept six hours in the last three days and I got fifteen pounds of iron hanging under this shirt.* And he doesn't like this room with only one way in and out. He bites his lip as a pained expression floods his flushed face.

Seeing his turmoil, a nuance of concern comes through the aggravation. "You all right?" Jesse asks.

"Ah, I don't know exactly how to say this, but could you do me a favor?" he asks in a voice pitched so low it barely carries over the squeaking of the machine's handles pumping back and forth.

"Like not piss on you when you're drowning?" She's instantly back on guard.

"More like scratch my back, right under the left shoulder blade."

"You gotta be kidding."

"I've never been more serious."

Jesse thinks about it. He's crawled back into that very grave-eyed tone-of-voice thing he does. Curious, she releases the handle and reaches over with her right hand and digs her fingers into the heavy cotton material over his shoulder and encounters a hard pad of webbing. Her eyes enlarge as she feels down his left side and encounters a compact hog-leg shape. Now *she* lowers *her* voice. "What are you—*strapped*?"

"Yes, ma'am. Not so loud," Davis answers.

"Jesus, Lemmer . . ."

"That's not my name," he says. Then he tilts up his head, balancing on the moving pedals, and probes one eye, then the other with his finger and holds up two contact lenses. His eyes are still rimmed with fatigue, but now they're green. "Joe Davis," he says in a barely audible voice, extending his right hand across his chest.

Okay, it's just too weird, like being swept along in a dreamlike funhouse moment, bobbing side by side on the machines. But she's curious about what he'll say next, so she lowers her elbow to offer her hand and, dodging the seesaw motion of the trainer handles, their hands clasp. "Jesse Kraig. What, ah, is going on?"

"Either the dumbest thing I've ever done in my life, or the most important thing in yours—if me and some people are right," he says in a hush.

She frowns. "Could you be a little more specific?"

"I'm here to get you out of this hospital."

"Oh, boy." Jesse swallows. "*You* came here looking for *me*?"

"Keep working the machine and listen," he says. "I'm out of time, so you can yell for those guys"—he nods at the aides standing on the other side of the glass panel wall—"and it'll get ugly. Or we can work together. It's your call, Captain."

There is something about his tone, the leaden focus of his eyes, and the way he says "Captain."

"You're serious," Jesse mutters, staring straight ahead, pumping the handles and the pedals. Talk about running in place.

Then a clatter erupts down the hall, followed by a muted yell and the crash of something heavy hitting the floor and glass breaking. Tony and Neville go alert and face in the direction of the noise.

"Now what?" Jesse blurts, skittish, teeth on edge.

"Shhh." Davis raises his hand like a conductor signaling silence, and the look on his face is moving way past serious into something else entirely, and pins and needles are doing a scary tickle up her back.

A man in maroon scrubs darts into view on the other side of the paneled wall; he's tanned, and his streaked blond hair is askew.

"Get ready, I got a bad feeling." Incredibly light on his feet for such a burned-out-looking guy, Davis hops from the machine.

Maroon Scrubs waves his hands at Tony and Neville. "We have a problem in physical therapy. This patient's gone ballistic, and we need some help," he yells with a slight accent Jesse can't place.

Tony turns to Davis and Jesse. "Stay put," he orders, reaching for a small staff radio stuffed in his hip pocket, as he and Neville hurry down the hall.

This time when Davis reaches for her wrist, she doesn't pull away. Together they dash for the door and then pause, gingerly listening to the commotion in the physical-therapy suite. Davis sweeps her behind him in a sudden forceful motion. His right hand hovers.

"Hey," Jesse mutters. *You're making me nervous, guy.*

"Whatever happens, do exactly as I say." Cold, direct; an order. "Now let's back out of here real slow until we get to the corner. Then we run for it." He is now balanced, poised on the balls of his feet. Seeing her confusion, he adds, "I'm on your side."

"Great," she mutters. Fighting a trapped sensation, her eyes travel up and down the hall.

"Look," he says, trying to calm her. "I know your dad, Conrad, farmed for twenty years; now he works for the Ag Extension. Gail, your mom, volunteers a lot at the Big Pembina Lutheran Church in Langdon."

"Now you *are* scaring me," she gasps.

As the sounds at the end of the hall cease, they hear footfalls behind them and turn and see two well-groomed men in green scrubs come up the corridor. They have sleek, styled black hair and light-brown skin. Jesse notices that their smocks bulge around the waist. The perception coils icily in her stomach: *Way too tough-looking for VA staff.* One pushes a wheelchair. The other carries a clipboard with a syringe in a plastic sleeve pinned under the clamp. He stops and smiles at Jesse. "Captain Kraig?"

Before she can answer, Davis steps between them. His posture and the intense smile on his scarred face now definitely move her past nervous into galloping tachycardia. Casually, Davis holds up a metal cigarette lighter and turns it in his fingers in front of the two guys. Like he's showing them the embossed circular emblem.

"*Hola*," he says amiably in Spanish. "*Vamos a fumar algo de hierba.*"

For a heartbeat they both stare, narrowing their eyes, at Davis as he pockets the lighter. Then they lunge. One grabs her arm. Davis crouches, torques right, and staggers one of them with an elbow smash. Simultaneously he hooks his foot behind the ankle of the guy grabbing Jesse's arm, twirls him off balance, and breaks his grip. "Run!" he shouts.

Jesse is frozen, flatfooted. *What? What?*

The second guy recovers, and the three men flail for advantage in a crackle of punches, blocks, and counterpunches. Jesse has been in enough grappling training to know that Davis is real good. But so are they. And there's two of them. Now one of them has a Taser and, with more luck than skill, he jabs through the swinging arms and hits Davis in the throat. Jesse winces at the sizzle of electricity and tenses to run as Davis grunts, his eyes flutter, and he staggers back. Then the man with the Taser brings up his other hand and Jesse sees a blur of dull metal as he chops an automatic handgun, butt down.

Davis takes the glancing blow along the side of his head. His knees collapse, and he falls to the floor.

Time elapsed, three seconds. Jesse's mouth forms a circle, but the scream is stuck in her throat.

Then the guy who zapped Davis turns and holds the prongs of the Taser up to her face. He grins and keys the spark an inch from her eyes as the other one slaps a piece of duct tape on her mouth. The guy in maroon scrubs, who drew off Tony and Neville, comes out of the door to physical therapy. Alone. He has another Taser in one hand and a pistol in the other.

Strong hands pin her arms as they confer quickly and check their watches, then look up and down the deserted corridor. One of them grabs Davis' feet and hauls him into the exercise room, comes back out, and closes the door.

Jesse braces against the suspended glide of shock, and finally she reacts and tries to wrench from their grasp, brings up her knee to . . .

The vicious punch to the stomach doubles her over and takes her breath. Her vision tightens to red-rimmed pinholes and she almost vomits into the gag.

The man who hit her says something—sounds like Spanish—to his comrades. They all laugh. Then he turns to Jesse, who is gasping, sagging on wobbly knees, being held up by the Taser guy. He smiles with cold-eyed amusement and says in a conversational tone, "Hello, Captain Kraig. I'm Dr. Jaurez. Your X-rays are back from the lab, and we know what your problem is."

Then they open the first door past the exercise room, a bathroom. Maroon Scrubs retrieves the syringe and the clipboard from the floor, joins Jaurez, and they shove her inside the small bathroom. The third man stays in the hall. Jaurez shuts the door as the other guy pushes Jesse against the sink. Their demeanor is terse, workmanlike.

She bolts for the door, but they easily manhandle her back against the sink. For a moment there's only the sound of her panic breathing through her nose.

Then the one in maroon gives a tight little smile and says, "Hi, I'm Hector. You don't remember, but we met before in Walter Reed, but you were kind of out of it at the time. I promise you this won't hurt; it's just a sedative. You're going for a ride. I think I like you with your pants down. I think I'll give it to you in the ass." He eases the syringe from its plastic sleeve, holds it up to the light, and flicks it with a manicured fingernail.

Very distinctly Jesse sees a bead of moisture glisten on the needle tip.

The one who calls himself Hector nods at Jaurez, who, grinning, forces her toward the toilet stool, groping one hand at the hem of her sweatpants, yanking them. When she feels the back of her bare thighs hit the plastic seat, an insane rage gathers in her very bones. It's beyond life and death. It's about bathrooms and freakin' *privacy* and *goddamned pushy men*!

Then.

Three fast gunshots crash in the hall. Hector and Jaurez whip their heads toward the skitter of a ricocheting bullet. This time, as the shots echo, Jesse's body finally gets it. All the drugged, demented, passive hospital days fall away, and she explodes. Before they turn back to her, she surges to her feet, pulls up her pants, and dropkicks Jaurez in the groin. Windmilling like a wildcat, she's all over Hector, clawing and tearing and punching, and she manages to pry the syringe from his hand and stab it overhand into his arm. Frantically he extracts the syringe and flings it away like a repulsive insect. In that flash of distraction, she ducks, sidesteps Jaurez, jumps toward the doorway, twists the handle, bolts into the hall, and rips the tape from her mouth as Jaurez swears, "*Puta!*"

She freezes when she sees the third man stagger at the end of the hall, sees the pistol in his hand. In slo-mo fascination she watches the gun swing up. The tidy hole in the muzzle levels on her heart as she sees a dark stain spreading on the left side of his ribs. A prickly cordite haze hangs in the close air and raises an instant rash of goosebumps on her bare arms.

Davis is pushed up on his left hand in the exercise room doorway. Blood trickles from his hair. Black and blue bruises from the Taser swell like vampire bites on his neck. He holds a Colt .45 in his right hand. An ejected cartridge casing twinkles, still rolling, on the linoleum floor.

The man with a bead on Jesse's chest turns to face something to his left. Tony stumbles in the physical therapy doorway, dazed, his arms outspread.

"No," Jesse yells as the bleeding guy fires at Tony, but the big orderly jumps back into the room and the shot goes wild. The gunman shifts to face Davis, who is on his feet now and swings the Colt up in a two-handed grip and pitches forward from the waist, making a smaller target. Instinctively, Jesse cringes to her knees as a second volley of shots crash up and down the hall. Blasts stab her eardrums and bits of flying plaster sting her face, and the wounded man smashes back against the wall and slides to the floor as Juarez pops his head out of the bathroom. Davis, sagging against the wall, one hand gripping his side, yells, "Run past the gym!" as he swings on the bathroom door and fires again. Juarez ducks back inside.

Jesse blurts, "What the hell?" as she stares fixated on the gunman, who sprawls on his back with a hole punched in his forehead. Reflex. She spies the familiar shape of the 9mm Beretta on the floor where the dead man dropped it.

"Forget it. Run, dummy!" Davis commands.

Like hell I will. She scrambles and snatches up the weapon, sees Davis push off the wall, sees blood drip on his pants. "You're hurt," she says.

"Run." Then he fires two more shots into the bathroom as she sprints past the gym. Davis is right beside, pushing her on.

A junction of halls confront them: green signs to the left, purple signs to the right—which way out? The place is a goddamned deserted maze.

An overhead PA fills the empty hall: *There is an intruder alert in Section C; all patients stay in your wards.*

Tony must be okay, Jesse thinks, *and has his radio working.*

They race to the right and see a bank of windows and a sign: Elevators. Davis pushes Jesse into another corridor adjacent to the elevators, ducks out, checks the direction they came from, then leans out and pounds the *down* buttons. He checks the intersection of corridors again and sees two terrified female nurses slip out of a doorway and crouch across the hall.

"Get back, outta the hall," he yells. Too late. The elevator door opens and the panicked nurses make a dash for it.

A flurry of shots snap down the hall. The windows next to the elevator shatter, and both nurses flop down in a loose-limbed tangle. "Oh God, oh God!" One of them screams, batting her hands around her head like she's fighting off a swarm of bees.

"Cover," Davis yells and sprints into the open, ripping off three shots. Jesse drops to a crouch, peeks around the corner, and sees Jaurez and his partner hug either side of the hallway, flattened into doorways. She leans out, gripping the nine two-handed, and fires steadily down the hall until the slide locks back. Empty.

But it drives the two gunmen to deeper cover in office doorways. From the corner of her eye she watches Davis execute a speedy coordinated maneuver. He tosses his pistol to Jesse as he snakes out his left leg and catches the elevator door with his foot before it closes. At the other end of this lunge he grabs a frantic nurse in each hand and physically drags them and then heaves them into the elevator. The door closes.

Sighting down the heavier, unfamiliar .45, Jesse isn't prepared for Juarez, who appears at the bottom of a doorway, lying prone. Jesse adjusts, but Juarez gets off two quick shots and snakes back out of sight as Jesse returns fire. She blinks, amazed at the amount of lead that just went up and down the hallway.

Davis is back. They lock eyes.

"Okay," she pants, hyperventilating. "I'm a believer. Now what?" She winces at the bruised, bloody mess over his eye. He does not mention the nurses. He reclaims his pistol. "Hold onto the nine," he says as he stabs a quick look down the hall to where the gunmen are hiding. "Stairs." He nods toward the Exit sign down the short corridor across from them. He thumbs the magazine from the Colt, tucks it under his warm-up, and replaces it with a full one. Cold metal clashes as the slide snaps forward. Then he swings out, crouching in the open, and yells "Go" as he fires three, four, five rapid shots. Jesse dives across the hall and comes out of the roll. Jaurez is a green blur, Hector in maroon; they flatten into the shallow cover of the doorways. Loud *whiz*. A bullet cuts the air next to her ear.

She runs for the stairway door and slams it open with Davis right next to her. Scrambling down the stairs, he releases the empty magazine, sticks it in his pocket, and reaches under his sweatshirt again. A flash of his muscled belly slick with blood. He wears a harness thick with flat pouches, from which he yanks another mag and slams it in the Colt. Thumbs the slide.

Jesse cringes as a bullet splashes cement from the stairs and clips, ringing, off the metal rail. Cement particles bite her face.

They dash through a stairway exit, and they're on the second floor, where packs of patients and staff huddle in the halls listening to the overhead announcement. People scurry as Juarez appears at the end of the corridor waving a pistol.

"They don't quit," Jesse says.

"Fuckers are taking it personal," Davis says, pulling her back out into the now-frenzied hall. Then the crowd parts in front of them and two VA cops in blue uniforms jog toward them. Both have radios held to their ears. They've drawn their pistols. They see the blood on Davis' face and approach on the run.

"Hold it right there," one yells, raising his pistol. Davis yanks Jesse by the arm, jerks a look back down the corridor, and sees Juarez and Hector coming at a dead run. Juarez fires. The cops fire back. Davis hurls Jesse left, shielding her, as rapid-fire shots ring out behind them. One of the cops staggers. The other one drops to one knee and is also hit as he aims a shot, and he sprawls as someone screams. People scurry, double over, lie flat. Several aides pushing an elderly man on a gurney freeze. One of them covers the patient with his body. Down the corridor, a middle-aged man holding a bouquet of flowers slumps against the wall, clutching his hip. A huge atrium panel collapses, and Jesse knows her eyes are taking snapshots she'll never forget. A pudgy man with *Blackwater Aviation* stamped across his shirt crouches, shaking, against the wall. Next to him a bearded older guy—jeans, beribboned cap: Viet Nam Vet—stands nonchalantly wearing his black MIA colors on his chest like some ghost shirt, invulnerable to the flying bullets. With a remote quizzical expression on his seamed face, he comments to no one in particular, "Fuckin' A."

"Gotta get away from population," Davis grunts, wrenching open another exit door. They plunge down the stairs to a landing. A man in a custodian's gray uniform stands at an open door on the landing, fumbling with a set of keys. "Get outta here," Davis yells. "They're right behind us." The custodian's eyes swell, and he hurries down the stairs, leaving his keys in the lock.

"In here." Davis grabs the keys and shoves her through the door, and they plunge into a cramped, dimly lit walkway. Sprayed messages cover the sheetrock walls like gang graffiti. Machinery whirs, faint emergency lights, tubes and pipes and ducts wrapped in silver insulation. They scoot off the walkway into the maze of pipes. Davis fires two more shots, blasting out the nearest emergency lights. As the shots echo away, they hear their pursuers entering the dark space.

Davis pushes her ahead of him, and she senses the chasers have split up and are picking their stealthy way through the machinery. Jesse tries to control her deep, sobbing breaths. No time to think. It's all headlong senses, a hot bath of sweat, adrenaline, and fear.

"Go ahead, stay low, make some noise," Davis whispers.

"What?"

"Draw fire. Go." He gives Jesse a shove. She lurches forward in a crouch, thinking how she always wondered what it was like for the grunts she ferried in Tumbleweed Six. *Well, girl, now you're getting a crash course.* A moment of ringing silence. Eyes adjusting to the quarter-light. Christ, she can feel the sweat on Juarez's face out there. Everybody still-hunting. Waiting. As she cautiously steps, she eases a hand along a metal shelf and feels a box with some kind of containers in it. She takes one and hurls it into the darkness to her left and ducks low. The moment it clatters, two muzzle flashes stutter to the left and right, and the sound is deafening as Jesse hears the death scramble among the machines resolve into a staccato burst of closing shots that throb in her ears like incandescent wires. Then she counts out the long silent seconds holding her breath.

"You recognize my voice?" Davis calls out.

"I do," she answers.

"Don't move. I'll come to you."

CHAPTER SIXTY-TWO

When Davis finds her, he stands motionless, catching his breath. The Colt hangs loose in his right hand, and his bloody face is a gaunt shadow. Neither jubilant nor contrite, he stoops like a workman who has survived an ordeal of particularly hard physical labor.

The moment passes, and he quickly checks to make sure she's all right. Then she follows him to where the final shots played out. Efficiently, using a pencil flashlight, he examines the two bodies; Jaurez curls in a fetal clump, wedged under a pipe, as if he crawled into the silver woods to die. Hector lies on his back with his hands and feet retracted to his chest, like a singed spider. Jesse takes a close-up look at the multiple chest wounds, at sheer physical death. They look like two piles of dirty laundry, like whoever was wearing their bodies left in a hurry.

"They're clean—no ID, no identifying marks—but I know who they are," Davis says between clenched teeth. "Here." He hands her two full magazines of 9mm he's stripped from the bodies.

"Who are they?" Jesse asks.

"Los Zetas. Sometimes when the agency plays dirty, they hire them as contract killers. Strictly off the books."

"Spooks." Jesse says it without heat, almost like an afterthought. As she stuffs the mags in her sweatpants pocket, she points at Hector. "That one was going to give me a shot. He made a joke about meeting me before. In Walter Reed." She raises her eyes and studies Davis' face in the faint light. His skin is shiny and tight, annealed like hammered metal.

"He said that, huh?"

"Yeah."

Then he cocks his head to assess the emergency tempo they can hear over the whir of the machinery above and below them. He tugs her arm. "Over there, where we can see better." They hurry down the catwalk, and he sinks to the floor beneath one of the faint emergency lights. Trembling now, pouring sweat, he pulls up his shirt, unclips the harness, pushes it aside, and cranes his neck to get a look at the ragged skin bleeding on his right side, below his ribs. Then he leans forward. "Check my back, see if there's an exit wound."

Jesse, getting blood from a gunfight on her hands for the first time, squeegees blood away with her palm and studies the torn flesh along his side. Then, as she checks his lower back, he unpacks a compress, disinfectant, and tape from his harness.

"No exit wound," she says, fiddling with the vest. "It hit a buckle on your rig. So you have a huge bruise on your hip and this really ugly, really deep flesh wound on your love handle." Their eyes meet. "But you don't have love handles, you skinny bastard."

First she cleans and tapes an adhesive strip on his gashed forehead. Next she sprinkles Betadine on the side wound, applies pressure and a compress, and winds the tape under the harness around his waist. The hard edge evaporates from his face, and she can almost see the tension release off him in waves. She looks up and down the cramped walk space that still reeks of cordite and fresh blood. "So now what? Not like we can call the cops."

He emits a shaky laugh and his eyes swoon. "Cops come through after the fact, after the lions do the damage. I used to be a cop . . ."

Jesse points down the walkway toward the bodies. "They work for somebody high up, right? You're saying the government is trying to kill us?"

He gives a mirthless grin as he slides the Colt back into his vest and pulls down his shirt. Then he hooks quote marks with his fingers in the air and says, "Not *the government*; someone *in* the government."

"I'd like to believe that's cynical bullshit," she says, hugging herself.

This time his laugh is stronger. "Take it from a recovering action toy—I'm sure this started as somebody's really great idea, and now, what we got here . . . Ted Bundy on his best day couldn't invent something this fucked up. No, this takes patriotic, church-going white guys sitting around a table . . ."

Revived by his cryptic little speech, Davis gets to his feet. "Something we gotta do. C'mon." He motions her back down the narrow walkway. Squinting in the gloom, Jesse watches as he hoists Juarez and slings him over his shoulders in a fireman's carry. "You drag that one," he says, pointing at Hector. "We're going to hide them in the machinery." Bent over, favoring his side, he disappears in the dim light among the silver-wrapped pipes.

Jesse discovers it's hard dragging a body, especially when above and below her she can hear the scurry of feet, like bats in an old barn, flitting to the muted emergency voice on the PA.

Davis returns and helps her wrestle Hector's corpse deeper into the machinery. "Okay, good enough," he says. His face is now pale and dripping sweat from the exertion. He flops down and sits on the catwalk. "I need a minute," he says.

"So Mexican hit men. You gonna tell me what's going on?" she asks.

Absently, as her voice echoes in the machinery, he pulls a crumpled blue pack of American Spirits from his kangaroo pocket. Then he holds up the metal lighter and smiles. "These guys are all about drugs," he says softly.

"What?"

"Something this old FBI buddy said . . ."

"FBI? Are they here too?"

338

When he pops the lighter and lights the cigarette, she ducks instinctively and darts a nervous look back toward the tangle of machinery. Then she squints at his face that gleams, sweaty yellow, in the faint emergency lights. "How'd you know that stuff about my parents?" she asks.

He takes a drag. "When you were nine, you fell out of an apple tree and broke your left forearm." He exhales a lungful of smoke. "You went off birth control pills when you were living with Terry because of the water weight." He winks. "You're vain. You like your coffee black—no cream, no sugar—and your period comes around the 23rd of the month."

"You got a real way with women, don't you? I say again, what's going on?"

He cocks his head and says, "Near as I can figure, you saw something in Iraq you weren't supposed to."

Jesse grits her teeth. "How do you know that?"

He shrugs. "I don't know that. I *suspect* that. And I suspect there's some people, probably in the CIA, who think the rules don't apply to them anymore. It's an ongoing dilemma from Runnymede to Watergate to now. Is the king above the law? So it's all right for them to whack you and your crew to protect their devious bullshit."

"And where do you fit in?" Jesse asks.

Davis grimaces as he experiments with moving his torso. "I was sent by another group, in, ah, other agencies, who think they went too far. It's kinda like when the elephants fight, the grass gets trampled. And right now, you and me? We're the ants in Dumbo's footprint."

"You're a big help."

"Yes, ma'am." He pushes up, tests his balance, grabs her hand, and yanks. "C'mon. We gotta move. One more stop, and then we get you outside." He takes a second drag on the cigarette then stubs it out and sticks the butt in his pocket.

Back in the stairwell, Davis locks the door and pockets the keys. Then he leads her down the stairs to the basement. The underground warren of halls is practically deserted. Jesse sees a figure dart in the distance, crossing an intersection, like a panic scene below decks in *Titanic*. Davis heaves the keys into a trash container.

"Where are we going?" Jesse asks.

Davis points to a sign at the end of the corridor: Inpatient Pharmacy. Then he reaches under his shirt, digs in his vest, and pulls out a square of putty-looking material the size of a cigarette pack. He removes a jackknife, flips it open, and carves a small chunk of the putty and then fiddles with a device that Jesse assumes is a timer detonator. "I'm going to blow that door, but I just want to destroy the lock. Could still be people inside. I don't want to hurt anybody."

Jesse almost laughs. "You don't want to hurt anybody?"

"Uh-huh," he says, either missing or ignoring the irony. "Wait here." Then he pulls up the hood to his sweatshirt, jogs down the hall, and slips into the recessed doorway. In seconds he's back.

"C'mon." He leads her back down the corridor, through several turns, and they reach a stairwell as a muffled explosion shudders through the halls.

"Explain," Jesse says.

"Maybe the cops'll think they came to smash-and-grab the pharmacy—confuse the reporting, buy us some time," Davis says as he reaches over and untucks her T-shirt so it covers the butt of the Beretta in her waistband. Then he takes out a pack of moist toilettes from his vest, gives one to her to clean the blood off her hands, and uses another to touch up her face. Finally, he takes out the knife again and cuts off her electronic bracelet along with her patient band and then his own. A minute later they come out of the stairwell on the first floor and blend into the jostle of foot traffic heading through the lobby toward the visitors' entrance.

CHAPTER SIXTY-THREE

Jesse stares at him amid the bustle. "How'd you get a gun in here?"

"Same way they did. There's no metal detector," Davis says. "I could have brought a .50 cal in here one piece at a time."

"What was that place with the machines, where we left the bodies?"

"Interstitial space." He jerks a thumb at the levels above them. "You notice how there's seven feet between the floors? That's where they put the mechanicals that run the hospital."

"And you know that how?"

"I studied the floor plan. C,mon." He urges her ahead of him.

The overhead PA drones: *There has been an intruder incident in Zone 3B. Disaster Management Plan is in effect. The Hennepin County Sheriff's Department has been called into the hospital. Remain calm and return to your wards. If you are near a main exit, you may go outside. Remain calm.* The hospital is somewhere between lockdown and evacuation.

"They'll never evacuate this place; it's too big," Jesse thinks out loud.

"They did once, just hours after 9/11. Some sick asshole called in a bomb threat, totally unrelated, and they moved every single person out on the lawn—except a couple operating theaters that were in mid-procedure. I shit you not," Davis says.

"You shit me not, huh?" Jesse hears her voice, which is off, a touch shrill. "So where did the phony name Lemmer come from?"

"Got me. The guy I work for made it up."

"You really a soldier?"

He manages a pained grin. "Stand by, doggie. I was a Marine."

"What then? C,mon, I need to talk right now."

He turns to her as they walk, and seeing his sweat-drenched face, Jesse thinks, *He's assessing me for shock. And he's holding himself together by sheer will at this point.* In a steady voice, he says, "I'm the only friend you have in the world, remember?" After a beat he asks, "You all right?"

"No, I'm not. Keep talking."

"In a minute. Right now we have to get you out of this place before they cordon it all off. I think we still have time. C'mon, this way." He eases her past the diminutive smiling statue of Bob Hope and through a door where they mingle in a tense crowd of patients and staff milling outside. The sweltering summer afternoon is strobed by emergency flashers as cops rush everywhere, trying to direct the press of bodies. Car horns blare in the parking lot. A SWAT team lumbers down from their van and deploys in cumbersome body armor and shields. Davis directs her, and they angle away from the crowd. He stumbles and takes her shoulder as they hurry toward the sprawling patient parking lot where the aisles are clogged with bumper-to-bumper cars trying to flee the bedlam.

"C'mon." He leads her to the back of the lot, and they stop at a Ford Escape. He scans the immediate area, then sinks to the curb between the parked cars and pulls her down next to him. "Get me out of this harness."

She helps him peel off the sweatshirt and unsnap the harness, which looks like a modified survival vest. He tugs open one of the pouches and takes out a syringe and some pills. He tears the packaging with his teeth and gulps the pills. Then he reaches down and pulls off the compress. "Help me," he says, "This syringe? Put the whole shot right in the wound."

Jesse blinks. She's not sure what happened in the last twenty minutes. Except she's alive and some other people aren't—people who were trying to kill her.

Then this guy . . .

"C'mon," he urges as he gingerly touches the wound and gnaws his lip. "Infection's the problem. Those Zeta creeps like to dip their rounds in the toilet after they take a dump."

"What is it?" she asks, taking the syringe.

"Antibiotics and a DARPA cocktail—keeps the wounded walking. Demerol and anabolic steroids. Do it."

Amazed at her calmness, Jesse takes the needle, forces it into the torn, bleeding tissue, and presses the plunger. She's not surprised anymore when he barely flinches.

"Now," he says, "use the needle to dig out any pieces of the buckle, any debris from the vest in the wound. Clean it the best you can. Don't worry about the bleeding for now."

Willing her fingers to be steady, Jesse uses the syringe needle to probe and worry several twisted shards of metal from the welter of torn, oozing tissue. Then she slaps on a fresh dressing and helps him struggle back into the sweatshirt, and his eyes roll back in his head and he leans over and vomits on the pavement. "Better," he says. Bracing on the cars to either side, he pushes up to his feet and surveys the light show in front of the wide building that flashes like a red and blue hornet convention.

"They haven't set up a perimeter yet; traffic's still getting out. I think we can make it."

They get in the car, and he stows the vest and the pistol and her nine under the seat and brings a liter bottle of water off the floor and hands it to her. "Drink. Save some for me."

After they finish the water, he hands her some more moist toilettes to clean her hands and starts the Escape and bulls his way into the clutch of departing cars. As flashing vibrations of the running firefight lurch inside her head, the rest of her body moves at a herky-jerky stop-and-go pace. They loiter in a queue of cars moving a frantic inch at a time to get out the front entrance.

She shakes her head and says, with awe in her voice, "Up in that hall, with the nurses. All the rounds flying around, and nobody got hit."

Davis gives a tired snort. "The only guys who can hit anything in a handgun fight are the heroes in cop thrillers."

And Jesse thinks but does not say, *You seem to do okay.*

Finally, they edge up to the head of the line, where a tense sheriff's deputy is swearing into his radio and gesticulating at the cars jockeying for position to leave. Davis sees a hole, guns into it, and they are off the campus.

Davis makes the turn onto East 55 and merges into the anonymous rush-hour traffic. "One more thing I have to do," he says as he takes out a cell phone and punches a preset. After a moment, he gets a connection.

"Mouse, it's me. What? You monitored already? Yeah, I got her out. Uh-huh. Three more of our Mexican brothers. If we're lucky, it'll look like they came in to hit the pharmacy. And I stashed two of them where the cadaver dogs won't find them until they get ripe." Pause. "They didn't give me a choice; they came on like gangbusters." Another pause. "I know it's a mess. Work with me here. No, I'm not all right . . ."

He blinks rapidly, listening. "No, you listen. We need some cyber magic. They shot the place up. There's casualties all over the place. Do the presto-chango. Put her face on the tube, skew the reporting. She went AWOL before. Well, she's AWOL again; maybe it'll look like they got her. Try'n buy us some time. Have Bobby Appert stand by. I'll get her clear and debrief her. Right, in Hayward . . . might turn up something."

Exasperated, Davis holds the phone away from his ear, then puts it back to his mouth. "Dammit, Mouse, Appert told me to *find him a bad guy*; tell him I'm working on it!"

The Escape is drifting into traffic in the next lane, so Jesse reaches over to steady the steering wheel. Davis calms down and says in a quieter voice, "Okay, nothing crazy. And dump my VA file." He ends the call and engages Jesse's wide-eyed expression.

"Who's Mouse?"

"The guy I work with."

"And?"

"Not now," he says in a thick voice. "I'm too goddamned tired."

The freeway has moderated into a divided highway metered by stoplights. He turns at the first light and parks on an empty stretch of parkway. "I am flat beat. I need you to drive so I can catch some sleep," he says. "Can you find your way to Interstate 94?"

"I can do that."

"Follow it into Wisconsin to Highway 53 and turn north. We have almost a full tank of gas. When you get to Spooner, turn right on 70. When you reach Stone Lake, wake me up, and I'll take it the rest of the way. Got it?"

"Got it. Rest of the way where?"

"Someplace safe, where we can regroup."

"Is your friend Mouse there?"

"No," Davis says patiently, "Mouse lives in the woodwork at the National Security Agency." He smiles tightly. "Jesse, please, I haven't slept for three days."

"Okay, then; can I ask you something totally unrelated?"

"As long as it's not too complicated," he says, sagging back in the seat, taking out a cigarette, and cupping the lighter in his hand. His face is sunken in the flame; his eyes roll up, his eyelids flutter.

"You have sisters?"

"Two of them."

"Younger or older sisters?"

"Older, both of them. Real ballbusters."

"Thank you. Just one last thing. Will you tell me who you really are?"

"Yes, ma'am." He gathers himself, grimacing with the effort. "April 12th, west of Samarra, me and Greg Colbert dug you out of your chopper. I was the code name he was hauling in Tumbleweed Five..."

Jesse blinks, totally energized by the sudden memory. *Sam's Snake Eater.*

Then he says, "You got shot down on my mission, Jesse. You're not alone anymore."

Jesse has never melted before. She does so now, sinking into his shoulder as hot tears streak down her cheeks.

Davis puts his arm around her shoulder and leans his cheek into her matted hair that smells like fear and sweat and gun smoke. He'd like to stop time and stay right here forever, feeling her heart beat against his chest.

But since that's not on, he dabs her tears with the sleeve of his sweatshirt. "Nerves," he says softly. "Adrenaline flameout. You can drive, right?"

"I can drive," she says, straightening up.

He opens the door and flips away his cigarette as she gets out and comes around to the driver's side.

CHAPTER SIXTY-FOUR

The moist sensation eases into the dreamy stupor, and when Davis opens his eyes, he sees Jesse's face striped by light filtering in through venetian blinds. The varnished yellow pine car siding that panels the walls is familiar, and through the bedroom doorway he sees a corner of fieldstone fireplace and the cathedral windows. Hayward. His eyes travel back to her face, and it's not the fright-mask face from last night; this is a scrubbed, morning face that is more relaxed, and her hair is shampoo fresh. She's wearing his Recon T-shirt that is also clean. Well, mostly clean. In fact, everything's clean. The sheets are clean, and he's clean except for the blood-caked bandage on his right side.

And he's buck naked.

Davis reaches down and grabs the sheet that drapes across his thighs and tugs it up to his chin.

"You have a nice body in a mangled sort of way," she says as she sets aside a basin of warm water and a washcloth.

"What?" He starts to sit up, but the stiffness in his side pins him to the bed.

"Easy there, cowboy. You were really out. I'll bet you don't even remember taking the wheel at Stone Lake and driving on the back roads. You unlocked the place and walked straight for the bed and slept for almost ten hours."

Davis sits up more slowly, gritting his teeth, using his elbows to hoist himself.

"You must feel safe here because you didn't wake up until the end of your sponge bath," she says.

"My sponge bath?"

She heaves her shoulders. "We were both pretty nasty, so after I woke up and showered, I decided to clean you up. There's a washer and dryer downstairs, so I washed our things. Hope you don't mind me wearing your shirt. I'm operating off a limited wardrobe at the moment."

Davis sniffs. "Is that coffee?"

As she gets up off the side of the bed, he sees the T-shirt hem swing against the fine golden hair on her bare thighs. The hair catches the sunlight, as does the rust-colored bloodstains that dapple the bottom of the shirt. "Coming right up. I can't vouch for the quality first time out, it being a strange kitchen and all," she says. For a moment her eyes linger on his, and in her enforced calm, he detects the obvious question: *Are we clear or is more coming?*

She leaves the bedroom and returns a moment later with a cup that he takes in both hands. Briefly he inhales the invigorating steam, then takes a sip. After the second sip, he shakes his head. "You're right. I don't remember driving in."

She takes the cup from his hand and sets it on the bedside table. "C'mon. I'll help you up. You'll feel better after you brush your teeth. I did."

"Ah, Jesse, all I got on under this sheet is a bandage."

She studies him, perplexed and faintly amused. "I saw you kill three guys last night. You really think I'm going to faint at the sight of your dick?"

He can't think of a fast comeback to that, so he lets her help him to his feet and out the door. The bath opens immediately to the left. A clean pair of boxer shorts is folded on the vanity counter next to a toothbrush, a tube of Crest, and a bottle of Listerine.

"I found the brush and stuff in the drawer. This place is stocked with everything. You need help getting into the shorts?"

"I can manage," he mutters.

As she leaves, she closes the door. After brushing his teeth and rinsing with the mouthwash, he does feel better. Getting into the shorts is more of a problem than he anticipated. The simple act of raising his right knee, then his left, feels like inflamed wads of adhesive tape ripping apart in his side. By the time he gets the shorts on, beads of sweat have popped on his forehead, and he knows it's past time to get the bandage off and assess the wound for sepsis. He opens the door and leans on the jamb.

She's right there—patient, waiting, smiling—close enough for him to smell her minty breath. "Hell of a blind date, huh?" he says.

"Ball's in my court. Next time I'll take you flying."

"Oh, yeah." Davis' eyes flare, and he staggers back against the doorjamb.

"Your, ah, face is turning white," she says, steadying him with a hand on each of his arms.

"Getting old. Don't bounce back like I used to," he says apologetically. The hint of intimacy promptly packs up and departs her face and is replaced by a practical Little Dutch Girl expression.

Davis grins weakly. "You don't strike me as the domestic type, but how are you at sewing?" he asks.

First he sends her out to the living room to bring his vest into the bedroom, where he reclines on the bed with pillows propping up his back. He takes a small, sterile surgical kit from the vest that contains a curved needle already knotted with thread, a forceps, and a small scissors. As she puts on a pair of vinyl gloves, she wonders, "I thought you have people a call away. Wouldn't they be better at this?"

"Sure, they'd meet us at the nearest hospital with wall-to-wall federal agents; they'd take you into protective custody. You want that?"

"Not until I figure some things out."

"Okay. First we have to clean this wound and stitch it up, then we'll talk."

All business now, she peels off his shorts. Then she removes the crusted, yellow-fringed bandage and places it in the wastebasket next to the bed. Next she wipes down the needle, forceps, and scissors with a piece of gauze drenched in disinfectant.

The five-inch gash in the skin above his right hip is a long pucker of infected yellow edged by red, then purple and black bruising. It's open in the center, creating a puss-filled crater, and looks like an inflamed state of Florida lying on its side.

"Okay, I did this once in training, on some poor sedated pig they shot, and a couple times in the field," he says. "But I can't get an angle on it or see well enough. So you're up."

"Great."

He hands her a syringe from the kit that is enclosed in plastic. "This is lidocaine, to numb the laceration. Open the sanitary wrap and inject the sides of the wound. Say, twice on each side."

Jesse strips away the protective covering and carefully empties the syringe in four different locations in the tear.

"Okay, now you have to probe around with the needle to make sure no pieces of the buckle broke off in there."

"I think I got them all out in the hospital parking lot," she says.

"Take your time," he says with a ginger smile. "I'm numbed up, so I won't feel a thing. Theoretically . . ."

"Cripes, this is like a high school biology class when we dissected the frog," she mutters as she digs delicately with the needle. Satisfied that no metal is left in the gash, she sets the syringe aside on a clean towel.

Craning his neck to see, he says, "Now scrub it clean with some gauze and the Betadine. There could be particles of the webbing tore off in there. You have to make sure it's clean before you close it."

Slowly, methodically, she washes the upbraided tissue with the disinfectant. Twice she finds small threads of foreign matter that she carefully edges out with the gauze. Then he picks up the forceps and shows her how to manipulate the needle with a double loop of thread over the forceps tip and how to draw the free end through to create a knot.

"Got it," she says, taking the forceps in her gloved hand.

"Now, you have to make the first suture inside the deepest part of the opening, to close the dead space. First one side, then the other."

Calmly, Jesse curls the curved needle into the torn muscle, draws it through and repeats the process on the other side of the wound. Then she pulls the suture snug and does the double loop, draws the free end through it, and repeats the looping three times to get a tight knot. After snipping off the knot with the scissors on the deeper suture, she closes the rest of the wound with ten evenly spaced stitches and ties them off.

She lets out a deep breath and stares at the job as Davis uses a piece of gauze to blot the sweat from her forehead. "So what do you think?" she asks.

He gives a shaky grin, reaches out, and lightly touches her cheek. "It was good for me. How was it for you?"

An hour later, after breakfasting on scrambled eggs and toast, they sit on the deck overlooking Dummy Lake. The late-morning sky is deliciously moody, shadowed with clouds, and a breeze fans ripples across the water. Davis now has taken a careful shower and wears a fresh bandage on his numb, stitched side and, with two prescription-strength Tylenol on board, has changed into a light cotton robe Jesse found in an upstairs closet. She still wears the Recon shirt, and Davis is thinking he's never going to get it back. Cradling his third cup of coffee, he twirls an unlit cigarette in his fingers and studies the brooding expression on her face. She has soldiered through the drama of fight and flight. Now she's waiting for some answers.

"So," he says.

"Wait, I want just one normal moment." She turns and leans into the deck railing and tilts back her head and closes her eyes as an eddy of wind shivers through her hair. Then she turns to him and says, "Yesterday at four in the afternoon, I was on the elliptical on the third floor of the Minneapolis VA, and now I'm across state lines feeling like Bonnie and Clyde."

Through a mild lethargy of lidocaine and Tylenol, Davis manages a fond grin. "You did sort of look like Bonnie Parker putting rounds down that hall . . ."

She does a brief little curtsey with her eyes, and then the brooding expression is back. So Davis lights his cigarette and gives her the Cliff's Notes version—him getting in trouble asking questions after the crash, being sacked and sent home, his Memphis trip, the talk with Noland's ex-wife, and then the attempt to kill him in the woods off the Maryland Parkway.

"Spooky. This Mouse guy gave you a new identity, and the FBI went along?"

"Not *the* FBI, *an* FBI agent and a couple of his friends. Then Mouse intercepted a phone call from a Rivard County cop to your shrink about the stolen car and how you made a remark to Rivard about a chopper going down in Turmar. That got me cracking to Minneapolis. So what we want to know is, how the hell you got onto Rivard?"

"Hold that thought." Jesse gets up and goes into the house. She returns with a small black fanny pack, which she unzips. "I guess I can trust you," she says, holding up a dog-eared envelope and a folded piece of paper.

Nonplussed, Davis' cigarette drops from his lips. "You guess?"

CHAPTER SIXTY-FIVE

First Davis reads the letter. Then he points at the photo-copy of Morgon Jump's military ID above Sam's longhand and looks Jesse straight in the eye. "No bullshit. You saw this guy at the crash site?"

"No bullshit. He shot my crew chief, and probably my gunner."

Then he spends an hour rigorously questioning her about the VA psychologist's intercession with the North Dakota cop with an emphasis on Sam Dillon, what he told her during the hospital visit, and her assessment of his mental health. "I know, ironic under the circumstances, but . . ." Then he starts chain-smoking and talking on his cell phone in cryptic one-minute snatches. Sam's letter is pinned under an ashtray on the deck rail as Davis paces.

He looks up. "Rivard's gone. He had a heart attack. Shit." He leans back to the phone, stares at the photocopy on Sam's letter. "That still leaves this Jump guy. What if we follow on Sergeant Dillon's advance work, pull the security camera tape in Balad, and ID him? What? No way she thinks Dillon was a candidate for suicide. And neither does the North Dakota cop who's investigating. So we let him lead with the questions, get with Appert? They can locate Colbert, depose him about the phonied-up report. Okay, I'll be here." Davis ends the call.

"So where're we at?" Jesse asks, refilling their cups from a fresh pot.

"You and your shrink were on the right track. Sam's death is the best place to start. As for the rest of it?" Davis shakes his head. "Cops and spooks is way more complicated than cops and robbers."

Davis sees a new color dial into her eyes: murder blue. She fairly spits the words, "You're saying they can kill my crew, and maybe Sam, *and get away with it?*"

"Slow down. There's a lot of dots here, and we've only connected a few of them. Say we're right, and this was a black op. Tactically, the way they think, you were in the way. Words like 'regrettable' come to mind," Davis explains. "We'll probably never know the reason Jump was there. Obviously something Noland, the missing contractor, was mixed up in. Jump himself might not even know. He's a soldier, Jesse, like us. It's all about who, when, and how. We don't really get to ask why, do we?"

"This time we do, goddamn it. I can identify him as being there."

"Okay, look. We can get Appert to bring you in, to someplace safe, take you into protective custody as a material witness, but . . ."

"But what?"

"Game it out. A prosecutor will say you're not a reliable witness. The drugs, the diagnosis, AWOL."

"I don't get it. Can't you declassify covert missions? Or out them, you know, play dirty pool like Valerie Plame?" Worry lines form at right angles to the scar on her brow. "Why not this Jump?"

Davis shakes his head. "Sure there's the culture of secret systems. When I was an Agency asset, I did covert. But the target selection involved analysts, intel interpretation from human sources, satellite, and drone platforms, along with the logistics of getting in and out. I got a feeling this is different. Rivard and Jump don't come with an operational tail. It's totally self-contained. No record whatsoever to declassify."

"So you're saying he's untouchable?"

"When I was in the game, we used to joke about who ran those kinds of deep black missions. We called it the Office of Perfect Crimes. A name gets passed in a dead drop. Nothing is written down. The only way it comes out is if somebody on the inside goes on the record. A whistleblower. Something like this, you're not risking your career, more like your life."

Jesse furrows the scars on her brow for a moment, deep in thought. Then she blinks a few times and stares at Davis. "Jump's a good soldier, so he'll never talk," she says slowly. "And Rivard can't because he's dead. But . . . what if there's another person?"

"What other person?"

"When I made my face-plant at Rivard's place, there was this woman—a young woman with dark hair, kind of pampered, classy-looking. And she stayed close to Rivard . . ."

"Yeah, so?" Davis narrows his eyes.

"Well, the thing about it was the way she looked at me. She had this *extreme* reaction. I mean, she literally had trouble keeping her balance. She turned white, Davis, *like she'd seen a fucking ghost.*"

"Hmmmm." Davis studies her face; the anger is still palpable, but now it's focused, intelligent.

"Can your friend at NSA find out who she is?"

"Sure . . ." Davis draws it out and nods his head back and forth, intrigued.

"I'd sure like to know what it was about seeing me that bothered her so much."

"It's a real long shot, Jesse."

"You bet."

"What the hell." Then he thumbs a preset on his cell. "Let me run it by Mouse. It'd mean another trip to Michigan. But, you know, everybody might still be gathered for Rivard's funeral. We'd have to stake the place out ourselves, try to get a line on her. It's too thin to bring in Appert for starters . . ."

★ ★ ★

Davis is negotiating a pain-default swap, sending the agony in his side down the line to be paid for later and all the time thinking, *Okay, we're running on fumes here. Dorothy and the Tin Man off to see the Wizard.*

But I like the company.

Mouse texts and sends a photo confirming the identity of the dark-haired young woman as Rivard's granddaughter, Amanda, who presides over the Rivard Foundation board of directors, runs the grant-making and management committees, and is basically a one-woman show. He allows that approaching Amanda could be a shot in the dark, but bottom line, it is worth ruling out. He says he's discussed it with Appert, who is less sanguine but has discreetly alerted allies in the Detroit FBI office as possible backup. "But be careful," Mouse stresses. "Don't overplay it."

And Joey, try not to get anybody else shot.

So they load up the Escape and hit the road, and Davis stops at the first Target store to augment Jesse's wardrobe with a new pair of shorts and a top. Midway across Wisconsin they pick up spot news on the radio about "the confused shootout at the Minneapolis VA hospital yesterday afternoon that local authorities are calling an attempt to steal narcotics." So far the casualties include an unidentified staff member as a fatality, two VA cops in serious but stable condition, six visitors and patients injured, and a number of missing patients, one of whom was listed by name, a Captain Jessica Kraig. The disinformation campaign is holding for now.

Davis and Jesse exchange a look. So they haven't located the bodies stuffed in the pipes yet. An hour later Mouse calls and informs them that the security tape from Balad has gone missing. So no help there. They spot a Starbucks and pull over to fuel up on caffeine and take inventory. Soon the table is covered in napkin sketches as Davis grills her about everything she can remember about the Rivard estate—the grounds, the sight lines, the road access, security.

Jesse rubs her eyes, leans back, and then reaches over and touches the ripple of scar tissue on Davis' cheek. "Hey you, relax," she says as she withdraws her hand and runs her finger down the cleft denting her chin.

Davis looks up from his diagrams, raises an eyebrow.

Jesse shrugs and peruses the other clientele who—standing or seated—hunch, heads bowed, over iPhone and iPad screens. Suddenly self-conscious about her damaged face and the scars on her bare right knee, she thinks out loud, "Gee, whaddaya suppose they make of us?"

Davis rolls slightly feverish eyes. "For them, soldiers only exist in movies, and wounded soldiers don't exist at all." Then he taps one of the sketches. "How close can we get to the house using available cover?"

"A hundred yards. But that's academic if we run into Jump."

"We don't *run into* anybody. This is a surveillance," he insists. "We try to establish the granddaughter's whereabouts, her pattern. If we can catch her alone, we try an approach to feel her out."

"Right. That's why there's a briefcase in the trunk stuffed with fifties and hundreds along with a first-aid kit and assorted rifles and ammunition."

★ ★ ★

Now it's getting toward midnight, and Jesse finds herself back in upper Michigan, on US 2, east of Escanaba. Davis slouches behind the wheel in a dogged zone beyond fatigue and pain and has the windows cranked open because he's smoking. Like on her solo trip down this lonely stretch of road, the night air that flocks against Jesse's face suddenly fills with demons.

"I keep thinking," she says, "that day in the desert, if I would have broke to the right instead of left, none of this would have happened."

After a moment, Davis says, "Your dad was army infantry in Vietnam, right?"

"Yeah."

"He talk about it?"

"Not much."

"Maybe because he once committed an atrocity and an act of heroism in the same half hour. Don't pay to mindfuck a war, Jesse."

"So what's that say about the guy we're after, Jump?"

Davis has no answer and keeps his eyes fixed on where his high beams fade into the darkness.

After a dozen more miles, the silence stacks up in the front seat until Jesse finally comes out and says it. "I gotta ask. Since you and Jump used to work out of the same shop—another time, another place—were you ever the man in the desert who couldn't afford to be seen?"

Davis squirms behind the wheel to reposition the ache in his side, very aware of Jesse's measuring eyes. He's thinking how once the rules were fairly straightforward, not unlike the center line on the two-lane blacktop that stretches into the gloomy furnace of the upper Michigan night. Right there is your basic compact of trust. Impulse balanced against control. You take it for granted the guy coming at you at sixty miles an hour will stay on his side of the white line.

"First thing that went to hell in Baghdad was the rules of the road," he says.

His hand moves to the stalk on the steering wheel and twists off the lights. It's an old road game he played when he was younger and more in thrall to a death wish. And when he had a much faster car. Once his eyes adjust to the moonlight it's easy enough to track the blacktop, the shoulder, the fields on either side ticking with cicadas. So he eases the wheel a quarter turn and drifts across the line into the left lane. In the distance, perhaps half a mile, he sees the flare of oncoming headlights. As he steps on the accelerator, he reminds himself, *High beams give you a hundred fifty yards of depth perception.*

"What the fuck are you doing?" Jesse braces against the seat.

"Educating you." Leaning back, elbow resting out the window, one hand on the wheel, he calculates the approaching lights, watches them flicker and disappear in dips, come back on.

He is aware of his breathing, which is normal. His pulse is barely elevated.

Just yards from the forward edge of the onrushing lights, he swings back into his lane. The other driver wobbles slightly toward the shoulder as Davis' shadowy Ford appears out of nowhere and hurtles past.

After he switches the lights back on, Jesse releases her grip on the seat cushion and twists to watch the other car's taillights fade in the dark. "So it's like we were never there." She mutters as she turns back to Davis. "Like Jump wasn't there in the desert or you weren't there at the hospital. And if somebody killed Sam, he wasn't there either."

"You catch on fast," Davis says.

After a few more minutes of cryptic silence, he asks, in a more relaxed tone, "So what got you interested in flying?"

Jesse leans back and says, "Summer after my sophomore year in college. My dad got me on a road crew with public works; you know, the girl in the orange vest holding the stop-and-go sign directing one-lane traffic through a torn-up stretch of highway. We have a saying—North Dakota has two seasons: winter and road construction.

"So I'm standing there in the hundred-degree heat with steaming asphalt and wheat fields all around, and a guy in one of the backed-up cars falls on his horn. Heart attack. So we're trying to make him comfortable after we call emergency services, feeling pretty helpless, actually, out in the middle of nowhere, and I look up and see this helicopter coming in low and fast—a Eurocopter EC-145, with the twin tail booms. Life Flight out of Grand Forks."

She shrugs. "Just something about how the pilot brought that airframe in so cool and Johnny-on-the-spot, and I decided right there that's what I wanted to do instead of winding up in some freaking cubicle."

Davis glances at her. "Big difference between flying a civilian air ambulance and Kiowa Warriors and Black Hawks in a war zone."

"No-brainer. The military has the best schools, the best hands-on; and by going through the Guard, I don't have as much obligation as the regulars. Plus, as an officer I pick up management experience."

"So you never considered going regular army?" Davis asks.

Jesse shakes her head. "In the Guard I could keep one foot in the civilian world, where the jobs are. And besides, the women in the regulars, flying cutting edge in Iraq and Afghanistan? They're all divorced, getting divorced, or turning into military nuns." She smiles tightly and says, "It tends to get hard on relationships. I'm willing to do my part, but I'm nobody's martyr . . ." Jesse arches her back to work out the kinks. "I was headed for fixed wing. Up until this happened, I assumed I'd have a life."

"And do what?"

Jesse takes a moment to reconstruct her dreams. Before *this* happened. "Get my pilot's license, fly someplace big and open, where they don't have deserts and where no one's shooting at me." Her eyes drift out the window into the black jack pine. "Alaska, maybe . . ."

After a moment Davis asks, "You were engaged to that Terry guy. So how come you never got married?"

"Lots of things, but it came down to this one night. I was making a list of potential bridesmaids sitting there in my trailer at Balad, and I couldn't come up with a single close girlfriend. I mean from our quote-unquote 'circle.'"

"Tomboy?"

"Hey, I was runner-up for homecoming queen my senior year in high school. Of course, it was a small high school. And I had a boyfriend. But we spent a lot of time working on his car. Some of the things I did just went better with guys, like my brothers." Jesse holds up her palm to clarify. "But don't over-interpret; I read more Jane Austen than *Popular Mechanics*."

"Give me an example of the 'some' things."

"Okay, once when I was fifteen I caught this big frog by the pond and tossed him in a pot of boiling water to see what'd happen."

"So what happened?"

"It was a deep pot. The water won."

CHAPTER SIXTY-SIX

They stand stark as crows in their black mourning clothes on the cobble beach in front of the big house—Amanda in a dark sleeveless dress, Morgon, Roger, and Brian Cawker, who cut his vacation short to attend the funeral. They are waiting for Roger's pilot, who is taking the estate helicopter on a test flight. Before the pilot lands, he will drop John's ashes over the lake.

The quiet ceremony was specified in John's will; he wanted his ashes scattered in the surf in front of the house. Nothing fancy; he left it to Amanda to recruit the farewell party. Morgon shifts from one polished dress shoe to the other. In other words, in Amanda's present mental state, it was up to Morgon to name the new inner circle that would stand witness.

It is, in effect, a changing of the guard. He will explain this to Amanda in more detail later, when she is feeling better. He appraises her, standing stock-still, staring to the north—pretty, of course, and as composed as the Zoloft can make her. Ambien gets her through the night. Considering the meds, she conducted herself with surprising aplomb during the memorial service at the Lakeside Episcopal Church, flanked by the family lawyer and the accountant. Morgon stayed in the background and could have been a deacon in his dark suit.

But the lines of authority were made clear in a discreet comment by one of the CIA elders in attendance. A white-haired man in a tailored two-thousand-dollar suit took him aside briefly and commented that "they" were still interested in continuing their "special relationship" with the Rivard Foundation. When that old fucker hobbled away, he left Morgon privately feeling like the island of Britain.

The next time there is a coded call to the Rivard mansion, it will be Morgon, in John's place, traveling to a face-to-face rendezvous. Brian Cawker will replace him on the sharp end. Cawker's assessment of the Zetas as blunt instruments is borne out by the distressing news coming out of Minneapolis in fragments off the news reports. Apparently the pilot's kidnapping has been accomplished during a ham-fisted shooting spree that included a raid on the hospital's narcotics depository. And now Roger is getting nervous. His ace boy, Juarez, has not reported in and may have helped himself to a stash of class-A dope.

Morgon tilts his head and watches the silvery-blue striped helicopter appear, flying about a hundred feet over the waves. It tips slightly to the side, and they see a mist trail briefly from the cockpit window and then scatter in the prop wash. He glances at Amanda. John's death has hung over them like a dark cloud since he returned, like she blames him for precipitating the heart attack because of all the blowback from the Iraq fiasco.

And now it's a literal cloud, drifting down through the air.

As the helicopter circles and flares toward the hangar, Amanda remains facing the beach, eyes closed, face upturned.

A shift in the wind brings a dull powder—like soft gray sparks—that sprinkles over them and, as Morgon brushes the errant particles of John's ashes off his sleeve, he notices that Amanda doesn't move and some of the ashes melt into the tears on her cheek.

Then she puts a hand on Morgon's shoulder and lifts first one foot, then the other, and takes off her two-inch heels. She manages a vague smile and says, with her medicated, bored drawl verging on sarcasm, "It's not that bringing in Roger to look over the chopper and the books is a bad idea; we don't need an aircraft on the place anymore, and another set of eyes doesn't hurt." She raises her slim cool hand and pats his cheek. "But I'd like to be in the loop on the front end, not after the fact." A genteel sneer peeks in her overdilated gray eyes as she says directly, "Don't take me for granted, Morg. I'm not arm candy. We need to talk, you and me, about what we do around here going forward. Things are going to change." Then she brightens with a tight, possibly manic smile. "Now I'm going to change into something casual and unwind."

"Sounds like a good idea for all of us." Morgon leans over to kiss her cheek, but she steps away, turns, and walks stiffly up the lawn.

Roger joins him and asks, "Amanda's sounding a tad scratchy?"

"The strain, the heat." *The drugs,* Morgon thinks but does not say. Then he and Roger and Cawker fall in line behind her and trod back to the Gothic house like a funeral-weary Addams Family.

It's turned into one of those overcast, sultry early afternoons. Diffuse sunlight casts mossy shadows. Martha sets out a sweating beaker of iced lemonade on the veranda and retires to the kitchen to marinate steaks. Roger, nervously checking his phone for messages about his missing soldier, Juarez, excuses himself and takes the golf cart to the hangar to talk to his pilot. Cawker emerges from the house changed into a loose T-shirt and cargo shorts. Morgon joins him in a pair of faded jeans and a polo shirt.

As they sit and sip lemonade, Cawker surveys the rolling lawn and says, "Nice here, quiet; out of the way. But no security? I thought you'd have some cameras, at least."

Morgon removes his shoes and socks and wiggles his toes, relaxing, letting it all unspool. "We take good care of the sheriff's department, and they take good care of us. I make a call, and we'd have three cars on the road in five minutes."

Cawker nods and sips his lemonade, then inclines his head toward Roger, who paces back and forth by the helicopters, his cell phone still held to his ear. "Fuckin' Juarez. All we get is scraps of information off the news reports."

"I already told Roger, no more Zetas. Next time out we'll be talking to your Brit SAS alumni," Morgon says.

Cawker raises his glass in quiet agreement. Then they both look up when Amanda saunters out the front door in running shorts, a halter, and Nikes. Her face is rinsed clean of makeup and apparently any lingering funeral doldrums. As she twirls her hair into a ponytail and fixes it with a binder, she toes Morgon's bare foot. "I'm going to run the road to work out the kinks before we eat. You interested?"

"Pass." Morgon leans back and holds up his lemonade. Then as she descends the steps, he calls out, "Stay close to the house."

Amanda throws him a mocking hand salute and sets off in a graceful warm-up trot down the driveway. As she nears the entrance to the estate, Morgon turns to Cawker and says, "Do me a favor. Trail along and keep an eye on her. Between the funeral, the meds, and now, with the heat, I'm a little worried about her."

Cawker nods, sets his drink aside, briefly tightens the laces on his cross-trainers, and adjusts the pistol in the hideout holster positioned under his shirt in the small of his back. As he comes down the steps, he marks Amanda's left turn at the country road and then sets off in a comfortable lope across the lawn at a diagonal to cut through the stand of woods and come out on the blacktop behind her.

Morgon watches Cawker thread his way into the trees and then fingers one of John's blue-tip matches from his shirt pocket and inserts it in his mouth in lieu of a Camel. He gazes across the shimmering lawn in the direction of the hangar, where he sees Roger and the pilot walking around the Bell that is parked next to Roger's red fashion statement of an aircraft.

Go easy on him, Morgon decides, rolling the matchstick across his lips. *Show some forbearance. You still need his business acumen.* Briefly he listens to the soft flop of Lake Huron behind the house and imagines John's ashes and bits of bone moving in and out with the tide wash.

It occurs to him that John probably never sat on this porch and thought of himself as lord of all he surveyed. But then John was to the manor born and didn't hatch out of Jump Hollow near Greenwood, Mississippi.

CHAPTER SIXTY-SEVEN

Amanda Rivard has been running along this road since she was a little girl and can recognize the knots in the birch and oak trees and the pebbles on the soft shoulder that crunch beneath her shoes. It's her road. Her county. She still detects the scent of the damp orchids and lilies that filled the church yesterday afternoon. They linger, twined in her hair like a garland of soft thorns. She still sees the stringy Christ spread-eagled above the altar in the nave window with a tortured face like Edvard Munch's *Scream* in the red and purple stained glass along with assorted lambs, shepherds, and angels.

She slows to a walk, looks up and down the road, and then eases a small baggie from the waistband of her shorts. It contains the last joint Kelly Ortiz rolled for her and a small Bic lighter. Fondly she remembers Kelly's magic fingers rolling marijuana cigarettes as she fires up the number and the crackle moves through her lips, into her lungs. She exhales and expels a wave of tension in a long vibrato sigh. Patiently she waits for the boost from blood to brain to smile. *Not your daddy's dope. Hydroponic GX13. This is some strong shit.*

She has no idea where to get the stuff in town with Kelly gone. And it's doubtful Morgon will score dope for her. He's a real handy guy to have around the house, but she's never seen him get high on anything.

Except lately, maybe ambition.

Briefly she pictures the cannabis doing its deft, faintly illegal, softshoe into the plodding Zoloft in her bloodstream. Probably pushing it, but what the hell. Hit by hit she imbibes the numbing tactile glow, and by the time she lets the charred rem-

368

nants drop from her fingers, she's back, softly remembering about the church service.

"A man for the ages," pronounced the reverend James Tindsdale. "A man who saw and accomplished great things. A man who was a generous friend to all gathered here."

And in the good reverend's eulogy she understood the torch passing to carry on the foundation work *in her county*. The thoughts are delicate wind chimes in her head, echoing off into the steamy air. She breaks into a languid trot and finds that running when high is a dreamy, floating sensation. This is the first time she's run the road when no one in the family is waiting for her to return. With John gone, she is alone.

Alone. Alone. Alone. Like a tattoo, her shoes beat out on the gravel. But alone can also translate into freedom. And Morgon doesn't seem to grasp the subtleties of transition and succession. A Rivard will always have the final word, here, on these grounds in Rivard County.

A dusty, muddy, blue SUV with tinted windows passes slowly. A Ford, she thinks; nothing special. *So you are never really alone, are you?* There are always other people, as Morgon relishes pointing out—reading to improve himself—in a quote from Sartre. Hell is basically other people. The Ford disappears around a bend two hundred yards up the road.

She slows her pace as she admits that she misses Kelly, whom they drove away with their dark, mismanaged bullshit. He was someone more her age she could confide in about her mother's suicide, her father's cancer. Not like Morgon. You don't confide in Morgon; you shelter in his powerful shadow.

John had started grooming Morgon from the first day he set foot on the place. Such a foolishly transparent gesture— Morgon was the strong son he never had and all that patriarchal crap. Now Morgon is presuming on his welcome and is taking the bit in his teeth. Now he's brought in that slippery

Roger Torres and Cawker, who is like a scary, diminutive Morgon in process.

He expects me to marry him and have his children. She actually laughs when she flashes on the final scene in *Rosemary's Baby*: Mia Farrow seeing past the cleft hooves and claws and fangs in the crib and cooing as she surrenders to maternal instinct.

We're not bad people, are we?

Not anymore.

"Yeah, well," she thinks out loud. "How about never again."

A flare of sunlight breaks through the overcast and briefly drops a net of shadows across the road. The peek of sun flames out in the bronze hair of another runner, a young woman who approaches around the bend, coming toward her. Amanda notes that this runner has a syncopated gait, favoring her right leg when it strikes the road. The runner stops, kneels facing away from the road, and occupies herself with tying her shoe. Amanda knows most of the joggers she encounters on this stretch, near the house. This one's new. She may be someone's guest or a tourist. Amanda nods and strides past, and a few steps later, a clear, chiseled voice sounds behind her.

"Amanda."

Turning, slowing to a stop, Amanda watches the young woman stand up and walk toward her. Something funny here. Amanda's smile, meant to be polite and curious, twitches across her face, and she feels the Zoloft stability heave beneath her on a cannabis trampoline and, with a sudden chill, she regrets smoking the whole joint.

The woman is attractive in what her New York friends would call a "Midwestern" way: her abbreviated hairdo could have been styled using a bowl for a guide, and her shorts, sloppy untucked tank top, and shoes are strictly box store. In fact, a slender plastic tie protrudes from the side of her shorts like a fishing leader, neglected after the price tag was torn off.

"Yes?" Amanda cocks her head, and now she feels a trickle of ice water in her knees and the rational observer in the back of her head is saying, *Yes, Zoloft is effective at smoothing out normal anxiety, but not so good at buffering a walking nightmare because, hello, you've seen this apparition before . . .*

The woman is close enough now for Amanda to clearly see that something is seriously wrong with her pretty milkmaid face. These slender earthworms thread through her chin and pop out over her lips before burrowing into her cheek to emerge over her right eye. More of the slick purple worms are knitted into her bare right shoulder under her shirt strap, and there's a whole glistening nest of them on her right knee, curling up into her quad and down into her shin.

Amanda dry-swallows and teeters slightly. She recalls that, in some cases, Ambien and Zoloft can interact badly and produce hallucinations. Add a bale of marijuana, and you get this witches' brew.

"We were never properly introduced," the woman says in a cordial voice. "Captain Jessica Kraig. I made a surprise visit to your house around a week ago. You were having a party."

"I . . . yes . . ." Amanda falters, momentarily stunned by the triumphal, barely restrained anger blazing in the girl's intense blue eyes. *But you're dead. Morgon said so on the way to the memorial service.* Amanda looks away from the burning blue eyes and casts her gaze up and down the road, but there's no help in sight, and she truly is all alone out here with this ghost. She fights a surge of panic to bolt. The woman is suddenly very close and bristles with a physical presence that would easily overpower her, and Amanda recalls John's words: *Some farm girl from North Dakota.*

"You can call me Jesse," she says.

Striving to recover, Amanda's fingers pluck at her own face, and she mutters, eyes lowered, "Now I remember the, ah, scars..."

"Yeah, they're a bother, but what are you gonna do?"

Now Amanda's knees have started to buckle. "I'm not well. I'm on medication. My grandfather just passed away..."

"I'm sorry to hear that," Jesse says, stepping in closer, her hands hovering to catch Amanda if she falters.

Now the blue Ford SUV is back, and a lean man with close-cropped, curly brown hair gets out and opens the rear door. He wears faded blue jeans and a loose gray T-shirt. Amanda's association with the Morgons and Cawkers of the world have taught her that most guys with flat bellies tuck in their shirts unless they're hiding something stuck in their waistband. Like a gun. He's another of the Wormwood People with his face marked with diagonal scarring from cheek to cheek, and a tiny stipple of bright red blood has leaked through the right side of his shirt. He's smiling, but his greenish eyes remind her of Morgon's eyes, the eyes of a wild animal that has learned to pass for tame.

"Why don't you get in, Miss Rivard?" he says. "We'll give you a lift home, because you don't look so hot."

"Don't hurt me," Amanda says under her breath, playing for time, as she shuffles toward the open car door.

★ ★ ★

Brian Cawker's first impulse is to reach for his phone when, from the cover of the trees, he sees Amanda being intercepted first by the woman, then by the man, who pulls up in the blue Ford Escape. As he recalibrates from leisurely afternoon to all-hands-on-deck, he watches Amanda get in the car and drive away.

As the SUV rolls past, he commits the Wisconsin license plate to memory and has his phone flipped open. But before he selects Morgon's number, he sees the brake lights flash as the car turns in toward the estate on an overgrown logging trail maybe 150 yards down the road. He's thinking he should keep Amanda close and do a little recon before he calls.

Falling into an easy rhythm, grateful that the shirt and shorts he pulled from his bag are green and tan and blend in, he backtracks through the woods and takes up a position a hundred yards from where the Ford has now pulled into a thicket. He's always had good bush eyes, so at this distance he easily recognizes these two interlopers who have detained Amanda Rivard and now stand talking to her next to the car.

He assembled the dossiers on them for Roger Torres.

Now they leave the car and work their way cautiously to the tree line. The pilot, Kraig, raises a pair of binoculars to her eyes, then lowers them and continues to talk with Amanda. The man—Davis—joins them and takes the binoculars and studies the house across the rolling lawn, where Morgon sits in a chair on the veranda sipping lemonade.

Cawker takes a deep breath, exhales, and eases the Beretta from under his shirt. Then he thumbs the cell phone, selects Morgon's number, and hits send. Across the lawn he watches Morgon pick up his phone from the table next to his chair and raise it to his ear.

"Stay absolutely cool, mate," Cawker whispers. "Show no reaction. We have company, and everything we know is wrong."

CHAPTER SIXTY-EIGHT

Staying absolutely cool, Morgon fingers his chest pocket for his cigarettes as he listens to Cawker, and it's like the tectonic plates are shifting beneath his feet as this massive, grimy glacier intrudes on the day, studded with skeletons, and plows under the manicured grass.

His hand comes back empty. No cigarettes. *Left them in the carriage house to please Amanda.*

When Cawker finishes running it down, Morgon plucks the matchstick from his lips and casually flips it away. Then he takes a few beats to look across the lawn at the tree line. Not good. Clearly he has fumbled his first management assignment. "Fucking Roger and his low-rent Zeta pukes," he mutters. Then, quickly, he orients to work the problem. "Okay, so where are they?"

"In the trees. Roughly at your eleven o'clock, a little over two hundred yards."

"And nobody's talking on phones?"

"No. They're talking to Amanda. No sign of backup so far. Looks like they're on their own."

"But they couldn't put all this together on their own, could they?" Morgon states the obvious.

"Not likely. The cover story in Maryland involved the FBI and the state patrol. Who knows what strings they pulled to skew the reporting from Minneapolis. I'd say we're eyeball deep in crocs."

"And there's Grand Forks," Morgon thinks out loud. *And that wasn't sanctioned. You called that totally on your own.* "Well, fuck it; that's what lawyers are for. And maybe it's a good thing they're talking to Amanda. Right now talking to Amanda can drive you crazy. Okay, here's what we do. First, is Roger's pilot in the game?"

"Nigel? Sure, ex-Rhodesian air defense. He's merced his ass all over Africa."

"I'll have Roger spin up the bird and stand by. Then it'll take me three minutes to go in and grab something out of the gun safe. I'll set up at the south end of the house in the junipers. Can you see where I'll be?"

"I can see it."

"You're carrying, right?"

"Morg, I got a Beretta nine and one mag. Fifteen rounds. That's it. I'm more than a hundred yards away. This Davis wouldn't come in here light. I did the background on him. He's real trouble."

"So are we." Morgon, coldly furious, has already made his decision. "But for now they're alone. Okay, here's the drill. Keep a safe distance. They're just inside the tree line, right?"

"Roger that."

"So you throw a few rounds their way, they might bolt into the open . . ."

"It's possible, but what about Amanda?"

"Yell for her to run for the house, that you'll cover her."

"Yeah. But what if she doesn't?" Then, "Maybe we should take a step back and think this through."

"Dammit, Cawker. Work with me here. If they don't move, I'll come in to you, and we'll have to do it the old-fashioned way, won't we?" He squints across the lawn. "First let's see if you can get them moving."

"What are you thinking?"

"We finish it right here and now. Once they're down, we dress them in logging chains, load them in the chopper, drop them in the fucking lake, and be back in time for supper. Let the people who give me my marching orders worry about the damage control."

"Like they were never even here. Sounds like a plan." Cawker's voice is rock steady on the phone, but as he tucks his cell away, he allows himself a long inward sigh.

CHAPTER SIXTY NINE

The initial panic has subsided. Now mere dread squeegees her raw nerves as Amanda strives to adjust to the prospect that these two people—one of whom she was assured was dead—have taken her hostage. As the Ford pulls into the logging trail, she notices that the weeds are beaten down and she surmises that they've been in here earlier; in fact, they've probably been watching the house.

Staring straight ahead, she braces herself for what happens next. The man is obviously injured; they both have a hot fix to their eyes, a rankness to their clothing, and a flush to their scarred faces that signals extreme fatigue.

As Jesse motions for her to get out of the car, Amanda attempts an opening gambit. "Look. I don't know what this is all about, but I have access to a great deal of money if that's what you're looking for."

"What I'm looking for is an explanation of why you freaked out when we first met." Jesse says it cold but civil.

Now the man has come around from the driver's side and asks a series of questions about the people at the house and the helicopter activity. Amanda patiently explains they are the last guests to depart from the funeral ceremony. One of them is test-flying the estate helicopter that is now for sale. In an effort to establish a touch of gravitas, she states, "If you know who my grandfather was, you understand that his friends are not to be trifled with."

"Right," the man says. Then he hands Jesse a pair of binoculars. Amanda watches Jesse raise the glasses and lens Morgon sitting on the porch. "That's him," she says. "That's the guy who shot my crew chief."

Then they both pause to observe the effect of Jesse's words sinking in.

"So," the man says, "the question is, Miss Rivard, why did three guys come into the Minneapolis VA last Friday and try to kill Captain Kraig?" He adds, "And don't tell me that comes as a surprise."

Amanda takes a jarring moment to experience her life turning upside down. "I misspoke. Obviously this isn't a problem that money can solve." As her words crash-land on their stone expressions, she adds, "So what's going on here? Should I call my lawyer?"

The man composes a nuanced smile on his face, scar by scar. "Let's say there's a ring tightening around you that involves several federal agencies. Let's say you should check with your attorney about any exposure you might have—say to a federal grand jury—about having prior knowledge about a conspiracy to silence and then, that failing, to murder Captain Kraig. Not during some botched hush-hush operation in Iraq—but in a Minneapolis veteran's hospital."

"Sounds serious. May I see a badge?" Amanda asks.

The man continues to smile and points casually across the lawn at Morgon, doll-sized, sitting on the porch. "Does he carry a badge?"

Despite the heat and the stress and her addled blood chemistry, Amanda fully grasps his meaning. "So that's how we are," she says.

"That's how we are," Davis confirms. He jerks his head at Jesse. "You thought she died in Minnesota. You thought *I died* in Maryland two weeks ago. We are not making this shit up, *alone.*"

Even after smoking a world-class doobie, Amanda has near-perfect recall for names. "Davis," she says simply and doesn't even attempt to follow all the weird pictures that start in her head: funeral flowers and stained-glass windows and the crumbling Zoloft-buffered edges and Iraq not staying inside the fucking TV where it's supposed to. And now here's this green-eyed killer with his crooked smile, back from the dead and wandering in across the lawn like another of Morgon's loose ends.

On a goddamned fishing expedition!

It's so patently absurd she puts her hand to her mouth to stifle a laugh.

Davis moves in closer, studying her eyes, then, gently, he takes her right hand, raises it, and sniffs her fingers. He releases her hand and turns to Jesse. "She's stoned."

Amanda shrugs and addresses Jesse. "You should pick your men friends more carefully, honey, because, believe me, I know this type, and they'll let you down every time." She's standing waist-deep in thistles and weeds, and gnats are swarming around her bare arms and legs and face, and she's started to sweat, and she's wondering if this is a multiple-choice test like the Lady or the Tiger. Open the wrong door, and you get eaten by several federal agencies. But maybe what's behind the other door might solve all of her Morgon problems. "You appreciate my late grandfather's line of work?" she begins. "Well, then you understand that it's pretty ugly stuff that he was tasked with doing, and I guess you got caught up in it," Amanda says, not faking the conflicted roll to her eyes.

Davis and Jesse exchange measured glances.

Amanda pauses until she has their full attention. Then she turns to Jesse. "Look. I know who you are, and yes, I was surprised at the way you keep coming back on us. For what it's worth, I spoke up against what they did to you. When the Iraq job fell apart, I was in the room when my grandfather got the call about you surviving and being in the hospital. And I heard him make another call, to someone in Germany, about how to deal with you."

"It would be helpful to know what I flew into in Iraq."

"Sorry," Amanda says. "I just make the travel arrangements around here. For that other you'd have to ask John, and we just sprinkled him along the beach. You could try the general information number at the CIA, but I suspect they'll put you on hold."

Jesse looks directly into Amanda's calculating gray eyes and asks, "So what did they decide to do about me?"

"After they failed to get to you in the hospital . . ."

"You mean *him*," Jesse interjects, pointing toward the house. "The guy on the porch with the scar. You know him, right?"

"Sure. About 90 percent of the time he's a perfect gentleman, and the other 10 percent he's the Creature from the Black Lagoon."

"Why'd he kill my crew?"

"Let's say you have to sink pretty far down to get to where Morgon works. There must have been an accident. You can understand that, being a pilot. Women and kids and GIs get blown away in Iraq by pilots all the time."

"We're talking about my crew." Jesse bites off the words.

Amanda accepts Jesse's incensed farm-girl stare as the price of doing business. "After they failed to get to you in the hospital," she repeats, "John suggested that the operator in Germany slip you a maximum dose of PCP. They hit you again at Walter Reed. That way you'd present as psychotic and they'd medicate you accordingly. Which, I gather, they did."

Jesse shows gritted teeth in the rictus of a smile. "So I'm not crazy after all. How nice."

Amanda ignores her and turns to Davis. "For conversation's sake, are you offering me a deal?"

"For conversation's sake, I can put you in touch with an FBI man who has that authority. You make travel arrangements; I'm just a messenger."

"I'm not saying we're there yet, but I assume you have a name and a number?"

Davis hands her a slip of paper. "Special Agent Bobby Appert. It's the smart move, Miss Rivard," he says.

After a quick glance at Appert's number, she folds it and closes it tight in her sweaty fist. Her gaze drifts through the foliage to Morgon sitting on the porch. "There's a few federal agencies that'll circle the wagons around him, you know," she says quietly.

"Sometimes you have to pick a side."

Amanda weighs it. "And he'll go away?" She nods toward the house.

"That's the idea," Davis says.

"So nothing's for sure."

Davis holds up his phone. "Call the number."

"How soon can they be here?"

Davis wings it in his best game-face voice and says, "Be best if we relocate, meet them."

"And then what?" Amanda swats at the bugs swarming around her face.

"They take your statement, get a warrant, and arrest Jump and shut them down."

Amanda gives a sardonic smile. "Shut them down? Really? How do you know some oversight committee won't dither for six months and decide John was just a bad apple running a rogue operation? In the meantime, if Morgon can't make bail, there's no guarantee they won't send another Morgon at you— or me, if I talk—just for spite. God knows they've been training a limitless supply of them the last ten years. And I suspect, Mr. Davis, you're one of them."

Davis shrugs. "We're burning time here, Miss Rivard."

"Flip on Morgon?" Her sweaty fingers tug at the widow's peak in the center of her forehead. "Jesus, the lawyers will cost a ton, and I'll have to call in most of my chits."

Davis senses she's reaching the tipping point and moves in closer. He draws a look from Jesse as his voice changes up, positive. "But in the end, you'll get immunity and keep this place and what you do here."

"I want that in writing, with my lawyer present."

"You got it," Davis assures her, taking her by the arm, nodding to Jesse to start moving toward the car.

Amanda balks as she remembers a lecture from medical school about the difficult transition from student to practicing doctor. How you have to respond rapidly and correctly to acute situations. She feels the pressure of Davis' fingers on her bare arm. She has to make a decision.

"You coming?" he asks.

"You're asking me to snitch."

"I'm showing you a way to survive."

She tosses one last look back through the trees toward the house and Morgon and the world that was. *Lady, tiger? Live lady trumps dead tiger. Do it.* "Okay. I'm in. Let's get the hell out of here."

Hunched, furtive, she hurries through the itchy waist-deep weeds, swatting at mosquitoes, but then she dares to hope, and every step starts to feel like freedom. No Morgon. And it starts to come out in a rush. "For openers, I can give him how they funded the operation through anonymous donations to the foundation. And I can show you how the money was disbursed to pay subcontractors, like the men who came into the hospital. They look hard enough, they should be able to trace it back to somebody's budget." Then Amanda turns toward Jesse with a tense smile. "Sorry, honey. Taxpayer dollars killed your crew."

But Jesse isn't listening. Bringing up the rear, she's lensing the house one last time with the binoculars. She lowers the glasses. "He's gone off the porch. And you hear that?" Past the house, at the far end of the grounds, a helicopter turbine coughs and begins to crank.

Davis, phone out, about to punch in Appert's number, jerks his head around. "Move," he shouts. "Run." They dash to the car, and Davis yanks open the driver's-side door to shove Amanda across the seats. Jesse has her hand on the back door handle when a single gunshot cracks and the Ford's rear hatch window blows out in a bright shower of shattered glass.

CHAPTER SEVENTY

Ah, shit! So go to plan B.

Davis hurls Amanda to the ground, dives, rolls through the tall grass and ferns and thistles, and comes up pulling open the Ford's rear door. Fast look around. Where'd Jesse go? As he heaves in and reaches over the back seat for the rifle cases in the boot compartment, another shot smashes through the rear windows, and pellets of glass sting along his arms, his face, and in his hair. But he grabs the cases and the first-aid kit. As he rolls back into the grass, he pats his empty right trouser pocket.

Somewhere in the confusion, he lost his cell phone. So much for backup. Amanda crouches, shivering, six feet away, with her pupils dilated and her face striped by the dense bottlebrush grass, and she's jumpy as a bead of grease on a hot skillet. Any minute she's gonna run.

"Stay down," he commands, looking around for Jesse as he unzips the longer case and slides out the rifle and a plastic strip that contains ammunition. Quickly, expertly, he feeds four rounds into the Remington, pushes the bolt forward, and sticks the remaining ammo in his back pocket.

"Oh shit, oh shit," Amanda mutters and Davis swings his head in the direction of her fixed stare and sees Jesse crawl around the back of the car with a fringe of golden hair pasted in a wet, red pageboy against her forehead. More blood makes a gory nimbus on the top of her head.

"Not bad," Jesse grunts. "Glass just cut the scalp. Superficial head wounds . . ."

" . . . bleed a lot," Davis finishes the thought as he tosses the shorter case toward Jesse, who now crouches, trying to rub the blood from her eyes and making a mess of her face.

Then he turns to Amanda, who's halfway to her feet because the blood smeared on Jesse's face is starting to look like a deal breaker. "Lie flat on your stomach. Do it," he orders. Shaky, hyperventilating, Amanda complies.

He turns back to Jesse. Eyes wide, she's holding her breath but looks steady as she inserts a magazine into the AR15 and pulls the operating rod to load the chamber. They both exhale. Davis tears open the aid kit, tosses Jesse a compress, then scans the silent, shadowed trees. "That was a pistol," he mutters. His side is throbbing like hell to the backbeat of buzzing insects, the drip of sweat, and his pounding heart. So here he is again in one of those deadly, frozen moments.

"We're blind," Jesse whispers. "Can't see shit hiding down here in this freakin' stuff."

Davis raises his finger to his lips. Moment like this, up against pros, you only get one move. World Series of your life, bottom of the ninth, two out, two strikes, three balls, and Mariano Rivera is winding up. One throw, one swing. So who's going to blink first?

They do.

"Amanda," a voice yells, deep in the trees. "Run for the house; I'll cover you."

Three rapid shots rattle through the overhead, whipping up a tiny storm of bark and bits of green. As the debris filters down, Amanda tenses up on her palms and the balls of her feet and the fear spins in her eyes like gray icons on a slot machine. Another flurry of shots cracks high and wide, and her eyes swell and she jumps to her feet and crashes, wild, through the brush toward the open ground beyond the trees. Jesse squats in the weeds with the Beretta stuck in her waistband. Squinting from under the hasty bandage around her head, she swivels the black assault rifle, looking for the shooter. "We blew it. There goes Bobby Appert's perfect material witness," she hisses through clamped teeth.

With a grimace, Davis rises like a sprinter on starting blocks. "Shit. Don't fire unless you have a clear target." Then he's in motion, and it's like he's running through this banner with big block letters on it: DUMB. More shots make a racket through the trees, but he forces himself to ignore them because it's a pistol and the voice that called to Amanda was out of pistol range. But they managed to hit the car twice.

Gaining on Amanda, he breaks from the cover of the trees and instinctively crouches and shifts the rifle across the open space. Some primal alarm in Amanda's stoned cortex also seems to get the message because she stops running and shifts nervously from foot to foot as her face turns waxy with apprehension. The imposing house is almost two hundred yards away. They're in plain view and the red helicopter's engine revs and its blades beat an ominous tattoo in the air.

"Get down," Davis yells, inching toward her. "Make yourself small. We'll crawl back to the trees." He eyes the roll of the ground. "There's some defilade . . ."

"Some what?"

CHAPTER SEVENTY ONE

Oh, this is perfect. It's gonna work. Not so much a thought as an imbedded process of orienting and reflex and ranging as Morgon raises the barrel of his rifle at the corner of the house and shifts his bare feet in the thatch of dry juniper needles that sting among the wood chips because, after he alerted Roger, he came through the house and opened the gun safe and grabbed the Remington and a box of shells and his .45 so goddamned fast he didn't take time to put on his shoes or say anything to Martha, who watched him pass through the kitchen in open-mouthed shock.

Absolutely perfect. Cawker's shots stir the pot, and Amanda bursts from the trees and then stops running as if suddenly intimidated by all the open space. Then Joe Davis— an apparition from a Memphis photograph who now becomes available in flesh and blood, in the optics of the ten-power scope—slows to a tense crouch and approaches her with one hand outstretched like he's trying to calm down a spooked colt.

Soft *click.* Safety off. Greedy for the shot, he decides to forego the supported position. *Just do it. Swat these interlopers who have ruined your day.* In the slightly wavering scope he can clearly see the sweat pop on Davis' determined expression. *Musta forgot everything they taught you—showing your ass like this. Must be a fuckin' Boy Scout.* Then it all plays out in the tight, intimate world of the sniper scope, which, depending on your stomach for seeing the pores on your target's face, is a curse or a secret delight. The precise black crosshairs caress the ripple of scars on Davis' cheeks. A little tricky; he's still moving in a crouch, using the rolling ground for cover, and just now Amanda is in the way.

C'mon, c'mon. Just have to time it right. The first stage of the sensitive Camjar trigger releases, and Morgon takes up the slack, and the rifle stock recoils against his shoulder. Shit. Rushed the shot. He moved again. But then —*yes* —he sees Davis twirl and fall.

Amanda screams, but Davis doesn't hear it or the shot, because the shock tears into his left temple and the smackdown pinwheel of gray sky becomes green spinning grass, and then it all goes black.

Morgon has his phone out and hits a preset. "Roger. It's cool. One down. Bring up the bird and work the tree line. I'll call Cawker and see if he can get a fix on the girl."

He racks the bolt and loads another round and watches Amanda, who now is walking, head down, arms folded tightly across her chest, across the lawn toward the house. Cautiously, he leaves concealment and carefully steps forward, steadying the rifle across his left forearm, covering Davis' crumpled body. He jerks the rifle barrel to wave Amanda out of the way and puts it back on line as he thumbs his cell phone in his left hand. Now he holds the rifle in one hand to free the other to talk. "Cawker. Yeah. Davis is down. So far so good. We're going to push the trees with the bird, see if we can flush the girl. Keep your eyes open. We gotta assume she's armed." Then he slips the phone into his pocket and starts to circle because Davis sprawls behind a slight rise in the ground and Morgon can only see his head and shoulders. Amanda continues walking, eyes downcast.

Across the twenty yards that now separate them, Amanda raises her chin and stares at him with her eyes hard and shiny as ball bearings. "I hope to hell you know what you're doing," she says.

"I know what I'm doing," Morgon answers. "Where's the girl?"

She ignores his question and goes on in a cryptic tone, saying, "Because if you don't know what you're doing, I still have to look out for myself."

Morgon winces at her. "Calm down. You did good. Now where's the girl, goddammit?"

"Her head's . . . all bloody." Amanda clamps her eyes shut for a second, then looks away.

Morgon nods. "Now go to the house, take Martha down in the basement, and wait until I get back. This ain't over yet."

Amanda's icy stare goes right through him, and she repeats, "I hope you know what you're doing." Then Morgon, who's had enough of her spacey bullshit, waves her away, and she continues on toward the house.

Morgon is on the phone again, to Cawker. "Amanda says you hit the girl. I'm going to sweep the tree line. Stay put." Then he calls and updates Roger. "Buzz the tree line and see if you can spook her out. Just clean up now." More confident, he stands up straighter as he puts the phone away and turns his full attention back to Davis' body that lies in a slight depression a hundred yards away. Circling, he's looking for the rifle he was carrying. Must be under his body. From the corner of his eye he sees the red helicopter levitate off the ground and start forward, tail lifted, nose down. He takes a firm grip on the rifle and places the crosshairs on Davis' bloody head as he slowly steps forward.

Crouched just inside the foliage behind a fallen tree, Jesse hears the shot and sees Davis spin and fall and lay motionless, and she doesn't look away. She takes in every detail to include the way that cold bitch, Amanda, doesn't even look twice when Davis goes down and keeps walking across the lawn. Then Jesse bares her teeth when she sees Morgon Jump come out of hiding and start his stalk across the grass. So there he is, the motherfucker who's still killing her buddies.

Quickly she faces about and probes the barrel of the AR15 at the surrounding thick brush. Deep breath. Sweat and blood blur her vision. She uses the bandage to wipe away the sticky haze, then tosses it aside. Just a maze of trees out there. Nothing. Jump's in front, and she doesn't know how many others are to her rear. And they got a chopper in the air. She has one magazine in the rifle, another one stuck in her waistband, and the Beretta.

She takes a few beats to study the red helicopter that's starting her way.

Then her heart catches in her throat because—*Oh, you skinny bastard*—she sees Davis' right hand twitch, low, next to his side, and the fingers flutter, feeling their way along the rifle tucked in under his right arm and walking down the stock toward the trigger guard. He turns his hand, curls his fingers into a fist, and gives a thumbs-up sign.

Okaaay. Jesse carefully leans the AR-15 against the tree trunk and takes out the Beretta. Then she's up and moving, stepping from the trees into plain sight because their relationship is founded on her drawing fire, right, and she waves her arms and screams with everything she's got:

"Hey you! Yeah, you, fucker!"

A hundred yards away, Jump turns away from Davis and instantly fixes on the slender figure with a red-smeared face that steps from the trees. *And it's, no shit, not a phantom in a dream, but there you are out in the open where I can see you. I should have wrung your neck in Balad, but this will do just fine.* He grins when he sees her raise the puny handgun, and it's back to how it all started. Amateur hour.

Now the red helicopter is swerving directly toward her, getting close enough to clearly see the yellow pyramid logo on the side. Jesse squats and grips the pistol two-handed, holds two feet high, and fires four rapid shots at Jump, which at this range is like flipping rocks with a catapult. And she notes that Jump, the smug bastard, doesn't even duck, obviously contemptuous of a female banging away at extreme range with a pistol.

Just you wait.

Then, before he gets the rifle up, she drops, rolls, and scrambles back into the safety of the tree line, snatches up the black assault rifle, and yells, "Davis, if you can move, crawl toward the trees because all hell's gonna bust loose!"

Davis' left eye is plugged and sightless and his whole body is a shivering tuning fork of screaming nerves. Impossibly, he hears the crack of four shots and Jesse's voice somewhere behind him. So the game is still on and the pitch is still on the way and there's a roar of approaching engines, and he takes a chance and twists his head and feels his left eyebrow hang and flop against his face like a wet forelock.

"Crawl!" she shouts.

Okay. I think I can crawl.

He flings one painful look behind him. Morgon Jump stands, barefoot, maybe ninety yards away. He swings his rifle, looking for a target in the trees.

Trying not to think about the mess on the left side of his head, Davis turns in an agonizing, crablike belly crawl toward the sanctuary of the cool, shadowed trees. Any moment he expects to be hammered into the ground by someone in the looming chopper. Then the leaves in the tree line stutter in a green frenzy as a rapid-fire volley of shots rips the air.

A hundred yards over Davis' head, Nigel, the Rhodesian pilot, yells in alarm as the *tick-tick-tick* of impacting bullets tears into his tail boom. "Fuck this," he says and turns the helicopter sharply away from the trees.

Roger Torres, who is having a real bad day, shouts, "But Morgon's in trouble down there."

"Your *girl* knows what she's doing," Nigel shouts back. "She's trying to take out the tail rotor. My pedals are jumping. I'm putting down behind the house."

As the helicopter veers off, Jesse swiftly swaps out the empty magazine, slaps in a fresh one, hits the charging handle release, and finds the now backpedaling Morgon Jump in the peep sight. She takes a supported position on the tree trunk and puts the blade on his chest. Then she squeezes the trigger as fast as she can. Ten, twelve, fourteen rounds chew up the turf around his feet, and he goes down like a string-cut marionette. *Gotcha.* No time to celebrate because Davis is out there. She bites her lip as she tosses a wary glance to her rear. *How come they're not shooting? Screw it.*

She drops the rifle and bolts from cover and grabs Davis by the waistband of his jeans and one arm and drags him into the protection of the trees. Gasping with the effort, she turns him over and forces herself not to recoil from the swollen left eye. The dangling eyebrow. Red exposed bone gleams in the ragged flesh.

"How bad?" he croaks.

"I don't know."

"It's a simple question. You see bone or you see brains?"

"Bone. I think."

Then he growls, "Grab your piece, goddammit; they're still out there in the woods!"

Jesse snatches up the rifle and scans the silent trees around the Escape. Then she turns to the scene on the lawn. Jump is on his butt clutching his right thigh, and the helicopter is doing a wobbly retreat. As the Bell flares and lands behind the house, she sees Jump struggle to his feet and, using his rifle now as a crutch, start to hobble toward the house.

"Jump's hit," she yells.

Now a dark-haired man runs out to help him. Jump drops the rifle and throws his arm over the man's shoulder as together they do a stumble, skip, quick-step toward the helicopter that's still running, out of sight.

"They're helping him back to the bird. It landed behind the house. I don't know where the other ones are." Jesse's voice is a fever of adrenaline as she scans the woods behind them. Davis has managed to sit up and experimentally feels at his head. He tries to get to his feet and collapses back to the ground.

"Aid kit, by the car," he mumbles, taking the AR-15 from her and squinting with his good eye. While she fetches the medical bag, he attempts a sight picture on Jump and his rescuer, who are now getting closer to the house. Never happen. Too much blood in his eye. Shaking too much.

Jesse returns and drops the bag at his feet. When she doesn't open it, he follows the direction of her bright eyes that fix on the silver helicopter parked next to the hangar, the one that they used to scatter the ashes along the beach. And Jump is getting away, and it's all there in her fierce blue glare. "I'll be fine," he says. "Stay to the edge of trees 'til you're even with the hangar. There's some terrain relief. I'll cover you."

On impulse she leans over and kisses his mouth, and his blood on her lips tastes like warm, wet copper.

Then she's up and off, sprinting through the brush at the edge of the trees. Davis read the ground right, and there's just enough downside to the roll of the ground to mask her run. All she can see is the roof of the mansion against the overcast sky. Ignoring the pain in her right knee, she tosses the Beretta aside because it slows her down. Just like worrying about catching a bullet slows her down, so she lets that go too. Then she makes her break into the open, toward the hangar and the Bell Long Ranger, which is the first bird she ever flew at Rucker. It's gassed up and ready to go and waiting for her, and she's less than a hundred yards away now, and her lungs burst with the effort.

Davis watches Jesse dash in a low crouch, using the ground to conceal her approach. *Good girl.* He swings the AR-15 in an arc, but the woods behind him are silent, so he sets the

AR-15 aside and, wiping away blood, quickly ties a compress over his temple. Jesse is now just yards away from the silver-blue helicopter. Then she's in. Okay, he sees the chopper blades slowly start to rotate. She made it.

Gingerly he probes the bulky dressing and decides that Morgon Jump has damn near shot off his left eyebrow and maybe carved a new wrinkle along the left side of his skull. But, aside from all the glistening, needle-pointed pain in the goddamn world and his left eye plugged and swollen shut, he can still function.

Sort of.

So he retrieves the Remington, checks the action, and hopes the scope isn't cattywampus. Reflexes. Even head shot, he hugged the rifle protectively into his side as he went down. With his good eye he watches Jump being hauled behind the house by the dark-haired man and hears the chopper revving.

Okay, Marine, back to basics. Square away. *Improvise. Adapt. Overcome.* After taking a few experimental steps, he bears down and sets off toward the gabled, turreted house feeling like a crippled caddy on a fucking golf course.

Brian Cawker sees it all unfold from behind the sturdy trunk of an oak tree and takes a quick inventory of his options. He has an empty pistol, no ammo, a few hundred cash in his pocket as well as a thousand in traveler's checks, his credit cards, and his passport. What the hell was Morgon thinking? Showing himself like that before they located the girl? And now he's hit and Roger will be running scared and the Kraig woman has apparently managed to ding Roger's helicopter with an assault rifle nobody knew she had. Davis is back from the dead and looking very much alive and now is on his feet with a scoped rifle. Any minute Cawker expects the cavalry to arrive, probably in blue windbreakers decorated with big yellow letters: FBI.

And it's pretty clear from the last twenty minutes that, in this crunch, Morgon Jump is not up to being another John Rivard. *So fuck it. Just have to disappear from the grid for a while and get some new ID.* He can always find a berth someplace where they run a tighter ship, like maybe Singapore.

So he decides it might be more sensible to see how this plays out from a discreet distance. Say, from Sydney. He turns and jogs off into the woods.

CHAPTER SEVENTY-TWO

Vaulting into the cockpit, Jesse's hands and feet touch the pedals, the cyclic, and the collective, and the helicopter's latent avionics pour into her. For the first time in months, she knows exactly where she is. *Can't fly, huh? Okay, Janet. Watch this!*

Cranking on the double quick, she cracks the throttle, engages the starter, and wraps it up fast through flight idle to 100 percent and pulls pitch before she even fastens the seatbelt.

Like riding a freakin' bike.

It's maybe four hundred yards to the house where the red Bell is still on the lawn by the beach. Squinting, she sees the pilot is out of the aircraft, checking the tail boom. *C'mon, c'mon.* She wills the blades to turn faster and grab air. Then okay. Skids up. She's off the ground, and a deep chill crackles inside her as she inhales the sweet bloom of avgas and it's like she's firing up neural systems that have been too long dormant. She zooms past Davis, who is hobbling across the lawn. Comes even with, then passes, the house. Okay, so what's the play; which way's the pilot gonna go? Glancing to her right through the windshield, she makes out the red blur of the other helicopter in the trees. *He's taking off, hovering, turning toward the beach. Same direction as me.*

She ignores the gauges, instinctively figuring time, distance, angles, and wind speed. *Okay, you can't do this by the book.* Then she smiles ruefully and thinks, *Well, one book, maybe.*

Hugging the contour of the ground, she skims forward, picking up airspeed, feeding in power, swiveling her head to track the fleeting red image trailing at her five o'clock. Through the hundred yards of woods that separates them, she sees that he's still headed in the same direction, along the beach. Back maybe five hundred yards. *Stay close to the deck so he can't see you. Got a little wobble to him, so I musta hit the boom after all. Okay.*

So how about Chickenhawk Rules!

Here goes.

She hauls in on the controls and puts the Bell to starboard in a steep turn. *So take a chance. So aim for a meager clearing in the trees.* Like a daredevil from another generation, she's hell-bent on testing the Bell's potential as a chainsaw.

Ohhh shit! Bit of pucker as the airframe shudders and the props growl in protest. A whirligig of severed branches and shredded foliage slaps the windshield. But it gets her through the trees. Shaky but still airborne, she pops out over the beach ahead of the red helicopter and keeps the turn going, and there's only one option now. White-knuckled on the controls, she heads straight at the red Bell that fills her windscreen until she can see the pilot's startled face.

He tries to evade to the left, but she swings out, and there's no room or time, and he takes the only other choice, which is to flare right, into the tree canopy. Jesse braces herself, passing the other helicopter so tight she knows their fans overlap, and then, as the red Bell commences to eat itself to pieces in the trees, she executes a rivet-twisting but adequate emergency landing and brings it down with a tremendous jolt in the surf.

Now billows of black oily smoke obscure the overcast sky, and Jesse is out and drops to her knees in the cold surf. She scoops a double handful of lake water to her face to douse the red-hot adrenaline shakes and clear her eyes. Not done yet. She gets up and wades through the water. Then she's walking on cobbles, then sand, as she watches two men, the pilot, presumably, and the dark-haired man, crawl from the smashed helicopter and scramble, limping and tripping, headlong down the beach.

Morgon Jump, abandoned, makes slow progress away from the wreck on all fours. Blood mixed with dirt soaks the right side of his jeans, and his shirt is fouled with oil.

Without breaking stride, Jesse leans over and plucks up a sturdy length of driftwood. Jump sees her now from the corner of his eye and rolls on his side and then uses his elbows and then his palms to push himself up in a sitting position and fumbles, yanking at the Colt .45 jammed in his waistband.

At a distance of ten yards they glare at each other, and it's *déjà vu* on steroids. The crippled helicopter. Seeing him up close, with the gun in his hand and the livid scar throbbing on his neck. "Didn't get away this time, you bastard," she says in an even voice, gripping the driftwood.

Morgon's face is lacerated and his lips have been split in the crash, so he coughs blood as he shakes his head. In the distance he can just make out a corner of the porch where he was sitting just minutes ago, sipping iced lemonade. A sound — part cough, part cold mirth — escapes his bloody lips as he waves the Colt toward his feet. "Shit, I started out barefoot in Mississippi, and now here I am again."

Jesse, all in, grits her teeth and brandishes the stick, determined to try a rush.

Then Morgon's face turns grim and he raises the Colt and extends his arm. "That what they taught you in the North Dakota National Guard? Bring a club to a gunfight?"

Davis sees Jesse thread the silver helicopter into the trees and then hears the crash on the other side of the woods and sees the black plume of smoke and tries to run, but his body won't do it. Gasping, he makes it to a clearing past the house where it's open down to the shore and sees a shimmer of red in the smoke and spots Jesse leap from the other helicopter that has landed, tilted, in a foot of water. Helplessly, he watches her walk toward a man who is crawling on all fours across the beach.

He swings up the rifle and lenses them herky-jerky in the scope. Jesse with her stick. Morgon Jump sitting up and pulling out the pistol, and it's no good because it's more than two hundred yards and a futile chill clamps his chest to ice. He can't keep the trembling rifle anywhere near steady—offhand—in the condition he's in, standing, one eye swollen shut and his head coming apart and still shaking like hell.

Then his good eye fixes on the limestone wall about a dozen feet away, around a gazebo, and the ground behind the wall is still excavated, not filled in. So he scrambles to the wall in three fast strides, rolls across its broad flat surface, lays the rifle on the warm, solid stone, and snaps in.

Nothing fancy. Center mass. He drops the crosshairs between Morgon Jump's shoulders, squeezes the trigger, and sends the shot like a prayer.

CHAPTER SEVENTY-THREE

Davis swoons and smells fresh-turned earth and imagines sunlight. The sound of surf. Sirens. He squints through his one good eye and locates Jesse jogging up from the beach, and he marvels at how she's come through all this batter looking so clean, like she's finishing a long cross-country race. Or maybe it's him who's finally feeling clean, but more likely he's just slipping into shock. So he sprawls behind the wall and waits for Jesse, but Amanda Rivard appears first like a gliding vision with a geisha fright mask of clenched ivory and ebony for a face. She bends over him and opens a first-aid bag.

"Cops?" Davis wonders, thick-tongued, the words furry. "You call 911?"

Amanda stares toward the beach and hugs herself to contain a full-body tremor. When she stops shaking, she nods as she pries the clumsy compress away from his head and assesses the wound. "I called the sheriff direct. He's prompt, because I reminded him who bought his new fleet of Crown Vics."

The sun has come out, and Jesse now casts a shadow over them. Amanda looks past Jesse, down toward the beach, with a question in her spooked eyes. "Is he gone?" she asks in a dry whisper, gnawing her lower lip.

"He's dead,"

"You're sure?"

"Trust me; now see to the living." Jesse kneels and puts her hand on Davis' shoulder.

"So you got him," Davis sighs, going in and out.

"We got him."

Davis tries to sit up. "Need a phone, gotta call . . ."

400

"Shush there, cowboy; take a break." Jesse eases him back down. Then she eyes Amanda coldly and nods at the wound on the side of Davis' head.

Amanda stares at them for several beats with her facial expression misfiring. Then she turns back to Davis. At first her voice fails, but then she swallows and composes herself. "I'm reluctant to touch this. You need a trauma center. I think it furrowed the temporal, but only X-ray and MRI can confirm whether something broke off and penetrated." The medical opinion exhausts her, and her fingers spasm and her cheeks jerk and she collapses to a seated position on her backside. "You'll tell the FBI I tried to help," she mutters. The color drains from her face as she watches the police cruisers and ambulance race toward them across the lawn, along with a fire truck that veers toward the smoking crash site on the beach.

"Hey," Davis mumbles, "I don't mean to presume on a first date, but could you maybe undo my belt and, ah, remove my shoes and elevate my feet . . ."

"Got it," Jesse says, brushing some dirt from his cheek. "Clear the airway, stop the bleeding, treat for shock." Then she waves to the ambulance that swerves to a halt ten feet away. While the EMTs unload a gurney, she turns back to Davis and smoothes her fingers through his fouled hair.

"So you ever thought of going to Alaska?" she asks.

Davis blinks because the sun blinds him, or maybe it's the last fierce blaze of determination leaving her face. "Ah, remind me what's happening in Alaska?"

"DeHavilland Beavers. Bush pilots. Me."

"Sounds like a hell of a deal." Davis attempts a crooked smile as two paramedics rush up and bend over him.

Not Sure What to Read Next?
Try these authors from Conquill Press

Jenifer LeClair
The Windjammer Mystery Series
Rigged for Murder
Danger Sector
Cold Coast
www.windjammermysteries.com

Brian Lutterman
The Pen Wilkinson Mystery Series
Downfall
www.brianlutterman.com

Christopher Valen
The John Santana Mystery Series
White Tombs
The Black Minute
Bad Weeds Never Die
Bone Shadows
Death's Way
www.christophervalen.com

Coming Soon

Apparition Island by Jenifer LeClair
Broker by Chuck Logan
The Search For Nguyen Phem by Chuck Logan
Windfall by Brian Lutterman
Ithaca Falls by Steve Thayer
The Darkness Hunter by Christopher Valen

For more information on all these titles go to:
www.conquillpress.com